S0-AXK-645

Tor Books by Elizabeth Kerner

Song in the Silence
The Lesser Kindred
Redeeming the Lost

REDEEMING

THE

LOST

ELIZABETH KERNER

A TOM DOHERTY ASSOCIATES BOOK/NEW YORK

This is a work of fiction. All the characters and events portrayed in this book are either products of the author's imagination or are used fictitiously.

REDEEMING THE LOST

Edited by Claire Eddy

A Tor Book
Published by Tom Doherty Associates, LLC
175 Fifth Avenue
New York, NY 10010

www.tor.com

Tor® is a registered trademark of Tom Doherty Associates, LLC.

ISBN 0-812-56876-1
EAN 978-0-812-56876-9

First edition: June 2004
First mass market edition: December 2005

Printed in the United States of America

0 9 8 7 6 5 4 3 2 1

To
the Glory of God
and to
Martha Newman Morris Ewing
and
Sarah Alice Morris Gramley

The Marvellous Morris Girls

My mother, Martha, so desperately missed,
so dearly loved,
even if we did fight like cats and dogs
for quite a few years:
so far away in death, and as near as my mirror
where I sometimes catch a heart-stopping glimpse of you—
the ache in my heart that never forgets that you are gone,
the joy that remembers all that you were
and the indomitable warrior spirit in you
to fight for those who could not fight for themselves

My dear Aunt Sarah, whose love and affection have upheld me
in the good times, the bad times, and the dry, hard times—
whose strength and tenacity and sheer zest for life
have inspired me for many years,
whose faith in me has braced a flagging heart,
and whose truth-speaking is as rare and precious a gift
as the loving heart that prompts it—
to you, who have become my second mother

I dedicate this work

Prologue
Maran Vena

Bone to iron, blood to flame—
hammer, anvil, tongs, coal,
water, air, fire, hammer—
thus the blacksmith's soul.

At last. Nearly there. I can find the way from here, and have finally been able to release the Silent Service guide who has led me thus far. I've a feeling I should arrive on my own.

I have been running after my daughter these last six months, across half of Kolmar. Wretched girl. When I saw her return from the Dragon Isle with that man who was no man, when I saw my dear friend Rella stabbed the moment she stepped off the boat, I knew the time was come when I would have to face my child at last.

I have had to watch my daughter all her life from a distance. From her first step to her first kiss I have been with her half a world away and she has known nothing of me. She passed through all of childhood's more dreadful moments well enough, as far as I could tell, but when she came up against a demon-master I realised I could dwell in shadows no longer. What worse could happen, after all?

I can hear you. Already you have decided who and what I am. You think me evil, or at the very least unfeeling and unnatural. You are wrong. Listen with a mind open to wider possibilities and you may learn something.

Or perhaps there is some justice to your point of view. To be honest, I wonder about it myself in the long nights. It's not an easy question, and there's no simple answer that I can find. Life's like that—messy and mixed, heroes and cowards in the one skin. It's only in the bard's tales that good and evil are so cleanly divided.

Or in people like my daughter.

When I was young and just coming of age I was desperate to leave my home to see the wider world—not unlike Lanen, as it happens. My mother loved me well enough, but it suited her that I should go a-wandering, for I was not to her taste as a child. My blacksmith father Heithrek loved me best of all his children and feared for me out in the world alone. I have never been a fool and understood the dangers well enough, so I waited, but each day the waiting grew harder.

Working beside my father made it at least bearable. When I first grew taller than my brothers, he laughed and put me to work in the forge. As I stayed and learned the beginnings of the craft, he would have me tend the iron in the fire, pumping away at the leather bellows until the sparks and the colour of the metal told him the iron was ready to work. I loved the fire, the warm darkness of the forge, the music of my father's hammer against the anvil, the air of mystery and creation that blew through the glowing coals as he transformed stubborn iron into well-behaved tools. The forge called me unto itself as some are called to serve the Goddess, and I answered gladly.

My father was pleased with me, but the whole idea of a female blacksmith unsettled my mother who soon asked him to dissuade me from such a strange pursuit. Heithrek did his best. He put me to drawing down the pig iron, hoping that the sheer weight of the stuff and the dullness of the work involved would put me off, but I found it a challenge and laughed with delight the first time I managed to draw down half a pig in a day without having to stop and rest.

Each of my three brothers had come to the forge to try if they were true smiths. Each one left after a short season when he found it was not in him. The eldest has become a scholar, the second a farmer, the third a shaper of wood rather than iron. My two younger and more delicate sisters, Hildr and Hervor, simply thought I was insane, and told me so when they were old enough and brave enough.

"Maran, you'll never find a man if you spend every waking moment with fire and iron," Hildr told me. "The only time the lads ever see you is when you're soot-black from the forge." She had a point, but there again, given the lads in our village, I didn't really care. It wasn't those puny lads I wanted to know more of, but the world that lay about me, enticing, so wide and so unknown. We lived in Beskin, on the edge of the Trollingwood within sight of the great East Mountain range. I grew up in the sight of mountains that reached halfway to the sky, and my heart longed for them as other maidens longed for a man.

The wanderlust grew as the years passed, as I worked beside my father and grew to my full height and strength. I had known for years that the village lads would never be a match for me in any sense. Truth be told, I was all but ready to set out into the wide world alone if there was no other way, but as luck would have it there came through our village, just in time, a mercenary looking for work. He was well-enough looking, built small but wiry, and there was that about his eyes that intrigued me—a strangeness, as of pain long borne; an otherness that spoke of distant lands; a depth in him that I could not fully understand, but that spoke of wisdom hard-gained and worth the knowing.

In any case he was obviously a man well able to keep himself. He came looking for work, and said he'd be willing to act as bodyguard—well, my father knew that I would leave soon in any case, and Jamie was a good compromise.

Jamie. The man I have loved best in all the world, though my best love has been shoddy enough. Not Lanen's father, though he should have been. Jameth of Arinoc. My Jamie.

Rella's Jamie now, damn it.

I can hardly grudge them their happiness. I left him alone to raise my daughter, and Rella has known me and been my faithful friend these twenty years gone. I should have known this would happen were they to meet.

I knew they travelled together with my daughter, some three moons past now. When I saw Jamie every day as I watched Lanen, I tried to convince myself that the long years had loosed Jamie's hold on me, but when finally I realised that Jamie and Rella were become lovers I felt a pain sharp as a knife in my breast. Part of me cries even now, like a spoiled child, *but he was mine!*

Aye. If he was mine, I should have been with him.

Why wasn't I with him, a neat near-family with Lanen as our daughter, and mayhap other childer for our own?

Ah. It never was meant. And it's all the fault of Marik and that Hells-be-damned Farseer.

Jamie and I had travelled together some three years, and we had been lovers much of that time. He asked me to wed him, several times, but I was young and did not want to be tied to the first man I had ever known. Fool that I was, too stupid to realise how fortune had favoured me! He taught me to defend myself, and though I never took to the blade properly, I learned enough to keep my head on my shoulders. We roamed the length and breadth of Kolmar together—oh, the tales I could tell!—until, upon a day in early autumn, in Illara during the Great Fair, I met Marik of Gundar.

A kind of madness took me. For the first and last time in my life I was stricken as by a blow by the sheer presence of a man, and I desired him with all my being. I've never done nor felt such a thing before or since, and I have long wondered if even then he was practicing demon-craft.

Alas, I fear he was not.

Marik and I were of a height, which was unusual enough, and although he was easy to look at—his hair was golden red, his eyes the yellow-green of the first grass of spring, and his nose bent like a fine hawk's—it was not his appearance alone that swayed me, nor even the fact that there was a scent about him that made my knees weak. No, the truth is, I heard him speak only once and I was lost. Dear Shia. His *voice*. Goddess preserve us, it was pure seduction. Light, clear as crystal, with the soft accent of the East Mountains, and his every word sang to some part of me that had nothing to do with words. Or with thought, come to that.

I fobbed Jamie off with some stupid excuse, which he recognised for what it was, but he was older in the ways of the world than I. I can only think that Jamie assumed I would enjoy a night's pleasure with this stranger and come back to seek him out again the next day, ashamed but with this madness out of my heart. Would that I had been so wise.

Marik and I were lovers that very first night, and many nights after. For two months we—well, never mind. At the end of it I learned, purely by chance, that he was dealing with a demon-master name of Berys to gain power for his Merchant House. Between them, Marik and Berys created the Farseer, sacrificing an innocent babe in the making, and promising further the life of Marik's firstborn to the demons that made it. The Farseer itself Jamie and I took with us, to keep its power from the benighted souls that created it. I have it yet, an innocent-looking smoky glass globe about the size of a small melon.

Marik knew no more than I did that Lanen lay under my heart already. He meant to rise to power through the stupid thing, to make a way for demons to enter Kolmar under his control, for his own profit and power, with never a thought of the evil that would come down upon us all. Jamie and I stole the Farseer from him the instant it was made and took it with us when we ran. We escaped, but only by the width of a hair, from Berys's revenge. Jamie and I kept running, far to the north and west, where I met Hadron of Ilsa, a horse-breeder in an obscure corner of Kolmar. He fell head over heels for me and I wed him.

Well, what would you?

Of course I should have wed Jamie, of course I knew it, but Jamie—oh, Hells. I hate this.

Still, I have sworn to myself to write the truth here, lest I forget it amid all the lies I have told myself and others over the years.

I feared that the demons would find Jamie and me, find us and rend us and send us screaming down into darkness. And if they were going to take my husband, I could lose Hadron well enough, but if Jamie came to harm through me I would have gone mad. If I had told Jamie as much he'd have married me anyway, and I couldn't let that be. Instead I told my dearest love that I needed somewhere stable and safe for the growing babe, and that Hadron would do.

Jamie stayed with me and I will never know why. Surely no man could love anyone so deeply?

You know, it's amazing, you get in the habit of lying to everyone and in the end you lie to yourself. I've always been a damn good liar. Comes of being honest most of the time. When I lie, hardly anyone can tell. Even I lose track on occasion.

I knew fine that Jamie loved me truly and I took ruthless advantage of it. And when Lanen was born, I could see in his eyes that he yet had some hope that she was his. I never told him she wasn't. Truth be told, I wasn't absolutely certain who her father was. I prayed it was him, but deep inside I suspected she was Marik's.

I lived with Hadron for nearly a year after she was born, my shining girl, and I honoured him with my work and my body as best I could. Jamie's every look, every movement, burned in my eyes and in my heart, but for his sake I never spoke word or let him see my own desperation. I would not, for my own comfort, give him hope, shame Hadron, and then leave them both. That would have been too great an evil even for me.

To say truth, before she was born I tried to hate my babe because it was very likely the child of Marik of Gundar. Before she was born I had some idea of abandoning the child to Hadron's tender mercies and leaving with Jamie, because I was going to hate it, of course I was.

Yes, yes, I know, I was an idiot. I've known it for many, many years, so you can keep your thoughts to yourself.

Flesh of my flesh, whom my father would have adored had he lived to see her—tiny, helpless, this stranger who had shared my body for nine moons now alive, breathing for herself, shaking the air in her demands for food—how could I do anything but love her? It was not her fault that her father was such a man. From the moment she first drew breath I thought her the loveliest, most incredible child in all creation. What mother does not know this to be so? Her eyes, the smell of her hair, the feel of her at my breast, the wonder I knew as I watched her first steps: at least I have had these memories to keep me company through the long lonely years.

And yet I left her, for the demons came.

They pursued me always in dreams, from the time I arrived in Ilsa, and then one terrible day during a late winter storm one came in truth. Like an idiot I fought it with my knife—they can't be killed that way, though they don't like being cut—until I started thinking and put my free hand to the silver Ladystar I wore on a chain. I prayed then, aloud, for help, and the next time my blade touched the thing it disappeared. I went straight to a Servant of the Lady that I knew of thereabouts and had myself shriven and my wounds dressed in secret. I asked the Servant if she knew how to deal with demons, but she seemed to think I had brought it on myself by summoning demons, no matter how often I denied I'd done any such thing. I couldn't tell her about the Farseer, of course, but I knew I'd been standing next to it when the creature had appeared.

I took the short sword that Jamie had taught me to use, found my way into the forge at night, and managed to grave the sign of the Lady, the Goddess Shia, Mother of us All, on both sides of the blade. It worked much better the next time, and the next—but then they started coming once every se'ennight. The worst was the time I was feeding Lanen when one arrived, and it scratched her. She screamed to shatter the sky as I fought it, and I was scarce able to breathe for terror by the time I had dispelled it. I washed the scratch with water tinged with honey and she stopped crying. I did not. I knew that Marik had promised the life of his firstborn child in payment for the Farseer, though he'd had no idea then that she was already growing in my womb. Lanen was their prey, I was sure of it, and I was convinced that they sought her through the damned Farseer and through me.

I left that night, taking the Farseer with me. I released Hadron from his vows to me, that he might pursue any chance of happiness left to him without hindrance. Hadron I never worried about, Goddess forgive me, my cold heart, but Jamie—Jamie I left without a word, and Shia knows I have cursed myself roundly for that for many a year. I prayed he would stay and watch over my Lanen, and he did.

I know not what fate awaits us all after we die, but, dear Goddess, if there is a judgement awaiting all souls I dread it to my bones. So unspeakable a trick, to abandon them all three together. I knew I was doing ill, but all I could see in my heart was a vision of Lanen torn from my arms and sundered by cackling demons. I killed all the love left to me in the world that day and I would have done so ten times over to keep my daughter and my best-beloved safe.

What life have I had? A very quiet one. I came home, to Beskin in eastern Eynhallow, to my father's forge, long cold. I had learned at his shoulder the working of iron, and in time I made a decent blacksmith for the villages round. It has kept me here, unremarkable save for my profession—for even here in the North Kingdom, where women are vastly more independent than in any of the other kingdoms, I know of no other female smiths. I have remained safe and largely unnoticed, while I have studied the service of the Lady and used the Farseer to watch over my daughter Lanen.

Why did I not destroy the Farseer? I have been tempted, a thousand times. But I learned in that dark hour when Jamie and I saw it made that there can only be one in the world at a time. If I smashed the thing, Marik could make another and all my sacrifices would have been in vain. He would have found us in an instant, and Lanen, Jamie, and I would surely be dead in moments.

Yes, yes, of course I was a fool. How could I know then what I have learned since? It has taken me years to discover that the Farseer has its own defences as part of its making. Jamie and I escaped with the thing nearly the moment it was made and its makers spent vast resources trying to find it. The results of nearly all of Marik's fortune and Berys's power at that time were those few Rikti that found me and attacked me in Hadronsstead. The Farseer is invisible to the Rakshasa, those few that found it and me must have been a few out of thousands sent all over Kolmar, discovering by chance a needle in a hay field. Berys has not given up the hunt, over the years, but I have studied and spent a great deal of time in prayer to the Goddess, and I have learned that if I invoke Her name and bless the thing when I use it, and have myself shriven afterwards, the stink of it is dispelled and the demons can't find me.

I had owned it for sixteen winters before I learned that. I could have gone back then, when Lanen was fifteen, I suppose—but by then she was at one of the hardest times of life, and I didn't want to—oh, Hells. It is so much easier to lie, and I'd sound so much more like the person I wish that I were.

I didn't dare face Lanen and her anger—Jamie's anger—Hadron—I told you I was a coward. Had it been Lanen in my place, she'd have done it. The girl fears nothing. But it wasn't Lanen, it was me, and I couldn't bear it. I had abandoned her as an infant, for the love I bore her and for her safety, and I was convinced that she would never believe me. Or forgive me.

You may think that love from a distance is easy, and in some ways you are right. But every time she was in danger, as she lived through childhood's diseases, when pain and sadness visited her, I watched for hours and hours despite the cost to my soul. Jamie and my Lanen have been dearest in the world to me, despite the years and the distance, despite my daughter not knowing I lived. Or cared.

I could not bear the thought of seeing hatred in her eyes, or in his.

I met Rella about a year after I first returned to Beskin. She was always coming and going, but in the end it was she who eventually helped me learn how to protect myself from the dark influence of the Farseer. When her daughter Thyris died—Goddess, may I never see such a parting again—I sought to hire the Silent Service to help me find out how to use the damned thing in safety.

I was astounded when Rella was assigned, I had no idea she was a part of that guild, but she told me she had asked to work with me, and that it was time there was truth between us.

Then half a year ago, I looked in on Lanen and found that she had left the safe haven of Hadronsstead and struck out on her own. Even Jamie only managed to go as far as Illara with her. I begged Rella—truth to tell, I paid her—to go after Lanen and guard her for me, and she went with a good will.

And of course, my daughter was not content even with all the lands of Kolmar, oh no, she had to take ship away west and seek the Dragon Isle, where grow the lansip trees whose leaves are the most powerful healall in the world, and where dwell the True Dragons of legend—great winged, clawed creatures the size of a house, able to speak and reason. In the ballads they are clever and powerful, but all the songs agree that they left Kolmar long ages since. There is one ballad, the Song of the Winged Ones, that tells of them in their new home and touches briefly on their leaving, but even that tale has no more than a hint of why they left Kolmar. Something to do with demons, it seems, but the words are vague. In truth I had thought the True Dragons no more than myth, but Lanen—ah, Lanen not only found them, she fell in love with one.

Just goes to show she's truly my daughter. Mad child. As best I could tell, though, that great silver dragon who caught her heart came to love her as well. What happened then I'm not entirely certain, for there were times in that crowded few days when she was gathering lansip and losing her heart to a dragon, when I could keep my eyes open no longer—but when the dust settled there was no more silver dragon and Lanen was helping a man with purest silver hair learn how to walk. They returned to Kolmar and were wed this Midwinter Festival past. That was when I realised that I had to find her myself, to tell her of the greater danger that awaited her and those she loved. I left my home just after midwinter and have been travelling the three moons since. It has been a hideous journey and cold as all the Hells most of the time. Thank the Goddess for the river, though I could not ride its broad back at first—the Kai is too rough and rocky where it springs from the earth to support a boat. Not for many a long league of walking could I hope for rest. Still, I finally reached the great crossroads of Kolmar, the city of Sorún where the Kai and the Kelsun meet. I have been moving swiftly south ever since, on the river when I could, towards the hills north of Verfaren, the city of the Mages.

The worst of it is that I don't know what has happened. Lanen is no longer with them. I watched in awe as she and those who travel with her helped bring about a new race of creatures, the little dragons who now bear the same great gems as their larger cousins, but I am only human. I fell asleep, and when I woke and demanded of the Farseer to show me Lanen, I saw her lying in a crumpled heap on the floor in some cramped stone room. I know not how she has come there, or why she is alone. When I spoke Rella's name, I saw her in solemn conference with the others, and glimpsed Jamie's face looking—dear Goddess—looking like a lost soul bent on damnation.

I can only guess that Lanen has been stolen away and that the others seek her. I might be able to help them find her. I have learned that what I see in the Farseer is only the vaguest of directions if I cannot recognise the place I am shown, but from all I can tell I should meet up with Rella, Jamie, and the others in the next few days. There is one of the True Dragons with them now as well, though why in all the green world it has come hither I cannot imagine. Indeed, it seems that the green world is changing profoundly even as I stand here, and my daughter is in the midst of it.

Dear Goddess. I hope I live through it. I fully expect her to do her very best to break my jaw when finally we meet. Or my arm. I would, in her place. I don't intend to let her have things all her own way, mind you. At the very least I am bright enough to keep out of arm's reach until her temper cools.

Oh—and there is the one last thing I have learned about the Farseer. It corrupts the soul. It was made with the help of demons, after all, and that darkness inhabits it and taints any who dare to use it. I have resisted that taint for more than twenty years, paying in the coin of prayers and devotions to Mother Shia, and in having to live with the Raksha-stink when I could not be shriven immediately. It isn't a smell, really, more a deep sense of gut-sickness. I have borne it for a very long time, and I fear that all the shriving in the world will never cleanse me of this prolonged contact with demons.

But if that is the price of watching over my daughter, I will bear it until I break.

i

The Return

Shikrar

The joy of our homecoming was too soon over. None had the strength left to stay aloft for long, and we all soon drifted, weary but grateful, to the ground. My heart was pulled in a dozen directions at once. My joy at seeing my people come safe again to their ancient home, after an exile lasting full five thousand years, was uppermost. The Kantri, we whom the Gedri—no, Shikrar, in their tongue they are called humans—we whom the humans call True Dragons, were come home at last, to share this vast land with the only other creatures who speak and reason. I knew fear also, of course. In this place where we were largely forgotten as living creatures, where we were become little more than tales to frighten children, we had no way to know what our welcome might be. Behind and through all, however, was deep heart's-sorrow for Varien, my soulfriend Akhor, whose beloved wife Lanen had been stolen away mere days before.

I had not the leisure to give any of these feelings the attention they deserved, for I was bound to go and welcome my people to a land I had only known for the last four days. It was enough,

I think, for most of them to see me here before them—Eldest, Keeper of Souls, guardian of our people in the place of their transformed King, Varien.

Most of the Kantri lay exhausted where they had landed. We all had flown, with only one brief rest, for many days on the back of the Winds. Our home for so many years, the Isle of Exile that the humans name the Dragon Isle, was gone. The earthshakes that had plagued us these last years had grown worse and worse, and at the last the fire mountains had erupted, spewing molten rock over our home. It was gone forever. We had had no choice. Kolmar was the home of our ancestors, after all, and it surely must be clear to the Gedri that neither caprice nor passing fancy drove us to dare the crossing of the Great Sea. The Winds had decided for us that it was time we returned. Our oldest teaching was clear: "First is the Wind of Change, second is Shaping, third is the Unknown, and last is the Word."

I could only hope that the Gedri would see it the same way.

There were a number of our folk ranged along the edge of the field, where a shallow little stream danced over stones, drinking thirstily. I wandered among the weary souls, scattering praise and encouragement where I thought it would be accepted.

As I passed, I noted that the great sealed golden cask containing the soulgems of the Lost was safe, resting now between the forelegs of my son's beloved mate Mirazhe. The Lost! The cursed legacy of the great evil that was the Demonlord, the reason the Kantri left Kolmar so long ago. Born a child of the Gedri, the Demonlord sold his name and his soul for a terrible power over us. In the dreadful final battle fully half the Kantri alive in those times, two hundred of our people, had their soulgems ripped from them by demons. They fell from the sky, reduced to the size of mere younglings, and the powers of speech and reason were taken from them; it was that day upon which they were first called the Lesser Kindred. The Demonlord was eventually destroyed— but he died laughing. It is widely believed even now that he will return to trouble us one day. In the normal way of things, when one of the Kantri dies, the soulgem shrinks to a quarter of its size and resembles a large faceted gemstone. Every soulgem is retained reverently, for they are the means by which, through the Kin-Summoning, we may bespeak the Ancestors when need arises. When the soulgems of the Lost were gathered up, however, it was seen that they flickered with some unknown inner fire. From that day to this we have tried to contact them, but neither the Kin-Summoning nor truespeech nor heartfelt prayers to the Winds have made any difference.

Mirazhe managed a nod to me, and lifted one wing slightly to show the sleeping form of her youngling Sherók. I breathed again. Strange, is it not? I knew that Sherók must be well, but it was not until I saw him safely asleep with his mother curled round him that my heart believed it. A little beyond Mirazhe, piled carefully on the ground, were the lansip trees we had brought with us, the only remembrance of our old home. The Gedri prized lansip, leaf and fruit, beyond all imagining. For thousands of years it had grown only on the Dragon Isle that lay now below the sea. I foresaw a thriving trade in a few years, if we managed to plant the trees quite soon. If they would grow here. The poor creatures who had borne them hither also slept, even more tired than the rest.

Their weariness was not to be wondered at, for they had flown high and far for the best part of three days and nights, without cease and without hope of rest—and before that, two full days of flight to reach the tiny isle where we had rested and drunk from a small, brackish pool. None had eaten since the fires of the earth had taken our island home from us, and although we do not normally require large amounts of food, we were all in desperate need of sustenance.

Here, however, came one in whom pride was stronger than exhaustion—Idai, weary but unbowed, striding towards me from the eastern side of the field. She it was who, following me, had led the Kantri through the everlasting Storms and across the wide expanse of the sea. I walked to meet her and bowed formally, in the mingled Attitudes of Joy and Praise, in acknowledgement of all that she had accomplished.

"Iderrisai! My heart rejoices to see thee safe," I said aloud, adding in truespeech, *"Safe and well, and with all our people. It is a great thing that you have done, Idai. You will be remembered among the Kantri forever."*

"I thank you, Hadreshikrar," she said gravely, aloud. She remained silent otherwise. I turned to follow her gaze—ah. Yes, she would not bespeak me on seeing him, lest truespeech betray her deeper thoughts. The Gedri—no, human, I must remember—the human called Varien approached us swiftly from the edge of a small stand of trees in the west. Varien, the Changed One. He who had lived a thousand years as Akhor, the Lord of the Kantrishakrim, soulfriend and dear as a son to me, and who for most of his life had been dearly loved by Idai. Poor Idai. Akhor had never returned her love or encouraged her regard: but even among the Kantri we cannot choose whom we will love. It was less than a full year past that he had been changed, through a kind of death and rebirth, impossibly, from his true form to a creature with the form of the Gedri children, but with his soul and his mind as they had ever been.

I glanced again at Idai and knew the pain in her heart, though she tried to hide it. Truespeech does not always require words, after all. She had loved Akhor for most of her life, knowing full well that he did not return that love but unable to deny her own heart. For her to see him now was little less than agony. It was a measure of her greatness of soul that she did not hate Lanen, who had caught Akhor's heart between one breath and another while yet he was of the Kantri. She and Lanen had made their peace: but now Lanen was stolen away by great evil, and all Akhor's thought and all his mind and all his soul were focussed, waking and sleeping, on getting her back. A lesser creature would have rejoiced inwardly at Lanen's misfortune. Idai has a great soul.

I had known Akhor from his birth, a thousand and some winters past; he was soulfriend to me, and apart from my son was the only soul on live who knew my full true name. He had possessed the form of a human for less than six moons. It was still very hard for us all to accept, this strange being who was undeniably Akhor in his soul but withal so very different. So small, so fragile! I prayed to the Winds that he would not be so short-lived as the children of the Gedrishakrim usually were. By all rights he should live yet another thousand years, in the common way of our people.

Varien hurried over to meet us. Idai bowed her head low, and without thinking he leant over and stretched out his neck as if to greet her in the Kantri manner. The very feel of it must have stricken him wrongly, though, for he swiftly stood upright. Instead, he reached out with his hand and placed it, oh, so gently, upon her cheek, where the solid faceplates of my people curve back to protect the great vein in the neck. She trembled a little at the contact.

"Idai! Oh, welcome and welcome, my namefast friend, my heart soars at sight of thee," he said. He dared to gently stroke her dark copper faceplate, gazing into her steel-grey eyes. "When we parted I feared I would not see you for many long years, and lo, even in this dark hour, the Winds have sent you as a flame to brighten my soul's darkness. It is good to see you, Iderrisai." He smiled then, and his soulgem—no longer part of him, as nature meant it, but worn in a circlet of gold that held the stone against his forehead—burned for that moment bright and clear. "I see you were not content to let mine be the only great tale of these times! You and Hadreshikrar have between you accomplished a work that will be remembered as long as our people live and memory lasts. You have brought us all home." He leaned forward and touched his soulgem briefly to Idai's faceplate, a deeply personal gesture used only between the nearest of friends.

I was grateful that Idai closed her eyes in that moment, for Varien's sake. He could not see the years-long sorrow rise in them, pain and weary loneliness that struck my own heart in the instant. I had to close my eyes against the depth of it. By the time Varien pulled back from the contact, though, Idai was in control of herself again.

"You are well, then, Ak—Varien?" she asked. Her voice wavered only slightly. Varien might well put it down to her weariness.

"I rejoice to see thee and my people safe at last, but in truth, I tell thee I have seldom been worse, Idai," he said, and as his voice deepened I heard the anger in it rising. If he had been in his old shape his wings would have begun to rattle. In this body, his hands curled in upon themselves and the skin of them began to turn white. "Hath Shikrar told thee of the great ill that hath befallen us, Lady? That a demon-master hath stolen away my beloved from my very side, and I helpless to stop him?" A tremor in his voice betrayed the depth of his feeling. "And that I know not where she bides, or whether she is quick or dead?"

Even I was shaken. Varien in his fury was using the style of Gedri speech he had learned hundreds of years before. "I have told her, Varien," I said aloud, adding silently, *Your speech betrays your anger. You must not fail now, Akhor. We are here and our strength is yours. Do not let your heart's wound blind you. We cannot fly in force and destroy this Berys at once—he is a demon-master and we know not the extent of his strength. Remember the Demonlord, who destroyed the half of our Kindred upon a single day! I do not counsel cowardice, my friend, only prudence. And such a battle, such a war, would not be kind to those innocents around about. We are new-come to this land. Would you arrive as a destroyer?*

"I would arrive as one bent on saving the life of my beloved!" he cried.

"We will find Lanen, by my soul I swear it," I answered solemnly aloud, "but we must go softly at first, lest we break all hope of living here in peace with the Gedri, or break ourselves like fools upon the power of this demon-master."

"Oh, I expect you'll have a good chance of living in peace here," said a calm voice from near the ground. The Lady Rella stepped forward and bowed briefly to Idai. "Welcome—you're the Lady Idai, aren't you?" Idai nodded once, and Rella grinned. "I remember you from the Dragon Isle. I don't think we ever exchanged names, but Lanen told me about you. Well-met, Lady, and welcome to your new home. I for one am delighted to see you."

Idai hissed her amusement. "Rrrellla, the strong arm that kept Llanen safe from her own kind. Yess, I recall you. Well-met, and I thank you for the welcome, but I do not know if it will outlast my first request." She turned to me. "Have you eaten, Hadreshikrar?"

I instantly wished she had not said that, for of a sudden I was aware of my empty belly and a raging hunger surged through me. "No," I replied shortly, and both Rella and Idai laughed as a noisy rumble from my interior nearly drowned out my answer. "No, I have not eaten, apart from a morsel here and there since I arrived. The prospect of fighting a Raksha has sustained my spirit, but my belly longs for meat."

"As does mine. We have none of us eaten since we left the Dragon Isle sinking into the sea below us, and we have endured many days of desperate toil. We are hungry and we are weary, Shikrar, and we thirst. Whither shall we go now to find sustenance?"

"This is where I come in useful," said a quiet voice, and a man with golden hair and light blue eyes stepped forth. He bowed to Idai, his eyes taking in the host of the Kantri behind us. I was impressed that he managed to contain his astonishment as he spoke. "I'm Willem of Rowanbeck, but only my mother calls me Willem, I'm Will. I live near here, and I know of a farmer not ten miles away with a herd of good cattle. If you have anything to trade for them, I suspect Timeth wouldn't mind being the first in Kolmar to have dealings with dr—with you."

Idai stood in Concern. "We have brought the lansip trees, Shikrar, they are safe, but they must be planted soon and cared for. When once they are established the leaves and the fruits will serve us for trade—but what we shall do in the meantime I cannot imagine. What else have we to offer the Gedri?"

"There is *khaadish*, Idai," said Varien, at the same time that Rella said, "You have gold, don't you?"

"*Khaadish?*" asked Idai. Concern flowed into Confusion. "What might be done with *khaadish?*"

"Even a very little of it can do a great deal, Idai," said Varien. "It is peculiar, I know, but the Gedri value *khaadish* greatly. A small quantity, enough only to fit in my hand, will purchase food and a place to rest for us all." He turned to Will. "Would that suffice for your friend?"

Will raised one eyebrow, and I marvelled again at the mobility of Gedri faces. "I expect he'll faint dead away. I don't think he's ever seen gold before. But his farm is two long days distant, in the steep hills to the north—"

A hiss of amusement from behind me took me unawares, and Kédra, coming up beside me, laughed. "Ah, my father, it is good to know I can still surprise you!" he said. We touched soulgems by way of greeting, as only parent and child ever do. "You are not known to me, friend, but as you stand with Lord Varien and the Lady Rella I trust that you are a good soul. I am called Kédra, the son of Shikrar."

"Willem of Rowanbeck," said Will, bowing. "I am glad to meet you, Kédra, and I don't want to be rude, but we were talking about finding a way to get you and your friends something to eat."

"That is why I arrived so swiftly to offer my services," Kédra said, his eyes alight. "I heard your objection. A two-day walk up-hill for one of the Gedri is a very, very short way to fly, I suspect. Will you come with me in token of our good faith, and treat with your friend on our behalf? For I have *khaadish* with me." He opened his hand, and there between the great claws was a small lump of *khaadish*, gleaming and pretty enough but useless for most purposes. Why the Gedri value it I will never know.

Will, however, choked. "Sweet Lady! Here, Kédra, Timeth is a friend of mine, but even I won't lie for him so far!" He bared his teeth in the Gedri expression of friendship. "That would be riches beyond his wildest dreams. Half of it would be very gener-ous payment indeed for his kine and a sure guarantee of a place to rest for the next few months, while he gets his breeding stock back to work. There is a good stream on his land as well. But for pity's sake don't offer him that dirty great lump of gold! His heart would stop at the sight of it."

Kédra bowed, his eyes alight with amusement. "Are you of the kindred of Lady Lanen?" he asked. "Your words remind me of hers. Very well." He carefully cut the lump of *khaadish* in half and dropped it in Will's outstretched hand.

"That's more like it," said Will.

"And now, Master Willem, will you trust me to bear you?"

asked Kédra. "I have flown thus before, carrying one of you Gedri."

"Aye, and you managed well enough then," said Rella, her voice light. "You never dropped me once."

"Mistress Rella!" cried Kédra, bowing to her. "It gives me joy to see you."

"Same here, my lad. Welcome. You can trust him, I reckon, Will."

Kédra hissed his amusement. "I thank you for the recommendation. Come, Master Will. Shall we go swiftly? Be assured, I know how to counterbalance with a weight in my hands—and my young son is very, very hungry."

Will

I couldn't help it. I knew it was rude, but I hesitated. No matter what Rella said those claws were bloody huge. This one wasn't nearly the size of Shikrar, thank the Lady, but it was still immense. And it—he—wanted to carry me in those—Hells, it would be like travelling in a cage of swords.

Hmmm. It had carved gold like butter with a single claw.

A cage of *sharp* swords, wielded by a giant.

Kédra didn't rush me, though; he just watched and waited. I had come to like his father, Shikrar, over the few days I had known him. For all his overwhelming size and power, I was beginning to see in Shikrar simply another soul. Different, having lived a different life in a very different body, but for all that there were similarities. He had destroyed the Raksha that attacked us up on the High Field in the hills, as we would have if we had had the power; he treated all of us poor weak humans with respect, when clearly he had no need to do so; and it was obvious that he was worried sick about his friend Varien, and about Lanen.

Besides, I had raised my dragon-daughter Salera from her earliest youth, when I found her dam dying in the woods and she so lost and alone. I had fed her and raised her until she had grown to her full stature and left me, but I knew her and loved her as she did me. She trusted Shikrar absolutely. Surely I could trust his son?

And the idea of flying—ah, now. All those dreams of soaring made real. *That* was temptation.

I swallowed my fear. "Very well, Master Kédra. I'd be pleased to come with you and show you the way."

Kédra nodded, and it looked very like approval. "It is well. Come apart with me, then, and tell me where this farm lies."

"Right now? I mean—I—don't you need to recover a bit first?" I asked nervously. For now it was come to the point, my palms were moist with sweat.

"The need of my son for food is greater than my own need to rest, though I thank you," said Kédra. I wondered if that was amusement I heard in his voice. "Come, let us go a little apart. I will need room to take to the sky. And perhaps I should warn you, it may be a little violent at first."

"Aye, well, birds always seem to have to flap harder when they're taking off, I suppose it makes sense," I said, only realising that that might come across as an insult after I'd said it—but no, it was much, much worse than an insult. He was curious.

"Flap?" asked Kédra. "What means 'flap'? I do not know the word."

"It means to—to—you know, move your wings fast," I sputtered, gesturing uselessly, trying to avoid what I knew was coming, but Kédra was none the wiser. I sighed. "Like this," I said, and I swear to you, there in front of all those noble people and ancient dragons I started flapping my arms, as you do with childer, pretending to be a bird.

Great peals of laughter rang out from away behind me, and I swear that wretch Aral's was the loudest, but Kédra gave a great hiss and nodded. Thank the Lady I'd learned that hissing is the way dragons laugh or I'd have run a league. Hells take it, his teeth were *huge*.

"It is a good word. Yes. I shall have to flap harder to leave the ground," said Kédra. "Shall we go?"

"Aye," I said. The sniggers coming from the direction of my friends stiffened my backbone as we walked a bit apart from the rest and I pointed out the direction Timeth's farm lay in and tried to describe the way there. The memory of looking like an idiot helped me steel myself to step on to the palm of Kédra's hand. His other came around to protect me, and with a sudden leap and a series of wrenching jerks we were in the air.

Blessed Lady aid me, I'm for it now, I thought as I fought to keep my stomach under control. *I'm going to have to come back with him, too.*

Marik

I went to visit her, the day before it shattered. It would be my last chance. I wanted to gloat.

It wasn't as if I had known her. Hells, I only met her the autumn before, as a grown woman, and I only had the word of Berys's demon informers that she was my child. As far as I was concerned, she was the price to be paid to end my pain and no more.

Don't ask me why I went down there. Hells knew she'd caused me enough trouble. I think I was just—curious. I expected to find her proud independence laid low by helplessness, and I was looking forward to seeing that. However, as I am not a fool, I took with me one of the large armed guards that Berys had infested the place with. In case she made trouble. I had just enough experience of my daughter to know that she might well try something stupid.

We were, after all, still in the College of Mages at Verfaren, where Berys was the respected Archimage. He did not wish to reveal himself until all was prepared, so he kept Lanen in bespelled silence that she might not cry out and alert some passerby, or use Farspeech to call for aid from the damned dragon that was somewhere up in the hills a few miles away. I persuaded Berys to change the nature of her silence at midday, that I might speak with her in private. For that brief hour her voice would work as normal within her cell, but nothing she said in Farspeech could get beyond the walls. He didn't like doing it, but he owed me that much.

I even took her food and drink. Berys didn't want me to do that, either. He was still nursing a grudge and a sore throat from when she tried to strangle him, but I finally convinced him I needed her alive and healthy to pay off the demons later that night. The College cook was most generous when I requested a tray of hot food to take away to my chambers. The woman seemed pleased that I was finally hungry. I hadn't been hungry for months. I think I had some idea of a last meal for a condemned prisoner.

I remembered just in time to wear the amulet that Berys gave me to ward off the Rikti he had set to attack anyone who opened the door. The guard took up his station just outside. I left the door a little ajar, in case I needed him: out on the Dragon Isle she had knocked me unconscious with one blow. I didn't care to risk that again.

The cell was small and simple, originally meant for solitary study. Moving the locks from the inside of the cell to the outside had been all that was required to make a serviceable dungeon. Thick stone walls in good order, a tiny window for light and air, a heavy old wooden door bound with iron. It was enough.

She was asleep. Berys's spell was set to change only when I entered her cell, so she never heard the door being unlocked. I made no sound. The scent of the food must have roused her, or the change in light—in any case, she rose swiftly to her feet, and almost as swiftly staggered back.

I had forgotten until the moment I saw her astonishment that the last she had seen of me was when I was out of my mind. Helpless, in fact. Perhaps there was some symmetry there.

She stood and stared at me, openmouthed, as I put the tray down on the desk where she had been sleeping.

"Marik?" she whispered, and flinched in shock.

At the noise, as it happens.

"Sound—what—VARIEN! VARIEN, TO ME!" she screamed, staring wildly around the room as if she expected to see someone else hidden in the shadows.

"Save your breath," I sneered, quite pleased at her desperation. "Your voice won't go beyond these walls. And neither will your thoughts." She shut up then, staring with wide eyes. "Oh, yes, we know about your Farspeech. Or to be more exact, I know about it." I grinned at her. "Do you know, your dragon friends did me a great service when they broke open my mind. I can hear them, just like you." I didn't bother to tell her that I only heard two of them clearly and could not respond. Only enough information to make her worry harder. "Not that I thank them for it," I added sourly. "They never damn well shut up."

She gazed at me for a moment in silence, completely unreadable. It was annoying.

"What?" I snapped.

"I have that problem too. Or I did, before Berys cut me off from sound." She stood and began to pace. "Goddess above, but it's good to hear something."

"Keeping you quiet is no more than a sensible precaution," I replied, trying to ignore a flash of memory—the vision of a head larger than my body, jaws agape, coming for me. I shuddered in my turn. "I remember that big silver bastard, the one I half killed, coming through the wall. I'd rather not have that happen here."

When first I tried to honour my bargain with the demons, out on the Dragon Isle, I nearly managed it. Berys's apprentice, Caderan, had summoned the demon in question, Lanen was given up to it, and I thought all was accomplished—when that bloody great damned silver dragon came through the flimsy wooden wall of the cabin, destroyed the demon, and stole away my sacrifice. Caderan and I ran for safety, but that moment has haunted my nightmares ever since.

"You are right to fear it," she said, calmly. I was impressed despite myself. "I don't think you'd live through the experience a second time."

I laughed in her face. "Forgive me if I'm not impressed by your threats, girl," I said. "Besides, why are you wasting your time talking? Your supper is getting cold."

"Do you really think I'm going to eat anything you've brought me?"

"Idiot. Why should I bother with drugs or poison? Berys has spells for that."

"True enough," she said grudgingly.

"It's just food. I thought you'd be hungry."

She frowned her suspicion at me, but I expect the smell rising from the tray soon made up her mind for her. Cutlets of pork in a mushroom gravy. Berys must not have fed her since he captured her two days since, she ate like one starving. It gave me a strange sense of satisfaction to watch her eat. Like feeding the goose you know will soon grace your table at Midwinter Fest.

When she had mopped up the last of the gravy with the last of the bread, and finished the jug of watered wine, she sat back and gazed at me as if waiting for something. After a moment she said, "You know, I find it hard to believe you've had a rush of fatherly feeling, Marik," she said. "Why are you here?"

"Why not?" I replied. "I'm bored, girl." To my own surprise, it appeared to be true. With Maikel gone, I had no one to talk to apart from Berys, and he was as boring as last week's soup when he wasn't indulging in his deep-laid schemes. I didn't care to spend more time in his company than was necessary. At the best of times Berys made my flesh crawl. Still, he was useful. I would soon be rid of my pain at last! Yes, this girl was going to be of use to me in many ways. I promised the soul of my firstborn to demons before I knew she existed, long years since, when Berys and I created the Farseer. I had been suffering for it ever since. Demons don't like debtors.

"And so you come to me. Goddess help us all." She stared at me, shaking her head. "How did you manage to get your mind back? Last time I saw you, you were drooling."

"Thanks to your scaly friends," I snapped. "Berys helped me out of that particular hell."

"Not Maikel?"

"He left me," I said shortly.

"Wise man," she said. "I suspect everyone you have ever known has left you. I'm just surprised he stuck around for so long. He was a good man." She looked straight into my eyes. "And he seemed to be genuinely attached to you." When I did not respond, she shrugged. "Ah, well. There's always one idiot in every crowd."

I stared back at her and said angrily, "You fool. Have you forgotten that I have been in constant pain since your mother stole that Farseer? I promised my firstborn to the demons as the price of its making, and in a few hours you will pay with your soul." I felt a nasty grin spread slowly across my face. "There's a bit of doggerel verse Berys keeps quoting: 'Marik of Gundar's blood and bone shall rule all four in one alone.' You're quite useful, really. Your soul to demons to ease my pain, your body to wed Berys so the prophecy is fulfilled and he rules with you. So insult me all you like. I win. You and your harlot mother lose."

I should have known, I had been expecting something of the sort, but I still didn't see it coming. She stood all in a moment and struck me across the face as hard as she could, which given her height and her strength was impressive. I cried out but was too taken aback to react instantly and she had time for another blow. I reeled, but somehow managed to grab her wrists and stop her before she could land a third. We were both furious, but before I could repay her in kind she arrested my gaze with her own. Her eyes were blazing.

"Is that it, Father?" she asked, her voice a low snarl. "Is that what you wanted? Penance for your evil? Punishment for the blackness of your soul, that would murder an innocent babe without a second thought and deliver the life of your only child to demons? And all as payment for a thing of no use in the world save to make you richer!" She fought to free herself, but I had been battered enough and held her still. "How dare you call my mother harlot, you bastard!" She kicked my shin. The pain made me yell, and the guard opened the door.

"Sir?" he said.

"Will you leave off?" I asked her.

"I won't touch you more," she said, and wrenched free of my loosened grasp. She went as far away from me as possible, to the far side of the little cell, and leaned against the stone wall, her arms wrapped around herself. "You can send your tame bear away."

I nodded to the guard. He backed out of the room and pulled the door nearly closed.

"They told me you never even knew your mother," I said. Even as I spoke I wondered why in all the Hells I didn't leave. What *was* I doing there? What possible reason could I have to speak to this woman?

Curiosity, I thought. *Pure and simple. She's your daughter, until they take her soul away in a few hours. This is your last chance to find out what she's like, before you rejoice that she's gone.*

Lanen

What in the name of sense was he doing? I couldn't fathom it. Even now, years later, I have no idea what in all the world he was after that morning. Perhaps he didn't know either. Perhaps there is a connection of blood and bone that cannot be entirely denied even by the most soul-dead.

Or maybe he just wanted to taunt me one last time.

And to be honest, I was less concerned with his reasons than with my own anger. I had not pulled my punches when I hit him. I should have been afraid of killing him, but to say truth I *wanted* to kill him. There was a part of me that was annoyed that I hadn't even managed to knock him out this time. By fortune, by chance, by the fact that I'm terrible with a sword, I had never killed anything on two legs that didn't also have wings, but the fire in my heart blazed at full fury and I would gladly have murdered him then and there if I had the chance.

For the moment I did what I could to answer his questions.

"Whoever 'they' are, they're right. I don't remember her. She left when I was no more than a year old and never came back."

"Then why such a spirited defence?" he asked.

"Good question," I replied. I stood up again and started to pace, rubbing my sore knuckles, trying not to let Marik see that I was shaking with anger, lest he take it for trembling in fear. "I'm not certain myself. Perhaps I cannot imagine that anything she did twenty-four years ago could be as dark an evil as that which you plan for me. Perhaps I'd defend the Lord of the Seventh Hell himself if you cried out against him." Then, without thinking, I added, "Perhaps it's because I'm—Hells take it—" I forced myself to stare him straight in the eye. "You can't wed me to Berys, I'm married already. I was bloody well going to have children one day, you bastard, and of their two grandparents I know which one I would have let them meet."

Goddess help me, I'd almost let slip the one piece of information I didn't want Marik and Berys to know. I always say too much when I'm really angry.

"Oh, that's a small problem. Whoever your husband is, he surely won't be that hard to kill. Take heart, Daughter," he mocked, falsely cheerful. "You might yet bear children, though to be honest I've never thought of Berys as one to indulge in so—normal an activity." He smirked. "In any case, whatever of you is left is unlikely to enjoy it much."

"Curse you to all the Hells," I snarled, "and take Berys with you for good measure."

"Too late, in his case," he said lightly, and called for the guard to come get the tray. When the guard opened the door, the instant he stepped in, I cried out in truespeech as loudly as I could. *Varien beloved Berys holds me captive, I'm here I'm here to me my love swiftly, they steal my soul this night come succour your childer swiftly to me to me!*"

Marik slammed the door behind the guard and whirled to face me, his eyes blazing. "You tricksy bitch! 'What might have been,' indeed—you are with child even now!" His grin had a certain mad edge to it. "And Berys and I are neither of us such fools as to let you yell for help. The guard and I are the only ones will have heard your shout, and the spell against Farspeech encloses the room no matter if the door is open or shut." He laughed. "Berys will be delighted. Hells, I've never heard *you* before!"

I strode the two paces across the room to strike him down, but he danced away from me and called out for the guard. Nothing happened.

I felt a terrible grin distort my face, the match of Marik's. "He can't hear you. You shut the door, idiot. And you can't get to the door save through me."

He swore and tried to get around me, but I never moved. "My soul to the Lady, you're a dead man, Marik," I said. My voice surprised me. It was quite a lot higher than my normal speaking voice, very strange indeed. But very clear. "Shrive yourself, for by all I hold sacred I swear, I am going to kill you with my bare hands."

At least he didn't waste time saying something stupid like "You wouldn't dare." I suspect it was quite clear that I bloody well would dare, and then some. "The guard will be back any moment now, I was right behind him," he squeaked, dancing away from me as best he could in that small space.

"Then I don't have very long," I said, and lunged. I caught an edge of his tunic and hauled him towards me with all my strength. He was no weakling himself, but somehow all the helplessness, the fury of being a prisoner, and now my desperate fears for my unborn babes, combined to give me a strength I had never known. I tripped him up so that he measured his length on the floor and fell heavily on top of him, kneeling on his chest with my hands about his throat. I squeezed with all my strength. He turned red, then purple, awfully quickly. I never let up, not for an instant.

Not much longer now, surely. My arms were starting to shake. I thought of my children sacrificed on Berys's obscene altar and squeezed harder.

To my astonishment, he stopped fighting to get my hands away—he was reaching for something—

With a snap as of breaking crockery and a hiss like an angry snake, the room was suddenly full of Rikti and they were attacking me.

I couldn't do it. I couldn't keep my hands around Marik's throat. The instinct to survive is too strong. I struck out at them as best I could, but they were all around me, biting and clawing at my back, my arms, my face. I got up off of Marik and ran to put my back against a corner. I was bleeding in a dozen places. One dove directly at my eyes, its claws extended. I turned my head away and threw up my arm to protect myself, and though it clawed my arm, it didn't get any further. I dared to look again.

Marik was gone, the door just closing behind him. There didn't seem to be nearly as many demons as there had been, and the half dozen that remained didn't seem to be in a hurry to attack me. What in the world?

I waited. The nearest seemed to make up its mind and flew at me swiftly with extended claws. I grabbed for its leg, meaning to smash it against the wall, but I missed. It didn't. I felt the claws bite deep, cried out with the pain, saw the stream of red as my blood flowed from the slash—

And then the damned thing burst into flame and disappeared.

The others cried, "Kantrishakrim!" and winked out of existence as swiftly as they had arrived.

I tried, with teeth and shaking hands, to tear bits off the bottom edge of my tunic to use as bandages. It was the only time I cursed at the quality of my clothing, because I couldn't do it, the cloth was too strong. At least it kept my mind off of things for the time it took to make the attempt. The bleeding eventually stopped on its own, but my wounds burned and stung as though I'd scrubbed them with nettles.

And I was left alone with my thoughts, tumbling one after another like a torrent down a fall. It was to be tonight. It was already past noon. Marik knew I was pregnant. I was exhausted, shaking from the effort, and badly wounded by the demons. I crouched in a corner, full of fury unspent, angry at myself for not finishing the job—and deep inside there was a terrible quivering in my belly as I began truly to despair for the life of my babes. I feared I had only hours left to live.

It wasn't until much later that I realised what the Rikti had said. Kantrishakrim. It was Old Speech for "the Wise People," the Greater Kindred.

Seems I had changed rather more thoroughly than I had thought.

Idai

As Kédra left, Varien and Rella begged my pardon and returned to the other two Gedri who waited still at the field's edge,
near a small wood not far away. I took the chance to look about
me. Shikrar was well enough, despite a few injuries that plagued
him yet. When all had been resolved, he would surely fall into the
Weh sleep for a few years and all would be well when he woke. It
would be difficult, for being new-come to this place we had as yet
no knowledge of where we might establish our Weh chambers.
We are desperately vulnerable during the Weh sleep: it comes
upon us whether we will or no when we are badly injured, and
every fifty years or so in any case, for we continue to grow
throughout our lives. While in its thrall we sleep and cannot be
wakened, and our armour burns off to allow the new armour, yet
soft, to grow. We cannot even guard one another during the Weh,
for the guard will be taken by the Weh as well. Now that we were
back among the Gedri, it was vital that we find a safe haven.

Shikrar had explained it to me, but I still could not compre-
hend the bizarre Gedri liking for *khaadish*, which was the root of
the trouble. Where we sleep, we turn the ground to *khaadish* after some years—it is simply what happens. *Khaadish* is pretty to
look at, shiny and yellow and very soft for a metal, but there are
only so many uses for it. The Gedri covet it insanely. We of the
Kantri do not forget, and the story is yet told among us of one evil
night long ages since, when a helpless child of the Kantri was
murdered by marauding Gedri during the Weh sleep for no more
than the *khaadish* she slept upon. From that time, we have sought
out hidden Weh chambers, both for our safety and that the Gedri
might not be tempted.

I breathed deep in the clear morning. It would not be a hardship to fly over these lands seeking hidden chambers. Kolmar was
lush and inviting, what little I had yet seen of it. I would enjoy
that particular task.

Kédra bespoke us then—they had already found Will's friend,
and had sent Will on ahead. Will, seemingly, had talked him out

of simply appearing at the farmer's door. I snorted. Kédra was impulsive as ever, and the flight across the sea had not improved his sense of humour.

Akhor, though—Varien—alas, he was changed yet again. I gazed after him. The joy that had filled him when he left our old home with his beloved was gone. That joy that had sustained me, knowing that he had found his soulmate at last, though all my years of hopeless love fell like dead leaves around my heart. He could barely speak for his anger and he was wild with helplessness.

I could look at Varien no longer and wandered about, trying to distract myself. Rella was rummaging in her pack for something. Beside her stood two other humans, solemn and unmoving, but some creature was joining them from the shelter of the trees. It stood beside them—what—

"Shikrar!" I cried. "Whatever is that bright creature that waits with the Gedri children? It—is it—by the first Wind that ever blew, it looks like—"

"Come, Idai," he said, amusement in his eyes. "Come, I would introduce you to my friend, the Lady Salera."

Shy as a bird the bright one stood as I came near, raw courage holding her unmoving in the face of awe. I lowered my head slowly to look closer—oh, she was of our Kindred, that was certain. She appeared to be no more than the merest youngling. And gleaming in her shining copper faceplate were eyes blue as a summer sky, and a soulgem the same—colour—a soulgem. A *soulgem.*

"Hadreshikrar, I will beat you for keeping this from me," I swore in truespeech. *"Name of all the Winds that ever were. A soulgem. The creature has a* soulgem. *How has this come to be?"*

I could not stop staring, but to my relief it was mutual. Shikrar took refuge in speech.

"Idai, this is Salera, the first of the Lesser Kindred to come into her own," he said, and his own wry amusement was transmuted now to a kind of awe. "She and her—Kindred—are younger than the moon. They were brought into the light of reason but three days since." His voice danced with it. "New-come to the world, new-come to speech and reason. It is a great wonder."

I could barely speak myself. "How, Shikrar?" I asked, never taking my eyes off the littling.

"I was not there, Idai," he replied gently. "Why do you not ask Salera?"

I shook myself and bowed to her. "Your pardon, Salera. I am the Lady Idai. Little one, you are a wonder and a mystery. Of your kindness, will you tell me how you come to be here, as you now are?"

"It was the Silver King Varien and his Lady Lanen who opened our minds," said Salera calmly. "We all were called by some deep song in our hearts, we met all together in the High Field, and— the Lord and the Lady wakened us." She bowed her head briefly, that we might see her faceplate more clearly. It touched my heart, for it was the same gesture every youngling of the Kantri makes for a time after their soulgem is finally revealed. "Where before was darkness, now our soulgems gleam as bright as yours. The Silver King opened our minds to speech that day, and the Lady Lanen guarded the narrow way, that we might pass over in safety."

Even Shikrar looked surprised. *"I have not heard this version, Idai,"* he told me in truespeech. "What did she guard you from, Salera? What threatened you?"

"Fear," replied Salera. She gazed at the two of us steadily. "We could barely understand what Lord Varien offered us, but we knew deep within that it was change beyond measure, and that it could not be undone once it was done. It was . . . frightening." She fluttered her wings in remembered agitation. "Frightening is too easy a word. Fear, and fear, and fear beyond that. Even I resisted, and I knew that my father was on the other side of that change. But Lanen—she showed us her heart, we saw that she too was Changed and become more than she had been, and the great joy she had in her new life. Her gift was to awaken our courage. It was a great gift indeed."

She bowed slightly then, as if it were a strange movement to her, and said, "If you are answered, Lady, can you now tell me where is my father gone?"

I blinked. "Your father, littling?" I asked, confused, but Shikrar interrupted, "He is gone with my son Kédra to find food for the Kantri. He will return swiftly, I have no doubt."

She relaxed visibly—

"Name of the Winds, Shikrar, they use Attitudes but a talon's breadth removed from our own!" I cried in truespeech.

—and continued, "It is well." She saw that I stood in Astonishment and laughed. "Lady, forgive, you cannot know—Will raised me from a kitling, he is the only family I have ever known." Her speech was a little slow, a little stumbling, and she sometimes managed the more difficult human sounds and sometimes did not. Without thinking I addressed her in truespeech.

"Salera, might I bespeak you? Human speech is difficult, and I know not if you have yet learned our own language."

She sat bolt upright, in the absolute image of Astonishment, and stared wide-eyed at me. Her speech instantly became all but incomprehensible. "How iss thiss done? Hwat iss this hyou ssay? I hear hyourr voice yet you haff not spoken!"

"Hadreshikrar, do you mean to say you have not bespoken this child?" I said, turning to Shikrar in amazement. "You, who are the first always to introduce younglings to truespeech!"

To my delight, he could not answer at first. It is not easy to surprise Shikrar, the Eldest of our Kindred, and it always pleased me when I was able to do so. "I—before she, before they were—oh, Idai, I have not even *tried* to bespeak her since she and her people awakened!" He turned to her, tenderly, and spoke quietly using the broadest kind of truespeech. *"Lady Salera, I beg your pardon. My friend Akhor—Varien—told me that you could not hear him, but that was before you came into your own."*

"Hwat iss thiss bespppeakking?" she asked him, her wings fluttering in her agitation.

"Calm yourself, little one," I said, trying to be as gentle as I could. *"It is natural for our people. This is the Language of Truth, the language of the mind. With it, we may speak to one another when we are far apart, or when we are aloft and the wind will not carry sound between us."*

"How isss it done?"

"It is done with thought, littling," said Shikrar calmly, and aloud. "Where most thought is scattered abroad, like clouds in the sky, truespeech is more like to a single star—focussed." He continued in truespeech. *This kind of speech, which we start with, may be heard by all who care to listen. It is the first kind we learn and the easiest to master. There is another kind, whereby we may speak only to one particular soul at a time.*" He paused a moment. "*That usually takes some years to master, but you are not as young as you appear, I would guess. You might achieve that level of concentration much faster than is usual.*"

"How shall I do thiss?" she demanded.

"*Let us begin slowly, and with a warning,*" said Shikrar, still speaking broadly. I managed not to laugh. I recognised the very words. It was the same speech he had given to every youngling he had ever taught. Teacher-Shikrar indeed!

"*Thoughts are truth, and truespeech will reveal your inner thoughts, whether you want it to or no, until you have become accustomed to it. It is impossible to lie in this speech, for the lie will burn like a beacon, and in any case your underthought will give you away.*"

"Hwat iss to lie?" Salera asked, in all innocence.

Shikrar bowed. "It is to say that which is not so, little one," he said aloud. "Forgive me. I suspect it is not within you."

She glanced at him shrewdly, for all her youth. "I suspect it is within me if it is within you, Master Shikrar. Though perhaps not yet." She gazed back at me. "I hwill try this truespeech. I cannot sshape my tongue around words sso well ass you." She bowed her head and closed her eyes in concentration.

I heard nothing.

Shikrar, however, had taught younglings for many, many years. "Littling, I cannot hear you." He stood in Patience. "Will you try again?"

"Can you not hear me call my father? He does not answer. Said you not that distance is no bar to this speech?"

"Ah, littling, forgive me!" replied Shikrar. "I never thought to tell you. The Gedri do not have truespeech, as a rule. Only the Lady Lanen in all of history is so blessed. I fear you will not be able to bespeak Willem."

"The Silver One, Hfarian, he cannot speak so?"

"Varien is a separate case, littling," said Shikrar. "He is—different."

"And so my father is different," answered Salera. "I have learned his tongue, can he not learn this one?"

"Alas, I fear he cannot," said Shikrar, sadly. "Lord Varien is of our own blood, and has the soulgem he has borne for a thousand winters. The Lady Lanen has been blessed by the Winds and the Lady. You must not hope for this, Salera. It will not come to be."

Salera hissed her frustration, her tail whipping round her. "That is—that is darkness in daylight! Why should this be? It is not hwell!"

"Alas, you are right, littling, it is not well; but in all the lives of our peoples we have found nothing that may be done to change it."

And she surprised us again. Still, perhaps I was the more taken off guard; Shikrar at least maintained the appearance of calm.

Clearly and angrily she bespoke us both, as she gave a great leap into the clear morning sky. *"What use then is this speech, when I cannot use it with the one I love best? I go to find him."*

We both stood silent for some time, and Shikrar sighed. "Idai, my friend, I grow old," he said wearily. "What world is this we have come to? That youngling just managed her first words of truespeech most beautifully—"

"I heard her, Shikrar. I expect everyone else did as well," I said wryly. Younglings were not known for subtlety, and Salera's people were apparently no different.

I had managed to raise the shadow from off him for an instant. "Truly," said Shikrar, amused. "She is a delight, that one. And yet, alongside the gift of truespeech that should be so great a joy, she knows now a sorrow that did not afflict her but moments since." He sighed again. "Idai, my friend, what is this place, where Gedri and Kantri are so oddly joined, even for the best of reasons, that the differences between us become a source of pain rather than of delight?"

"Perhaps it has ever been so, Shikrar," said Varien, who had now drawn near with the other Gedri.

"And still, my friend," answered Shikrar, curiously sad, "it leaves me wondering what we have come to in this green land."

"Life, Shikrar," said Varien quietly, his eyes steady. "Life and change. It is well. Perhaps it will be our task to add something unchanging to this mixture, but we ourselves arose in this place. Surely, in ages past, Kantri and Gedri have formed friendships, and the Kantri have grieved for the brief lives of those companions. Should we then seek to avoid the company of our fellow creatures?"

"Her first use of truespeech, Varien. It is a moment for great rejoicing, a step towards a deeper life, and it has brought her only frustration."

"Shikrar, Shikrar," said Varien, managing a lighter tone. "It has been too long since you have taught so young a kit! She will come around to joy soon enough, I promise you. She is very, very young yet." He managed the turning up of the corners of his mouth that the Gedri name a smile. It looked well on him. "But I see you are up to your old ways. Name of the Winds, Hadreshikrar, could you not wait even an hour to instruct Salera?"

Shikrar glanced at me, and I was glad to see a hint of his usual self returning. "This once I cannot claim the honour, Akhor. Idai it was who first bespoke the youngling."

Varien bowed to me. "It was well done, Lady. I never thought to—I have been—"

"You have had your own troubles, my friend. And Shikrar says you tried before and found no response."

"True enough. Salera and her people are a joy and a wonder," said Varien lightly enough, but I heard his voice fall back into sorrow as he added, "but they are not the Lost, my friends. Still our duty to those trapped souls lies unfulfilled. Salera's people, the Lesser Kindred, descendants through five thousand winters of the beasts left when the Demonlord ravaged our people, were my great hope for restoring the Lost. I dreamed that somehow we might reunite the creatures with the soulgems of the Lost—I never thought that they would be developing on their own. They are a great blessing, but all my hope for the Lost is now foundered." He shook his head and muttered, "As is so much else."

"You never let up, do you?" said the Gedri female beside him. "Life is short, Varien, or whatever your name is. I know your heart aches, but can you not spare a moment to rejoice in the good when it comes your way?" She bent in half before me. The Gedri bow so awkwardly. "Forgive me, Lady—Idai, is it? I am Aral of Berún, a city far to the east of here." She smiled. "Varien would probably introduce us in a few weeks, but I don't think we have that long."

I gazed now more closely at the two Gedri who stood with Varien. Young as he looked, they looked younger still. Mere children.

Until you saw their eyes.

The girl-child, Aral, had about her a kindly air, and a strange familiarity that I could not explain, but that spoke well of her— indeed, something about her altogether spoke of the Kantri and it inclined me to favour her, but it was the youth beside her who shook me from my complacency. For all his lack of years, for all that I knew so little of Gedri faces, when our gazes locked he seemed for an instant to vie with me. Perhaps he sought to test me in some way, as younglings do on occasion, but for that brief moment he was unguarded, and I drew back. In that instant I had seen a raging torment behind his eyes, as of a searing flame, and a deep sense of power that surprised me. I sniffed, but there was not the least Raksha-trace upon him. This one would need to be watched, though not by me. A thought arose in my deepest heart. *Let his enemies beware.*

"You shame me, Mistress Aral," said Shikrar. "Your pardon. I am not yet accustomed to the swiftness of your kind. Mistress Aral, Master Vilkas, this is the Lady Idai, known among us for her wisdom. Idai, these two have taught me not to judge by appearances, for they are great Healers in this land."

"Healing is a most noble use of power," I said, gazing full at Vilkas. "I confess to astonishment, however, Master Vilkas, that you two are so at your ease among us."

"We've had practice," said Aral, while Vilkas returned my regard. "We chanced upon Lanen and the rest of them—Lady, was it only a week gone? We were escaping from Berys and his damned Rikti, and when we stopped for food and shelter there they all were, and she in dreadful need of healing." Aral bared her teeth. "We've barely stopped for breath since, but we were there when the Lesser Kindred were awakened." She stood taller. "We helped heal their soulgems."

I listened to her, but I did not look away from Vilkas. "There is a great work behind your eyes, Healer," I said. "It is not unseemly to take a just pride in accomplishment. And unless I am deeply mistaken, it has to do with Varien's beloved."

"How the Hells did you know that?" he asked, but his gaze did not waver either.

I hissed gently. "I am She who Knows without Knowing, littling. That is the meaning of part of my name."

He drew himself up, the very image of the Attitude of Pride if he had had wings. I envied the Gedri their mobile faces, but found it interesting that they used Attitudes much like ours to convey emotions. "Lanen was dying," he said simply. "Her babes are half Kantri, half Gedri. Her body could not support them, so I changed her blood to match theirs. She is altogether changed now, for you cannot change only the blood. The rest has to match."

I dropped my jaw in astonishment and heard Shikrar draw in his breath sharply. "Do you tell me that Lanen is also half Kantri now?" I breathed. "Surely that is not possible!"

"It is done," said Vilkas. "Whether I should have done it or no, I have." One corner of his mouth turned up. "At least now they'll match."

"Name of the Winds, Varien, you never told me that!" exclaimed Shikrar. His eyes were wide.

"I—to be honest, my friend, I cannot say it has been

uppermost in my thoughts," replied Varien. "So much has happened since, I—"

He broke off, for Shikrar had moved his wings into the Attitude of Surprise, with a touch of Accusation, and the movement had caused him pain. I glanced more keenly at Shikrar, for I had finally realised what it was that had so altered him in so short a time, aside from the taking of Lanen. "If these Healers are so great as all that, Shikrar, why have they not healed you?" I replied.

Vilkas—it is hard to explain—he seemed to sharpen, as if something had broken through the mist he kept about himself. "We did not know he was ill or injured. Have I your permission, Lord Shikrar, to see if I may learn what is amiss with you?"

"It is nothing," said Shikrar swiftly, "I am well enough, I . . ."

"His right wing is damaged, in the first joint, and the wound he received in his left shoulder last autumn has not had the time to heal as it should," I said, annoyed. "Don't be a fool, Shikrar. Perhaps they can help."

"In all the long ages when our people dwelt together, even the strongest Gedri Healers could do very little for the Kantri," replied Shikrar indignantly. I judged that was better than dwelling on pain.

"Ah, but we have done better since," said Aral, her smile broadening. "When Salera's people were—becoming themselves, we healed every one of them. Mind you, there wasn't much to do, but it *did* work." She gazed up fearlessly into Shikrar's eyes. "May we have your permission to help? Or would you rather be brave and in pain a bit longer?"

Shikrar threw his head back and a flicker of flame shot skyward. All of the Gedri but Varien stepped back, shocked. Well, perhaps they had never seen a real laugh before.

"Come, then, heal me an ye may," he said, his eyes dancing. "Name of the Winds, these Gedri have no fear!"

"Say no sense, rather, and you'll be closer," said Aral, who had moved some distance away from Shikrar. "What was that all about?"

Varien smiled, banishing just for an instant the deep well of

sorrow behind his eyes. "It was a laugh, Aral, no more. Lanen"—
ah, and it was back—"I surprised Lanen so, the first time. It is
nothing to fear."

"Oh, I don't know, I think I'm safe enough in fearing that,"
said Vilkas dryly. "You may not burn readily, Varien, but I do."
Turning to Shikrar, he continued. "If you would be so kind as not
to be amused while we treat you, Master Shikrar, I would be
greatly obliged."

His eyes gleamed, but Shikrar answered, "You have my word,
Master Vilkas."

"Do you want any help, Vil?" asked Aral.

"Yes, come on, we both need to learn this," replied Vilkas, already distracted.

It was fascinating to watch him. He who had been all shifting
mist, hidden even from himself as he strove to hide his inner self
from others, became all in a moment a soul sharp and gleaming,
edged and poised for use like a sword. It was extraordinary to behold. "It's all new to me too, the more eyes here the better."

"I will leave you to their tender mercies, my friend," said
Varien, and the ghost of a smile flitted across his face. "I expect to
find you vastly improved when I return." He bowed and wandered off to speak with Rella and they were soon deep in talk.

Vilkas and Aral began what looked like a swift set of ritual
passes through the air. A gentle blue light surrounded them both,
until they joined hands. The gentleness was still there, but the
light was much stronger.

Vilkas

Aral and I sent our power towards Shikrar. It *would* be the
largest of them we'd begin on, I thought. Why start by halves? I
had no idea what we might find. Human anatomy we had learned.
Dragon anatomy was a complete mystery.

Until now.

I was pleased to learn that injury was injury no matter what the
vessel. Dragon blood and bone were not the same as in humans,

but for all that they were still blood and bone. The wing joint was badly inflamed, and the shoulder was still badly damaged for all that I could see it had been worse. With Aral's help, I had a long look at Shikrar's healthy shoulder, and then we got permission from Idai to examine her, to be certain of what healthy tissue looked like.

"Remember, Vil," said Aral, as with the Healer's deep sight we gazed into the tissues of unwounded Idai, "all of these creatures are completely exhausted. You can see it in Shikrar, but at least he's had a few days' rest. This lady and all the rest of them have just pushed themselves to the very limit to survive—look at the buildup of the waste products in the muscles. At least"—and her voice faltered slightly—"it looks like something that shouldn't be there. Drat." She sighed. "I'm not sure we could find a normal example anywhere just at the moment."

"Mmmm, that's the problem, of course. I'm with you, that particulate in the muscle looks like fatigue poison of some kind. It's clear enough, in any case."

"Yes. The wing muscles are the worst, of course. I'd guess the leg muscles are probably the nearest to their normal state—not the ones that have been holding the legs close to the body, the other ones, between the two farthest joints."

I started to move, without thinking, and a wing appeared before me. *The muscles at the edge are not so badly affected,* I thought stupidly, before I looked up, blinking away my Healer's sight. Idai's face was before me, and I glimpsed the covering of amazingly tough hide and the blood vessels beneath, stretched over the heavy bone of the mask, before my normal sight returned.

"Are you always so heedless of those whom you heal?" she said, and I was briefly surprised by the fact that I could hear the annoyance in a dragon's voice as clearly as I would in anyone.

"Your pardon, Lady," I said, nodding to her. "I—when we are so deep in the Healer's sight, it is difficult to remember that there is a person—and with you, there is so much to learn—"

Aral appeared by my side and interrupted. "Lady Idai, please forgive my colleague. He concentrates harder than any three people I know. I've seen him get so immersed in what he's doing he forgets to eat for days on end. And yes, he gets a bit heedless of his patients, but that's what he needs me for." She jabbed her elbow, surprisingly subtly, into my ribs. "May we have your permission to examine your—er—back legs?"

Idai obligingly extended a leg, glancing keenly at Aral. "I see. I have known others so lose themselves in their work. Somehow it does not surprise me that males of both our Kindreds have this in common," she said. Aral grinned up at her before getting back to work.

It was clear in a moment when we saw the healthy muscle—we had to look deep, but there is something unmistakable about bodies that are working as they should. The deep tissue of the unused muscles still had that silver glow of health about it, though the bloodstream was carrying the fatigue poisons throughout the body.

"Well, Vil, I can see what needs done," said Aral shortly. "You?"

"Yes. It looks easy enough."

I felt another jab of Aral's elbow, but I'm not stupid. I was just about to speak in any case.

"Our thanks, Lady. With your assistance, I think we can help Shikrar."

Idai dipped her head and a sinuous wave followed down her long neck. Very odd indeed, but she seemed happy enough.

Aral is right. I do tend to lose track of the social graces when I'm working.

We moved back to Shikrar's side. "We'll do it as usual, eh?" I said. "You compress and provide the pain relief, I'll shift the inflammation."

I looked up at the vast form now above me. Truly, things could be easier.

"My lord Shikrar," I said, not knowing if they used such titles. Better than nothing. "Will it please you to come closer?"

His head was suddenly very, very close to mine and I couldn't help but flinch. Goddess, he was huge. "Have you any hope, truly, of healing me?"

I almost laughed. Honestly. Everyone always thought they were different. "The Lady's power heals all, my lord, rich and poor alike. I cannot think why it should not heal you."

"But we do not worship the Lady of the Gedri," he said.

"Maybe you should start," said Aral, grinning. "Have we your permission to try, Shikrar?"

He lay right down then, putting his wing gingerly upon the ground. It was still going to be hard to reach that affected shoulder, but—first things first.

"You may try, Aralishaan," he said kindly.

Aral

We moved together to the wing joint, getting it clear before our eyes, seeing exactly what needed to be done. We joined hands and sent our power forth.

At least, we tried to. I felt Vil increase his own strength until he glowed even in broad daylight, but it wasn't going anywhere. Our power went no farther than the ends of our fingers.

Shikrar, watching closely, closed his eyes. "Alas. I feared it might be so. In all our history, there have been few of the Gedri who could help us to heal." He sighed. "Perhaps it was too much to hope that the two of you might have been among them."

"Don't move!" I yelled angrily to Shikrar. "Don't give up yet, Vil! We healed Salera's people, I know we can—wait—wait, of course!"

I had felt a slight burning for the last few minutes, where the pouch around my neck touched my chest, and it had finally occurred to me that when we had healed Salera and her kin, I had held the gem in my hand. Perhaps that would do it.

I let go Vil's left hand and fumbled with the pouch and finally managed to get out the large gem. I held it tight in my hand.

I wish someone had told me. That kind of thing shouldn't happen to the unprepared.

Shikrar

The Kin-Summoning is a ritual among our people, requiring days of fasting and preparation and the burning of special herbs and leaves. As a part of our choice at the dawn of Time, we were given a way to remember all that has gone before. The soulgems of our ancestors allow us, when necessary, to speak to those who have died.

Or so it had ever been before. Though on those occasions, it has always been the Keeper of Souls who gave way to the Ancestor being summoned.

Aral, with her Healer's power about her, drew forth the soulgem she had in her keeping. I spared a moment's thought to commend that unknown Ancestor to the Winds, and to pledge silently that I would soon rescue her from this Gedri child who held her all unwitting, when Aral suddenly stood straighter and looked into my eyes. The Healer's glow about her was reduced to a flicker.

"What are you called, my kitling?" she asked, and her voice was as near to the voice of a Lady of our Kindred as a human could manage it.

I could think of nothing to say, though my mind began to race. Kitling, indeed! I was the Eldest of the Kantri alive at that time.

"Come, come, what are you called? I hight Loriavaitriakeris, daughter of Kai the Old and my dear mother Tethrik. You may call me Loriakeris." Aral smiled. "So you see, there is no need to be rude. What is your use-name?"

"I hight Shikrar," I said, entranced. "Lady, I know of you. My soulfriend Akhor is of your lineage, but—but we thought you lost these many ages past!"

"Not lost, young Shikrar, no, no, not lost. Just . . . spending my time with the Gedri." Aral's smile softened. "This is not the time for this discussion. I believe that with my help, these Healers can do their work. Do you permit?"

"Yes," I stammered, and in the instant Aral was back, with her Healer's aura deep blue about her, and the soulgem in her hand glowing brilliant ruby.

"Hells' teeth, what was *that*?" she cried.

"Later, Aral," said Vilkas, his voice stony, his gaze still locked deep in my injuries. "Are you well?"

"How should I be well? Some dead dragon just took over my body, how in all the Hells could I be well!" she yelled.

Vilkas wrenched himself away from studying me and took Aral by the shoulders. "Aral, not now. We need to work. Are you injured?"

"No," she said sullenly, shaking off his grasp. "Just angry."

"Then help me. I need you, and we need that—Loria-what's-her-name. Now."

"I'll do what I can, but don't ask me to work, I'm far too angry."

"That's fine for now," said Vilkas, turning back to stare into my wing. "Just you open that door and let me in . . ."

Aral, mumbling, laid her left hand on his shoulder. Her right still held Loriakeris's soulgem—and in the moment, I felt a wave of power, and blessedly, there was no more pain. "You've damaged this ligament," muttered Vilkas as he worked, "shouldn't take long to—there, that's it—now the inflammation . . ."

It was fascinating, the link that was forged. Not that he could hear truespeech, or that I could hear him precisely, but there was most certainly a connection. I wondered if other Gedri were aware of it when they were being healed.

And then, as I was concentrating on the link between us, I noticed for the first time a strange undercurrent to my thought. There was something of truespeech in it, but there did not seem to be many words. It was more like a distant murmuring. I wondered briefly if Salera was teaching all her people about truespeech, but that did not seem right—as I have said, younglings cannot normally keep their early truespeech under such control. However, a swift sharp pain, like a stiff muscle unlocking, brought my thought suddenly back to those who were working to assist me.

This Vilkas, I noted, was a most extraordinary soul. I had never heard of such a man. For all his usual reserve, for all that he

fought the very essence of himself with every breath, he could
yet give of his gifts without stint and without restraint to accomplish this healing. A gift indeed. It was over in mere minutes, but
in those minutes, what a change! By the time he had finished,
Vilkas was sweating and breathing like prey running from a
hunter. He was moving towards my shoulder, but I stretched out
my forearm and stopped him. "Enough for now, Master Vilkas," I
said quietly.

"No, that's just the easy part, I need to—"

I did not let him move. "It is enough for now. You will exhaust
yourself, and that will serve no one."

Vilkas opened his mouth to argue, but Aral interrupted.
"Quite right. Thank you, Shikrar," she responded loudly. Then
she quietly muttered something to Vilkas that I could not hear. It
must have been a powerful argument, for he released his healing
power and sat heavily on the ground.

I was concerned for him, but as I opened my mouth to speak
to him a great noise arose from behind me. *Name of the Winds,
does this day hold no peace?*

And there, in the back of my mind, a little louder now but still
faint, that distant murmuring, like waves on a shingle shore.

ii

The Wind of Change

Idai

It was just as well that Varien had gone apart with Rella, for I had to protect the Gedri with my body from those who sought to harm her and I could not have protected him as well. I had barely glimpsed the creature before I had to save its life.

"It reeks of the Rakshasa!"

"Move away, Idai. It is evil!"

Great flutterings of wings, great agitation, exhaustion, frustration, and very little thought. Shikrar and I had long feared this moment and spoken of what we should do. I was learning, yet again, that plans are never complete enough to deal with life. I could smell the demon-trace around this woman as well as any, but Shikrar and I had made oath to each other that we would not harm nor allow harm to come to any who came to us in peace no matter what they reeked of. It would take a great deal to make me trust this Gedri, but first I must keep her alive.

"This is not yet our home!" I shouted, trying by sheer volume to break through the anger of my people. "On the Island of Exile we were alone and accountable only to ourselves. Here we must learn to bear with the Gedri; we must learn to live among them whatever they may reek of. They were given Choice by the great Powers!" I summoned calm and let as much concern as I could find show in my voice. "That gift of Choice is with them until they die. Would you steal this soul from the Win—from the Lady of the Gedri, before it has a chance to repent?"

This won at least a moment of silence. The Kantri are fire-hearted, and the reek of the Rakshasa fans the flame terribly, but we are not stupid.

A muffled voice came from the region of my chest. "For goodness' sake, my soul to the Lady, I am in Her service! It's not me they're reacting to, it's this thrice-damned Farseer. If you'd just give me a moment to speak . . ."

I opened my talons, looked down, and there found that which would in all likelihood make me trust her, for looking up at me was the very image of Lanen, if you added enough years and lines and turned half her hair to grey. "My thanks," she said, nodding to me. She bore a large pack on her back and I still held her close. "I suspect I owe you my life. May I ask your name?"

"I am called Idai. You are the mother of Lanen," I said. It was not a question. I bespoke Shikrar and Varien as I gazed down at her. *My friends, there is someone here whom you must meet. Come quickly. I feel the need of your counsel.*

The Gedri's eyes, clear and relieved before, clouded. "Yes. I am Maran of Beskin." She stood straighter—*for courage,* I thought— and something of desperation came into her gaze. "Have you found her?"

"No," I said quietly. "Have you?"

"I think so," she replied, never glancing away.

Shikrar

I hurried to answer Idai's summons, still weary from the curious aftereffects of my healing and leaving Vilkas and Aral where they stood. I found Idai surrounded by many of our folk, nearly all of whom stood in the Attitudes of Anger or Frustration. More worrying, I felt also an undercurrent of Fire, that flame that arises in us in the presence of our life-enemies the Rakshasa. Varien arrived about the same time I did.

Before I could speak, though, Rinshir cried out, "The Gedri that Idai defends reeks of the Rakshasa, Eldest!" He too stood in Anger, but his was moving swiftly towards something stronger. "Are we come to this, that we should protect the Raksha-touched?"

"We are new-come here, Rinshir. Would you then destroy this child of the Gedri, in its own land, with no thought of its life or its laws, without even troubling to ask why it has come among us?" I resisted my own anger and the temptation to shame Rinshir further. "You are weary, my friend, weary and hungry and unsure of what lies ahead, as are we all. Let us not begin our lives here in our ancient home by murdering an innocent."

"Hardly innocent, Master," interrupted the Gedri from Idai's shelter. I could have cheerfully swatted it myself. Stupid creature! *Just like Lanen*, I thought, *no sense of when to hold its peace. Are all the Gedri so foolish, I wonder?*

"Shall we let all the demon-touched pass unharmed, then, that they may murder us at their ease?" snarled Rinshir. "I do not like your reasoning, Hadreshikrar."

"I do not appeal to reason, Rinshir," I replied as calmly as I could, "but to mercy, and to patience. Remember, Raksha-trace can linger where the soul has been attacked as well as when it has had traffic with the creatures themselves."

"If you would just bloody well listen to me, I could explain!" cried the Gedri, its voice muffled by the protective cage of Idai's hands. "I am not a demon-caller! Name of the Lady, I've spent half my life fighting the damned things. It's the Farseer you feel, I swear it on my life!"

And finally, I heard the voice that uttered those words, even though I could not see her face, and my resolve sharpened. "I will have your word, Rinshir, that you will not harm this daughter of the Gedri, that you will keep silence and let her speak in safety," I said quietly. "I will take it upon my own soul to vow that she will not call the Rakshasa down upon us."

Varien had reached us then, and came to stand near Idai. He glanced at the Gedri in her hands and drew in his breath in surprise.

Rinshir moved away slightly, his Attitude of Concern warring with that of Anger. "Shikrar, don't be absurd. Your soul's pledge for a demon-tainted Gedri? What could make you do such a th . . ." He drew back, standing in Amazement, but only for a moment. Then his eyes widened in realisation, and he moved in the instant from Amazement to Fury. "Surely she bends your will even now, Eldest!" he cried, and faster than thought he drew in a breath to flame the evil where it stood.

I could do no more than stare at Rinshir, astounded at such hatred, entirely unprepared. Idai, blessedly, was ready for him. When he arched his neck and aimed at the creature Idai was protecting, she knocked his head back with her own, so that his flame scorched only air. I was most impressed; I had never seen Idai move so swiftly. While he was recovering from that blow, she knocked his wings aside with her own, loosed the Gedri woman, and wrapped her right hand around his throat, just under the jaw where we are most vulnerable.

I kept well out of it. If anything, I'd have assisted Idai.

"You fool, Rinshir," she hissed, her talons poised at the great vein in his throat. "How do you dare to attack that which I guard?"

"It is demon-stained, Idai!" he yelped in his own defence. His voice was none too clear.

"Thrice fool and blind," she snapped, her teeth worryingly close to his throat. I began to fear a little for Rinshir's life, but there, defying Idai was the act of one who cared little for life in any case. "And did you not see this other Gedri standing here, who would also have died in your flame?"

Rinshir looked down, but he did not recognise what he saw.

"Good morrow, Rinshir," said Varien quietly. "I had hoped that your travels might have stretched your mind as well as your wings, but alas, I see no evidence of it."

Rinshir flinched at that voice, distorted as it was through

Gedri throat and tongue. Varien, for all the changes that had beset him, was still our King and held our fealty.

"I have lived eight hundred winters longer than you, fool of a *dhraisek*," hissed Idai. "Are you then grown so very wise in so very short a time that you can see that which is hidden from me, while it lies yet between my talons?" Her eyes glittered and her wings rattled with her anger. I was glad to see that Rinshir had yet some sense left, for he finally tried to move away from her. He did not get far, as she did not loosen her grip on his throat.

"Do not think to challenge me, Rinshir," she hissed, keeping her body between Rinshir and Varien. "There is a very old and very simple reason why we of the Kantrishakrim respect our elders. I am twice your size, and by all the Winds that ever blew, I will fight you if you do not heed me." Without apparent effort she overbalanced him and bore him to the ground, her talons still around his throat and her face a blink away from him. "And know this, fool," she snarled in his ear. "If ever you bring even the least harm to Lord Akhor, to Varien, by my name I swear I will have it out of your hide."

I had never seen Idai so angry, and in that moment I was sincerely grateful that I had followed my own deepest instincts and had kept on her good side ever since she was the merest youngling. To speak truly I do not know what would have happened had not Varien walked up to put his hand on her forearm.

"Idai, my friend, it is enough," he said gently. "Let him go. We are unharmed, all is well. Let him go."

Idai

Varien's voice shook me out of my self-indulgent anger. I stood back and let go of Rinshir. I don't think I have ever seen him move so quickly. I turned to Shikrar, who stood beside me, and winked. Just as well he should never know how near I had come to murdering Rinshir for even thinking of putting Akhor in danger.

"A moment, if you please," said a voice from near the ground. The Gedri woman, who had very sensibly moved away while I was instructing Rinshir, had returned, and now she laid her hand on my forearm as Varien had. "I have you to thank for my life," she said simply. "I am deeply in your debt."

Varien stepped forward and stood beside her. "As am I, Idai. As ever. Again."

I hissed my amusement. "It was worth it to see Rinshir's Attitude change. From fury to absolute terror in a single moment. Most satisfying." I glanced down at the Gedri woman, then to Varien as I said, "And now, if you please, Maran of Beskin, you will tell us what it is about you that so reeks of our life-enemies."

"I've been using the Farseer to keep up with Lanen," she said simply. "Whenever I use it the stink wears off on me. I must be overdue to make my devotions to the Lady. I never meant to set everyone off. Seems you folk are a lot more sensitive to it than we are." She scrubbed at her face with both hands. "The damned thing's barely worth the bother of keeping, when all's done," she said wearily, "but as long as I have it, Berys can't bloody well make another one. That's the only reason I didn't smash it twenty years ago—though I'd never have found you in time if I had." She paused for a moment. "Do you have the first idea where Lanen is?"

"No," said Varien cautiously, "though one of our number has gone to seek her in Verfaren."

"Thank the Goddess," she said, and unfamiliar as I was with Gedri faces, even I could recognise the relief in her voice. "It's Jamie, isn't it?" It wasn't a question.

"Yes," said Rella, speaking quietly as she appeared behind Maran. "Well-met, my friend," she said, nodding to the newcomer. "Jamie's gone after her."

"Blessed Mother Shia, we might have a chance yet," Maran replied, but before she could say more I heard Kédra's voice calling out to us all. At least *he* sounded pleased.

Shikrar

Kédra and Will returned at just that moment and provided a much-needed distraction. The sounds at the edge of hearing were growing noticeably louder. I could nearly make out words. And it seemed to be coming from somewhere near at hand.

While he was still high up and a little way distant, Kédra called aloud to us all on the ground, "All is well! We have food, my friends, and water in abundance, and a place to rest as long as we need it!" Kédra landed awkwardly, allowing Will to drop just the little distance from his hands as he backwinged frantically. As Will picked himself up and brushed the earth from his clothing, I bespoke my son.

"Kédra, how fare you? Is it well, truly?"

"It is very well, my father," he replied aloud, though his eyes were troubled. "I must speak with you soon, Father," he said in tightly focussed truespeech, then continued aloud, "Farmer Timeth is presently recovering from the acquisition of sudden wealth, but his kine are healthy, his water is good, and his farm backs up to a high rock wall to the north, under the shelter of which there is room for us all."

"Blessed be the Winds," I murmured. "Good news at last."

Mirazhe came to join us then, her tiny youngling Sherók awake now and riding between her wings. He looked so terribly small and fragile. When I frowned a little at Mirazhe and opened my mouth, she hissed a laugh and said, "Fear not, Hadreshikrar. Your son's son is perfectly safe, and the soulgems of the Lost are in Gyrentikh's keeping."

I shut my mouth with a snap and turned my head away briefly in embarrassment as Kédra and Mirazhe laughed. "Am I so transparent, my daughter?"

She replied, her eyes dancing, "You are, my father. But none the less valued for that."

Sherók, for his part, was delighted with the view despite the hunger that he was broadcasting in waves. Kédra greeted his son by touching his soulgem to the raised spot on Sherók's faceplate where his soulgem would eventually break through, and Sherók's thoughts turned from hunger to joy in the instant. The wash of his pleasure at seeing his father again was as the dawning of a second sun to my weary soul, and I stood and called to the

Kantri, aloud and in truespeech, telling them Kédra's news.

"It is nearby, dear heart," muttered Kédra to Mirazhe. "I have not eaten, but it will not be long now." Indeed, most of the Kantri were preparing to depart when Vilkas came running up to me.

"Lord Shikrar, please, you must not let them eat right away!" he cried, a little out of breath. "Will told me what you were doing, but you must listen. Don't let them eat at first! Start by drinking. And when you kill the cattle, start by drinking the blood."

I stared at him. "Surely how we eat is no concern of yours," I said, annoyed at his tone of command.

"Please, I beg you, listen to me. Your bodies are very similar to ours, I saw the results of fatigue in your blood and muscle. Just exactly like us. And I tell you, if you eat meat too quickly after such desperate exhaustion and hunger, you could die of it. Even water is not the best. Blood has salt and enough sugar to help you back to enough strength to eat. Drink the blood, I pray you, and wait an hour until you are recovered. Then drink water, slowly, and very small amounts of food at first—that is the most important. Eat much less than you want, lest your hearts stop from the shock."

"We have managed to live so long without your assistance, Master Vilkas," I said dryly. "I thank you for your concern, but—"

"Shikrar, didn't you tell me once that some of the Ancestors died when they reached the Isle of Exile?" asked Varien quietly.

"Yes, the greedy ones who gorged themselves on the few large creatures who lived on the island, and left the rest to—oh."

I closed my eyes and sighed. When I opened them again, I bowed to Vilkas, to his great surprise. "Master Vilkas, forgive my foolishness. We will do as you have asked."

Vilkas nodded to me, an attenuated bow, and strode back to where Mistress Aral spoke with Will. I called out in truespeech to all the Kantri, who, groaning and complaining, nevertheless began to rise and flex stiff wings. I took a moment to bespeak Kédra.

"What did you need to say to me, my son?" I asked, but he did not answer immediately.

I was just as glad, for the murmur in my head was growing now with every breath. I listened again—nothing distinct yet—and shook my head to clear it. And watched my son do precisely the same thing.

"*Kédra, do you hear this whispering?*" I asked urgently.

"*Nearly shouting now,*" he replied, frustrated. "*But I can't make out the words. Have you the faintest idea what it is or where it is coming from?*"

"*Not the least,*" I began, but I was interrupted by a loud mind-voice under very poor control.

"*The Hollow Ones have risen! Be 'ware, my elders, the Hollow Ones follow me close!*"

We all, every Kantri on live, looked up into the western sky. Salera was flying on the Winds' wings, desperately powering ahead of a great cloud of . . . of . . .

Of the Lesser Kindred. But as they drew nearer, I could see that these were the Lesser Kindred as we had known them of old, as our Ancestors spoke of them: no soulgems, no sign of intellect, no spark at all. They appeared to be mobbing Salera as crows will mob a hawk, but when she flew past at speed and just as I was preparing to fly to her aid, they all came to land. There must have been nearly two hundred of them, all dark of hue like rusted iron, falling clumsily to earth in a great crowd. The Kantri, now fully roused, surrounded them—but even so I was not prepared.

Gyrentikh let out a great shout. "Shikrar! Shikrar, quickly, here!"

I leapt into the air, blessing the work of Vilkas and Aral as I climbed just a few tens of feet that I might see Gyrentikh. I might have saved myself the effort. He was at the center of a circle of the strange creatures. None came closer than one of their own body lengths, but every pair of dull eyes was focussed unblinking on—Gyrentikh?

No. On that which he guarded.

I backwinged in shock, fool that I was, stalled, and fell to the ground. I hadn't done that since before I had seen seventy winters.

"Shikrar!" cried Varien. "Shikrar, what—"

"The Lost. The soulgems of the Lost!" I shouted, climbing to my feet. "That's why they're here." I stood now beside Gyrentikh, facing all those desperately intent beasts, and I shook to my bones. "Name of the Winds, Akhor. What are we to do?"

I found that I was shouting, for the whispering was turned now to yells, and it was coming from the golden cask over which Gyrentikh still bravely stood guard.

I could hear words now. Cursing, screaming, wordless shouts, and one cry repeated over and over.

"LET US OUT! LET US OUT! LET US OUT!"

Varien

I hadn't the faintest idea what was going on. I was about to try to push my way into the midst of that unnatural crowd when Salera came running up, Will trailing behind her.

"Lord, these are the Hollow Ones!" cried Salera, terribly distressed. "They have our shape but they are beasts. They know neither speech nor reason. Beware, they have killed our kind before!"

"Whence came they?" I asked. "Quickly, Salera!"

"I was following Lord Kédra when several of my people hailed me," she said rapidly. "I had only begun to speak to them of truespeech when we all became aware of a terrible darkness below. We have had to fly from the Hollow Ones before, but only ever in ones and twos. This—this is very wrong." She shivered. "We all chose different directions and scattered, but the Hollow Ones followed me. I thought my death had chosen me. What is it they seek, Lord? What has called them here?"

"The soulgems of the Lost, it seems. Why, I have no idea."

Maran strode up, her pack on her back, Rella, Vil, and Aral behind her. Maran's eyes were fixed on the dark agitated crowd of the Hollow Ones. There was now a great fluttering of wings among them, that in the Kantri denotes rising anger.

"What in all the Hells is this about?" asked Maran quietly.

I opened my mind to bespeak Shikrar and staggered from the noise.

"LET US OUT!"

Shikrar

I could bear the shouting in my mind no longer. I could think of nothing else to do, so I picked up the golden cask that contained the soulgems of the Lost. Instantly there was silence, from the beasts and in my head.

"Go, Gyrentikh," I commanded him quietly. "They are not come for you." He walked slowly through the beasts, who ignored him, while I tried desperately to think.

When one of the Kantri dies, the soulgem remains. It shrinks to half its size in life and is preserved with all honour in the Chamber of Souls, in appearance like a great gem. These gems are dark until the Keeper of Souls has cause to summon an Ancestor. At such times, the soulgem of the particular Ancestor will glow gently as it did in life, until the Summoning is over.

When last the Kantri lived in Kolmar, five thousand years before, a great and nameless Demonlord had arisen. In the terrible battle that ended in his death, we found to our despair that he had learned how to destroy us. A single word, a single gesture from the Nameless One, and one of the Kantri would fall from the sky: they dwindled to the size of younglings and their soulgems were ripped from them. Even after the Demonlord was dead, we could find no way to restore those who had been defiled. They were become as beasts, and their soulgems never turned dull as with death—ever they flickered, neither alive nor dead. We came to call them, our family, our dear friends now taken, the Lost. That we might not take our revenge from the innocent Gedri who remained, we flew west, to the Isle of Exile, taking with us the soulgems. None now lived, or had for three and a half thousand years, who had known any of the Lost in life. Since the day it happened we had tried to restore the Lost, to no avail.

I had no idea what was happening now or why, but in the silence of my heart I was forced to admit that there was nothing to lose.

I lifted the cask high and with one talon incised a circle in the top of the golden cask in which we had carried the soulgems with us across the Great Sea. I gently removed the circle and dropped it in the grass.

The soulgems of the Lost were not flickering, as they had for so many centuries. They were blazing.

The soulless creatures surged towards me. Had we been of a size, I had surely been overwhelmed, but I am the Eldest and thus the largest of the Kantri. They were like so many younglings.

I was uncertain of what to do next when a cry of pain drew my attention.

It was Maran.

Maran

I had ignored the rising heat at my back until that big dragon opened that damned golden egg. In the instant I felt as if my back were on fire. I threw my pack from my back and turned to stare at it.

The leather was burning. In a circle.

In moments the Farseer was revealed, a globe of smoky glass about the size of a small melon. I gingerly moved my hand towards it, expecting extreme heat—but there was nothing. I touched it, picked it up: no heat at all.

When I looked up, the Farseer in both hands, I was confronted by a sea of blank faces. The little dull dragons, though they stayed in a circle around the big dragon—was he called Shikar, something like that?—they were staring at me now.

"Hells' teeth, what's in that dirty great golden bowl?" I asked anyone who would listen.

And there at my elbow, with several other people, was the silver-haired man my Lanen had married, telling me swiftly about those he called the Lost.

As he spoke, as I forced myself to listen and to ignore the fact that I still didn't know his name, something chimed in my memory. I had studied the disciplines of the Lady—at one time I thought I'd have to become a Servant to escape the demons—but I couldn't remember. Something about balance.

As if he read my mind, the tall young lad with the silly beard stepped forward. "By the Goddess, it just might be," he said, his eyes alight with possibility. "The Lost were dragons transformed by the Demonlord, a man who sold his true name and his very soul to demons. It took all three races together to create the Lost. Perhaps . . ."

"Perhaps it will take all three to restore them," said the silver one, his glorious voice deep and resonant and full of a wild hope. His eyes were gleaming and he was shaking with excitement, and I have to admit I caught some of it. "Come, Maran, perhaps your Raksha-taint will serve us after all!" he cried, pulling me with him into the middle of that uncanny circle of creatures. "You as well, Vilkas," he cried, and the tall lad followed.

As I came close to Shikrar the beasts started fluttering their wings again, a dry rattle that sent a shiver down my back.

Varien

"Shikrar, put them down," I said quietly. "Vilkas thinks—it might be—we may be able to do it, Shikrar, at last. Restore the Lost."

"What must I do, Akhor?" he asked softly, laying the cask on the grass at his feet. His control was extraordinary. His voice hardly trembled at all.

"Lift out a single soulgem," I said, my eyes never leaving the beast-eyes that stared intently at the three of us. Shikrar reverently picked up a blazing violet gem. A single creature stepped forward—it happened to be the nearest—and lowered its head. There in the faceplate was a shallow depression. I took the soulgem from Shikrar and, shaking, placed it in the hollow.

Nothing. The creature did not move.

"All three, Varien," said Vilkas quietly. "All three."

I took Maran's hand and Shikrar's talon and brought them together to touch the gem.

Nothing.

"I may stink of the things, but I'm not a real demon," said Maran quietly. "This was made by them." She lifted the Farseer to touch the soulgem, but she had overbalanced. It slipped from her fingers. All three of us—Shikrar, Maran, and I—moved to catch it at once, and were all touching it at the same time.

Upon the instant a great blaze of light streamed from the Farseer, dazzling even in daylight. I tried to let go of it and could not, and neither could the others. When I thought to look, I realised that the Hollow One still stood before us, unmoving, soulgem in place.

What was there to lose?

"Together, then. Touch the Farseer to the soulgem," I said. It took but a tiny movement from us all—a little farther—contact.

The soulgem caught a portion of the Farseer's blaze. There was a grotesque sizzle like fat in a fire, and the creature stepped back. Its eyes were wide, surprise warring with furious joy for just an instant—and it *changed*. I had never understood why that simple word was so important in the tale of the Demonlord until I saw it happen.

In reverse.

In an instant.

Light and colour spread out from the soulgem, flowing swift as flame over the creature, first changing that rusty black faceplate to one of bright iron, then extending the full length of the beast—which was a great deal more length than it had before. In moments, impossibly, there stood before us a full-grown adult of the Kantrishakrim, dazed, blinking in the daylight, astounded.

Shikrar, eyes wide, somehow managed to croak, "Welcome, Lady. I hight Shikrar of the line of Issdra. Who art thou?"

"Tréshak. I hight Tréshak," she managed, and cried out in agony.

Idai hurried up to her. "Lady, what ails you? What may be done for you?"

"Not me," she moaned. "Help them. The rest of them. Free them, quickly, in the name of the Winds!"

And so we did. As the three of us were yet bound to the Farseer, Vilkas drew forth the soulgems and held them in place while we touched the Farseer to each in turn.

I had dreamed of this moment for many long years. Our people had striven to restore the Lost since they had been torn from life by the Demonlord. In the thousands of years since, there had been endless debate about the flicker of the soulgems. Were the Lost in some way still alive and aware? Were they tormented by demons? Would any of them still be sane if we did manage to bring them back after long ages of whatever imprisonment they endured?

It seemed in the end to depend on the individual.

Many, blessedly, were largely undamaged. Their imprisonment had seemed little more than a long, uneasy Weh sleep, and they simply awoke in their new bodies with little sense of the passage of time.

Some had been aware for part of the time, crying out, feeling trapped in some desperate place. They said that they had drifted in and out of consciousness. They thought perhaps several tens of years had passed while they were ensorcelled. Somehow they had managed to cling to hope, but they were furiously angry.

The first of these to be released saw Gedri standing before it and drew in a breath of Fire. I cried out to Shikrar, who managed to deflect the blast upwards. We did not condemn him—the last thing he recalled clearly was a treacherous Gedri, the Demonlord, who had stolen his life from him. He was taken away by the Kantri to a part of the field far from the Gedri, where he was told as gently as possible what had happened in the intervening time.

Vilkas took a moment to warn Rella, Will, and the Healers to move out of sight until all could be explained to the confused souls. They disappeared in the direction of the Dragon's Head, an inn hard by the field.

There were a few, though, who wrung our hearts from us. A score of souls found themselves in the green world, cried out in agony, and threw themselves into death.

It is rare that a child of the Kantri will willingly choose death, but we can do so if the pain of life is too great. It is very simple. There is a—a something in the base of the throat. The nearest that humans can understand would be a flint. It would be as if you filled a room with oil-soaked straw, threw in a lighted match, and closed the door.

When we die, in the natural course of things, the fire within is released from our control and we burn to ash very quickly. This was even faster. The first of the Lost who chose death passed to the Winds in less time than it had taken for its new form to appear. Shikrar, his voice trembling, asked Vilkas to collect the soulgem and bring it to him: when he saw it clearly, he heaved a deep sigh of relief. It was small and dull. The poor trapped soul was released to death at last, and could rest.

It took nearly five hours to restore them all. We were exhausted by the end, but we had no choice—the Farseer clung, blazing, to our hands, until the last of the Lost was restored. The moment all was accomplished, the thing dropped to the grass, dark and lifeless.

Shikrar, Maran and I followed in much the same fashion.

Berys

What a fine chance! I had only just sent along a Rikti spy to report on what the damned dragons were doing, and behold, what piece of news it has brought me! If I understand it aright, it appears that those whom the Demonlord had thought destroyed have been restored. How very *resourceful* of them.

So, the number of my enemies is doubled. And these new creatures were created by the Demonlord, whose imminent arrival will doubtless rouse them to fury and to the foolishness of acting in anger.

How interesting. It will be useful to see how he deals with them.

On the whole, I believe that I am pleased. What fun would all this be if it were too simple?

Marik has confirmed the Rikti's report. How kind of him to keep me informed, and how charming that the damage the dragons inflicted upon him has allowed him to hear the thoughts of those two creatures. Shikrar and Akor. Altogether delightful.

I was uncertain as to when I would unleash all those lovely healers of Marik's. There they sit, so demure in House of Gundar trade establishments throughout the four Kingdoms of Kolmar, no sign of their slightly suspect allegiance. And I never coerced one; they have come to us of their own free will. Ah, how easily the lust for power corrupts.

It is astounding how many folk are unhappy with the power they have, and how willing they are to take part in something they know to be wrong. Just a little corruption at first, a fortnight to try out the new power available to them before they must choose. Nearly all, having become accustomed to the greater level of power in those few days of the trial, are seduced by the good they can do.

They are under no illusions. Even the most ignorant village Healer knows perfectly well that power is either the gift of the Lady or the price of the Rakshi. Barely one in a hundred has had the moral courage to resist. Barely one in ten of those has refused entirely. After all, it is such a *little* price. A lock of hair. Not much to ask. Hair grows back.

And now they are there in their hundreds, all over Kolmar, ready to my hand. When I activate the link, those who have submitted to this will be, swiftly and simply, taken over by a demon. They will retain half their natural power for the demons to make use of—and demons are very good at making use of power—and half the power of every single Healer who has made this pact will flow into my hands, to do with as I will. Once I set them in motion, with the simplest of rituals, they will go forth and take the darkness with them. Slaying patients, destroying crops, burning homes—whatever the demon fancies.

If I send them out before the Demonlord arrives, they will cause extra chaos: a nice distraction. If after, they will give my foes yet more to worry about, piled upon already burdened hearts and minds. Both are attractive—hmmm.

Chaos, I think. I should just have time for the ritual this evening before my treat.

As for the Demonlord himself—that Black Dragon is damnably slow. I feel every beat of its wings and it is exhausting. Just as well that I have the body of a young man now; I do not believe that my old self would have had the pure strength to bear it.

I have already accomplished the impossible, of course. The fools I am surrounded by should bow down and worship at my feet. They have no idea—but ah, they will learn. Very, very soon.

I, Berys—no. No, I need hide no longer. I, Malior, only living Demon-Master of the Sixth Hell, have performed the greatest work of my life but these few days past. It has taken me many long years, much learning, much sacrifice, and quite a bit of blood— some of it even mine—but at last I have summoned the Demonlord, he who gave up his name for all time in exchange for power. Five thousand years ago, before he faced the great dragons in battle, he performed the spell of the Distant Heart. His own beating heart was removed from his chest, placed safely in a box of gold, silver, and lead, and taken by the Rakshasa to a far distant place where none would ever find it and he would live forever.

He was no fool. When he started destroying the True Dragons, thus fulfilling the deepest desire of his soul, they fought back. The spells and demon-protections he had established kept him alive for some little while, and half the dragons died that day, they say. However, they finally managed to exact vengeance by destroying his body. It is written that he laughed even as his body was burnt to a cinder, and no one knew why.

I know why. Because he knew through his arts that one day, a demon-master possessed of great power would create for him a new body, untouchable this time by fire, and that he would live again, this time forever.

Ah, life is sweet.

For I have found it, not two moons since. The Demonlord's Distant Heart. Every demon-summoner alive would murder cheerfully for the knowledge I now possess.

A few days past I summoned the Lord of the Fifth Hell, who told me that the Demonlord could only be destroyed by a creature that bleeds both dragon and human blood when cut. Such a thing must exist for the spell of the Distant Heart requires a counterspell to be effective, but I could waste years searching for it and still never find it. After all, demons are not truly aware of time as we know it. This creature might have died out centuries ago, or not been born yet.

I knew that before I summoned the Demonlord, knew that I could neither banish nor destroy him immediately—but there are ways and ways to deal with demons. The binding spells that hold him can be renewed easily enough, for as long as I like. Perhaps my arts will, in time, allow me to fabricate such a creature. It is not beyond possibility—and after all, I will soon have a wife! Given sufficient preparation, surely I can create a child that would answer that need. And in the meantime, I will have the means of my eventual success at hand. For what would be the good of finding the creature of mixed blood if I had not the Distant Heart in my possession?

And I have found it by pure chance.

This autumn past, poor deluded Marik of Gundar, who has relied on me to bolster his power for many years, took the risk of travelling to the Dragon Isle to gather lansip, that marvellous leaf that grew only in that one place in all the world. Healall, good for everything from headache to heart's-ease, and when taken in sufficient quantity, able to reverse the effects of time itself. All in all, I suppose I should be grateful for Marik's delusion: it has given me back half a century of life, and it drew my attention to the Dragon Isle. I has prudently avoided that place for many years, for the Kantri, the True Dragons who lived on that island so far to the west, have a natural power over the Rakshasa who serve me. However, as I began to search some months ago for the proper material out of which to create a body for the Demonlord to inhabit, all suddenly came clear.

A body untouchable by fire must be made of fire, or of stone. A body of fire is unworkable, for fire—even demonfire—must have something to burn upon, however small, and that would soon be exhausted. I could have fashioned him a body of granite, but it would take years and years, and I have no wish to wait so long. It is also the case that hard stone is unforgiving, and it can be shattered given sufficient strength. No, the Dragon Isle held the answer. It was volcanic in nature: fire and stone at once, fluid and ready to be shaped to my will, and vastly lighter than solid rock. I had only to call forth the molten stone from the heart of the island.

When I began the work I meant only to shape a body that would hold the Demonlord—I intended the shape to be a figure of dread to the dragons, that they might feel that one of their own had become their destroyer. However, I had barely begun the making when I felt suddenly, even at that great remove, the presence of something burning with a fire hotter even than molten stone. I turned my mind to it, I probed with my thought and with all the power nature had granted me, and lo, there it lay, open to my thought, and just where it would be of most use.

The making of the Black Dragon took all the power I possess. I had to goad the quiescent voice of the island from a rumble into violent activity, then to raise the casket containing the heart into the midst of the material I used to create the body of the beast. Once the shaping was done, though, it was—it is—a perfect creation. It houses the Demonlord, bound to me inextricably by blood and bone, and it bears within itself its own destruction. That pleases me. And when I offer to ensoul it at last, give it life again—well, the other main stricture of the spell of the Distant Heart is that body, soul, and the Heart cannot ever be combined again in the one creature. If that were to happen, the spell would be broken and the Heart would become mere flesh again.

It is truly said that if you put all your energies into a single task, all of life comes together to aid you. However, the wise man does not put all his trust in so insubstantial a thing as life.

Since I provided Marik with numerous demonic artefacts, among them a means of keeping off the dragons, I received half of the lansip harvest for my pains. I have used almost all of it already, bar a few boxes I have retained to control those demons who crave it: but the distilled essence of lansip has proven the legends true. No more the protesting joints, no more the weakness, the thousand small ills, the dimmed eyesight, the fading hearing—no more the tread of death behind me or its shadow in the glass before my eyes.

I have conquered time itself. Behold, I now have that which all men desire—a mind honed by seventy years of study and nearly ninety years of living, and a body no more than thirty years old to carry out the demands I make of it. I had forgotten the power of this age! Every nerve tingles with strength and youth. By all the Hells, it is a wonder.

Of course, I do miss my hand.

I had to cut it off to bind the Demonlord to my will. The sacrifice will be well worth it—it was only my left hand, after all—but the place where my hand once was itches constantly. It is of minor interest. I suspect the illusion will end in time. Perhaps I can find a smith to create a mechanical replacement. It is damned awkward getting dressed. Still, that is what servants are for.

It irks me that I have been so weak these last several days, but even I must needs recover from such great works as the binding of the Nameless One and the making of the Black Dragon. I labour even as I rest, to keep the creature in the air as it flies to Kolmar from the distant west. And I have had a rasp in my throat from the choking I had off that witch-daughter of Marik's when she attacked. I have ensured that she has nor food nor fuel. The weaker her body, the easier it will be to dominate her will.

I know that one of the True Dragons, the Kantrishakrim as they are called, is here—it nearly stopped me from capturing the girl. The rest will not be far behind. Marik has done so much good, at least: I know the Kantri are coming. Truly, that surprised me. It seems that in the making of the Black Dragon the island was overwhelmed in fire. I had not planned that. However, it is all moot.

If the Black Dragon arrives first, all well and good, for it houses the soul of the Demonlord, and will be the death of the Kantri. I do not hope for this, for the thing is a golem, living stone despite the half-demon soul that animates it. I must support its every wingbeat, and even I grow weary on occasion. I shall have to make another sacrifice of blood—not mine, of course!—this night before I face the Mages. It is proving a great deal harder to support the creature than I had anticipated, though I am well equal to the task.

If the Kantri should arrive first—well, I have a demonline ready and waiting, and in a breath I can be hundreds of leagues distant and the way closed behind me, and they with no way of knowing where I might be. And the Black Dragon, the Demonlord incarnate, will arrive eventually. In that moment the fate of the Kantrishakrim will be sealed.

I am thankful now for the foresight I showed in establishing this cantrip which records my thoughts in this book even as I think them. It is vastly easier than sitting and writing for hours. I have one operating on Marik as well. It has helped me to check that he is telling me the truth. The poor idiot is too stupid to lie, it seems. It is well. And for myself, when I come into my own, it is good that there will be a true record of my coming to power, that the slaves may know how they came to their slavery. Despair is truly the most satisfying sauce.

The next step takes place this very night. I have commanded an assembly of the College after the evening meal and they will all attend. After all, why should they not answer the summons of their beloved Archimage? I have hidden my true self, the power of my arts, for many long years. I have cultivated the goodwill of my fellow Mages even while despising them, for it has taken so very long to prepare myself—but tonight, kind, caring Archimage Berys will die, and in the place of that weakling I will stand revealed to them at last, in my true self. I will offer the choice to my College, to join me or to die. I expect most of the fools will choose death, but I may perhaps gain a few willing souls from among the students. There are many who desire more power than has been given them by the Lady.

And if all else fails, they will make splendid demon fodder.

iii

The Wind of Shaping

Varien

I woke to the sound of Idai's voice in truespeech. *"Come, Akhor, it is not like you to miss a meal,"* she said, her voice light in my thoughts. I sat up, disoriented, rubbed my face, and opened my eyes to find myself little the wiser. It was late afternoon. The sun was falling behind the western hills, and a chill wind was beginning to swirl around us, as if it were not certain which direction to come from. Wrapped in a cloak I had not been wearing, asleep beside Shikrar and Maran in the middle of a field—but where—*oh*.

"Idai, where are the Kantri? Where are the Lost? How do they fare?"

"Peace, my friend," she said quietly. "All is well." I rose and walked with her, a little away from the others, leaving them to sleep. "All of our people have followed Kédra to that farmer's field, to eat and drink and rest. The Lost—ah, it is long and long since they were trapped. Imagine if you went into the Weh sleep and woke five kells later! There is a great deal for them to learn. We must not expect it to happen overnight." She sighed. "Oh, my friend. Think of all the Kantri who have worked towards this day—three full generations, birth unto ending—so many who dreamed of a joyous release for those trapped souls. I am such a fool. In all my hopes, I never imagined that the restoration of the Lost would be so heart-searing." She closed her eyes for a moment. "Akhor, the last thing that most of them recall is throwing themselves at a treacherous Gedri who had killed their mates, their parents, their children; I do not know if there is enough time or reason in the world to overcome their hatred."

"If time and reason are not enough, we shall have to see what compassion may do," I said resolutely. For all my exhaustion, I felt now braver and brighter than I had for days. "Come, Idai, throw off this gloom! I too longed for a day of glory for the Lost—but I will forego that pleasure for the wonder of their restoration, however painful."

"Ah, yes. You remind me. Tréshak has said that they now wish to be known as the Restored, Dhrenagan in the Old Speech, not the Lost any longer. We have taken to referring to them so." She sighed once more, then drew herself up, into the Attitude of Resolve. "You have the right of it, as ever, Akhor. We will surely be able to help them. Damaged they are, certainly, and confused, but time is our great ally. Time will heal the heart's wounds and show the restored mind the way of reason."

I could not help it, I laughed aloud. "So it will, Iderrisai, therefore be not afeared of giving them time to come to realise that they are free! That must be a shock nearly as great as finding themselves imprisoned." I smiled, though I somehow felt a traitor to Lanen at doing so. "Idai, think of it. The Lost are restored to us. At last they are free, after all this dreadful march of years! Bless every Wind that ever blew! Whether they are yet able to rejoice surely is of less moment than their return." I let out a deep sigh. "And I will at last be able to sleep peacefully, without the memory of those flickering soulgems to haunt my dreams. However it has come about, whatever the consequences, this is a wonder." I dropped into truespeech. *"Even for those who chose the swift fire of death, my friend. We have done them the greatest service of all. At last, after so many kells of torment, they may rest."*

"You have the right of it," she said, dropping down again from the formal Attitude. "Name of the Winds, Akhor! This has truly been a day of wonders, but I would give a great deal for it to be over. I am weary as I never thought I could be, weary in heart and wing and soul. I could sleep for a full moon. Can it possibly be that we only arrived here with the dawn?" She hissed her amusement. "My word on it, Akhor. I never valued peace and quiet nearly enough."

"Perhaps none of us did," I replied with a smile. We moved back to the others and Idai woke Shikrar. She spoke with him in a low voice, doubtless telling him what she had just told me, as she walked him slowly over to the little stream, where clear water and half a cow awaited him. I sat down beside Maran, too weary yet even to walk to the inn. She still slept—and in every line of her, I saw my beloved Lanen. My throat began to tighten, and though I knew it to be useless, I could not stop myself sending out to her in truespeech. *"Lanen, beloved, can you hear me? My heart declares that you yet live, for it beats still, but my life is airless darkness without you. Where are you, dearling?* Kadreshi, *beloved, where are you?"* A sudden thought occurred to me—perhaps she could hear but not respond? *"Lanen, beloved, we are searching for you! I will not cease, I will not rest until I find you, and by my soul I swear I will come for you though all the Hells should lie between us."*

No answer but silence.

I bowed my head, sorrow and a deep emptiness round me, until a short while later a glorious scent, entirely out of place in an open field, came wafting past me: bread and meat. And was that chélan? I turned—and there, preceded only by the scent of what he bore, was Will arrived like the wind of heaven, bearing food and drink. He put down his tray and woke Maran gently. She sat up, moaned, and reached for the chélan. I was astounded at the reaction of this body. As one of the Kantri, I would not even consider eating when sorrow wrapped my soul, but this Gedri body craved fuel and I reached out for it.

"Aye, you're as bad as the Healers," he said, shaking his head. "They need to eat like horses when they've been working. Get this down you." He handed us both trenchers of fresh bread, spread with butter, softened with gravy, and with slices of roasted beef draped over all. I had never tasted food more clearly, or needed it more. Though there was something—

"Will, where is Salera?" I said, between mouthfuls.

"She's gone with the Kantri," he said, and smiled. "They were all so taken with her, and she is fascinated by them. She said she'd come find me in the morning." He shook himself. "As for you two, there's plenty more away back at the inn, but I'm blessed if I'm going to bring it to you. Up you get."

"Blessed indeed, lad," said Maran, gulping down the last of her chélan. "I've seen you often enough in the stone, Goddess knows, along with that tall lad and the fine lass, but what are you called?"

"Willem of Rowanbeck, Mistress," he said, grinning. "The tall Healer is Vilkas, the young woman is Aral. You're Lanen's mam?"

"I am that," she said, grinning back, "and it's not making my life any easier, I can tell you. I'm Maran of Beskin. And you!" she cried, turning to me. I had risen, and now reached down to give her a hand up. When she stood, we were of a height, and her gaze locked on mine. It was the first time I'd looked at her closely. Name of the Winds, she appeared so like my beloved Lanen that my heart ached with it. "I've seen you nearly every day since Lanen found you, but I've no idea what your name is."

"I am called Varien, Lady," I said.

"Varien," she repeated softly. "It's a good name. And you can call me Maran, lad," she said, grinning. "I'm a blacksmith, not a lady. Goddess, what a voice you have on you." She stared at me, frowning, her gaze suddenly gone quite serious and her voice very low. "And you—I must know. Unless I'm mad, or unless that damned thing deceived me, you're no man. You're a dragon; transformed, somehow, but a dragon—that great silver one who watched over Lanen out on the Dragon Isle."

"What!" I cried, taken aback.

"Don't waste time being coy, man! Is it true?"

"You are neither mad nor deceived. I am both dragon and human," I answered. Not for the first time, I wished that my mind might be more under my control when faced with the unexpected. The Kantri are seldom surprised. The Gedri, it seemed, were seldom otherwise.

She paled. "Bloody hellsfire. Then it's true. A transformation of kind. It's started." She grasped me by my shoulders. "Do you have any idea how this was done, or who did it? How you were transformed?"

In my astonishment I answered without thinking. "I have no idea. Lanen and I thought it was—all we could imagine was that it was the Winds and the Lady."

"Oh, save us all," she said, sounding much like Jamie in a bad mood. "It probably was exactly that. Now all we have to do is find out who or what on the other side has undergone the same transformation." She began cursing under her breath and strode off towards the inn, leaving me a moment or two for thought.

That this woman was Lanen's mother I never doubted for an instant, though how Lanen could have grown so similar to one she had never known was a wonder. The same headlong rush into action without thought of the cost to herself, or indeed to anyone else; the same wildly focussed intensity and determination about her. And the Winds bear me up, the same eyes in a face so achingly familiar.

I stopped and blinked.

If she knew I had begun my life as one of the Kantri, what else might she have learned?

I ran after her. I was better at running these days. Time was, if I were lagging behind, I would have fallen by instinct onto my "forefeet" that I might fly to catch up. My hands and knees had not been that badly scraped for some months now. I was still far, far too slow to suit myself, but at least I remained upright. Will trotted easily beside me, tray in one hand, mugs in the other.

Vilkas and Aral awaited us outside, Rella beside them. Aral watched Maran suspiciously, and I could not blame her—whatever else might be said of her, she still reeked of the Rakshasa. As we approached I noted that Aral had begun to summon her power, just in case. Vilkas, however, simply stared.

As well he might. For the moment she was near enough, she took his right hand in hers and went down on one knee before him, bringing his hand to her lips. She might have been a great queen kneeling to honour a subject who had served her well, for there was nothing of servility about her, kneeling there in the twilight before him.

"I beg you to accept a mother's blessing for saving the life of her daughter," she said.

"Lady, arise, I pray you," said Vilkas gruffly. I tried hard not to smile. Vilkas was, after all, a very young man. "I did what was required. I only wish I had been able to keep your daughter from the clutches of that bastard Berys." Between his clenched teeth, he added, "We don't even know where she is."

Maran rose and grinned, and for a moment I saw her as one of the Kantri—for this was not delight. This was baring her teeth, and woe betide him who was its object.

"Ah. There I can help you. Did anyone think to bring my pack?"

Rella

"As ever, Maran, I have looked after you," I said, pretending weariness. We grinned at each other as I handed over her pack. I'd begged a double handspan of thick leather and sewn it, with double stitches, over the gaping burn hole, so that it was as good as before.

We had been friends for nearly twenty years. I knew she would have done the same for me, twice over. It still hurt. Like it or not, Jamie stood between us now like a burning brand. It appeared that we were both going to ignore that particular raging fire until we were forced to deal with it.

She grinned, looking over the patch. "You do fine work. I never knew you were so good with a needle." She drew out the

Farseer once more, and I saw her flinch when she touched it. *Time she found a Servant of the Lady and got herself shriven,* I thought. *She's getting twitchy.*

"This is the Farseer that Marik and Berys created ere Lanen was born," she said, handling it as though it burned her fingers. "I have used it for years, but when Lanen left Hadronsstead, I—well, you may assume that I have a rough idea of what has taken place."

Varien stood beside me, and I could practically hear his heart pounding. "Do you know where Lanen is now?"

She turned to him, her eyes bleak. "I'm not certain, but I know she's in Berys's power. Where he is, there we will find her."

"Can you not see where Berys is, that we may be certain where to look for her?" asked Vilkas.

"He's wherever he has been living these ten years past," said Maran shortly. "I've never seen the place in person, I don't recognise it to give it a name. It's a stone building with a large walled and cobbled courtyard closed by two wooden doors. There's a guard on the doors, there are usually lots of people around—"

"It's Verfaren right enough," said Aral flatly. "It's just over three leagues distant from here."

"Then in the Name of the Winds and the Lady," Varien cried, "let us be gone to Verfaren!"

"Patience, Master Varien, it isn't that simple," I said, hating to have to quench his resolve. "For one thing, these three"—I pointed to Will, Aral, and Vilkas—"are accused of murder in Verfaren, and I'd rather not have to fight off King Sulis of Elimar's Patrols unless and until I'm forced to. For another thing, you must remember that whatever we may know about him, to the rest of the world Master Berys is still the head of the College of Mages, very highly respected and virtually untouchable. The College more or less owns the town. In effect we'd be storming all of Verfaren, and we don't really have enough troops for that."

Varien

I could not restrain the wild frustration that was sweeping through me. "Even a few of the Kantri could easily overwhelm a Gedri town," I said urgently.

"Master Varien, I hear what your heart is saying, but Rella's right, it's a bad idea," said Will, unexpectedly. His voice was, to my ear, maddeningly calm. "I know you'd risk anything for your lady: but I had a chat with young Kédra earlier, and I don't think you want your people's first act in their new home to be one of violence."

"And don't forget that Jamie is there now," said Rella. "He'll not be sitting on his hands." She looked up. "Come, we're all here now. Let us go in and talk over food. We won't get Lanen back any the faster for starving to death."

"How can you think of food?" I cried. "Lanen—"

"Varien, you're human now, and you were rather busy earlier," she said sharply. "That body needs food. You're pale as midwinter snow. Eat before you faint." She grasped my arm and towed me into the inn.

I wanted to object, but she was right. I was ravenous. The first course that Will had brought us had barely taken the edge off my hunger, and it seemed that the others felt the same. Rella had ordered a good spread and for once we all ate our fill: there was a cold roast ham, the rest of the hot roast beef with a thick gravy, carrot and parsnip, fresh bread and dripping from the roast, and roasted apples and honeycakes. The beer was nut-brown and cold.

When I had eaten my fill I stood up. The fire was warm and the excellent food tempted me to stay longer than I must, but ever I thought of Lanen. Truth be told, I could think of nothing apart from a burning need to rush in and rescue Lanen as swiftly as I might. Alas, I had not the power of my old form, or I could have flown in and—

"*And what?*" interrupted the neglected part of my mind that was the voice of reason. "*Slaughter innocents who got between*

*me and Berys? Destroy buildings looking for her? Make the
Kantri appear as monsters to be dreaded? Where is the wisdom in
that? No. Wait. Think. Remember the Lost, five kells ago. If they
had stopped to plan, they might not have been so devastated by
the Demonlord."*

"Varien," said a gruff voice. Maran had come to sit beside me.
She was smiling. "Just so you're in no doubt, that was my daughter you married at midwinter, young—well, young *as* a man you
certainly are." She turned away suddenly, avoiding my glance.
"She looked—she was absolutely beautiful, wasn't she?"

It took a moment before I could trust myself to speak. "I had
never imagined that such a creature as Lanen could exist," I said
quietly, just for her ears. "Such beauty of soul, such strength of
heart and limb, and a glorious fearlessness that I am learning is
rare in any race. Yes, she is also beautiful, but compared to the
truth of her soul, I think her beauty is not important." Maran still
looked away. "She is a wonder, your daughter Lanen," I said.

Maran did not answer straightaway, but when she did, she
managed to look into my eyes. "I'm glad you know it, Varien. She
is indeed." She looked away again, and spoke as quietly as I had.
"And in case you wanted to know, I wish with all my soul that I
had never left her. I have wished that every day and every night
since I went away. I thought . . . my soul to the Lady, Varien, I
thought I was saving her life by drawing danger to myself."

"I hear the truth in your words, Lady Maran," I said softly.
"But I am not the one you need to speak them to."

To my surprise she looked back at me and smiled wryly. "I
know. I thought I'd try a practice run before it's time for the real
thing."

Suddenly I liked her, this woman so like my beloved in spirit
and in form. I drew her to me and kissed her cheek. "Do not fear
it, daughter. She has a large heart. It will take time, as it will take
the Restored time to adjust to a world forever changed. Trust her.
I know she takes pride in you, for she calls herself Lanen Maransdatter."

"Does she now?" she said, her eyes strangely vulnerable, a little half smile passing across her lips. "Well, well. There's hope in that, certain sure."

I was about to respond when I had the strangest feeling in my gut. I wondered briefly if I had eaten too much too quickly, but it was not that kind of feeling—more an urgency. It pulled me to my feet. I had gathered my cloak and my pack and was nearly to the door before I had a coherent thought.

"Whither away, Master Varien?" called Rella.

"I can wait no longer," I said, desperate to be gone. "I have played my part; I have welcomed the Kantri, I have helped to restore the Lost. What is there now to keep me here, when Lanen is so near?" None spoke. "I go to Verfaren," I said. "Let any who wish to join me follow after."

I strode out into the dark night, down the road to the south, where my dearest love was held by one who wished her nothing but ill.

Jamie

I did not waste those two days of early spring walking down from the Súlkith Hills. I spoke at great length with Willem of Rowanbeck, who had lived and worked at the College of Mages for many years. I teased from his memory every corridor of the place, every room, every turn, every scrap of information I could glean, like a greedy harvester picking through the chaff lest a single grain of wheat be lost. When he could recall no more I turned to the young Healers, Vilkas and Aral. They reinforced the map I had built in my head and added a few details that might serve me. Serve Lanen.

It kept my mind off the ache in my knees, and the chill in my bones, and the deep winter in my heart.

For all I knew, the exercise might have been in vain, for we knew not where Berys held her captive; but if there was the slightest chance that I might need to know how to move through that place this was my best chance to learn.

And it kept me from running mad with inaction as we hurried to the plain to meet the other dragons.

I did not wait. I saw them arrive from a distance: aye, I was there when the dragons came. A part of me knew I was watching the world change, and in truth it was a goodly sight, but I could not feel it as Varien and the others did.

I could hardly feel anything.

I swiftly bade farewell to my comrades and took the fittest of our horses, all of whom were complaining.

Rella took my arm as I made to mount. "You insist on this still, do you?" Her voice was calm, but her eyes were troubled in the bright morning.

"I will not stay while there is the smallest chance I can find her," I replied. My own voice surprised me. When had it gone so cold?

"Then keep to our plan. We will meet outside the gates of the College at the morrow's dawn."

"Or I will leave word with your friend—Hygel, was it? Your contact at that inn?"

She managed a small smile. "The Brewer's Arms. Try the baker's stall at the mercat square if you get there early and can't find him, he'll be the one buying bread by the basket load. Otherwise, take your midday meal at The Brewer's Arms, but mind you look sharp or you'll miss him. He's very, very good at not being noticed." She frowned then and gripped my arm tight. "Mind you do the same. Berys is a bastard, but he's no fool. Don't make us have to rescue *you*."

One tiny corner of my mouth lifted, almost against my will. "I may be getting a little old, Rella my dear, but I'm not so far gone yet." I laid my hand on her cheek for a moment, then mounted my poor horse despite its objections. "If you can manage it, why don't you bring a dragon or two when you come, eh?"

Her brows lifted. "What a fine idea. Only two?"

"I shouldn't think any more would fit," I said. I tried, I did, to lighten my voice, to respond to her, but there was no lightness in me. "Be well, heart," I said, and turning away from the gleaming dragons in that great field, headed southward.

Towards Verfaren.

I sat back in my chair, glancing around me, taking a deep draught of chélan. I could feel it hit as I swallowed, feel the borrowed wakefulness shiver through me. Goddess knows I needed it. We had all of us walked all day and as far into night as a safe descent would allow, sleeping as little as we could, on the way down from the hills.

The early afternoon sun fought its way through the small windows of the pub. Rella had told me the unlikely one to go to, where the members of the Silent Service met to exchange information— "Though you'd never know it," she had warned me. "It's a quiet place, and Hygel himself will be the one your eye passes over most easily."

I hadn't asked miracles of my poor weary horse, I'd ridden as gently as I could, but Verfaren was a good ten miles from the field where the dragons had landed and I had need of speed. The creature was too tired even to complain when we had finally reached the gates of the town at midday. I'd found The Brewer's Arms without difficulty, and the stabling was good enough to satisfy me. I left the bay covered in a decent stall, with a good warm mash and a promise of rest.

Lucky creature. I couldn't see any rest for myself.

I'd not been in the common room long ere I began to see what Rella meant. The conversations around me were held in normal voices, and the speakers might as well have been discussing the weather. I tried to concentrate on one pair near me, but when I finally managed to distinguish their speech from the others, it made no sense at all.

So, the Silent Service had its own cant. I should have known.

The landlord came up and refilled my mug, then made to turn away.

"Hygel?" I asked quietly.

He glanced down at me, disinterested. "Hygel's not here."

"Shame. I've news for him."

One corner of the man's mouth turned up. "You and all the world. You tell me, then, and I'll pass it on when he gets back."

"Sorry, friend, can't do that. Rella would skin me."

"Rella, is it? I know a Rella. Tall lass, red hair, sassy walk."

I wondered if I really looked that much of an idiot. "Hells mend you for a liar, friend," I said, gulping more chélan. "Hard to walk sassy with her back, truly, and if you think she's tall you must be walking on stilts." I glanced at him. "I'll not speak to the hair, though. Alchemists have nothing on a woman who's tired of her looks."

The man put his jug on the table and sat down. "Is she well?"

"She is. My name's Jamie. I've come on business."

He leaned his arms on the table. "What business?" He lifted an eyebrow. "You're not in the Service, that's plain."

I replied in mercenary cant. "No, I'm on my own. But a little co-operation could be profitable for both sides, if you're who I think you are."

"Enough of that," he replied in common speech. "I'll admit you're not just some idiot walked into the wrong place." His seeming-casual gaze was taking in every detail of my appearance. You don't get eyes like that being a landlord.

"Kind of you to say so, Master Hygel," I muttered.

"Yes, yes, fine," he said, brushing at the air with one hand as if to shoo away all such nonessentials as his name. "I'm Hygel. What are you after?"

"Not what, who. I'm after him they call the master of the College here. He's taken something from me and I want it back."

Hygel let out a short bark of laughter. "Ha! That one!" He sat back in his chair, crossing his arms and gazing at me through narrowed eyes. "Old son, let me give you a word or two of advice, and because you're a friend of Rella's I won't even charge you for it. First, don't say his right name this close to the place, because he'll bloody well hear you. And second—whatever it is you want to do, don't try. Don't even think about it. You might as well call yourself a goose and pick a spit, because sure as life you're roasted before you start."

I shot out an arm, grabbed his shirtfront, and pulled his face close to mine before he could react. "He's got my daughter, you bastard," I growled. "Do not dare to laugh."

I could feel the silence behind me, likely barbed or at least pointed, in the sense of several silent blades drawn and aimed. I ignored it—though truth to tell, there was a part of me that was howling at my own reaction. I shoved Hygel away and stood up. "She's just a girl," I snarled. "I thought we might exchange information, for I surely to all the Hells know things you don't, and I need to know how to get in there and find her. Fast. Before anything worse happens."

Hygel stared at me. I stared back, my fury at Berys beating time with my pulse.

He gestured, and I felt the pressure behind my back melt away. "Sit down, friend Jamie," he said quietly. "Perhaps we need to talk after all."

I took my seat again.

"You first, and make it good," he said, very quietly. "What you need to know is worth a by-our-Lady fortune."

"Would it surprise you to learn that there are dragons here?" I said, lowering my own voice as much as I could and still be heard. "Not the little ones. The real ones."

Hygel snorted. "I heard that one two days ago. A True Dragon, one of the big ones. I'd always thought they were legend, and I wouldn't have believed it if my best local man hadn't told me. Seems it went into the Súlkith Hills and hasn't been seen since."

"Oh, yes, that one did," I replied, sitting back a little. "Though it's come down again, not ten miles from here as we speak. But it's the other hundred and eighty-some you need to know about."

Give him credit, he never changed his expression, and he swore impressively in a calm voice no different from his normal speech. Finally he calmed down enough to say, "Hells' teeth and Shia's toenails, where did you hear that? And do you trust the source?"

"I saw them land. I was there. Dawn this morning." I smiled

crookedly. "And don't blaspheme the Goddess's toenails, we're going to need all the help we can get."

"Is it conquest, then?" he asked, still in a tone of voice that you'd use to discuss the weather. "Do we need to get away?"

"I doubt it, from what I've seen. Though surely the world is changed forever. They are here to stay, Master Hygel, but they are reasonable creatures, and from what I've heard they truly want to live in peace. Well, most of them do. Assuming we let them," I added. "And I don't care what you've heard, or who told you—they're bigger than that."

"Well, light my toes and call me a match," he said, staring at me long and hard. "That's news and no mistake."

"News enough for you to tell me how to get to the Archimage?" I asked quietly.

"I told you already, it can't be done," he said crossly. "Him over there is no fool, more's the pity. He's been right cagey with his wrongdoing. There's those at the College know he's corrupt—Magister Rikard for a start—but until they have proof there's damn all they can do about it." He snorted. "Rikard's been looking for years, but Be—Himself has kept his head down. If you can prove he's taken your daughter against her will, Rikard will have him dead to rights and thank you for it." Hygel grinned briefly. "And likely thank me as well." He shook his head and leaned forward, dropping his voice. "Problem is, that one's got demons protecting him, has had for years, and it's got a great deal worse in the last few days." He took a draught from my mug of chélan. "Like a stirred ants' nest that place has been, this last se'ennight. Word has it two of the students went rogue and murdered two of the Magistri."

"Damn fine students, then, if they could overcome those who taught them," I said dryly.

"Right enough. But the place is closed in on itself. The main gate is locked, as it hasn't been since I can recall. Even All Comers is closed. That's never happened in all my years here." Hygel lifted an eyebrow. "If you can tell me what's happened, I can surely get you inside. Undetected, if you're careful."

"I know those students," I said carefully. "They've done naught but save lives since I met them. One who knows them better has told me the full tale, that they had caught Ber—his eye, and he had his excuse to destroy four of them at the once. Magistra Erthik and Magister Caillin, found dead outside the students' door—but found there first by the students as they were leaving. They never touched the Magistri." He looked doubtful, and I added, "Given that they went on to save the life of my daughter, without even promise of payment, I'm naturally inclined to believe them."

"Mmm. That squares with what I'd heard," muttered Hygel. "Perhaps I might trust you after all." A ghost of a smile flitted across his mouth. "As far as I can throw you, at least. What do you know already of the place?"

"I need to know where he might keep her—where he keeps his prisoners. I've a fair idea of the layout, but I need to know how to pass if I'm found." A great coldness washed over my heart. "Hells' teeth. Are they all corrupt, there? Could he keep her openly imprisoned and none to question?"

"No," said Hygel instantly. "There are bad apples in any barrel, but there are fewer at the College than in most places. He'd have to keep her somewhere that none could happen by, and there's precious few spots like that. There is no dungeon, only the cells where—" Hygel swore. "Aye, that'll be it, it must be."

"Tell me."

"Detention cells, partly below ground level, where they keep the drunks who show up hurt and get rowdy once their wounds are seen to. Stone cells, with thick oaken doors and naught but tiny gratings in the outer wall to let in air and light. There are four of them but one has crumbled on itself—no no, long since, be at ease—so there are only three where she might be held. The gratings all open on to the central courtyard, just beyond the main gates: four gratings in a row, it's the third along from the right that's ruined. If she had cried out, a passing student might have heard her. If—"

"If?"

Hygel sighed and swore quietly. "If Rella ever hears I've let this out without extracting a price, I swear, she'll spit down my neck after she's taken my head off."

"If what, man?" I hissed.

"If her captor hasn't cast a silence on her. It's a demon spell. He's known to be fond of it. The victim can't be heard no matter how they shout. And those windows are too high up to reach from inside."

I knew as if I'd been there that she was held in that spell, else she'd have shouted the place down. My Lanen had never been one to suffer in silence.

"I'd been told of those cells. My informer said they'd not been used in years."

"Maybe. And maybe they have been but your informer knew nothing of it. I tell you, anything could have happened this last week."

"The central courtyard, you say?" I frowned at the table. "And All Comers is closed? Damn, I'd been counting on that as a way in."

"Shut tight and likely locked," said Hygel thoughtfully, stroking his chin. "But now I think on it, there is a way in." A slow smile crossed his face. "Magister Rikard owes me quite a favour." Hygel sat back, as if he had come to a decision. "I do believe I'll collect on it. He can get you in as a new servant—seemingly there have been quite a few leaving the place of late." Hygel looked me over. "But not this very moment. You're dead to the world, man." He fished out a key from a pocket and handed it to me. "Top of the stairs, second on the left. Two coppers for the room and I'll throw in supper. Get some sleep." I started to protest but he cut me off. "Don't be an idiot. You'll need all your wits about you, and Rikard comes here for his evening meal every day of the world. I'll introduce you tonight."

I took the key and stood up. Goddess aid me, I was swaying on my feet from weariness. Still—"If you have betrayed me, the Seventh Hell itself won't be deep enough to hide you," I growled.

"Strictly business," he replied, undaunted. "Your news is worth a fair bit to me, I'd not cheat you. No profit in it." He grinned. "And truth be told, Master, I wouldn't object to losing that particular neighbour myself. He's bad for business."

I nodded and staggered up the stairs, found the room, and fell across the bed. I had thought my anger would sustain me, but I was asleep before I landed.

iv

Father and Daughter

Lanen

Mother? Mother, where are you?

I woke, groggy, from my half dream, my wits scattered to the four winds, deeply unsure of time or place. Who was that calling for her mother? What did she mean, I wasn't there . . . no, she wasn't . . . it wasn't me . . .

I was slumped into a corner in a stone room. Why wasn't I in my bed? This was Hadronsstead, wasn't it? A flicker of thought told me Hadron was dead, I must be in the tent on the Dragon Isle—but that wasn't stone—the tiny Silent Service hut we—no, we all slept on the floor but it wasn't stone either—some strange inn?

Memory rushed back as I blinked and stood up. It wasn't easy, I was cold and stiff all over, and my wounds burned. Probably infected by the Rikti. I couldn't imagine how I had fallen asleep at all, but I suppose there is a price to be paid for the kind of mad strength I'd had. I hoped Marik's every breath burned his throat.

Unfortunately, I now remembered only too well where I was, and what lay before me. Berys's dungeon. Hell blast and bugger it.

As best I could tell that first moment of waking, it was mid-afternoon, but I didn't have time to pay much attention as there were two of Berys's bloody huge guards looming over me. The larger of the two pulled me to my feet and closed my wrists in manacles, heavy iron bracelets with a short chain between the two. I noted, still groggy, that it was very peculiar to see this all happening but to hear nothing. It was desperately unreal, as if it were happening to someone else.

The larger of the bears attached a second length of chain to the first, then bolted my leash to a ring set in the stones of the wall. It allowed me very little movement, which presumably was the intention. What worried me was why they were taking this precaution now—and there he was, Berys, waiting in the open doorway with a smug grin on his face.

Suddenly I was very awake indeed. I threw my weight against the chain and succeeded only in battering my wrists. I soon gave it up, but my heart was thumping horribly in my chest. *Goddess, this is it, he's going to sacrifice me right now*, I thought desperately. *Mother Shia, help me and my babes!* I cried out in true-speech with all the strength I could muster. Nothing. It was like shouting into a pillow.

I tried to speak to Berys, but his spell was still in force and I made no sound. He seemed amused by my attempt, so much so that he raised one corner of his mouth in a disturbing smile and waved his right hand. "You still haven't learned, have you? Feel free to exhaust yourself fighting iron chain. It amuses me."

"The only thing that would amuse me would be your violent death, sooner rather than later," I snarled, and was surprised to hear myself speak. Instantly I turned to the bear on my right. "He *will* break faith with you, you know. It's only a matter of time until he needs another sacrifice and you're the only one around," I said. The guard didn't even look at me.

"Just because I can hear you, don't assume anyone else can," said Berys smugly. "I'm really quite good at selective deafness. As you may have noticed."

But I had my voice back now, for a blessed moment. And at

that instant, even Berys's voice was better than nothing. Though I expected nothing soon enough.

"Hello again," said a cheerful voice from the door, and there was Marik bearing a torch and smiling broadly. His hair was wet and he smelled as though he had just had a bath, the bastard. I felt like I hadn't bathed in a year. "Oh, dear, looks like the Rikti had fun playing with you," he said, grinning. It was quite repellent and I wished he'd stop, but he didn't.

"Why are you so damned cheerful?" I growled.

His smile broadened. "Why do you think, girl? This day I am free of the pain that has afflicted me since before you were born. Do you have any idea what I have been going through?"

"Hideous torment, I hope," I replied.

"Knives," he hissed, all his lightness gone in the instant. He leaned towards me and I swear I could feel his hatred beating against my skin. "I have lived with knives stabbing into my leg, sleeping and waking, for more than twenty years. Pain at rest, pain in movement, pain in every step I have taken every day of the world, since I paid for the Farseer I never got to use, thanks to your dear mother. Yes," he said, straightening up, the manic edge coming back into his voice and manner, "you will do nicely."

"Stop wittering and help me," commanded Berys. Marik went to help him set up what looked like an altar on the hard bed, putting candles in holders, lighting the coals in a small brazier. My heart dropped like a stone and I struggled desperately against the manacles. I might as well have saved my strength.

Berys started so chant, quietly, and Marik wandered back to me. He came right up to me, fascinated by something. Far too close for comfort in any case.

His eyes never left mine as he said, "Do you know, Berys, I have been learning things again. I do believe you will find my latest information interesting."

"I don't give a damn what you've learned," snapped Berys. "Not now! Draw back her sleeve, I need a sample."

Marik, stung by Berys's scorn, sneered and muttered, "Then I shall save my news until it pleases me to tell you."

Dear Goddess, he hasn't told Berys yet that I'm pregnant. I sent a wordless prayer of thanks winging to Mother Shia for that strange mercy. It could not last long, surely, but every moment of my tormentor's ignorance was precious.

Turning to the guards, Marik snapped, "Hold her fast." He pulled back the sleeve of my grubby tunic and the dingy linen shirt underneath—and suddenly a knife appeared in Marik's hand and he sliced my arm open. I cried out, in pain and shock, while he told the guards to hold me still as he collected in a brass cup the blood that flowed freely from the deep wound.

"You fool," said Berys crossly. "We only needed a small sample." He gestured again with his right hand, as if he were throwing something at me—a bolt of dark blue Healer's power, shot through with black, struck my arm. For the first second it felt like Healer's power, but the instant it began to work I started screaming in earnest. The pain of the wound was nothing to the pain of this "healing"—it was as if he had applied a poultice of concentrated stinging nettle to my open wound. My blood flowed even more freely, as if to wash off Berys's attempt at healing, and somehow that helped. Berys frowned and gestured to Marik, who against his inclination wrapped my arm tightly. The bright blood bloomed through several thicknesses of bandage, but eventually it slowed enough to content Berys.

"What in the name of the Goddess do you need that for, anyway?" I asked through gritted teeth, trying to ignore the pain in my arm.

"I do nothing in the name of the Goddess, but if you must know, girl, I am preparing a great work," replied Berys. He seemed to have picked up something of Marik's mood and added cheerfully, "I simply need to know that all will go smoothly. You are going to be part of history. You should be honoured."

"You should rot in the deepest Hell, but that isn't happening either," I snarled. Berys laughed and turned away, starting to chant again.

And now Marik stood directly before me, still staring. He seemed to be looking for something in my eyes. I was determined that he would find only disdain and anger. Never fear. Never despair.

"Proud of yourself, are you, Marik?" I sneered. "So, I'm finally to be given to the demons. So impressive. It's only taken you, what, twenty-four years to find me? And now you have me, chained and helpless, one woman against you and your pet demon-master, and your—trained bears." The guard still didn't move a muscle, damn it. "Very brave. Well done. What will you do for your next astounding feat? And do you honestly think Berys is going to let you live long enough to manage it?"

Berys started moving his hand and his stump to make figures in the air above the altar. Marik leaned closer to me and spoke quietly. "Oh, you have no idea, girl. In a few hours the Healers in every outpost of the House of Gundar, throughout the Four Kingdoms, will turn the world on its head. Every city, every town with enough folk to make it worth my while, will soon be full of people in constant fear of what evil a nasty Healer might do. Even those we didn't manage to influence will be shunned, as there is no way of knowing the difference." He grinned, a wild, unbalanced grin, no more than one step from insanity. "When brave King Marik comes to rid them of this terrible demonic oppression they will hail him as their new master. With delight. I shall come to the throne of the Four Kingdoms on a wave of acclamation."

He was very near now, relishing his power over me, and floating into my mind came Jamie's voice, clear as if he stood beside me, from those midnight sessions where he taught me to defend myself without a weapon. *If there's a man you need to drop fast, Lanen . . .*

"You'll come to the throne bloody well limping," I growled. My arms were bound and held, but my legs were free. I lifted my knee as hard and fast as I could. He doubled over and fell to the ground, turning his back to me. Amazing. Just what Jamie said would happen. I aimed my kick just to one side of his backbone, between the hips and the ribs, and by luck managed to hit the place Jamie had told me about. It was wonderful. He appeared to be in agony, which suited me just fine.

The guards, bless them, were slow to react, but they finally thought to drag Marik away. Berys, turning, didn't seem in the least concerned. "Put him in the far corner, she can't reach him there," he said, disgusted. "Then leave us."

They laid Marik gently on the stone floor and covered him with the blanket. He was gasping with pain, but his great friend Berys turned to look at him, said, "You'll live," and turned back to his altar.

Whatever he was doing, it appeared to be working. He threw a few lansip leaves on the little fire, and for an instant there was a most incredible scent in that horrible place, the very smell of the Dragon Isle itself. I closed my eyes and inhaled. Just in time, as it happens, for the next moment a terrible reek and a great cloud of smoke arose from his little brazier, and the figure of a demon appeared. This one had huge eyes to go with its outsized mouth. It also appeared to be wrapped in a chain.

"Tremble, mortal, for I am—" began the demon, but Berys tugged at the chain and the thing screamed.

"You are in my power. Don't be stupid. You have the simplest of tasks. Taste this blood and let me know if it will be acceptable to—" Here he said something that I thought might be a name, but I couldn't understand it.

"Will it be offered in full or in part?" the thing asked, gazing hungrily at the cup in Berys's hand.

"In part, at first," said Berys.

"Give," the demon demanded, and yelped again as Berys twisted the chain around it.

"You obey me for the price," he said, and the thing bowed. "Take," he commanded, and offered it the brass cup full of my blood.

The demon took it and drank it all down at once, whereupon it screamed far louder and more convincingly than it had at Berys's hands. It didn't stop screaming, and as it didn't seem to need to breathe, the noise was appalling. It was obviously in agony. I couldn't tell, exactly, but it looked as though it was trying to rid itself of the blood but couldn't. It finally managed to say the words "broken" and "contract," and Berys yelped. He sent what looked like black fire towards the thing—a kind of reversed Healer's light—and a stream of blood, presumably mine, flowed out of its mouth onto the stone floor. It finally stopped screaming.

"What in all the Seven Hells happened?" cried Berys. "It is only blood, there is nothing in it that could—"

"Kantrissshakrim!" the demon hissed. "You fed me blood of the Kantrissshakrrrim! I will dessstroy you!"

Berys stood still as death, staring in utter astonishment. The demon tried to get at him, but the binding held. Berys shook himself and said, "Only your death would break the contract. All is done, you are released."

"Payment!" it cried.

"You were paid with lansip when I summoned you. You have not done as I demanded, you are owed nothing. Go!"

The demon hissed like a cauldron full of snakes and disappeared with a loud bang and a reek of rotten eggs.

Berys turned to me, frowning in frantic calculation, his eyes narrowing as he started to pace back and forth in front of my cell, muttering to himself. "How is it possible? You are human, I know it, your father lies there and your mother was but a vessel made use of. Human born of human. You cannot be other, but you are." He glanced for an instant at the smoke still hovering above the brazier. "Demonstrably."

Then his frown disappeared and his eyes opened so wide I could see white all around. And I thought he looked insane *before*.

"Kantri and Gedri blood. Can it be? How in the—no, forget how. You! Speak truth!" he cried, and cast a cloud of that darkness at me. I took a deep breath and held it before the cloud reached me. "Speak! Your blood is Kantri and Gedri mixed?" he demanded.

"Go to the deepest Hell and rot there," I said with the last of my air, when I knew I could hold my breath no longer. I was forced to breathe in that blackness—but I could not. It was like trying to breathe soil. I had choked nearly to death when he dissipated it. I knelt, desperately gasping sweet air into my burning chest, as he stared. And then he started to laugh.

That was worse than hearing the demon scream.

Berys laughed loud and long, and eventually came close to me. I shrank as far back as I could.

"I do not know what has changed you, or how, or why," he said, exhilarated, "but as of this moment, you are the most precious creature in all the world to me."

Marik stirred at this. His breathing was returning to normal and he sat up, wincing. "I don't see what's so wonderful about her," he said, his voice rough. "In any case, I'm sure it will still be wonderful when her soul is gone to pay off my demons."

"Hmm—true enough, I suppose. Though it's a bother I didn't need this night," sighed Berys, peeved. "However, I don't need her soul for anything in particular, and she will surely be easier to transport if her will is gone. I will perform the sacrifice this very night before we leave, if only to shut you up about it."

"About damn time," growled Marik, climbing slowly to his feet. He stood before me, just out of reach, his face distorted by the mixture of triumph and hatred. "These are your last hours, girl," he growled, adding in a voice only I could hear, "all of you." Then, louder, "Suffer as I have suffered, sure in the knowledge that before midnight your soul will be in thrall forever to a Lord of Hell." He laughed then, a soul-chilling laugh because it sounded so *normal*. As if he laughed at a slight witticism rather than rejoicing in the hideous fate he planned for me.

I stood up straight, summoned what defiance I could muster, and responded, "I am alone and unarmed. What you say may indeed come to pass." I forced myself to attempt a smile, anything to plant some seed of doubt in Marik's mind. "But you are, of your own free will, actively sacrificing your only child to the powers of darkness. How do you hope to escape the same fate I shall suffer?"

He smiled. "As long as you go first, I don't really care." He turned and left, whistling. Berys, once his bears had cleared away the trappings of his altar, stopped and grinned at me. "Soon," he said, as he summoned his Healer's power and gestured at me.

"Sleep," he said.

I knew no more.

Will

Well, I admired Varien's dedication, but you'd not get me running down that road in the dark so soon after a decent meal. I'd get a stitch in my side in no time, and I expected he would too. But there, he was following his love.

Well, so was I.

I glanced over at Aral, almost unconsciously sitting beside Vilkas as she spoke with Maran. As though it were her natural place. She chose not to notice that Vil, close as a brother to her, had never indicated that he felt anything other than that for her. I noticed. He had never said . . . we had never spoken of her in that way, but after these two years I knew them both well enough. That churning soul, never at rest even in sleep: he did not long for Aral as I did, as a man longs for a woman, but he needed her desperately. It was that she sensed. It can be a powerful attraction for a young woman, knowing that you make a genuine difference in a man's life, that you are truly needed. It is not enough, of itself, to make anything other than friendship, but Aral was very young. I knew she loved him and that he did not return it, and when we had all three been cast by Berys to float on the tides of the world, I had resolved to be with her when she came to need me, for that day would surely come.

I was interrupted by Gair, the landlord and a friend of mine. "'Lo, Willem," he said, cheerily. "You are right welcome, you and your friends who pay good silver in good time!"

I grinned. "Well, if you can't make your hints any broader than that, I'll not pay you until I see you next." To still his spluttering protests I drew forth a small handful of silver and paid the shot I'd run up over the last few months.

Gair took it with thanks, and said with some amusement, "You'll never credit it, but I heard some of the old lads talking about dragons this afternoon! Can you imagine? Dragons!"

I raised my eyebrows and stared at him. "You amaze me."

"Sure as life. They sat out there"—he gestured to the common room—"and said they'd seen dragons—not the little ones, the big ones! Like in the children's tales!" He laughed. "Perhaps I'd best cut the ale with more water next time!"

"Gair, where have you been this day long?" I asked, as innocently as I could. Goddess, it was hard to keep a straight face.

"Cooking all day, since before dawn," he said. "This is my baking day. You're lucky, I made extra bread and those honeycakes on a whim. Mind you, I expected that roast to last me all week. I'll have to start another tomorrow." He looked around. "You don't think all this food just appears from nowhere, do you? It's taken me most of the day, starting when late turns to early. Why, what's been happening?"

"Have you never looked out your door, man?" I asked, stunned.

"Only to look away south and wonder what was keeping the trade away."

I took him by the shoulders and drew him back into his kitchen, trying not to laugh. "Gair, my friend—the old men were right. There are dragons here. Now. Not just the little ones, the Lesser Kindred—though they are come into their own. They can speak and reason now, Gair, the little dragons. They are intelligent."

"Never!" he cried, eyes wide. "Impossible! I've seen the creatures in the woods for years, they're no brighter than cattle!"

"Believe me. Awake and aware and capable of speech." I started to smile, watching his face. "And, Gair—breathe, man, life has changed but all's well enough—the True Dragons are here as well. They arrived this morning."

He went from astounded to annoyed in the instant. "Nonsense!" he scoffed. "It can't be. They're not *real*, man!"

"Then I've been talking with tales all the day long, aye, and for some days since," I said, trying not to laugh.

"But—but in the tales they're huge, they couldn't come and—not be—seen—Will, you bastard, you've seen them!"

"Gair, you idiot, they only bloody well landed in your field!" I said, laughing openly now. "Damn near two hundred of them, not half a mile away—oh, no—I suppose it's nearer four hundred now."

"What!" I could see the white all around his eyes.

"Oh, don't worry, they're not breeding that fast," I said, snorting. "No, no. It was quite a show, but one of the big ones and two of the folk out there managed to—oh, never mind, it's too long a tale. But be told. They are here, they're as big as legend makes them, they're brighter than you or I will ever be, and they're—they're good folk, Gair. As long as you tell them the truth. They can spot a lie a league off."

Gair didn't speak. I don't think he could. I was casting about for some way to reassure him when Rella came to the door. "Have you run out of ale, landlord?" she asked brightly.

"D-d-d-dragons!" Gair yelled. "Dragons! It's the end of the world!"

"Don't be stupid, man. It's a new start, and you're one of the first to know about it," she said. That seemed to get through, a little. At least he was breathing again.

"A new—a new start?" he asked. "How? How can we fight something like that?"

"Goddess, man, there's no need to fight them! They're creatures of Order. Trade with them! They are new-come to this place, they have no food, no shelter." She grinned then, moved close to him, and murmured conspiratorially, "You do know what they say about dragons, don't you? Think, man! What do they sleep on, hmmm?"

At least he knew his children's tales. "Every fool knows they sleep on beds of go—" The transformation was nearly magical. Where a moment before horror had reigned, now greed opened his eyes wider and brought a mad smile to his face. I'd seen that smile earlier in the day, when I told Timeth of his great good fortune. Rella grinned. "Good lad," she said cheerily. I nodded to him and took the ale to where the others sat.

Jamie

I woke suddenly in darkness and was just starting to curse Hygel for a liar when there came a knock at the door.

"Master, are you waked?" said a young voice. "There's a man to see you i' the common room. Will ye come?"

"Aye. Come and light my candle, lad, I can't even find the door latch it's that dark in here," I replied. The voice proved to belong to a young lad of maybe ten years, who wandered in, lit the candle by the door from the candle he carried, and disappeared. I went to the basin and splashed my face with cold water, for I was still muzzy from sleep. It helped a bit.

The common room was lit by several lamps as well as by the fire, but despite that—or perhaps because of it—there was a generous helping of shadowy corners. Hygel came over to me, shook his head, and muttering something about what the cat dragged in, led me to a dimly lit alcove where sat a man of about my own age. He looked nothing special, short dark hair well salted with grey, a trim beard with more grey than dark, a nondescript cloak thrown around his shoulders against the cold nights of early spring. When he stood, though, his eyes gleamed in the firelight, and I saw the mind behind them awake and on guard.

"Magister Rikard, this is the man I told you of." Hygel glanced at me, muttered, "Good luck," and left us to it.

"I don't believe in wasting time, sir," said Rikard, swiftly seating himself. All his movements were quick and precise like his speech, and his eyes were sharp and bright. "I have known Hygel for years, and if he vouches for you, I am willing to at least begin with you, but he says you have impugned the

Archimage. How do you dare to speak ill of so good a man?"

"I've known him longer than you, if not as well," I replied cautiously. "Though to say truth, I would not so corrupt the word 'good' as to speak it in the same breath."

"I have had concerns myself," he said, equally cautious. "If you have a complaint to make against the Archimage, I pray you, tell me. He surely would not be pleased to know that there were those who felt ill-used by him."

I said nothing.

"Well? What's wrong?" he snapped.

"I don't know you, Magister. I barely know Hygel, and neither of you knows me from Farmer Jon's off ox. And none of us can afford to be wrong."

"Goddess knows, that's true enough," he said. "Though a legitimate complaint would have to be investigated. We healers are not ruled by the Archimage, but led by him. Even he is answerable to the Council of Mages assembled."

"Would the word of one man, unknown to any of you, have any weight in that Council?" I asked wearily.

"It might, if you have proof, or another witness," he replied. "Have you?"

"The proof of my own eyes and those of half a dozen others, of spiriting a"—I took a deep breath, and pitched my voice low that it might not crack—"of spiriting my daughter away from me and from her husband some four days since. But I don't know where he is. I need help."

To my surprise Rikard closed his eyes, as if in pain. "Shia keep you, Master Jamie," he said, wincing. When he looked up again, those sharp eyes were more gentle. "I really am a Healer, you know," he said quietly. "I've been doing this for forty years, I don't need to summon power to see your pain. The merest glance— very well. Let us start again. I am Magister Rikard, of the College of Mages. How may I help save your daughter? Is she ill?"

"No. She's in the power of the bastard you serve, and I fear with every breath I take that he'll murder her soon if he hasn't already."

Rikard caught his breath, and his eyes widened. "Why has he taken her?" he asked urgently.

"I have no idea, though I think it might be to put her in the power of Marik of Gundar." *Her father, as it happens, but you don't need to know that.* "What I don't know is where he has taken her. Is Berys here at the College?"

"I spoke with him not half an hour gone."

I felt a great weight lift from off my shoulders. "Blessed be Shia. If he's here, she's here."

"How can you be certain?" asked Rikard quietly.

"I can't, not entirely," I said quietly. "He might have murdered her by now; but if she lives he'll have her close. Likely in one of those old detention cells, if you don't know different. I know not what he needs her for, but certain sure he's not stolen her away for her health."

"May the Goddess bless you forever, Master Jamie," said Rikard, his eyes gleaming in the dim light. "I've been trying to get hard evidence against him for years." Suddenly he drew back. "Though I warn you, if you are lying, Healer or no I'll have it out of your hide."

"He really is a twisty bastard, isn't he?" I chuckled. "Goddess. If you're looking for treachery everywhere—no wonder he's grown so strong."

Rikard sat back. "It's true. Though I have no real reason to trust you." His gaze never left mine, and after a while he added wearily, "Right now, I don't even care. I'm sick unto death of it all. If you're working for him, so be it. I'd rather have an open fight than creep about suspicious of everyone for the rest of my life." His eyes began to gleam again in the firelight. "And if you speak truth—Goddess, I've been looking for proof against him for *years* now."

"You haven't been looking in the right places," I snorted. "Hells, I saw him murder a poor babe near twenty-five years gone, making a Farseer. He was a demon-master then. Lady Shia only knows what he is now."

"Will you denounce him in public?" asked Rikard. The change

in him was amazing—he looked now like a drawn sword ready to strike. "Will you dare repeat such things to the assembled Council of Mages?"

"I'll cry it in the town square if you like, but first"—I grabbed a fistful of his robe and pulled him close to me—"*first* I get my daughter out of his hands."

"Agreed," he said calmly. "Let go of me, please, and listen carefully. The passwords you will need are very simple."

"M'name's Gerander," I said, sweeping off my recently acquired cap. "I'm Magister Rikard's new man, come to sign in."

"Left it a bit late, haven't you, Gerander?" asked the man at the gate, suspiciously. As well he might be. I had been living rough for some time, I had put on my grubbiest clothes, and I had to admit that I looked more than a bit suspect. That was the idea. Let him see the clothing, not the man, and I could pass easily enough later without being recognised. "And you've chosen the wrong name to call, Magister Rikard is—"

"Is here, Norris, thank you," said Rikard briskly. "I know, he's not very prepossessing, but there's a good man under all that grime. I'll have him wash and get him a set of server's gear so he won't offend you. Or me," he said, with a wink at Norris. We both passed through the gates, I under intense inspection, and into the courtyard. It was not brightly lit, but the lantern I carried shed enough light that I could see the small gratings off to my right, where Rikard said she was most likely being held. I contrived to walk to the right of the Magister, stomping my feet a little that I might get an idea of the echo and the sound.

As I passed the third along I thought the echo sounded a little dull. That was the ruined one, I'd been told—but I didn't believe more than half of what I'd heard. Oh, surely those who spoke thought they spoke true, but they weren't nearly suspicious enough of Berys. I'd lay money Lanen was there, in that "ruined" cell. My heart beat faster—she was so close—if I had a dragon's strength I could have torn a hole in the stone wall and dragged her out, if I left now and rode like fury I could get Shikrar or one of the other really big ones—

No. No time. Rikard had said Berys had called on all the College to gather after they had eaten. That meant about now. I hurried to catch up with Rikard, who walked quite calmly until he was out of sight of the guard at the gate. Then he grabbed my sleeve and we both ran. His chambers were nearby and he locked the door behind us.

As I was throwing off my worst garments and swiftly darkening my face and hands with soot from the little grate, I begged a scrap of parchment and the use of pen and ink. I scribbled a brief note as Rikard went over the directions we had rehearsed.

"Back out into the corridor, turn left, take the first corridor to your right and then the little stairs down to the left. It's not very far along, mind or you'll miss it in the dark." I folded the little scrap of parchment and tucked it in my scrip. Rikard handed me the dark lantern he had lit from his own lamp, and a small key. "Once you've got her out, bring her back here to my chambers. That's the spare key to these rooms, so she can lock herself in here. Then you keep the rest of your bargain—keep straight along the corridor in front of this room, along to the end, then right, it's the fourth door on the right, a big double door of old oak. You listen carefully outside that to see how the wind's blowing. If you hear a lot of shouting, come in and be ready to defend yourself."

"I'll do my best. And Magister—" I caught his eye. "Thank you."

"Get her out, son, and then you can help me bring down that devil," he growled. "With Shia's blessing, we'll have done a fine night's work between us."

I nodded to him and slipped out into the corridor, dark lantern in my hand, keeping to the shadows and moving as fast as I dared.

Magister Rikard

I strode towards the meeting chamber. My heart beat faster, knowing that I finally might have a way to depose Berys. Hard proof, after all these years! I sent a blessing on Jamie's errand, wondering briefly if I should have asked him to bring the girl before the assembly as further proof. No matter, if she was wanted she could be fetched once he had her safe in my quarters.

The doors to the chamber stood open, but unusually there were guards at the door. I didn't recognise either of them, and they were roughly twice my size.

And very heavily armed.

If I had not chanced to meet with Jamie that evening, I truly believe I would not have noticed. Perhaps it was that little touch of fear, of his being discovered, that had me on the alert. The presence of two such large and well-appointed strangers at such a time was very peculiar indeed. I glanced into the chamber without going in. It was already full.

In fact it was brimming over. Every Magister—well, nearly every one, a few came along behind me and wandered in, chatting of nothing much—every student was there. Even the paid servers.

It was so very, very wrong.

And in the moment, there flashed before my eyes the sight of my old friends, Magistra Erthik and Magister Caillin, dead outside the door of the student Vilkas. I knew Vilkas, I had worked with him, and Erthik had known him even better. She had been tutoring him along with his inseparable friend, Aral. Those two young souls could no more have murdered Magistra Erthik than they could—

—than they could have withstood Berys if he'd caught them. He had called an assembly to denounce them for trafficking with demons even before the murders were discovered. I had never believed it for a moment.

I took a step back from the door. The guard on the right gazed at me. "What's wrong, Magister? The Archimage is waiting, you are the last to arrive." He reached out to grasp my arm.

I flooded his system with sleep and did the same to the other. They dropped between one breath and another. A second pair of like men were striding down the central aisle towards the doors, and I drew in a breath and made myself invisible.

Not true invisibility, you understand, that's impossible, but any who sought me would not see me unless they were as powerful as I. Their eyes would latch on to anything else, anything at all, that was not me. I moved swiftly and as silently as I could, lest the other guards should have better abilities than I feared. One, indeed, went to the place I had been, but the confusion took him and he could see only his sleeping comrades. He bent over and began shaking them.

I backed down the corridor, going as quickly as I could without making noise. The few scuffs of my shoes on the stone floor were covered by the commotion that swiftly surrounded the sleeping guards.

When I was out of their line of sight, I ran, down the corridors and out into the courtyard, as far as I could go.

And if you must know, yes. No day goes by, no night have I spent since untroubled by my memory of that terrible, terrifying cowardice. I knew as certainly as if I had seen it happen that most, or all, of the people in that room were going to be dead before morning. I also knew—or felt—or feared—that I could do nothing for them by bravely dying with them. It was too late for warnings.

Perhaps if I had shouted to them, before the armed guards killed me, more might have escaped.

Perhaps I'd have just been killed with them, and even greater evil would have blighted all of Kolmar.

Let you take some comfort, then, in the fact that the name of "coward" from others does not affect me in the slightest. For it can never have the force from other mouths that it has from my own soul, red with spilled blood and black with leaden guilt, every day of my life.

v

Despair and Hope

Lanen

I woke, groggy, with no idea what time it might be. There was no hint of moonlight, though whether that meant she was yet to rise or had passed me by, I didn't know.

I cursed to myself as I sat hunched on the hard bed, staring into the darkness and wondering with a kind of detached dread what Berys might have done while I slept. I felt no different, and to be honest, I suspected there was not a thing I could do about whatever it was at this stage. I ignored the possibilities as best I could, and quietly blessed my ignorance of demon matters. If something awful was going to happen that I couldn't do anything about, I'd rather not know.

I found, as my eyes adjusted to the low light, that there was a tray on the floor with food on it—bread, cheese, cold soup, and water. I was starving and ate every scrap. I knew absolutely that it wasn't poisoned. Berys would never be so kind.

For all that, I only just managed to keep it down. Thank the Lady, it wasn't the deadly sickness Vilkas had healed me of— sweet heaven, was it only a week past? a little less?—just the normal sickness most women have to put up with in pregnancy. It was quite a deal less bothersome today than it had been the last few days. I didn't know if that was because something was happening with my babes, or because after days of enforced fasting I'd had two meals this day, or if it was just the natural time for that kind of illness to end. I tried to remember what I knew of childbearing, but the little I could recall was that there seemed to be as many different reactions as there were women.

"Damn," I said out loud—at least, my lips and tongue moved, and my throat shaped the sounds, and air rushed through, but nothing came out.

Alone in silence. Again. Still.

At least now I knew how Berys had discovered that I could speak with the True Dragons, the Kantrishakrim, in their Language of Truth. Bloody Marik must have told him.

O blessed Shia. I turned cold in an instant, head to toe. Marik, who knew I was pregnant, and was only waiting for the advantageous moment to tell Berys. *O Mother of us All,* I begged, *blessed Mother, as one to another I beseech you, protect my babes. Let there be no good time for my unnatural father Marik to tell Berys what he has learned. Let Berys curse Marik six ways in a se'ennight if it will keep my babes from the evil one.*

I couldn't even hear my prayer myself. Berys's spell was strong and solid—I had tested it day and night ever since I had been taken, but as far as I could tell I was still held silent on all levels.

I cannot imagine how he managed to silence the Language of Truth. Until a few months past I'd only ever heard of it in legends, and now I missed it as I'd have missed a lost arm. There on the Dragon Isle where I first heard my beloved's voice in my head, and replied without thinking, Varien had told me that I was the only human he had ever known who could use it.

At least until now. I had shouted in truespeech and Marik had heard me, curse him.

What a damnable twist of fate. Shikrar and Akor, attacking Marik's mind, had opened it to truespeech. Which had been taken from me just when it would have been bloody useful.

Something caught in my throat and I coughed, silent still. Hells take it. Somehow the fact that I couldn't even hear myself cough made me furious. I screamed aloud, just because I had to, for the sheer frustration of it.

Nothing.

I managed to stop myself this time, before I yelled my throat raw. I'd done that the first day of my captivity, after Berys had left with the marks of my hands on his misbegotten neck. Nothing had worked, and eventually I had grown weary of the effort. Anger is a wonderful tonic, but even anger could not let me forget that I was alive only through Berys's distraction with other matters, and only until he got around to accomplishing my damnation. At best it would only be a matter of hours.

And what in all the merry Hells had he meant by saying I was become precious to him? Obviously because of my changed blood, though what it might mean to him I could not imagine. Kantri and Gedri mixed—yes, that was what I had agreed to when Vilkas saved my life. My babes had been killing me, for their blood was Kantri and Gedri blended and they all unwitting fought for their lives nearly at the cost of my own. I would surely have died if not for Vilkas, that tall, dark, reserved lad with so great a well of kindness in him. Vilkas and his comrade Aral put forth more power than I knew existed, and with my consent changed me into a creature neither truly human nor truly dragon. I yet reeled from that deep change; I yet knew not what it might mean for me in the march of time; but to my heart it mattered not a whit. My babes were safe, my body was able to support them, and that would do for now.

I tried to breathe deep, tried to relax, but it was no use. My heart began to race, my breathing quickened, as if I could hear the tramp of the guard through the thick blanket of silence that covered me. I think what bothered me most was that I could not rest. Every instant I expected the door to fly open, every moment that passed I waited for Berys to return and accomplish my damnation. Whatever that would feel like. Surely I would no longer be myself. A body without a soul, like a breathing doll, no volition, no intelligence . . . I shuddered again, from fear, from cold. The first gleam of moonlight had stolen through the high grating, reminding me of passing time. It couldn't be long now.

I forced myself to calm down and drew in a deep, shuddering breath. If I stopped to think about Berys and what was surely going to happen, I wouldn't have the courage to breathe at all.

Start small, Lanen. You're still alive, don't give up yet.

I had no idea how Berys had brought me to this place, but it had happened in the blink of an eye. As far as I could tell I had been imprisoned two, maybe three days. Maybe four. My beloved husband Varien and I, and the Healers Vilkas and Aral, had all been exhausted after we brought the Lesser Kindred to their new life. We all could barely stand from weariness and had taken a moment after that day and night of work to rest, when suddenly the air had turned thick with demons. I had been torn from Varien's side to be dropped at the feet of a man I'd never seen before, but whom I guessed from his association with demons must have been Berys. I had heard of him and knew that he was older than my mother, but this man looked barely older than me. He had grabbed me, stepped onto a small platform made of rock, and suddenly we were here.

It all seemed a great deal of trouble to go to. And why in the Hells was my peculiar blood so useful to Berys?

Back to that again, around and around my thoughts trudged like a dog turning a spit.

I shook myself, there in the cold darkness. Think of something else, girl!

Oh, yes. Something else. What will it be like to be a body walking about without a soul, once mine is stolen away. Where would *I* be? Tormented by demons for all time? Or somehow aware of my empty shell being put through its paces by Berys the Damned?

I shivered harder in the gathering cold. Goddess help me. Either one sounded terrible beyond belief.

Marik must hate me desperately, to hand me over to Berys. Well, it was mutual now, and all the Hells mend him because

I surely wouldn't. He knew about my babes, and he would surely tell Berys eventually if he had not already. For that alone I would kill Marik if I had the chance. It occurred to me that I should feel some kind of guilt at having tried to murder my father, but to speak truth I felt only anger at myself for having failed.

I had spent most of my life blessedly ignorant of all of this. I had known nothing of my true father and had been abandoned by my mother after little more than a year. My dear friend and heart's father Jamie had raised me as best he could, but it seems that even he could not keep my fate from finding me. For reasons best known to himself, Marik had chosen last autumn to make good his promise to the Rakshasa, and had hounded me across the western sea to the Dragon Isle.

There he had received his due reward. The Kantri—the True Dragons, the great creatures of legend that can speak and reason— had broken his mind. The last time I had seen him ere this, he had not been able to walk unassisted and he could not speak. His Healer, Maikel, had held out no hope of Marik's ever being able to regain the power of conscious thought.

I shuddered to my bones. Perhaps that would be my fate, afterwards. *At least I won't be there to know about it,* I thought grimly.

Then, even more grimly, *Probably.*

Enough, girl, I told myself sternly. *Think. The door was opened once. Maybe there will be another chance. When they come for you, perhaps?*

It would help if I'd had any faint idea of where I was. Nothing looked even slightly familiar. The walls were thick and stone-built, but that could be anywhere. I shivered, mostly from the cold, and began to pace the tiny room—no more than two steps from wall to wall, but it kept me from freezing.

The most maddening thing was that I kept gazing, will I or nill I, at the little barred window high up on the wall. It faced towards the south so that I never saw direct light of sun or moon, only the scattered glow of either but sometimes I could catch a glimpse— I went to drag the chair over, but the chain pulled me up short.

Though perhaps—I stood on the chair where it was, standing on tiptoe—yes, there she was! The rising moon. She was just past the full, the Ancient Lady of the Moon, and she smiled at me, fair and comforting even in this dark and desperate place. I gazed as long as I could, but I could only perch like that for a very short time. Eventually a wave of dizziness swept over me and I sat down, hard. I was in such a hurry to get down that my backside clipped the edge of the chair and I fell into a muddled heap, heedless now of the cold, my anger gone and with it my strength. With my legs drawn up to my chest and my manacled arms wrapped around my legs, I rocked myself back and forth, small movements, as if I were terrified even to admit to myself how frightened I was. I closed my eyes and tried to imagine Jamie rocking me when I was a child, disturbed by an ill dream, but thinking of Jamie made things worse.

And what did not?

The unnatural silence rattled me. All that I did happened in a complete absence of sound, bar those few moments with my tormentors. It made everything feel like a dream. No, a nightmare. A nightmare that never ended, that on waking was as hopeless as in the depths of sleep. All I could look forward to was a painful death—or worse yet, a short life in agony, if there was anything left to feel agony after the soul had gone to the deepest Hells. Left in this cage, without hope, without sound, with nothing to comfort me and all I loved taken from me.

My body began to protest the compression and I let go my legs. I felt my belly quavering, a peculiar movement, and it struck me—was that the first movement of my babes? Or only my stomach protesting the food I'd eaten?

Goddess, Mother, aid me, I thought, my heart pounding in my ears. *I can't even be sure I've felt my poor babes move. I can't even take my own life and protect my children from Berys by killing them.*

Damn Berys. Damn and blast him to all the Seven Hells, demons take his liver and feet it to the dogs . . .

My whole body was shaking now, fear and rage together leaving me unmanned, for I was furious with myself even as I trembled in every limb. Every time I tried to think my way out of this hole I came to this place of fear, of gut-tightening, muscle-cramping, uncontrollable terror. *Dear Goddess, what evil have I done to merit this end?* I cried in the depths of my soul, longing beyond reason for the ability to shout or scream if only to relieve my anger. And my poor children, my unborn babes—I had fought for them, poor little souls, fought already for all of our lives nearly at the cost of my own. I had consented to be changed to a creature not entirely human that they—that we—might live, and now my empty sacrifice mocked me to my bones. At the time I had blessed the Healers for saving my life. Now I wished I had simply died, and my littlings with me. At least then we might walk together in the High Fields of the Lady.

By now, whenever now was, Berys surely knew that I was with child. I drew my knees in again, gently, and wrapped my arms around my middle. It was the nearest I could come to embracing my poor childer.

I pray now only that we will all go down to death together, my sweetings, and I will protect you with all the fire of my soul until the Lady comes to gather Her innocents to Her breast.

I had no doubt that their lives would end in as much pain as possible once Berys learned of them.

I bowed my head as black despair washed over my soul, for I could see no escape even in death for us all three.

I realised as it crashed over me that I had never faced true despair before that moment. Sorrow, weariness, anger, fear—all of these are the common lot of humanity, but always before there had been hope somewhere behind all. Hope, for me, had always lain behind my days. Always there was a prospect of a brighter future, of a time when this ill would be past or that obstacle would be overcome: but now I could see the future, clear and sharp before me, and it held only pain and fear and horrific ending, and all too soon.

The wise say that it is only when hope deserts you that you find the underlying truth of your soul. Some find only a vast weariness that pulls them swiftly down to their ending: some admirable few discover true courage in some hidden corner of the self. At that moment, in that desert of the soul, in despair more profound than I had ever imagined, I was brought face-to-face with my own imminent death. In that cold dark place of stone my heart was as a lump of lead in my chest. I could barely force myself to breathe, as if my body wished to make an end to life on its own terms. I closed my eyes and longed for even the release of tears, but I tell you now, true despair is dry as the dust of ages.

And then, with my eyes tight closed, I saw in my mind a vision of a tiny flame far off, years distant from me but present. The faintest hint of fire, as when a single spark lands on dry tinder and sits for a brief instant, glowing red in the darkness.

Even as I sat there I drew in a breath, carefully, and breathed out slowly and gently, as though I blew in truth on a tiny physical spark to encourage it.

In my mind it glowed a little before it subsided.

I drew another breath in the silent darkness, and in that stillness felt something within me flutter. *My starving belly, poor thing,* I thought, and physically blew again on that tiny mental spark. It glowed a little more this time, and when I next drew breath it did not fade. Again, and it grew as large as my little fingernail, and it seemed to have the shape of a woman.

My belly moved again and this time my eyes flew open. That was not hunger. I moved my hands to sit over the small roundness of my belly.

Butterfly movements from within. Barely noticeable, save that I had sat so still.

Sweet Goddess, it must be.

My babes were moving.

For one breathless moment I thought nothing, felt nothing, apart from a mad, delirious joy that they lived and thrived even now.

And the next moment I laughed harshly into the silence. In that instant, to my astonishment, the tiny flame within had grown from distant star to brilliant sun, and it raged now within me, all-consuming. I did not recognise it but I surely welcomed it, for that fire was strength and home and love and all, it warmed my body and set my soul ablaze. I did not need hope. I had nowhere else to turn, and turning inward I found—myself afire. All those I loved were there, within me—my beloved Varien, our babes so tiny but alive and growing despite all, my heart's father Jamie, were the nearest, but there were others: soulfriend Shikrar, his son Kédra, Mirazhe, their tiny son Sherók gazing newborn into my eyes, Idai in despite of her pain a strength and a companion.

The only way to be certain that you will lose is to surrender.

Determination without hope. It is a dry and strange place in the soul, and I do not recommend it, but it is full of power.

I stood then, breathing deep into my gut where my littlings lay. It was a strange fire indeed that I had found. I was ready to fight or flee, ready for battle in a bare cell, but there was nothing to do but watch the slow departure of the moon's gleam as the Ancient Mother's stately dance took even the reflection of her light from me.

I needed to act, to do something that would force an action, that would get me out of this Hells-be-damned cell.

I had never spent much time in the service of the Lady, not in the way of those dedicated to Her. They beseech Her on their knees for all sorts and kinds of things—but somehow it always seemed to me that kneeling was unnecessary. It might be that, having no mother around me, I took the Mother of us All into my heart more completely than most. Greatest need brings greatest faith, they say. I stood, braced, and spoke my invocation, though not even I could hear it.

"Ancient Lady of the moon, rising in the east, who hast brought light to this dark place; Mother of the earth beneath my feet, in the very stones that surround me, whose fire rageth in my heart; Laughing Girl"—I faltered for a moment there, for laughter and water seemed both too distant from me—ah—"Laughing Girl of the Waters, who surrounds my babes within me—a boon I beg of thee, blessed Goddess! Do not leave me in this cold place of death." I began to shiver, whether from the deepening cold or from anger I could not tell. "Come fire, come battle, come rage to warm me! Shia, Goddess, in the name of all that is precious to you, *do not leave me here!*"

If there were poetry in life, my words would have echoed from the stone walls and given me heart—and perhaps been heard by a passing soul who might have been of some use to me. As it was, my throat was raw from shouting and neither I nor any other creature in the world had heard a thing.

I stood motionless, waiting, fire in my heart yet trapped in cold silence, for death to come and claim me and mine, when a light spilled into the room. But it was not the moon.

The light came from under the door.

Jamie

I found the stair swiftly, and the four identical oaken doors. I was delighted, in a strange way, to also find a huge guard pacing the corridor in the pitch-black dark.

He was sharp and well armed and he came for me the instant he saw me. *Good eyes*, I thought as I avoided his first blow. With some difficulty, it must be said. *It's bloody dark down here.* Well, well, well, and I just happened to have a lighted dark lantern in my hands.

I threw open the panel of the dark lantern and shone the light straight in his eyes. He swore and backed off. And dropped his guard.

I had no wish to murder him, the poor sod, but I had no choice. I could not rely on a deep wound, not here in the midst of the enemy. I despatched him as painlessly as I could, and when he stopped twitching I dragged him along the corridor out of my way. I searched the body for keys. No such luck.

I took a closer look at the doors. They were not particularly close-fitting, for they had been made chiefly to keep drunken louts out of the way for a night. Still, if you've nothing but your fingernails and you can't be heard, a door of thick oak will do as well as one of iron. No light shone under any of them.

She can't hear you. You can't hear her.

There was no one anywhere near; obviously Berys had trusted in that poor bastard I'd had to kill. I lifted the catch again and opened the dark lantern. Light blazed in that dark corridor. I stood before the first door, keeping the lantern on the ground that as much light as possible might shine underneath. I knelt there only a few moments, hoping with all my soul that she was awake, or that the unaccustomed light would waken her, but I didn't dare wait too long at any one door. Every nerve in my body jangled like shaken harp strings, out of tune, wrong. I desperately wanted to call out to her, if only for the relief of some kind of sound, but Rikard had warned me. The corridor would not appear unusual, sounds would behave as normal—they would just stop at the door. She could be no more than the thickness of oaken planks from me and I'd never know it.

I called to her in the silence of my heart, as you do to loved ones in peril—do you live, my daughter? Are you here, so near I might touch you? Was the guard a distraction, and are you a thousand leagues hence in some dread prison? Does your body lie rotting already in a shallow grave, my soul's child, my bright Lanen?

I held back a sob and mentally shook myself. *Cold, cold as revenge, cold as the depths of evil, lest your fears unman you.*

There was no response. Time was rushing past like a gale, bearing all my hopes into bleak darkness.

The next door. I was acutely aware that every moment made discovery more likely. I waited, my light gleaming unnoticed into silent darkness, where only dust was illumined, where she slept unheeding or crouched wounded, where she was held chained to the far wall being driven mad with needing to get to the door.

Then the next door. The one Hygel had said led to the cell ruined long since. The door was like all the others. *Blessed Lady,* I prayed in the depths of my cold heart, *Ancient One, riding serene above us all in your pale chariot, I beg you, if she sleeps waken her.*

I had never prayed half so fervently, for I had never before been so unable to do anything of use myself.

Let her see the light, let her notice, let it be that she can move so far—let him not have blinded her. Lady, Goddess, Mother of us All, I am helpless and I hate it and I cannot change it. Don't let her die in silent darkness, Shia. Have mercy on your daughter. On my daughter. On the only child I will ever have.

Somehow I managed to spill a little of the oil onto my foot, which made me look down. At the fresh bloodstains on the stone outside this particular door.

My heart was a deep drum, pounding out the seconds. I lifted the lantern and shone the light onto the keyhole. My hands were shaking as I drew out the lockpicks I'd borrowed from Hygel. My short sword was loose in its sheath, for I fully expected to have to deal with as many demons as Berys could spare. I knew fine that Berys was too bright to leave her protected only by a single guard, a paltry spell, and an oaken door, and I was prepared for everything I could think of.

I was certainly not ready for nothing.

Berys

Behold the advantages of long-term planning. Marik and I have been preparing for years, building up a legion of our own particular Healers. In exchange for a doubling of their inherent abilities, they have allowed us to link them to a spell. Oh, of course it would only be used in event of an emergency, of course. And most of them have been told that the purpose of the link would be to summon vast power from every corner of Kolmar to protect us all from some great evil.

Ha! If I could find a way to do that, I would not need the Demonlord to rid myself of the dragons!

The beauty of it is that all the work of activation, apart from the final ritual, has been done long since. Though I really must arrange to replace Durstan, it is awkward getting dressed with one hand. It has been easy enough to draw the double circle on the floor in my hidden chamber, and scribing the symbols is simple—but preparing the cauldron takes twice as long as it did.

I have only just finished crushing the leaves and pouring in the oil. Now to light the candles around the altar, so; tie my rope wards about my waist, damn, it's tricky, I really *must* replace Durstan. Now let me ensure—yes, I did remember to put the globe inside the circle. Check the wards one last time—ah, yes, renew that smudged one, my robes must have trailed over it—all is done.

"Come, ye servants," I said, lighting the oil-soaked fire under the cauldron where it sits to one side of the central altar. It bursts into flame even as three of the Rikti appear.

"Tremble, mortal!" the largest hisses.

"Foolish imp," I said, twisting the binding and making it writhe. "Do not waste my time. You are bound to me already, if you refuse I'll have your soul for a year and a day, and I am a Master of the Sixth Circle. I can inflict the True Death on you if I choose."

They all hissed, but were silent.

"Good," I said, and pointed at the largest. "You, go find the Demonlord who ensouls the Black Dragon. It flies over the Great Sea towards Kolmar. Bring me back word of when it will arrive here."

The first vanished.

"You, where are the Kantri and what are they doing?"

"Masster, need more help," it said, not moving. "Too many places, too many dragons for this one. You want old ones, found ones, little ones, what? All scattered."

"Find the largest group of them and watch for an hour, then come and tell me what they are doing and where they are. Go now," I commanded. It too disappeared.

"You," I said to the smallest. "A simple task. Lift that globe," I said, pointing, "and hold it above the cauldron."

The globe was made of glass, a large round vessel twice the size of my head, with a small opening in the top stopped with a cork. It was nearly full now of little locks of human hair, black to brown to red to gold to grey, all jumbled together. A few nail clippings from the bald ones.

The Rikti held the globe high above the cauldron. I raised my hand and my left arm, moving the stump in a pattern to match my whole hand, reciting the words. I have had so much practice with the major demons, these minor deeds hardly challenge me at all anymore. The demons involved yelled and tried to distract me, as ever, but I can ignore them easily now. When the last word was spoken, the oil in the cauldron burst into flame.

"Drop it!" I shouted, and the Rikti let go of the glass globe, hissed and disappeared. The glass shattered in the cauldron, while the hair and nails crisped in the flaming oil. The air was rank with the stench of burning hair and I felt slivers of glass in my hand. No matter.

I spoke the final word of the spell. As befits the final word of a great making, it had many syllables and grew harder to pronounce. The familiar sensation of a thick tongue—I ignored it, knowing it for distraction, pronouncing each syllable carefully—now, here, the last—

The spectre of the Demonlord appeared in the smoke, grinning hugely. "Boo."

I am not a Master of the Sixth Hell by accident. If I could not ignore such things I would have died long since. I spoke the final syllable, loud and strong, and the flaming oil was quenched as I spoke. The stench of burnt hair filled the room now but I barely noticed it. I started to shake, then to laugh, as the power of hundreds of Healers flowed through my veins. I fairly crackled with it, Healer blue shot with purest black.

I turned to the apparition, which to my surprise had persisted. "What do you want?" I asked, grinning back at it.

"You wanted a report. I will pass over the western shore of the South Kingdom in less than a day. I cannot tell more exactly than that."

"It is near enough. And I have a gift all prepared for you when you arrive, my servant."

"You keep thinking I'm a demon. I'm not," it said. "You are bound to me as surely as I to you. But no matter. What is my gift? If I like it I may try to fly faster."

"The Kantri," I replied, smug. "You recall those whom you turned into beasts? You will be pleased to learn that they have suffered ever since, but this very day before sunset they were restored."

The thing spat an obscenity. "And you give me the gift of having to do the work over again, do you? It cost me my life last time!" It blinked. "Well, nearly."

"Ah," I said, "behold the beauty of the pattern. The body you wear is made of molten rock, ash, and sulphur. You are living stone and the best weapon they possess is fire. How should they kill you now?"

And the Demonlord smiled and saw that it was good, and departed.

How strange. I am shaking as I don my robes for the assembly. Not the insipid blue robes of the Archimage: that time is past. My name as a demon-master I must keep secret from others, as would any who did not desire death from any number of curses, but at the least I will appear before my erstwhile companions as a Master of the Sixth Hell. The black and silver robes of my achievement fit well on my young-again shoulders. It is good.

Fear? No, I feel no fear at all. Anticipation, yes, and excitement from the power pulsing through me. And desire. Oh, yes, *desire*. To see so many faces pass through shock and disbelief, to despair before they die—ah, I shall savour this evening. If all goes as I plan, I should have enough bodies dead by my hand, the souls shocked and betrayed at the end, to feed even the Lord of the Fifth Hell to bursting point. Just as well, for I shall summon it to assist me—it will, I doubt not, make short work of my fellow Magistri, and give them something to think about apart from me when I decide to leave. It will be a mutual work, I think: food and exercise for one of the most powerful Lords of the Hells, the end of this weary College for me.

Underlying all, of course, there is the undeniable pleasure in knowing I have Marik of Gundar's blood and bone in my grasp. With the power now at my disposal, I do not need her to fulfill some foolish prophecy. I will still grant her soul to the Rakshasa, if only to shut Marik up, but her body I shall keep for another purpose. I need her blood, after all.

I do not yet understand what forces cluster around her, this strange creature. I have had any number of incredible reports, chief among which is that the Kantri have taken to her. They flew her out to the Merchant ship after it had left the Dragon Isle. They talk with her constantly if Marik is to be believed. The very first of them to arrive in Kolmar, weary and wounded, nevertheless came immediately to her assistance. It will be useful to have her in my power when I leave this place, lest the dragons are too cowardly to deal with my Black Dragon without encouragement.

Of course, I now have no further need for Marik himself.

I do not plan to use him this night. No, he will be worth a great deal to me when the Demonlord comes. Betrayal, despair, perhaps even fury; a tasty banquet for whatever it is that inhabits the Black Dragon. I will enjoy putting an end to his whining and his endless requests for assistance—let him live pain-free for one night. His despair will be all the more delightful when it comes.

Ah, but enough of such pleasant musing. I go now to claim my birthright. And when the Demonlord arrives and all the Kantri are dead, and with the help of the fool King Gorlak of the East Mountains and his armies, I have control of all of Kolmar, I will give to the Rakshasa a home for themselves in this world, that they may serve me more readily.

The time approaches. After I have released the Lord of the Fifth Hell to feed on my erstwhile colleagues and any students he can catch, I shall take Marik with me to collect his daughter. Let Marik feel himself fully healed for a day or so before I sacrifice him. He will have so much more to regret that way.

Ah, life is sweet.

Jamie

It had been too long since I'd had to use lockpicks, and I was as rusty as the lock. It didn't help that every instant I was anticipating the sharp claws of the Rikti in my back. I must have been there a full minute—it felt like forever—when I felt the lock go and I pulled open the door, shining the lantern into the darkness.

Lanen stood there, eyes blazing, manacled and chained to the wall. For all that, she stood holding a chair by its back, the legs aimed at whoever was coming in. I was proud of her, being prepared for an enemy despite everything. She caught sight of my face and threw the chair from her. I winced, waiting for the clatter, but of course it made no noise at all.

I was inside in a moment, lantern in hand, setting the delicate lockpicks against those rough manacles to release her from her chains. There!

And suddenly she was free and in my arms, my girl, my own Lanen. I stole enough time from our peril to hold her to me for a breath—forever—then I took her arm and pulled her with me. Every bone in my body was screaming at me to run.

Varien

The moment I reached the road I called out in truespeech. *"Shikrar, my friend,"* I cried, striding as swiftly as I might towards Verfaren, holding my fist to the stitch in my side. *"How fare you?"*

"I have eaten a little, and rested," he replied. *"I am still hungry, but that may be addressed in time."*

"There is no time, Shikrar, do you hear me? I am filled with the most terrible foreboding. I beseech you, my friend—my wings are gone forever, I must needs borrow yours. When will you be able to fly?"

My head ached instantly from using truespeech, my side was worse, and I noticed as I walked that the wind was rising. From the south, of course. I was headed directly into it.

There was the merest hint of a sigh from Shikrar. *"I am at your service, my friend. I have eaten but little, I am yet wing-light."*

"Then come now!" I cried, breaking into a run for a moment, despite the pain, ere I was forced to walk again. My heart pounded in my chest like a great river over rapids, and of a sudden I found I was terrified. I could not stop shaking, and I feared in my marrow that Lanen's death was near her. *"Come swiftly, soulfriend, find me on the road. I will not stop to wait for you."*

Even as I bespoke him, I felt the fear of death enter me. "*Shikrar, swiftly, to me!*"

Lanen

The moment we stepped outside the cell several things happened at once.

First and most obviously, we sprang Berys's trap, for more of the Rikti appeared and began attacking us—though they seemed to concentrate on Jamie. I fought them off as best I could.

The second thing that happened was that, to my infinite delight, I could hear again, and I could speak.

"*Varien!*" I cried, as loudly as I could in truespeech. "*Come swiftly, my heart!*" Then I realised—I had no idea where I was.

"Where the devil are we, Jamie?" I asked, beating off Rikti as I spoke.

"Verfaren, where else would you find half the Hells in the corridors," he grunted, between slashes at the Rikti and swerves to avoid being injured. "Come on, the farther away we can get the better. Run!"

We pelted down the corridor and I called out to Varien as we ran—

"*We Jamie and I **are in Verfaren** the College of Mages attacked by Rikti but I am free . . .*"

—and met Berys and Marik turning the corner not five feet in front of it.

"*Oh, Hells, it's Berys!*"

I heard only "*We come Lanen! Shik—*" before Berys waved his hand and the beloved voice in my mind was silenced yet again.

I was getting truly sick of that trick of his.

Berys

I felt the activation of the Rikti on the prison door and hurried Marik down with me, along with two of my favoured guards who bore lanterns and the makings of the small altar that was needed to work the demonline. There was very little reason for either of us to stay in the Great Hall any longer, after all. The Lord of the Fifth Hell was doing a fine job on its own.

I was tempted to linger. The pleasure of seeing those colleagues I had despised for so many years dying in pain, confounded by a powerful demon—for they had never truly considered the possibility of such a battle, leaving such studies to me—ah, it was balm to my soul. Deeply satisfying. Still, there was no more for me to do, and I did not wish to lose my new treasure.

I expected to find the hunchbacked woman or possibly the proud student Vilkas in a foolhardy raid being savaged by Rikti; instead we ran full into the prisoner herself barely at arm's length, with some servant behind her and the Rikti nowhere to be seen. I threw up a barrier and just managed to stop them barrelling into us and escaping; they were held motionless. It was as well I was so powerful at that moment, for they struggled wildly, but my will was implacable and my power ascendant. I grinned and with a gesture stopped her from using Farspeech as well.

"How very kind," I said lightly. "Now I have two sacrifices, and you have even unlocked the door for me. Very considerate."

The guards handed off their lanterns to Marik and bore the prisoners unceremoniously into the cell they had just left.

Varien

In the event, Shikrar was nearly upon me when at last I heard my beloved's mindvoice.

"Shikrar, I have heard her! She is in Verfaren and faces Berys—in the name of the Winds, come quickly!"

"I am aloft. Where are you, Akhor?" asked Shikrar. His mind's serene voice restored in me a tiny measure of calm, at least enough to answer.

"On the road heading south of the field where we welcomed our people," I shouted, running as fast as I could. I told him what little she had said even as I ran, and heard his distant roar through the darkness. It was balm to my heart, as was the sound of his

wings above me. I cried out to him in truespeech and saw him
looking back and forth.

*"I can't see, drat these clouds—grace of the Winds, there is the
moonlight—and there you are, all of you. I come!"*

All of us?

I turned around. The wind had been in my face, I had not
heard the others behind me. Aral and Vilkas were on foot, Rella,
Will, and Maran were mounted. Just for an instant I blushed in
the darkness. At least someone had thought of horses.

Although I was proved the shrewder in the event.

The poor creatures had objected strongly to Salera when she
had first arrived at the Dragon's Head—was it ten, twelve days
since? It seemed a lifetime—and even more strongly to Shikrar
when he joined us up on the High Field, in the mountains. They
were still not at ease around him, but they hadn't bolted. Or they
hadn't bolted when Shikrar was walking sedately alongside them
as we all came down the mountain. When he appeared suddenly
from the night sky and landed with a thump right in front of them
they did a spinbolt and disappeared into the windy darkness,
leaving Rella, Will, and Maran to rise up and brush the dust from
their clothes.

"Well, it was a nice idea," said Rella, grimacing.

"I cannot stay," I told them, as Shikrar gathered me in his
hands. "I will see you in Verfaren."

"Don't leave me here!" cried Rella. "Please—Jamie—"

"I have bespoken Kédra, he comes for you," said Shikrar, and
took to the wild sky. We were barely aloft when he let forth a
huge hiss of pure fury, stretched his wings, and flew at the ut-
most of his strength. I could feel it even as he held me, I knew
that bone-deep *change* between flight that is important and flight
on which life depends.

"Raksha!" Shikrar cried in truespeech as he flew. The wind
was fierce against us. *"Akhor, it is a Lord of one of the Deep Hells,
some* kairtach *has summoned a major demon!"*

The wind might have come directly from the Hells that night.
It blew in huge gusts, catching him on the upswing, throwing me

backwards as he tumbled. The gale fought him, swiped at him, almost seemed to be trying to knock him out of the sky, but he laughed fiercely at the challenge and rode the tempest.

My heart soared. No matter that we rode on the treacherous wings of storm—it was *Hadreshikrar* who held me safe, who for more than my lifetime had taught every youngling of the Kantri how to fly. He was not the teacher of flight because he enjoyed the company of younglings, or because he had endless patience with them, although those were truths as well—no, he had earned his position. Every year. Only the best flyer, the one with the most experience and the greatest proven skills, was allowed to teach. He had been the best longer than I had been alive. I felt it when he caught the feel of the winds, felt him begin to move with them, anticipating the gusts by some weather-sense I envied desperately even as the blankness at my back ached for what was not there.

And suddenly there below was Verfaren. Ten miles was not so far on those great wings, thank the Winds and the Lady. The lights in the town shone on winding streets, and lights in the windows gleamed in the darkness, but the College on the hill was dark as death.

vi

The Fall of the College of Mages

Varien

Shikrar landed hard outside what I assumed was the College of Mages—it was the largest set of buildings and had its own walled courtyard—and he didn't so much release me as throw me to the ground. I rose to find him facing the gates. A large Gedri, heavily armed, took one look at Shikrar and ran silently and with great concentration into the night and away from anything he might have been guarding. Shikrar ignored him.

The gates of the College of Mages were astoundingly strong, as it proved. They withstood a blow from the Eldest of the Kantri without breaking, which was one blow more than I had thought it would take. When Shikrar hit them again—harder—the entire frame came away from the stone walls and the still-locked gates fell to the ground with a great crash.

There was a single human figure in the courtyard, barely visible in the dimness. He called out, "Jameth of Arinoc!" and ran towards me, thereby striking me as being very clever.

Shikrar rushed into the courtyard and looked around frantically, echoing my desperation. "Where, Akhor?" he cried. His voice boomed and echoed in the cobbled square.

I ran up to the shaking man and caught him by the shoulders. "Where is Jamie? Where is *Lanen?*"

"I don't know," he said, and even in that darkness lit only by fitful glimpses of the moon I could see that his eyes were wide and staring. "Most likely there, you see those grates?"

He pointed to a row of small gratings to the right of the courtyard, maybe five feet above ground level. Light gleamed in one of them as we spoke.

"Shikrar! There, where the light shines, she is within!"

Jamie

I struggled furiously against the holding spell, but I might as well have tried to dig a well with a fork. Lanen, away to my left, was swearing at the guards, who ignored her. When we were all inside the cell, Berys had his guards shut and lock the door while he cast a silence around us. "Don't bother yelling," said Marik smugly. "No sound can pass those barriers. In either direction."

Berys busied himself directing the guards, who drew stones from their packs and started building something while he started drawing things on the floor. I couldn't yet tell what it was going to be, but I was certain to my marrow that it held my death. They might want Lanen for something particular but I was of no use to them at all.

I had nothing to lose. Might as well enjoy myself.

"Bloody Marik of bloody Gundar," I spat. At least I might enjoy a little Marik-baiting, if I could do nothing else. "Last I heard you were mindless and drooling."

"No change there, then," put in Lanen. Her face was white and drained, but her voice was steady as a rock.

Marik ignored her and came near to me, staring intently. "Who the devil are you to give a damn?" he asked, lifting a lantern and peering at me.

I glared back at him, unable to fight, unable to move a muscle. "I could have killed you stone dead back then," I spat. "Should have finished the job." A defiant smile touched my lips. "Though I hear you've been limping ever since. Some good comes of everything, seemingly."

"Who in all the Hells are you?" he asked again. "I don't remember you! No human gave me this limp, it was the demons when we made the—"

"Oh, no," I interrupted. "We gave you that limp right enough. Indirectly. And at the least, Maran broke a few of your ribs for you. I heard them go."

His eyes widened. "You bastard! You were the one who took on Berys while she knocked me out! You and that whore Maran ruined my *life!*" Marik cursed, throwing down his lantern. He grabbed the front of my tunic to steady himself and threw a punch at me with all his strength. I saw it coming and managed to turn my face away enough to save my nose, but my jaw hurt like hell—and I could do nothing but wait for the next one.

"Your courage astounds me, Father," drawled Lanen sarcastically as Marik drew back for a worse blow. "Striking a helpless man. Such daring."

He stepped over to where she was held and slapped her, hard. "Mock while you can, Daughter," he snarled, turning the last word into a curse. "You're demon fodder."

"Leave off, Marik, I need that one," murmured Berys. "Come, it's time. You," he called to one of the guards, "bring her to the altar." It was only a few steps. *No!*

"Damn you, let her alone!" I shouted, stupidly.

Lanen

It was come, then. My ending, or the start of some foul half-life I dared not even think on. I was still held by Berys's spell, which I could do nothing about. Terror gripped me, gut-wrenching, breath-stealing terror.

That was what did it, I think.

I have always gone straight from fear to anger, and the greater the fear, the deeper the anger. But what took me over was not anger, or not only anger. It was—it was most like that moment when you first become aware and leave childhood behind forever; or when you first had to deal with death and you realised that life is always too short. I felt the change in my breath, in my blood, in the very beating of my heart, and it happened between one instant and the next. My very vision changed—it was the difference between looking at rain through thick glass and stepping out into a thunderstorm, when you can not only see but feel and hear the downpour and smell every drop. And it was not vision only that was affected. I had always known Berys was evil but now I could see it, and worse yet I could *smell* it. He reeked, a stench like rotten meat but much worse, coming off him in waves. I was hard put to it not to retch. He was my death and he stood there smiling.

And the soul's-fire I had discovered in that dry hopeless place exploded like a newborn star.

I threw back my head and cried aloud, words I didn't understand, and a great pulse of power blazed from me. The guard screamed and let go, Marik staggered backwards and fell, and I could feel Berys's will shatter and saw him reeling from the shock. I could move.

I often wonder what would have happened next if the wall hadn't disappeared.

Marik

I was trying still to master myself in the face of whatever the Hells the girl had done when I felt it, a rumble deeper than sound that shook my feet—there was no more warning than that, thanks to Berys's brilliant idea to keep us all from being distracted by sounds from outside—and my nightmare rose howling before me.

I could neither move nor act, I could not think, I could only stare and scream. I had dreamed this so many times, dreading it both mad and sane, seen it again and again—but this was not in some distant place, half legend, where dragons dwelt and anything might happen. This was not some light timber frame wall being torn away. The walls of the College were of shaped stone, three feet thick and centuries old, and that monster pulled down fifteen feet of wall at once. It was twice the size of the silver one, its head barely fit within the room, its vast bronze jaws agape and roaring, tearing down more of the wall to get at me.

I felt someone take me by the arm to throw me to it. I fought with all my strength, but that grip was iron. A brilliant light flared before my eyes and I was tossed into it, whether I would or no.

A moment of nothing, a moment in which nor breath nor light existed, and I stumbled out onto a high platform under quiet stars. There were high mountains around about me with snow on their sharp summits, ghostly in the pale moonlight. It was peaceful, a good place, it almost looked familiar—so long ago—faint memories of years long past, coming to the top of this tower as a child, wrapped in a bear skin to keep warm, gazing with delight on the mountains in winter . . . bloody Hells.

I was home. Castle Gundar. Halfway across the *world*! Those were the East Mountains around my home. I knew them all by name, I'd spent years clambering among them—Old Woman, Cloud Catcher, Demon's Tooth, the Needle, the Three Sisters—only—how the Hells was I come here?

I took a step, tripped over a loose stone, and fell against something—someone—

It was Berys, at my side. Looking pleased with himself.

Lanen

As soon as Berys and Marik disappeared, Shikrar drew his head back out of the room—just as well, he didn't really fit. Jamie and I scrambled over the rubble of the wall. Shikrar for all his size was hard to see in the fitful moonlight, but there by his feet—a tiny figure—

Oh, dear Goddess.

Varien. Varien. Varien.

I ran towards him and we met with a thump, arms wrapped round one another, and held on as though we would never let go. I was swearing at him—"Damn you, Varien, where have you been, I couldn't hear you, I thought that bastard had killed you"—but I am not certain that he heard me. He was muttering much the same nonsense, after all, and we kept interrupting ourselves as we kissed frantically.

Of course, it couldn't last. He had just managed to control himself so far as to lean back within my arms and look at me, when with the loudest noise I had ever heard a great light burst into the dark sky, flames leaping high against the stars, and bits of masonry began to rain down upon us.

The College was burning.

Jamie

"NO!" cried Rikard, sprinting towards the doors. I managed to catch him and haul him back just in time, for Shikrar would have trampled him as he hurried towards the fire. I only just noticed Kédra landing outside the College walls.

I had only seen Shikrar briefly in the fight in the High Field, burning off the little demons: I had been dealing with my own distractions when he took on the big Raksha. After that, despite his great size, he had impressed me mainly as being wise and calm as we spoke together on the way down from the mountains. True enough, his sheer size was a threat, but it was hard to know what kind of real power he could wield. I had just watched him tear apart stone walls with no apparent effort, but I still wasn't ready. He moved across the courtyard like a snake through water.

"For Shia's sake, let me go!" shouted Rikard, wrenching himself free. He ran like a man demented and began pounding uselessly at the doors of the burning building, unlocked but unmoving. "There are people trapped in there!"

Shikrar stood before the doors. "Stand away, Gedri," he said, that vast ancient voice deep and resonant in the courtyard.

I hadn't thought Rikard could move that fast. Just as well I was wrong.

Shikrar tore open the doors like a child tearing a leaf of grass, and flung them to the stones. Several dozen people rushed out, fire behind them, terror in their eyes. Some were shouting, some were screaming, some were wide-eyed and staring and looked as if they would never speak again. Vilkas and Aral, borne hither by Kédra, ran to help their comrades.

Magister Rikard did well then, drawing them all away to the far side of the courtyard, asking, listening, calming. In moments he returned and began to speak, his voice impossibly steady.

"Berys has murdered the Magistri with the help of a huge Raksha and a horde of the Rikti—and when the Magistri were gone, he set them loose on the students and left." Rikard's voice cracked. "From what some of them said, he was dared to call on one of the Lords of Hell. These"—he gestured back at the little group huddled by the shattered gates—"only got out because the demons took Berys's guards along with everyone else. These folk were closer to the doors and they had the presence of mind to run. They—we—Shia save us," he shuddered, his voice cracking at last. "We are all that is left."

A huge voice laughed on the wind, a laugh that racked my body with one great shudder, so heavy it was with evil. We all turned to see the vast figure that rose up, surrounded by the flames that consumed the College, seeming to enjoy their heat. It was the size of Shikrar but more nearly human in form, though horned and fanged in a hideous mockery of the Kantri. "Soon not even you, little wizard," it cackled, and spat at Rikard. A ball of poisonous green fire burned towards where Rikard stood staring aghast. He raised the best shield of his Healer's aura that he could muster, but it looked pale and weak in the light of that obscene fire. I was too far away to help, too far away to do anything but watch him die—when the balefire was batted out of the air by a dark wing, striking the ground with a loud hiss and smoking poisonously on the cobbles.

Varien

> Shikrar flew high,   foulness spurning.
> Fury fuelled him,   fanned his anger,
> drove him upwards: urgent his desire,
> swiftly to deal   death to the demon.

Words cannot do him justice. I had never seen him fly so brilliantly, never in all our long lives together. Lanen and I held each other and watched in awe. He spiralled high on the updraft from the flames, keeping out of his enemy's reach, gaining height, watching the demon's every move keenly.

There in the midst of burning stone, grown vast on its obscene feast of flesh, was the Lord of the Fifth Hell, a huge Raksha. It grew in its wrath, trying to make itself as large as Shikrar, but it was trapped—it seems even Berys had some sense left, and had not loosed it to rampage where it would. The thing was bound, likely to the building: if the building were destroyed, it might find itself untrammelled.

The flames, fanned by the wild wind, bothered it no more than they did Shikrar, but it seemed to take a passing pleasure in the destruction the fire was causing. It started to lean over towards us, but Shikrar swooped down and breathed Fire upon it as he passed—not the puny flames that humans know, but the true Fire that is part of our being. The distraction worked, though the demon managed to move out of the way of the flame. For the most part. We all saw the scorch mark on its upper arm.

It laughed. I knew about the Lords of Hell and was prepared, but several of the students were violently sick at the sound. So would Death itself laugh to see a world dying of plague.

"So, the great Kantri are reduced to this? A little firebrand to tickle me. Eat stone, dragon!" it cried, and wrenching off a great lump of stone, threw it at Shikrar.

With the merest flick of his wings Shikrar avoided the missile.

This seemed to amuse the creature, for it tore off larger and larger sections of wall to throw at him. None of them came very close, for Shikrar watched the Raksha's every move. When it stooped for a moment to break off more stone, he darted in and struck with fangs and claws, tearing a great hole in its shoulder, ripping gashes in its flesh as he passed swiftly out of reach again, away from the long arms and poisonous claws. He was forced to swerve again and again as the thing grabbed at him, but it was soon clear that he was wearing it down, flying in, biting and away before he could be touched, tearing holes in the foul flesh, darting away out of reach as its claws tried to score his armour and failed to find purchase.

At last, though, his boldness was his downfall. The Raksha, in real pain now, grabbed for him as he shot past a little too close. It caught the tip of his tail, throwing him off balance in the air before the edged scales cut deep into the demon's hand. It cried out but held on. Shikrar beat his wings furiously but he could not get free.

Vilkas

I was glad I had not eaten, for when my stomach heaved when the thing laughed, there was nothing to come up. Being so near to so evil a creature sickened me to my bones. Aral held my arm when I doubled over, and I swear I could feel her thought travel through her hand.

"I can't fight it, Aral!" I cried, shaking her off. "It's too big!"

"What does physical size have to do with anything in the realm of the soul?" she asked, far too reasonably for my liking. "Even if you can just distract it from Shikrar, that would be something!"

I grabbed her arm and drew her to me, so that our faces all but touched. "Damn it, woman, don't you understand?" I snarled, barely above a whisper. "It's all I can do not to fall to my knees. I'm shaking so badly I can barely stand. I'm *afraid*, Aral. I am by damn petrified and I can't do a sodding thing about it!"

She shook me off, her anger matching mine. "If you could direct just a fraction of that anger towards the right object, we'd be a damned sight better off." She turned towards the battle. I could see her aura glowing around her, bright and strong, but then she stopped. Swiftly she drew out of her tunic the pouch that hung around her neck. "Please, Lady," she said as she drew out the great ruby and held it to her heart with her left hand. "Hear me. Your kinsman has need of your aid."

Suddenly her aura was twice as bright, and within the blue there shone a corona of red light clear as the noonday sun through finest stained glass.

The demon had hold of Shikrar's tail and was drawing him nearer, despite Shikrar's desperate effort to get away. Aral lifted her right hand in a fist and sent her power to surround the Raksha's hand. Her arm shook, then her whole body—and her fingers began to open.

So did the demon's.

The red light from the soulgem twined around Aral's sending, pulsing, and the Raksha shook to that pulse as it fought. It reached across, trying to grip Shikrar's tail with its other hand, claws grasping—Aral stood shaking as she used every ounce of her strength to hold the thing still, just for a moment.

It worked. Just for a moment, but it was enough. The demon, furious, could not move. Shikrar turned back and, using his rear claws, slashed deeply at the wrist of the hand that held him. Aral's strength failed and her aura winked out. The Raksha, suddenly able to move again, watched the sharp scales on Shikrar's tail slice through the remains of its ruined hand. It screamed and spat balefire at Shikrar as he climbed. The green fire landed on Shikrar's back, searing, and it was Shikrar's turn to cry out.

The Raksha's cry had been music to my heart. Shikrar's pain, I swear, screamed along my own back.

Varien

Shikrar, moving awkwardly now but out of reach, flamed his fangs and claws clean as he climbed. His fire appeared diminished, and he was favouring his injured shoulder.

He spoke then, and I truly feared for him: he sounded desperately weary, in pain and out of breath. "Be warned, creature. I am the Eldest of the Kantrishakrim. Quit this place and return to the Fifth Hell, or by my soul I swear you will know the True Death." And still he climbed.

It laughed again, despite its mangled hand. "As if you could deal it to me! I have been loosed among men, I have feasted on souls and flesh and fear this night. I will have a taste of dragon to season all, as none of my kind have known this long age past!"

It is very difficult to judge distances at night, especially if you are looking straight up. Shikrar had been beating his wings less and less often. When the creature began its speech, he seemed to reach the end of his strength and seemed to be falling. The demon laughed and opened its arms to crush and rend him.

But this was Teacher-Shikrar, who had instructed every Kantri youngling for the last thousand years in the art of flight, who had often boasted even to me that he had not taught us everything he knew. It is true, he *was* falling. Directly at the demon. Very, very fast.

The Raksha reached out with both arms, its ruined hand hanging loose, ready to grapple with Shikrar at last. The rows and rows of teeth in that distorted mouth gleamed in the light of the dancing fire. Shikrar was dropping like a stone, arrowing directly at its face, claws and wings held close as if he did not dare to attack— as if he were protecting himself—but—*he held his furled wings close by his sides, not tucked over his back.*

What in the name of sense is this, my friend? I wondered, but did not dare to use truespeech lest I distract him.

—and at the last instant he swerved and pulled up at what seemed an impossible angle, using just the tiniest bit of wingtip, arcing backwards and up and rolling as he went, along the line of his descent. He seemed to miss the demon entirely, except for his tail—which he struck deeply and embedded in the thing's torso as he passed. His momentum threw him around it at incredible speed, but at a bizarre angle that it didn't seem able to anticipate. Shikrar's long supple body quickly wrapped around the Raksha, but it managed to get one arm free and raised it to strike.

Its ruined hand dangled useless from the raised arm, mocking it, as Shikrar's full length was thrown around the creature's torso faster and faster. His razor-sharp foreclaws sliced around its throat as he whipped around, and he used the last of his wild momentum to slam his upper fangs against its armoured head.

By the time the Lord of the Fifth Hell realised what was happening it was already dead.

Shikrar had managed to lock his foreclaws about its spurting throat and—he closed his hands. The deadly claws sliced that hideous flesh like so many swords, and at the last the sound of bone snapping was sharp in the night air. The thing collapsed. Shikrar unwrapped himself from it, threw it off him, and drew in a deep breath. I drew my own with him, nearly choking as I tried to force my human throat to breathe Fire. He seared the head first, to ashes; then the body, scorching the surrounding stones clean of every drop of Raksha blood, every trace of balefire.

The wild winds had died about the same time as the Lord of the Fifth Hell, but the fire that had destroyed the College burned on. As Rikard began to organise the survivors to put out the blaze, I moved near to my old friend.

"Shikrar, my friend, I owe you everything," I said. "Life, love, and all. And to think I used to consider myself a decent flyer! Never will I say that again, my word to the Winds, while yet you live."

"If I'd flown a little better the damned thing would have missed me altogether," he said, his wings drooping in the Attitude of Pain and his voice strained.

"So you are not yet without flaw? Even after all this time?" I chided him gently.

It raised a tiny hiss of amusement. "It seems not," he replied, and his voice quavered a little.

"Shock, I expect," said a deep voice behind me, and the Healer Vilkas strode forward, pale in the firelight that still flared in the ruins of the College. "Or reaction. Or loss of blood. Most likely all three. Do you permit, Lord Shikrar?" asked Vilkas, drawing his power to him.

"As swiftly as you may, Mage Vilkas," said Shikrar, his voice shaking plainly now with pain and exhaustion.

"Aral?" said Vilkas softly. That lovely young woman moved to join him, the soulgem still clutched in her left hand, but before she could summon her aura once again Shikrar swiftly moved his huge head very close to her. I was proud of her, for she hardly flinched at all.

"Lady Aral," he said softly, "I had lost that fight ere I had well begun, were it not for your aid. I am in your debt."

She did not speak, but reached out her right hand, tentatively, and touched his mask. He bowed to her touch. I turned my face away.

Vilkas was glowing brightly. He led Aral around to the wound on Shikrar's back and right flank.

I would not have believed it if I had not seen it. Perhaps it was the strength of the soulgem, perhaps it was the response of Aral's soul to Shikrar's kindness, and perhaps it was simply that Vilkas, frustrated at being of no service in the struggle, was intent on proving his worth. They did not cover over the wound, as we would have done with *khaadish*. They healed it from the inside out: Raksha-trace washed away with Healer's fire, bone-scorch soothed and burnt muscle renewed, blistered flesh eased, torn and melted scale made whole before my eyes. It took them the better part of an hour, but they healed Shikrar as we watched. When their task was done, the only indication that he had been wounded was the outline of new scale, lighter than the rest, where that terrible burn had been.

Maran

"You who have not flown before, be warned," Kédra had said, flexing his wings as we climbed into his hands. "It is a wild night for flying. The air is full of sudden drops and cross-currents this night. It will be rough aloft."

That was when I learned that dragons are liars. It wasn't rough aloft, it was bloody terrifying aloft. Still, Kédra got us there alive, so I was inclined to forgive him. I did wish at the time that it hadn't been so dark, or so frightening, because I didn't expect to have the chance to fly again.

He landed outside the wall just as Shikrar released the survivors from the Great Hall. Vil and Aral went to join their friends; the rest of us milled about, helpless, but not willing to leave.

My eye was drawn first to a pair of observers—actually, they stood so close together it was hard to make out that they were two people. As it should be.

Once I knew that Lanen was free and safe in her husband's arms, I found a quiet corner from which to watch the proceedings. It was obvious that greater folk than I were needed, and they all rose to the challenge. When the students were taken to The Brewer's Arms I followed, and managed to get a room to myself. To be honest, I didn't want anyone around who might smell Raksha-trace on me and overreact.

Maran, you're at it again.

To be honest, I wanted to be by myself to think things over. I had seen Lanen in the wild firelight. Truth to tell, my eyes had not left her. She had stood, her arms around Varien, all through the battle. If she'd been in pain, injured, tortured, she could not have done so. In fact she hardly let go her husband all through the battle, all through the aftermath—and he held her every bit as tight.

What did she need me for? What would she gain by seeing me? At this stage, surely I would only remind her of unhappiness. I could leave tomorrow, while the rest of them were busy making whatever plans were to be made. Just slip away, unnoticed. No one would miss me, least of all the daughter I'd never known.

Aye, Maran. You've been saying the same thing for the last twenty years, but you're here now. You've come the width of Kolmar to get here and got the blisters to prove it. Goddess, you're a coward.

I shuddered. Truth is awful. I *am* a coward. That night, at that moment, I could no more walk up to my daughter and greet her than flap my arms and fly.

Weariness saved me, in the end. I was too damned tired to wake early and leave. As I laid my head on the pillow, my last coherent thought was, *Perhaps it will look different in the morning. Goddess be my aid, let it look different in the morning.*

Jamie

Rikard turned to me in amazement when Vilkas and Aral set to work. "Sweet Lady Shia! I'd no idea we could heal those creatures!"

"I'm not sure anyone else could," I said. I was well impressed. "I know young Vilkas is capable of astounding work with people, but this . . ."

"Do you have any food for them?" asked Rikard suddenly. "Healing a human is hard enough on the body. They're going to be starving."

"Hells. No," I said. I'd forgotten that Healers need food and drink and a great deal of rest after working. As do their patients.

"I'll arrange something, for all of them," said Rikard. He turned to go, then paused and turned back. "Ah—do you know what—er—dragons eat?"

I blinked. "I haven't the faintest notion. Cattle, perhaps?" I considered the creatures' teeth. "You'd think they'd need a great deal of whatever it is. Fresh meat surely never hurt anything with teeth like that."

Rikard went off muttering, but in the end he was saved the effort. Rella had more sense than the rest of us. She had held back during the fight—or at least, I hadn't seen her—but she appeared now, leading a cow with a rope, while Rikard was still trying to gather those students who were capable of movement. Behind her came Hygel, bearing bread and ale and a promise of beds, or at least a roof and a blanket, for those who required them.

Rikard very kindly obliged by looking after the rest of us—Lanen's infected demon wounds, my aching jaw and demon scratches. As for the others, when the last scale was restored, when they at last released their combined power, Vilkas and Aral drew a deep breath, drank each a full pint of ale without pause, and proceeded to eat enough for four men between them, along with another pint each. When at last they were replete, Rella, Will, and I helped them stagger after Rikard and the meagre remnants of the College of Mages towards The Brewer's Arms. They just about managed to stay awake long enough to fall into their beds. Rella and I left them there.

Shikrar and the one I learned was his son spoke at length, Kédra having a good long look at his father's now-healed wound. He did not linger once his father started to eat, but took off again, flying northward. Shikrar finished eating, gave a great sigh, laid his head on his forearms there in the courtyard of the ruined College, bade us good night, and slept.

Varien and Lanen were nowhere to be seen.

I was weary as well, but my heart and head churned too much to allow for sleep just then. I had started pacing and thinking when I heard a small sigh. Lifting my head, I found Rella leaning against the wreck of a wall, watching me. Her face had a glow about it that at first I put down to being too near the remains of the fire; then I blinked and realised that it was the first hint of morning.

The opening of another day, this one more full of hope than I had dared trust to since that terrible morning Lanen was stolen away. She was safe now—I had found her and got her out of that ghastly place—though truth to tell, I wanted very much to know what in all the Hells that was that happened when she yelled at Berys. I think that was the first time it truly struck me that we might not have found her in time. That she might have died at Berys's hands before we could reach her. I hadn't let myself even consider that before, not for a moment.

Rella came up to me and silently put her hands on my shoulders. I closed my eyes and clasped her to me with all my strength, like a drowning man clutching at his last hope of air. "Goddess, Rella," I choked, my lips against her hair, my voice fighting its way past a throat closing, stupidly, at the thought of what might have been.

"Not yet, heart, but I'm working on it," she said lightly.

"Rella, she could have died. What if he had murdered her, eh? What if I had been too late? It was near as a toucher, my girl," I said, starting to tremble. "Berys had us. He had me, Rella, and I couldn't do a damn thing."

Her arms tightened around me, strong but gentle. "I know, heart. I know."

"This is stupid!" I cried, evoking a whiffle from the sleeping Shikrar. "She is safe now, we are all still alive, all is well—"

"Jamie—"

"Goddess, Rella," I said, my voice barely a whisper, "I nearly lost her!"

I wept then, at last, bitterly, loosing the tears that I had locked away to make my anger serve me. Rella held me until the storm passed, then stood a little back and smoothed my hair from my eyes. "What happened?" she asked.

I told her and found that the telling eased my heart. Rella's staunch sense steadied me, kept me to the point, until I came to the last of the tale. When I told her of Lanen's outburst—"And I swear, Rella, she glowed like a fire for a moment there"—and what it had done to Berys, though, Rella drew in a sharp breath and made me go over everything in great detail.

"You have no idea what she said?" she asked, her eyes piercing.

"I've told you, I didn't even recognise the language."

And once again, Rella astounded me.

"Did it sound like this?" she asked, and proceeded to say the same thing Lanen had come out with, as best I could tell. This time, though, there was no pulse of light, no shattering of something I couldn't see, no yelling demon-master. Thank the Lady.

"Hells take it, Rella!" I breathed. "That's it, or near it as damn it. What in all the world?"

Rella shivered and looked away. "Goddess, Jamie. That's—I thought only Her Servants ever did that."

She fell silent until I prodded, "Did what? Rella, what did she do?"

Still staring at nothing, she replied, "Servants of the Lady for years and years, dear to Her, deep in Her Service, are sometimes known to overcome some dreadful peril through the gift of the Voice of the Goddess."

"Which is?"

"It's what it says it is, Jamie," she said, finally looking into my eyes. "Mother Shia blesses those individuals, just for a moment, an instant, and says those words through them. Nobody knows what they mean, but nothing can stand against them."

"That I can well believe," I said, frowning. "Berys was thrown and no mistake."

Rella shook her head. "It's not that easy, Jamie," she sighed. "The balance, remember? The great Powers always find balance."

"And what form does that balance take?" I asked solemnly.

"Death, usually. Oh, not the Servant, unless they are very old," she said quickly, "but—Jamie, every single time someone has been granted the Voice of the Lady, someone close to the Servant, someone they value dearly, has died within a se'ennight."

Her eyes brimmed with tears—she, my rock, who was strong and held herself distant from such displays, had tears in her eyes.

I took her by both shoulders and gazed into her eyes. "Rella, what will happen will happen. She is safe. Lanen my daughter is safe. I'm not worried about what happens to me now."

"Damn you," she snarled, shaking my hands off and dashing the tears from her eyes, "I am! Don't you dare die on me now, Jameth of Arinoc, I'll never forgive you!"

I reached out again and drew her to me, held her so close I could feel her heart beating against mine. We stood there, comforting one another in silence, until false dawn gave way at last to true and a shaft of brilliant sunlight suddenly blazed across us both. I shivered.

She drew away from me gently and shook her head. "Besides, that girl seems to break all the rules. Maybe she'll break this one as well," she said quietly, blinking in the brightness of dawn. "And you've never asked what happened while you were being a hero here in Verfaren. You missed a lot by leaving the rest of us early."

"I saw them land," I said, smiling.

"More than that, Jamie. Beyond belief more than that."

I waited.

"The Lost have been restored," she said quietly. "It was amazing, remind me to tell you all about it when I'm awake. That's why we took so long to get here. There were nearly two hundred of them. It was Shikrar who did it, and Varien, and"—her voice fell to almost nothing—"and Maran."

"What!" I cried.

"Yes, she's here," she said, her voice still calm and soft. "And with her, by chance or Fate or the Goddess Herself, has come our best hope of finding Berys again, if you're still determined to do so now Lanen is safe. There's a good chance we can learn where he is this very day."

Oh. Of course. "Maran's brought that Hells-be-damned Farseer, hasn't she?" I growled.

Rella sighed. "Yes. Still, I'm not disposed to object too strongly. Demon-made as it is, we can make it serve us. In fact it already has, that's how the Lost were restored. All three of them touching the Farseer." She turned her head away for a moment. "It wasn't like the little ones, the Lesser Kindred. There was precious little joy in any of them, and—Goddess—some of them had been aware the whole time. Five thousand years." She shuddered and looked back to me. "Those were the ones that killed themselves."

"Hells," I muttered. "What of the rest?"

"They seem to be doing well enough, for now. I don't think we'll really know how they are until they've all had food and sleep. They all went away to a quiet place a friend of Will's is providing. For a consideration," she said, managing a smile. "Salera's with them for now as well, though I don't think she'll stay away from Will for long. Or leave Varien and Lanen unattended. She and all her people practically think those two are gods, after all." She snorted. "The Lo—oh, no, they want to be called the Restored—they could barely stand to look at either Varien or Maran, despite what they'd done, and they studiously ignored the rest of us." Rella sighed. "I think that was the best they could do. Their hatred of humans runs awfully deep."

"Maran," I said, shaking my head, which was now filled with the most amazing visions, and smiling despite myself. "Helping dragons restore the Lost. And before today I'd wager my life she'd never seen one before. Took them in her stride, did she?"

Rella nodded, her own smile more strained now.

"How in all the Hells did she end up here, anyway?" I asked. "Unless she was—ah." I faded to a halt. "She came looking for Lanen, didn't she?"

Rella nodded.

I turned away, a mad mixture of relief, delight, anger, and hope fighting for first place in my heart. "Why now, after all this time?" I muttered, mostly to myself, but Rella's hearing is excellent.

"Seems she saw what was happening to us all and decided she had to—I don't know—make her peace. Help her daughter. Do something." Rella's tone of voice was decidedly dry. "Just don't ask me why she didn't damn well do this years ago. I've tried to persuade her to it since I met her."

"She's not an easy one to persuade into doing anything, as I'm sure you've discovered," I said wryly, evoking a muffled "ha!" of agreement. I turned back to face Rella. The sunrise had brought a flush of youth to her face, mantling her cheeks for that brief moment with the gentle rose of dawn—but the marks of old pain and a hard life were etched in her skin. They gave her a singular character, showed a deep inner strength that simple youth could never hold a candle to. "You look well in the light, you know," I said, reaching out to stroke her cheek.

She moved away from my touch. "You know that Maran has loved no one but you all her life," she said, locking her gaze on me. "It's very powerful, that kind of thing." She lifted her chin. "Seductive." When I didn't rise to the bait, she sighed and just looked at me. "What are you going to tell her, Jamie?"

"What is it you fear, my heart?" I asked, quietly. "That I will race back into her arms and forget all about you?" I frowned. This wasn't simple jealousy, which I might have expected. I should have known, nothing about Rella has ever been simple. It had the same tang to it, indeed, but it was something else.

Rella held her head high. "Lanen's the very image of her, Jamie. The years have been kind. She's tall and strong yet, she hardly looks her age—"

"Rella, what is this?" I interrupted.

She ignored me. "And her back is straight, and she's a good soul, and I have never seen anything but sheer adoration in her eyes when she speaks of you."

Rella, you wonderful idiot, I've got you now, I thought, for I realised now exactly what was troubling her. Goddess, I wouldn't have believed it if I hadn't seen it. "And she doesn't have your sharp edges, and really any man with eyes could only make one choice, is that it?" I said sharply, challenging her. Rella, risen to prominence in the demanding ranks of the Silent Service, a warrior with a brilliant mind and enough character for any three people, had no confidence at all in herself as a woman.

"That's it," she said stiffly.

I stared at her for a moment. "The dawn light really is lovely on your skin, you know," I said, touching her cheek gently. She sobbed and made to turn away, but I drew her to me and held her close with all my strength. "Do you think I'd let you go now I've found you?" I muttered into her hair. "And here I thought you were meant to be bright."

"Bright enough to know when trouble's coming," she said softly.

"No, my heart. At least, there's no trouble coming between the three of us." I loosed her enough to look into her eyes again. "I'm yours, Rella, as long as you want me," I said. "I won't pretend Maran isn't dear to me, of course she is. Lanen is my daughter in every way that matters, and Maran is her mother. I can't escape that connection, nor would I want to." I kissed her gently. "Maran walked out of my life more than twenty years gone without a word of farewell. It took me years to forgive her, but you may take my word upon it that I do not harbour any visions of lost love for her." I smiled. "At least I don't want to punch her anymore." Rella answered my smile with a rather more mischievous one. "The honest truth is that you fill my heart, Rella. There is room there for friendship, there is room for Lanen, but as for my heart's own—that room is taken by you alone."

After a rather longer and more intense kiss, I sighed.

"What now, dear?" she asked, comfortable in my arms.

"It has occurred to me that I may well have to introduce Maran to her daughter."

"Ow," said Rella, wincing.

"Indeed. I don't expect it to be a particularly loving meeting."

Rella grinned wickedly. "I do admire your capacity for understatement. I expect they'll hear them in Elimar."

I grinned back at her. "Well, in the end it's their headache, not ours. Still, it strikes me as strange. She must have left Beskin months ago. How could she know what was going to happen?"

Rella gazed at me. "It's not so very odd. I know Maran well, Jamie, better in some ways than you, now." She drew back, her arms still around my waist. "She has a damned strange way of showing it, but she has always loved her daughter fiercely."

"Just as well. Lanen deserves it," I said. "And 'fierce' is a good quality to have just now. I was so damned helpless, Rella. I thought I could fight any man or woman in the world, but Berys is pouring out his own power like water and using demons like a mad general uses conscripts—throwing them heedlessly into the front of any battle to disrupt the enemy. Us."

"We don't have to go after him, you know," she said. "He's gotten away . . ."

"Yes, that's the problem," I growled. "He's just killed who knows how many Magistri, and nearly the whole of the next generation of young Healers, and he's gotten away. Again. If I can track him down, I will, but I'll need help."

She grinned. "You know Vilkas was out for his blood before. This night won't have soothed his feelings at all. The good news is, we've got some damned fine help on our side. And by the Goddess, we've got the demons' natural enemies as well—three full by-our-Lady races of them! We'll just have to think of a way to work together."

I held her close again, not speaking. I had forgotten how much simple human comfort there was in the touch of one you love. And Rella, who knew me far too well even then, said into my ear, "Lanen's safe and well, Jamie, and if it means so much to you, we'll find that bastard and make him pay. I swear it by my back."

I straightened, moved a little away to look at her. "Your back?"

"It's the one real, true thing I can count on in this world," she said, one side of her mouth raised in a wry smile. "It may be crooked and it may not work overwell, but when I hear the creaks and feel the pains from it I never have any illusions about what's true and what isn't."

"I've given up my illusions," I said, holding her tight.

"Good, my heart," she whispered. "Truth is always better."

The Calm and the Storm

Lanen

I woke late that morning, safe in my husband's arms, to sunshine blazing through the windowpanes. I kept my eyes closed against the light for I knew, somehow I knew deep in my bones that I was right to treasure the night, and that the day was not my ally. I stirred, holding him closer, putting my head on his broad shoulder. His arms tightened around me and he turned to kiss my forehead, and I heard his blessed voice in my mind, pouring balm on my heart. There were no words. What words could possibly encompass all that we felt? There was simply love, sung strong as the mountains, deep as the sea, boundless as the sky, pouring between us tangible as light.

It was not until he touched my rounded belly that I began to weep. Gently at first, a few soft tears, then to my own amazement I was taken with uncontrollable sobs from the gut, shaking my body violently as I hung on to him for very life. "Beloved, beloved," he murmured, holding me in a grip of iron. It was just what I needed, feeling his strong arms about me, but still I sobbed without knowing why—when of a sudden I was minded of Jamie, as he spoke of the time my mother Maran bade farewell to her father.

"I tell you, Lanen, I hope never to see another such farewell in this world. Both she and her father wept bitter tears as they embraced. It was their last sight of each other. Somehow they both knew."

I gave a cry and drew away from him, rising to my knees on the bed the better to gaze into his eyes as if I feared to see his death therein. My newfound vision was with me still, it seemed, for I saw far more than love and concern in his emerald-green eyes. Death did not haunt him, blessed be the Winds, but I was shaken from my own sorrow by the depth of grief that I sensed in him. In that unguarded moment I touched the dark, still lake of it, deep as my own, heavy and cold, taking unto itself all hope and light. I reached out gently to my beloved, tracing the line of his brow, his cheek, his throat.

"Varien, love, what sorrow is this that lies so deep and cold?" I whispered. He opened his mouth to speak—I saw him swallow the easy response as he remembered our oaths always to speak truth to one another. He said nothing, he did not bespeak me, only returned my gaze. I reached out and took his hands in mine. "Speak to me, love," I begged, swallowing against a lump in my throat. "For my heart is shadowed and I cannot lift it. I know the day is bright and we are safe, and reason tells me to rejoice that I am with you again, but—oh, love, my fool heart mourns as if you were struck dead before my eyes."

"The Winds take your words and make them false, Lanen!" he cried, rising all in a moment and holding me to him so tight I felt my bones creak. I did not care.

"Sweet Winds of morning forbid such a thing—oh, my Lanen—would that I might laugh at you, but my own heart sings that same song of unreason," he whispered. We held one another without speaking, until I could feel his heart beating against my own. That very simple, very real thing steadied me. I managed to let him go a little. Enough to stop my muscles from cramping, at any rate.

"Do you know, *kadreshi*, I believe it is a just grief," said Varien quietly.

"How should it be just? How reasonable?" I objected, moving back a little but still in the circle of his arms. I swear, sometimes that Kantri calm voice of reason made me furious. And anger was vastly more comfortable than the desperate grief.

"Beloved, when you were taken from me, I called to you with all my soul." He shuddered. "Never will I forget that day, kneeling on the grass, dead to all else, pouring all that I am into truespeech as I strained to hear your lightest whisper upon the Winds. There was—nothing." He shuddered. "I was—my heart, I have shed barely a single tear since you were taken. I could not hear you, in mind or heart, anywhere in all the world. I did not dare to weep lest I could never stop. I feared"—that glorious voice faltered, and his arms around me trembled—"I feared you were taken entirely from life, I feared I never would see you again or hold you in my arms, and with your life mine was come also to its end. Beloved." He breathed roughly, drawing me to him once more, his strong body my rock in a swirling sea. "My heart is full of sorrow deep as time, that I did not dare to speak before, lest it destroy me and take away all my resolve while still there was something to be done. Now that you are with me—oh, beloved, now I am grown brave enough to weep." And so he did, for I felt his tears raining upon my cheeks even as we kissed and clung to one another, and my tears fell upon his face, and mingling they washed away our sorrow for that time.

And suddenly to my own surprise my sobs began to turn to watery laughter. I had been struck by the foolishness of it all. The pair of us standing there crying bitterly because we were no longer parted! Varien gazed upon me, and like the sun emerging from a cloudbank, the great weight of weary sorrow fell away from us both and we grinned like idiots, even as the tears dried upon our cheeks.

I could not help being distracted; the late morning light picked out all the contours of his body, turned his eyes to living emerald, and set his long silver hair to gleaming like metal new-forged. That strange spicy scent that reminded me of the Kantri tickled my nose. My husband. Impossible, that so splendid a vision was my own heart's other self.

I wondered if my sight had changed forever, or if this was the last shred of that strange gift from the Lady held over from the night before. Watching him, I saw the moment when he looked deeper into my heart. I had never noticed the difference before. There was so *much* I had never noticed before. There was around Varien a shimmering silver aura that I certainly had never seen. What it might mean I had no idea. It was full of movement, surely. I wondered for a moment if there might be a tree outside the window, casting moving shadows, but my eyes widened when I realised that the bright movement behind him came not from without. It was—sweet Goddess, I was looking at the moving shadows of *the wings he had lost*.

Varien

I stared and stared, hardly daring to believe what I saw, until she reached out and touched my face. "I didn't know you still had wings, my dearest," she said softly. "Even thus, even as shadows, they are glorious."

"Lanen, what sight is upon you?" I cried, joy rising in me as I had not dared to dream it ever would again. "You see me—your eyes—" I stared hard at her, and it was unmistakable. "By my name, Lanen Kaelar, you have the eyes of the Kantrishakrim!"

Of course she could not let that pass. "Well, I'm not going to give them back," she said, grinning at me. "What in the world do you mean, you daft dragon?"

For answer I leaned close into her and breathed deep. "By the Winds!" I cried, reeling as wonder took me. "Lanen!"

"Still here," she said as one corner of her mouth lifted in half a smile. "What *are* you on about, love?"

"You are changed in truth!" I laughed. "I thought Vilkas changed your blood and nothing else, but all is connected—you cannot change the blood without changing all else as well—Lanen, my heart, you are become as much a child of the Kantri as I am!"

I could read her truly, more truly than ever before. I could see all the layers of thought and deep emotion, I could see the wonder that began to fill her heart, and glory to the Winds and the Lady, when I glanced down I could see our babes as they grew beneath her heart. They were as yet no more than a shining in the region of her womb, but already I could see two separate gleams. I took her by the arms and danced about the room like a fool, the pair of us stark naked and laughing.

We sealed our joy with loving then, passionate, joyous, urgent with our need to give and to receive. As we lay in each other's arms afterward, Lanen said calmly, "We'd best enjoy this while we still can. It's not going to be so easy when I'm out to here with twins." She held her arms an improbable distance from her body and I laughed. "Aye, well, laugh while you can," she said, contented, teasing me. "You've never seen a pregnant Gedri, have you? I'm not kidding. It looks completely silly and I'm told it is awkward in all kinds of ways. And you can't see your feet." I laughed as she continued. "And women near their time all say the same things. 'I wish the babe would put its mind to the job and get it over with,' and 'I'm never doing this again,' and 'Goddess, but my feet hurt!'"

I was filled with a quiet delight to hear her so calm and so—so normal about her pregnancy. She had gone through seven Hells and nearly died with it; I had feared she might resent the babes, but no, not she, not my Lanen.

By good fortune we were up and dressing by the time Hygel knocked on the door. Why he bothered I don't know for he opened it even as he pounded. "Come quick," he said urgently. "There's a riot about to start and that bloody great dragon is in the middle of it."

Marik

I had forgotten. I haven't been here, my father's home in the East Mountains, for twenty-five years. I'd forgotten the smell of the place in spring. When we arrived an hour past it washed over me. There's always the tang of the evergreens, but this time of year there's some shrub that grows low on the foothills that has thousands of little yellow flowers and smells like—like paradise. Better than lansip. I'd forgotten.

I always thought Berys was a little crazy, but now I know it. I saw the result of that madness last night, in Verfaren. Before my eyes, his legions of demons destroyed the most powerful men and women in the world, the Mages of Verfaren, in moments, and there was precious little they could do about it. Oh, some of them knew how to shield against the little demons, but when the big one arrived, that Berys called a Lord of Hell, they could do nothing. I don't pretend that I felt much at their passing, those people have made my life difficult for years, but Berys *enjoyed* it. Not their deaths, I don't think. Before. When they realised that they were going to die. He is even more depraved than I had thought.

Depraved but powerful. Don't forget that, Marik my lad. And he's only on your side as long as you're of use to him. I wonder more and more how long that is likely to be.

I must say, though, I'm impressed at the way he keeps his head. We walked out of the Great Hall quite calmly, and later, when—when—when the dragon came I saw my death and could not move, but he had opened the portal and threw me into it. The next moment we're here at my ancestral home, this fortified bastion in the mountains by the shores of Lake Gand. Across the width of Kolmar. It's a thousand leagues if it's a step. He calls it "travelling the demonlines" and says they take forever to set up and are only good for one trip. Damn shame. It beats horses hollow.

The pain is back again this morning, worse this time than it has been for many a moon, and with no hope of relief now that Lanen has escaped my grasp. I should have insisted that Berys sacrifice her the moment he captured her, curse him! He was the one who wanted to wait, he never has thought my constant pain worth bothering about. He is less and less amenable to reason these days, and I am half mad that say it.

Damn the girl for escaping. Damn Berys for letting her. Damn it all to the Hells and back again. I hate being in pain. These days

I can't even count on Berys to relieve it, as temporary as that always is. Of late he often claims that he is weary and needs to rest. Not now, surely, that he has activated the Healers.

Heh. I wonder what kind of havoc that is wreaking across the three Kingdoms this day? Only the three, of course. Gorlak has ever been a support to our plans, so we have not touched any of the Healers from his Kingdom of the East Mountains. I wonder if Berys has had word of how Gorlak is doing in his battles? Last I heard he had taken the North Kingdom and was within a breath of victory in Ilsa. That would suit us well. If there is yet an "us"— though Berys did save me from that monster just now, perhaps he still sees my worth in his schemes. Without me he has no legitimacy in this Kingdom, where my family is very near to the throne. Only Gorlak and his fool of a son, Ulrik, truly stand between me and my rightful place. If you look at the lineage a certain way.

It occurs to me to wonder, more and more, what will happen when all the Kantri are dead? Berys was going to wed what was left of my daughter, for his own devious reasons—I never really cared much why. At least, that was what he told me when he was his natural age. It would give me time to father a son where I would. But now—Hells take it, he looks younger than I am! Mind you, I can't see him interested in a woman, or giving a damn about having a child to establish a dynasty. Giving a damn about anything other than himself, in fact.

I must watch him more closely. Never trust a demon-master, even when he is in your pay, for he has fewer scruples than a weasel and only stays bought as long as you are useful. However, I am secure enough here. True, Berys is more powerful than ever, but he is in *my* home now. I may have been gone for a few years, but I still know and am known by most of the folk here. They have worked for my family and been well paid for it for many years, first by my father and, for some time now, by me. Surely that is worth something.

I have seen Mistress Kiri already; she roused and came to meet me the instant word had time to spread. She is greyer, but otherwise much the same. She seemed pleased to see me despite the hour. My own mother died young; Mistress Kiri was mother to me most of my life. I think she may still have some affection for me, and at the least she and her family owe me their allegiance. My father, second only to King Gorlak, was more and more in the court from the moment my mother died, and he never saw me from one year's end to another. His influence and the power of the House of Gundar grew and spread as he worked through the years, and I was proud of him, knowing that all he achieved would be mine one day. I was well content that my father should never seek me out, for it meant I could do as I pleased.

The sun rises earlier here than in Verfaren by some hours, but it can damn well rise without me today. I have pulled the heavy shutters closed. I will sleep late, I think. I shall tell Berys what I have discovered about Lanen's pregnancy sometime soon, but tonight I am weary. It will keep.

Berys

I have accomplished the second great work of my rise to power. The first was the raising of the Demonlord; now the College of Mages is no more, and most of the Mages are dust and bone. I have sent one of the Rikti to discover what became of the Lord of the Fifth Hell. It did not survive. I had hoped it would be set free when the building was destroyed, to create havoc to its heart's content. Alas, it was not to be. Sent down to the True Death in a senseless battle by the dragon that stole away my prize. However, Marik tells me that this is the one called Shikrar, whose full true name Marik taught me some time past. That knowledge gives me a great power over it. If I invoke its true name in its hearing, I will have absolute power over it. What a lovely thought.

I regret the passing of that particular demon: all that power, all that focussed will so well controlled, now lost to my hand. I will have to think of a suitable return for that death.

It is curious. I did not realise that I would be so weary. I was not this spent when last I summoned the Lord of the Fifth Hell—though I suppose, last time, it wasn't killed either. Ah, well, such are the fortunes of war. And I have discovered that in all the activity, I have left my book of Marik's thoughts in Verfaren. It is annoying, truly, but of no great consequence, as I have the book of my own thoughts with me. I trust him as he trusts me, that is, not at all, but he is shaky in his sanity and his imagination has ever been greater than his capacity for action. He does not seem to have noticed anything amiss. If I were he, I would have demanded the sacrifice of the girl the instant she was captured, but he accepted my plea of weariness and other more important tasks to hand.

I must remind myself from time to time that he is not a fool. It is too easy to discount Marik. At least now that he needs me to keep his pain at bay, he will not easily rise against me. He does not seem to have his old ambition since I returned him from madness. Perhaps he fears me? That would be pleasant.

The Demonlord has sent one bit of good news as well. It says it can smell land. It should reach the Kolmar coast in less than a day, likely by early afternoon, Verfaren time.

There is so much to do tomorrow. I cannot hope that the Demonlord will arrive here in the East by nightfall: it will almost certainly take it at least another full day to fly the distance, possibly more, and the power I have provided it will run out at midday tomorrow. I must cast the spell yet again, send it my own energy yet again. Golems are draining. It is as well that I have the power of our tame Healers at my bidding. However, I do not wish to squander it. I believe I shall have to take up my alternate arrangement. If I understand the ancient scrolls of Pers the Hermit correctly, there is a way to ensoul a golem, a soulless construct, which will give it continued power and movement without further investment of time or energy from me. The trick is that the Demonlord gave up his soul many thousands of years since, so I will need another soul to enslave the golem that is the Black Dragon. Pers never thought of two minds in the one place, but extrapolating from his work, I think I will be able to arrange for the mind of the sacrifice to be superseded by that of the Demonlord. I suspect this all will make the sacrifice quite mad, but the man I have in mind is only a very short distance from madness at the best of times. No great loss. I have only ever promised to end his pain. There is little pain in madness, as a rule.

I will confess, I look forward to watching Marik's face when he realises that I have brought him along as a victim. His daughter would have been most useful, it is true, but she is lost to us for the moment. Favoured of the Goddess, pah! But the Holy Bitch is wanton and seldom bestows her favours for long. Those who speak with the Voice are often left bereft very soon after. I will seek out the girl again soon, for she is my link to Marik of Gundar's blood and bone, as well as holding the dominance of the Demonlord in her veins. Far too valuable to leave wandering the world. All I need do is let the Demonlord loose to work his will and destroy the Kantri, and she will have no more protectors.

As it happens, I have already thought of this. When I sent her into sleep against her will, I linked one end of a demonline to her boots. If I really need her before the Demonlord has got rid of them all, I will be able to reach her in the blink of an eye, no matter how many dragons cluster round her.

As to the more mundane side of things, King Gorlak of the East Mountains is consolidating the Four Kingdoms for me by conquest. He took the North Kingdom swiftly, and reports I received just before I left Verfaren would seem to indicate that Ilsa was about to fall. I'm only surprised it has taken him this long, everyone knows ancient King Tershet is childless and senile. Though perhaps he has good generals. Had good generals. Gorlak says Ilsa will be his in a matter of weeks, possibly days. He may not realise that the plague of Healer-demons I have unleashed will work in his favour. At the very least, it will distract his foes.

"Marik of Gundar's blood and bone shall rule all four in one alone." That was the prophecy made more than a hundred years gone by a great seer of the demon-masters, before Marik's father's father was even thought of. I have studied long, and I am certain that it means that Marik's only child, this Lanen, is destined to rule the Four Kingdoms of Kolmar, and so she will. At my side. Or under my foot. Depending on how you look at it. The line before that is "When the lost ones from the past live and more in light of the sun"—I am certain that that line refers to the restoring of those the Demonlord created nearly five thousand years since. That has come to pass, entirely without my assistance, but two days since. The prophecy is taking shape, and I will do all I may to help it come into truth, as long as Marik's blood and bone is bent to my will.

And with the Kantri gone and the Demonlord bound to her bidding and she to mine—well, it was never said how *long* she would reign. Accidents do happen.

Maran

I shared a late breakfast with Will of Rowanbeck. Nice lad. He told me what Lanen and her other half had done up in the High Field a few days since. I'd seen part of it in the Farseer, but I'd had no way of knowing what the true effect had been on the little dragons. The Lesser Kindred, he called them. He told me about raising Salera from a kit, and how he had loved her as a child even before she had been transformed. It was all intriguing, to say the least of it. I was looking forward to speaking with this creature.

Will didn't know when Salera would rejoin him, but said she had told him it would be this day sometime. He headed off to speak with Shikrar and Kédra. Dragon mad, that one. I excused myself and said I would join them later.

Once he was gone I sought out the nearest Servants of the Lady. It wasn't easy to find them; it seems that all the activity the night before had spooked nearly everyone. This pair, a husband and wife, were only a little better than useless. I was worried that such people could not truly pass on Mother Shia's forgiveness, but She is merciful and considers the intent rather than the messenger. I felt the usual deep-seated pain and then the release as the Raksha-trace was removed. I had never found anyone who could tell me why it hurt so much, despite making me feel a great deal better at a different level. I had begun to wonder if it were possible to—if perhaps I was losing a bit of my soul whenever I used the Farseer. It wouldn't surprise me anymore. I left a donation, said a fervent prayer, and went off to look for the others.

They weren't hard to find. They were in the centre of a circle of folk standing around a bloody great dragon sat in the ruins of what had been the College of Mages.

Well, whatever else happened, *this* was going to be worth seeing.

Rella

I keep hoping that people are going to surprise me. I don't know why I bother. Lanen is the only one in years who has managed to do so. Oh, and Jamie once or twice.

I had had a few hours' sleep, no more, when Hygel chapped at my door. "Mistress Relleda, you need to come. Now," he said quietly.

I knew that tone of voice, and in any case I'd slept in my clothes. When I opened the door and saw his expression I started moving. "Rouse Jamie if he's not wakened yet. Where do I need to be?"

"The College," replied Hygel. "I'll follow as soon as I may."

"Bring chélan!" I called as I headed out the door.

I ran down the deserted streets to find a large crowd gathering around Shikrar. Kédra was gone—just as well, really. I wished yet again that the damn great things had facial expressions; those faceplates of theirs looked like concealing masks. On some, like young Salera, they were beautiful. On Shikrar, who was the colour of old bronze, it just looked—impassive. Unconcerned. Other-worldly. *Other*.

I fought my way through a half circle, several deep, of the curious and the disbelieving, giving way at the front to the angry.

Oh, Hells.

"By my name I give you my oath, I did as little damage as I could, but there was the Lord of the Fifth Hell to fight," said Shikrar, his voice calm and reasonable. He lay, seemingly at ease, amid the ruin of the courtyard, with no one to stand beside him. Where in all the Hells were Lanen and Varien?

"What was a demon doing here?" shouted an old woman. "This is a blessed place, or it was until you got here!"

"Daughter, I did not summon the creature," said Shikrar gently. I shivered. His voice at least was much in his favour, so musical, so expressive. "The Rakshasa are our life-enemies, there is a hatred between us that goes deep in the blood. I fought and defeated it. Why do you aim your anger at me?"

"Goddess help us, the College is in ruins and all the Mages dead! Do you say that one demon did all that, with no help from you?" cried a large man at the front of the—well, yes, might as well call it a mob.

"They have not all perished," replied Shikrar. "One of the Magistri lives, and some score of younglings escaped as well."

"So where are they then? If you saved them, shouldn't they be here defending you?"

I had opened my mouth to speak when a loud voice behind me called out, "If you will seek them out at The Brewer's Arms, I expect you'll find them fast asleep." Jamie strode through the crowd. "It was near dawn when all was done. If you will only hear truth from one of your own then seek out Magister Rikard. The only innkeeper with the courage not to bolt his doors was Hygel, and he took us all in last night. Or this morning, depending on how you look at it."

"Who are you, then?" asked a voice from the crowd.

"Nobody," Jamie replied, grinning like a wolf. It wasn't a comforting sight. "I just happened to be there when all the fighting was going on last night." He bared a few more teeth. "Oddly enough, I don't recall seeing any of you."

Jamie, you idiot, that's not going to help, I thought, wincing as a low growl seemed to wander of its own accord among the crowd.

"That damned dragon killed the Magistri and destroyed the College, and there it sits in the midst of its handiwork!" cried one, pointing at Shikrar. At those words, a murmur of assent ran through the mob, and it began to surge forward. What they thought they were going to do to a *dragon* I can't imagine, but when you get that many angry people together, good sense is the first thing to leave.

"Foolishness," said Shikrar, sounding slightly amused and seeming to ignore the movement towards him. He was still lying down. *Well done, Shikrar,* I thought, realising that he had chosen his position carefully. *You're a touch less intimidating like that, and you look relaxed. Good thinking.* "At least allow me to be bright enough to fly away, having caused such destruction, lest the good folk of the town come in the morning to avenge my evil deeds upon my hide."

"Nonsense!" cried a loud voice from the back, and "Make way for Magister Rikard!" This sparked a swift-rushing murmur of "It's a Magister, one of them survived, it's Rikard, he'll tell us the truth."

Ah, Hygel, you old fox, I thought. *Small wonder you're one of my best agents. Good man, excellent man, as Shia hears me I'll see you promoted for this.*

The crowd parted and a double column of bleary-eyed student mages marched towards Shikrar, Magister Rikard at the rear. When they reached the open space before the crowd, the little group divided itself, one column to either side, Magister Rikard remaining in the centre.

"It cheers my heart to see so many of you come to offer your thanks to our preserver," he said as loudly as he could. "Were it not for the dragon Shikrar here, we would be in even worse case this morning than we are."

"What happened, Magister?" called a voice, and all the others chimed in asking the same.

"It was Archimage Berys," said Rikard loudly, at which silence fell like a leaden blanket.

"He was killed?" cried the voice, dangerously angry now.

"No, more's the pity," said Rikard. "He was the cause of the destruction."

"You've always hated Berys," accused the same voice as a short powerful man with grey-shot brown hair stepped forward. He continued. "We've all known it for years. Why should we believe you?"

"Because it's bloody true!" shouted one of the students. He was tall and gangling in the way of young men, his close-clipped red hair blazing in the morning sun. He strode towards the loud objector, until Rikard motioned him to stop short. "Who are you, then?" asked the lad aggressively. "I didn't see you here last night, when we were damn nigh killed."

Oh, lad, don't take your lessons in tact from Jamie, I thought, cringing. *You'll never make a friend again.*

"I'm Tolmas, stonemason and builder," replied the man hotly, "and I've a family, young man. I kept them safe last night. Fighting demons is your work, not mine."

"Fighting demons is work for all of us, Master Tolmas," said Shikrar quietly.

"Except for Berys," snapped Rickard. "He's the one that called that abomination down on us."

"How do you know?" replied Tolmas, undeterred. "And how did you escape and all? We thought all the Magistri were killed."

"I am the last," said Rickard, his face stony. "To answer your question, Tolmas, I escaped because I was suspicious, and when I saw the armed guards at the doors, ere ever the Archimage arrived, I ran. I am a rank coward but I live. Are you answered?"

I winced for him. He was a straight arrow, sure enough, but I didn't see the need for truth that stark. Maybe I could give him lying lessons.

"Then how do you know this was all Berys's doing?" snarled Tolmas, speaking still for the crowd.

"He doesn't. I do," said the tall lad.

"Aye, and who in all the Hells are you anyroad?" demanded Tolmas.

I heard rather than saw a slight movement at the back of the crowd. Will, Vilkas, and Aral had arrived, and behind them Varien and Lanen were moving swiftly towards us.

"M'name's Chalmik," said the lad sullenly. I couldn't blame him. Never mind sullen, I'd have been furious if some loudmouth had been annoying me after I'd fought for my life, but I think he was too weary for it. "I've been at the College for four years. I was to take my warrant exams next month. Wasn't doing too badly either." He glanced behind him and said laconically, "Not too many warrants going to come out of there, now, are there?"

"Was it really Berys?" asked a new voice. "Did you see him?" This was an older woman. Her voice trembled, poor soul. They had all trusted him.

"Yes, it was really Berys, him that was the Archimage." Chalmik's voice rose and he pitched it to carry to the back of the crowd. I was impressed. "He showed up wearing robes with demon symbols on 'em, asked us students if we wanted to side with him and the demons, and when we refused he called up his little pets and threw them at us while he laughed," said Chalmik. "I've never seen such coldhearted evil in my life. Oh, it was Berys alright, in the flesh and twice as ugly. And if I ever see him again, by the Lady's hand I swear I'll kill him."

Jamie murmured, "Get in line, lad," but very, very quietly.

"What did the dragon have to do with it?" someone cried. Oh, well, yes, it might have been me. Caught up in the moment. As it were.

The corner of Chalmik's eye shivered, but he never did so crass a thing as wink. "We were all gathered in the main hall, trying to get through doors that had been locked with sorcery. We were about to choose whether we'd rather be cooked in the fire or eaten raw by the demon when some voice the size of a mountain calls out to stand away and we saw this huge claw come through the wood like it was so much paper." He grinned back at Shikrar. "We thought it was another demon at first, but it pulled the doors off and let us out. If we'd been in there another minute, we'd all have died. My word to the Lady on it. He saved us."

A middle-aged woman moved out of the main crowd then. She was short and stout, but with a bright eye and a kind, worried, very pale face. It didn't take a Healer to realise that she was in shock. Ignoring Magister Rikard, she walked straight up to Chalmik and laid her hand on his arm. "My daughter is a student.

She's done really well in her Healer's work. Magistra Erthik said she'd be a fine worker with women and babes." The woman glanced along the scant faces of the score of students, her eyes seeking desperately what her heart knew was not there. "I don't see her. Her name's Elishbet. Please—please—where are the others? Where is my daughter?"

Chalmik, that great gawk of an awkward young man, leaned down and took the woman's hands in his, calmly. "She's gone to the Goddess, Mother," he said, gazing straight into her desolate eyes. "I'm so terribly sorry." His voice shook then, but only for an instant. "Elishbet was a friend of mine. You should be proud of her. She was a damn fine Healer."

The woman nodded once to him, stood motionless for a moment, then went over to Shikrar. Chalmik followed, at a discreet distance. So did we all.

Shikrar regarded her gravely. She stared at him. "You killed the demon, did you?"

"I did, Lady," he said simply.

"You're not even scratched."

"I was badly wounded," he answered, hearing the accusation under the statement. "Two of the students honoured me and healed me last night. If you care to look, you will find the new scale on my back and my right flank. It is lighter in colour than the rest."

He shifted himself so that she could see. She went right up to him and touched the new scale, noting the extent of it. It covered half his back, but at that moment it was her bravery that wrung my heart. "That's a right bad wound, sure enough. But perhaps you don't feel pain like we do."

"Despite the healing I feel it even now, Lady, I assure you," he said, keeping his voice level. "If the students had not been so kind to me I would be in agony for many moons to come, at the very best."

She stared up at him. "They had to heal you so you could kill the thing?"

"No. I killed it first."

"But you didn't kill it before it killed all the other Mages," she said, anger rising with every word. "You didn't kill it before it murdered my *daughter*, damn you!" She balled up her fists and struck out at him as hard as she could, again and again, putting her back into it, beating out her pain on that dark bronze hide. You could see that he barely felt it.

The crowd shivered but Shikrar ignored them. He lowered his great head to the level of her eyes, slowly, so as not to frighten her, and he spoke as gently as he might and still be heard.

"Lady, my only child still lives, so I cannot know your pain: but I swear on my soul that I destroyed the Raksha the instant I could. I am not a god." At that she stopped striking him and looked up, into those huge eyes so near her own. Shikrar's red soulgem blazed in the morning light. "I am not some beast out of legend, with magical powers to change the way things are. I am a creature of this world, like you, flesh and blood. I can fail, like you. I did what I could. If I could turn back time and save every single soul who died last night, I would do it, were it to cost my own life—but I cannot, and such words are empty. I grieve for your loss, Lady, as I do for all those whose loved ones are gone to the Winds, but I am not responsible for it. You must look to Berys for that."

She stared at him still, not even seeming to notice that she was starting to shake. Chalmik moved up to stand beside her. "Mother, come, let me help you, you're in shock—"

"I'm not your mother," she snapped. "My child is dead." Her anger gave her just enough strength to turn away from Shikrar, but at her first step her knees gave way. Chalmik caught her as if he had been expecting it and half led, half carried her gently away.

That was the turning point. It was as if a string had been cut, or a spell released. The crowd let out its collective breath. Those who had no one to look for drifted away. Of the rest, some few went to speak with Magister Rikard, but most moved forlornly towards the ruins of the College and started to shift the rubble.

It is such a human thing. Even when we think all hope is gone we still look, not able to understand such devastation and death, not willing to let such a terrible disaster be real all at once. We look, just in case there might be someone trapped, someone escaped by some miracle, who still needs our help, every slightest noise shattering through us as hope tries to return in the face of terrible tragedy, as we listen for what we know will not come— but we cannot help it. It is in our bones. Move stone. Shift rubble. Dig down to ground level. Look for survivors.

Look for bodies.

Shikrar, watching three men trying to shift a large lump of wall, rose with a sigh and went to help.

We had all been willing to do our part, but Shikrar did most of the work. Vil and Aral were gone, with Will as witness, to make their peace with their former comrades and Magister Rikard. The rest of us took a little time to rest and speak together. Jamie came over to join Varien, Lanen, and me, and Lanen stepped forward into Jamie's waiting arms.

Lanen

"Jamie," I whispered in his ear as we held each other tight.

"Lanen, my girl," rasped Jamie, stretching up to kiss my cheek. "Don't you ever do that again!"

I laughed, as he knew I would, my arms about him. "I swear, I'll avoid demon-masters in future!"

"Just you do that, fool child," he said, moving back a little and feigning a cuff at my head. He kept hold of one of my hands, though. "I thought I'd taught you better than that."

"I *was* fighting magic, after all," I said in mock self-defence. "But it's true. I owe you my life again." My hand gripped his and found an answering pressure the equal of mine. "Goddess, Jamie," I said, shivering, "I was sure we were dead—"

"Now, my girl, no need to go over it," he said. "It's done. You're safe." We embraced once more, and I whispered, "Thank you, my father," before I let him go.

Varien came to my side and without warning went down on one knee before Jamie and bowed his head. I ignored Rella's unladylike snort.

"I am more deep in your debt than ever I might repay," he said solemnly. "I was too far distant last night to help my beloved when her need was greatest. If ever I or mine may serve you, only let your desire be known and it will be done."

"I thought you owed me one anyway, for letting you marry Lanen," said Jamie, grinning.

Varien rose and returned the grin. "Then the score stands at two."

"I'm glad that's settled. Now if you two are finished posturing, there is still work to be done," said Rella pointedly.

Jamie had been watching the workers and shook his head. "No need, my girl." He nodded at Shikrar. "He's better than ten horses and two score men," he said quietly. "I just wish to the Goddess they had something worth looking for."

"They won't find all the bodies, you know," muttered Chalmik as Vil, Aral, and Will rejoined us. "That fire wasn't natural. It burned hotter than real fire, that's what set the stones ablaze. And the demon—I saw it pick some of them up and—and—" He stopped and turned away.

"And what, boy?" said Jamie sharply. "Say it!"

Stung, Chalmik whipped around and shouted, "It ate them!" far too loudly. "It ate them, right? It didn't even kill them first, they were all screaming until it bit—"

And Chalmik ran around a corner. The sound of a person being violently sick is unmistakable. My own belly heaved in sympathy. *Take it easy, little ones,* I thought to my babes. *All is well.*

Vilkas began to draw in his power, but Jamie put a hand on his arm. "No, lad, leave him be," he said. "He needs to get it out of his system. He'll be the better for it." Jamie glanced at Rella, who nodded.

"I remember what it was like, seeing violent death for the first time," she murmured. "Vomiting is the least of it. The nightmares that will come, if they haven't already—those are the worst."

I shuddered. Perhaps I hadn't been so badly off, there in my silent cell.

Chalmik returned. He looked rather greener than I prefer to see people, but he seemed to be a little better.

It's a shame, really, that Salera chose that moment to land more or less directly in front of him.

He cried out and stumbled backwards, but as no one else seemed to be bothering to panic he gathered his scattered dignity about him and stood firm. Amazed, but firm.

Will was at her side in a moment, grinning. "Welcome back, lass. I've missed you."

"And I you, Father," she said.

There was a thump from Chalmik's direction, which we all charitably ignored.

"Though I have spent my time well," she added. I noted with some pleasure that her speech was improving, though she still spoke slowly and carefully as her mouth grew accustomed to the shape of speech. "My people and I have made ourselves known to the Kantri and to the Dhrenagan, the Restored." Salera's eyes were gleaming, blue as a summer sky. "We live in a time of wonders! We are sso many, Hwill, and all so different! I never dreamed of this bounty ere we Awakened." Her wings were fluttering in her excitement. "So many minds, so many souls to see the world and learn from one another."

"Have they taken to your people, then?" asked Will, anxiously.

She lowered her head and touched his forehead with hers, just for an instant, to reassure him, for all the world as if she were a huge, bright copper cat. "Do not fear for us, my father. We all are the same Kindred. My people and I, the Aiala, the Awakened, together with the Dhrenagan and the Kantri—we are facets of the same soulgem. The Kantri"—and here she sighed—"the Kantri cannot help themselves, as yet. We appear to be younglings in their eyes, and in truth we are new-come to our true lives, but we are not nearly so young as they think. Still, all is new, all is changed. They will surely learn to see us in time."

Varien stepped forward. Instantly Salera bowed, the sinuous bow of the dragon-kind. He reached out to touch her jaw, a greeting, a brief caress. "Littling, I beg you, have patience with us," he said gently. "For thousands of winters we have sat round fires in our chambers, telling over the old tales to pass the long nights

For five thousand winters, Salera, we have told the Tale of the Demonlord and tried to find some way to communicate with the Lesser Kindred. In all our dreams of restoring the Lost, we never imagined that you were growing into a different people! Name of the Winds, it is yet less than a se'ennight since you and your people changed, and not even a full day since the Lost have been restored!" He grinned. "The Kantri come to Kolmar, the Lost restored—it is a winter's tale come to life, a wonder as great as your own Awakening. Bear with us, I pray you."

"We do not bear with you, Lord," replied Salera. "We rejoice in you. The wider world is yet so new to us, and we have much to learn." Her eyes twinkled. "We all have much to learn. The Kantri do not know this land, and there we may assist them. The Dhrenagan remember it, but not as it is. Much has changed over the long ages. They will have to learn again, an old song transformed, or a new one with echoes of the old. It will be difficult at first, but surely we will sing together in time."

"Bloody hellsfire," muttered a voice from near the ground. Chalmik hadn't bothered to stand up again, which I suspect was just as well. "What is this?"

Salera stretched her long neck around Will to gaze at Chalmik's seated figure. "I am not a what, Master Gedri, I am a who. I hight Salera, of the Aiala. What are you called?"

"Mik," he replied, staring wide-eyed. "How—you're—*talking!*"

"It is the way of a reasoning creature to use speech, is it not?" she asked.

"But—but I always thought—I've seen you in the forest, I thought you were . . . just . . ." He ground to a halt under her unblinking gaze.

"Beasts," finished Salera. Mik nodded. "We were, but the Wind of Change has blown upon us all. I believe you are the first Gedri I have met who was not present at our Awakening." Suddenly she glanced back at Will. "Father—there are words for a first meeting among Gedri, I can feel the shape of them in my mind, but I do not know what I must say."

Will could hardly keep from laughing and Varien was no

better. Men! I replied calmly, "You have a choice, Salera. You can say 'well-met,' or 'good day,' or you can give your use-name."

"I have done that," she said, worried, "but the shape of the words is not what it should be."

Mik stood up, brushing off his robes. He approached Salera slowly but without fear. Good lad. "Good morrow to you, Mistress—uh—Sa—"

"Salera," I whispered loudly.

"Mistress Salera. I am honoured to know you." He put out his hand as if to shake hers.

She stared at it for a moment and looked back at me.

"We shake hands, one Gedri to another," I said. "Will, come here, put out your hand."

Grinning like an idiot, Will obliged me and we shook hands. Salera sighed and extended her hand, twice the size of Mik's, each finger tipped with a long sharp talon.

"I cannot," she said sadly. "I would harm him."

For once in my life inspiration struck at the right moment. "Here, lass, you hold up your hand, but open it as much as you can." She did, and the talons spread wide, leaving the tough skin of her palm exposed.

"Here, Mik," I said. "You raise your hand too, and touch palms."

Mik touched Salera's palm briefly and said, simply, "Welcome, Salera."

"Well-met, Mik," she replied.

I couldn't help but smile at the odd solemnity of it, but withal I found myself moved. As it happens, Mik, all unsuspecting, was the first to use the gesture of greeting between Aialakantri and Gedri that is now commonplace.

It's a shame the moment couldn't have lasted a bit longer. Ah, well.

Shikrar

I had been crouched over moving stone for some time. My new-healed back began to ache, so I paused, stretched my wings on high and reached out with my head and neck, easing the stiffness. I had not considered the effect of my full height on the nearby Gedri—I heard some cursing and, glancing down, saw that most of them had moved swiftly away from me. I am ashamed to admit that my chief thought was that, all in all, it would not be a bad thing for the Gedri to remain a little fearful of us for a time. There were so few of us, so many of them; and I was certain that the mob that had come casting accusations would not be the last to blame all their troubles on the Kantri, and others might throw more than accusations. It occurred to me as well that in all this long time, perhaps they had invented some weapon that would do us harm.

In the midst of my musing, my eye was drawn to a robed figure riding towards the town. I paid no attention until Salera shot into the air not a wingspan from me.

My mindvoice was echoed by Varien's as we both cried out to her in truespeech.

"Raksssshi!" she hissed, and launched herself at the rider on the road.

I could not get airborne nearly as quickly as she, I had to run instead. Out the ruined gates of the College and swiftly north to where the rider sat in the road, his horse long gone, gaping up at Salera as she gathered the breath of Fire. I just managed to shelter him from her Fire with my wing.

"Raksssshi! Evil!" she cried, trying to maneuver around me for a clear shot. I had never seen her fly like this. She was amazingly agile in the air, turning on a wingtip.

"We do not judge the Gedri, Salera!" I cried, struggling to protect the creature. "Others of its kind must punish it if punishment is due. For all our sakes, control yourself!"

She screamed her frustration and wheeled away, breathing her Fire to the Winds in protest.

"You are wise, Old One," said the creature under my wing. The stench of the Rakshasa rising from it all but choked me. The moment Salera had given up her attack, I folded my wings away. It laughed, and the eyes of the Rakshi gazed back at me from that human face. I spat Fire, carefully missing it by only a talon's width.

"Take no comfort from my restraint," I growled. "I would sooner destroy you than not, and I would be less forgiving than the little one—but you wear the guise of a child of the Gedri."

"An excellent shield, is it not?" the thing mocked quietly. "And so hard for their useless eyes to see past."

"Goddess, it's Healer Donal!" cried a voice. Magister Rikard came running up.

"Perhaps it *was* Healer Donal," said I, cold fury in my voice. "It is now the shell around a demon."

"I was just riding down the road when those things attacked me!" false Donal cried, as more of the Gedri crowded round. They are ever curious, as a race. The students came along close behind Rikard. Vilkas's dark head rose above the others; at his side, as ever, kind Mistress Aral, and behind her the Lady Rella.

Jamie

"Friend, if either one of them had attacked you, we'd be looking at a pile of cinders," drawled Rella. Her voice was light but her eyes were flint.

"The big one didn't want to be seen to kill a human!" cried false Donal loudly, trying to back into the crowd. "It said so!"

"You poor man," said a new voice, with nothing of pity about it. I had not seen Maran approach but there she stood, at the side of the demon-caught Healer. "Here, this should give you comfort." She took something from around her neck and pressed her palm to false Donal's forehead.

He screamed and tried to fight her off, but she held him in a grip that regularly bent iron to her will. Eventually several men managed to remove her hand from his forehead, but still he screamed. There, as though it had been graven in his flesh, was a shape I remembered well. A star with many points around a central circle, the points in groups of three.

"What have you done to him!" cried one of the students, who

was drawing in his power to help the afflicted one. False Donal tried feebly to fight him off.

"Nothing that would hurt a true Healer," said Maran, scowling. "It's my Ladystar," she said, holding it up for inspection. "I had it blessed this morning. Just as well."

The student laid his hands on false Donal and sent his power into the creature. The Gedri stopped screaming and growled, a grating, hideous noise from a human throat. "Leave off!" it snarled, knocking over the Healer and standing up. "Gah!" It rubbed the black shape on its forehead.

Magister Rikard made his way through the gathered folk. His face was grim and he glowed a clear blue, far brighter than the hapless student. "Donal, in the Lady's name, what has happened to you?"

The thing started to curse. Rikard's eyes widened. "True names—perhaps—I call you, Donal of Ker Torrin, Donal of the East Mountains, Donal ta-Wylark, speak to me!"

The man shuddered violently, closed his eyes, and collapsed. When next he opened them, they were no longer the eyes of the Rakshi. A plain human stared back at us all. Shaken, revulsed, terrified, but human.

"Save me, Rikard!" he cried. "It is not banished, it lurks and waits its chance to take me over once more." He began to weep, suddenly, shockingly. "Shia's heart, Rikard, I beg you, kill me, don't let that thing come back!"

"How did this happen?" asked Rikard. His voice struck even me as being overly harsh in the face of such desperation. "Demons follow laws. How could they take over a man—a Healer!—if he did not invite them in?"

"I did, I confess it!" cried Donal. "For the love of Shia, I beg you, shrive me, kill me, I cannot bear it!"

"How did you fall?" demanded Rikard.

"Power," said Donal. He was trembling in the mild air as though he lay naked in winter. "They gave us all power, power to heal, so much more than the Lady granted! And all for so small a price, that might never need be paid." His whole body shook now, his voice thick with revulsion. "But they have called in our debt. I was drowning until you called me forth, Rikard. I know not how long I will last, I fight it with every breath as it is."

"How may it be banished?" asked Lanen swiftly. "What have we to do to help?"

"It depends. Did you sign in blood?" asked a cold voice, and suddenly Vilkas stood over the wretch.

"No, no, it was just a lock of hair, that's all they took from any of us." Donal's eyes grew wild. "Save me, Rikard, it returns. I beg you, take my life before I am lost forever!"

"You poor fool," muttered Vilkas. "From such a compact the only way out is the death of the demon-master who made the agreement with you."

"Who did you compact with?" demanded Maran, pushing her way forward. "Quickly, man, a name!"

"Marik of Gundar and Archimage Berys," Donal replied, panting, as one who has run a long race. "It returns—in Shia's name, I beg you, strike to the heart while yet my soul has hope of paradise!"

Maran went to draw her sword, Rella pulled out a dagger, but they were too slow. I went for my own weapon, but I was too late.

"Now!" screamed Donal, his face a mask of terror.

Shikrar's talons pierced his chest, four talons sharp as swords. The Raksha, forced outside the body now that it was dead, barely had time to scream its frustration before Salera and Shikrar flamed it into oblivion.

Shikrar

With his last breath, the poor Gedri sighed "Thank you" to bright Salera and to me, and left this life to sleep on the Winds.

I bowed and sent a benison after the departing soul, and began to speak aloud the ancient prayer for the dead. I had never known it to be used for a child of the Gedri, but the Wind of Change blew stark across us all. Perhaps it was time for the Wind of Shaping to speak while the world shifted around us.

"May the Winds bear you, Donal ta-Wylark, to where the sun is ever warm and bright. May your soul find rest in the heart of light. May you join your voice to the Great Song of Time, and may those you love who have flown before meet you and welcome you into the Star Home, the Wind's Home, where all is well, and all is joy, and all is clear at last."

The words were meant to give comfort, but I felt none. I had killed a Gedri Healer in full view of a hundred witnesses. No matter that I had done so to grant him release from bondage—no matter that he had begged for that mercy—it was an ill way to begin, and I did not like it as an omen.

Lanen

Varien had not flinched, even when Shikrar solved the problem of who was going to release that poor soul, but I couldn't bear to look at the mangled body. I turned away, deeply regretting my breakfast—and there she stood. We had been near the back of the crowd when I heard some woman saying something about a Ladystar, but I hadn't seen who it was.

Maran, my mother, stood at my left shoulder, gazing at Jamie and Rella as though her heart would break.

Healing and Healers

Rella

"Marik and Berys! He named them before witnesses!" I turned to Jamie, laughing with savage delight, and saw that his eyes burned with the same fire as mine. "Those bastards seduced that poor fool of a Healer into selling his soul to demons. They are now outlaws in every Kingdom in Kolmar. Fair game at last!"

I had been waiting years for this. The Silent Service had known for some time that Marik had been building up the House of Gundar, raising small branch Houses throughout the Four Kingdoms, each with its own supply of men and arms, and—rumour had it—its own sorcerer. I had thought that last an exaggeration.

"They have called in *our* debt," Donal had said. And "They gave *us* power."

Hells.

I grabbed Rikard from the frantic melee around Donal's corpse. "Where was he quartered, Rikard? Where did he serve?"

"He worked in a little branch of the House of Gundar some leagues north of here, towards Elimar," said Rikard, still gazing at the body. Rikard's voice was flat, though with anger or with shock I knew not, nor cared in that moment. I dragged Jamie a little apart.

"Hells' teeth," I whispered to Jamie, "that's it. The House of Gundar. We were right, damn it, the Healers are *all* sold to Marik and Berys the Bastard."

"Every one? In all the Four Kingdoms?" Jamie swore. "Hells, there must be hundreds!"

"And Donal said the debt had been called in. If that's an example—"

"Lady save us," muttered Jamie, and I'd swear he turned pale under his tanned leather skin. "Hundreds like him? Walking demons?" He shuddered. "What chance would anyone have against them if there were no dragons by?"

"Little to none," I growled. "But Vilkas said there was another way. The death of the demon-master who made the pact." And I felt myself smile horribly. The idea of Berys's death had always appealed to me.

"The sooner the better." Jamie's sudden grin frankly blazed. "I'm first in line!" he cried.

"Only one tiny problem," I said ruefully. "We don't know where he is."

"Ah," said Jamie, suddenly quiet. "It is just as well then, isn't it, that we've a Farseer to hand?"

And with that he strode over to face Maran, who stood, head high, waiting for him. I would have greeted her but she was too busy staring at Jamie, who was giving as good as he got.

They were both closed and armoured, hearts locked securely away. At least, I knew Maran well enough to see that's what she thought she was doing, the poor innocent. *You're a blacksmith at heart, my girl,* I thought, wrapping my own fragile heart in stone. *You've had no practice. You can't lie to iron.*

Jamie, now, he was a lot better at it, but when he saw her like that, so much older, so much like Lanen, and trying so hard to pretend that she didn't love him with every bone in her body— well, I had known it was coming, no matter what Jamie said. I was desperate to turn away. I forced myself to wait and watch.

"Jamie," she said, nodding to him, not trusting herself with more. I swear the sun could have turned green just then and she'd not have noticed.

"Maran," he said, nodding back.

Lanen, who stood astounded, watching, could wait no more. "Maran!" she cried. Lanen's eyes were huge with the shock, and I could practically hear the clang when her gaze locked with her mother's. They both just stared for ages, then I swear, with a single breath they both said exactly the same thing, with exactly the same inflection.

"Hells' teeth!"

I led the retreat. I think Jamie would have stayed, if only to ensure a fair fight, but I grabbed his sleeve and hauled. I made sure Rikard came too.

The poor souls. It was going to be hard enough without an audience.

Lanen

For the longest time I just stood there, staring at her. To be fair, she was returning the favour. Neither of us said anything after that first outburst. Everyone else must still have been there— I know Varien was somewhere near—but I saw no one but her.

She was my height or a little more, though she looked to have twice my strength: her thick linen shirt covered shoulders wider than mine, and could not hide the impressive lines of her arms beneath. Her hair, light brown like mine but with a generous coating of silver, was braided and wrapped round her head like a crown. Her eyes . . . ah, her eyes. I knew them. They were the same as those that stared out of my mirror. And hers were crinkling at the edges.

"Hullo, lass," she said, grinning suddenly. Her joy was mixed with a measure of panic, to be sure, but for all that it was overwhelming. "By my soul, Lanen, but it's good to see you in the flesh."

"Maran Vena," I replied quietly, my mind reeling, my belly

fluttering. Nervous, frightened, angry, floating on a sea of wonder and of fury and of longing that threatened to undo me. "Maran. Mother."

No, it wasn't yet real. Impossible, she was on the other side of Kolmar—"What in the name of sense are you doing *here*?"

"I do still have the Farseer, you know," she said, her grin fading to a wry smile, her self-control taking hold again. "I left Beskin while you were on the Dragon Isle. When it became obvious that Marik had recognised you and knew you for his. By the time you had started back with that new-minted husband of yours, I was well on my way. I'd swear it was chance that brought us to meet here," she said, her eyes narrowing, "but the world is a strange place at the moment. I'm not so sure I believe in chance just now."

I suppose I should have been shocked that she knew about Varien but, to be honest, in the face of her presence it seemed a minor point. A thousand questions, a thousand blessings and curses and demands coursed through me. *Why did you leave? Why have you not returned until this moment? Was I so terrible? Did you hate me? Did you love me?*

"Why did you want to talk to me?" I managed to choke out. Ah, well, it wasn't the most pressing question, but it was a start.

She sighed. "There is much I need to tell you."

"Is there, by all the Hells," I snarled. I hadn't meant to be angry with her. I could see her calling on every ounce of courage she possessed not to fly from me—but I swear, I felt possessed. The words that burst from me didn't even seem to be mine, at first. "Then why has it taken you twenty-four years to bloody well come out and say it! Goddess, Maran, was I so terrible you couldn't bear me even for a *year*?" And then it came out, the one thing behind all my bluster, the one thing every abandoned child needs to know with all her heart, no matter how great the fear of the answer.

"Why?" I demanded, my voice high and thin and not my own. "Why did you leave me?" Oddly, I seemed to be shaking, and my eyes stung. "Why didn't you ever come back?"

My mother lifted her chin, her eyes wintry, her face like carven stone. "Lanen, I swear to you, my soul to the Lady, I left you because I believed you to be in peril of your life."

"And was I?" I asked.

She shook her head, unable to speak, and finally whispered, "No. I was wrong. I didn't know it for years." She cleared her throat and managed to reclaim her voice, or most of it. "And even when I knew you were safe I didn't dare come back."

"Why not?" I demanded.

She smiled at me then, one corner of her mouth tilted up. "I was too bloody scared, what do you think? I know how I'd feel if I'd been abandoned."

"No you don't!" I shouted, my fists clenched. "No you bloody well *don't!*"

I didn't know whether to laugh or be sick. It felt as though a dozen mice were quarrelling in my belly. I had longed for this day from the moment I had understood, as a small child, that I didn't have a mother like everyone else. Jamie had done what he could and I adored him, but—every girl needs her mother. I had mourned for her, longed for a mother's touch, been desperate for the wisdom of an older woman, so many, many times—and now here she was. Now, when I had faced death not once but several times, now I had grown strong and been wed and had children growing below my heart. I didn't know whether I wanted to throw myself in her arms or punch her in the nose, though if I am truthful the latter was the stronger impulse.

She nodded. "No, you're right. I don't."

"It's terrible!" I shouted passionately, shaking my fists in her face, my whole body shaking with the terrible release. "Unloved, unwanted, abandoned—with only Jamie to look after me, and Hadron who hated me left to bring me up. How could you just walk away from your *daughter?*"

"Because I was young and stupid and I thought I was saving your life," she replied sternly. "Lanen, I can't change what has been or deny that I have been a fool and a coward—but I was hoping we might start again."

"You're too damned late!" I shouted, my voice soaring as years of hurt tore through me. Here I thought I'd got it out of my soul long since, the more fool I. "You're *twenty years* too late! Where were you? Why didn't you come before now?" I demanded. "Why did you leave me there, my whole life there at Hadronsstead, with that man? It was terrible! I thought Hadron was my *father*! He hated me, and for years I thought I was evil and twisted because I couldn't bear him either."

"Lanen—" she began, but I was fairly started now and I couldn't stop.

"He kept saying I was too tall and too like a man and not fit for anything or anyone!" I watched as my words struck her like so many daggers. Years upon years of that terrible loneliness poured over me afresh, and all the bitterness, all the years of desolation, came pouring out in an agonized flood—and she stood there like a rock in a stream and bore it. "I *believed* him. There was a time when I even thought of killing myself to get away."

Damnation. I'd never admitted that to anyone. I'd barely admitted it to myself.

"If it hadn't been for Jamie I'd have gone mad years ago. Goddess, Maran, how could you leave *Jamie* to look after me? Did you ever love him as he loved you? Did you ever even think about him?" My throat caught, then, as I stood a handspan before her and shouted past the tightness. I wanted her to shout back, cry, rage, anything, but she just stood there and listened. "Eh, Maran? Did you ever think about me? Did you *ever* love *me*?"

She never moved.

"Damn you!" I screamed, and without thought I drew back and struck her as hard as I could across the face.

She took the blow without flinching. A distant, cool part of my mind took careful note that, whatever else she may be, she was bloody strong. "I deserved that, Lanen," she said. Her calmness was infuriating. I went to strike her again, anything to get a reaction, but this time she stepped in and caught my wrist in a grip of iron. And held it.

"Listen to me, Daughter," she said, keeping her voice low and as steady as she could. Her eyes were the hopeless grey of a winter sky, but they were sharp and focussed entirely on me. "I don't expect you to understand or approve or forgive what I did, but you *will* hear me." She was breathless, suddenly, and had to stop and just breathe. I wrenched my arm, trying to pull away. I might have been a child for all that her grip loosened.

"When I left you I was sure I was saving your life," she said finally. She closed her eyes just for an instant, swallowed, continued. "The demons had found me. Found us. I didn't learn that I was wrong for sixteen years."

"Demons?" I repeated, suddenly shaken. A memory from before memory came to me then: a bright room, dark fear with red eyes, a flash of silvery metal.

"Demons," said Maran, letting go my wrist. "Have you never wondered why you have that scar on your right shoulder?" She reached out and touched the exact spot. How in the Hells did she know that?

I shivered. "Jamie said I hurt myself when I was—tiny—" I said slowly.

"It's a demon scar, Lanen," she said, her face unreadable. "You weren't even a year old. They came for me. I had learned how to get rid of them, but that time—that time there were more of them, and they hurt you as well." For the first time her gaze left mine as she lived that moment again. I wondered, in a quiet part of my mind, how many times she had lived it over the years. "It was such a tiny scratch, but you cried *so* hard. I had to fight you even to cleanse it. By the time I was done I was shaking so badly I had to put you down lest I drop you."

I waited.

"I was younger than you are now, Lanen. I knew so little of life," she said, and for the first time she let her guard down a little. "I knew it was wrong to treat Jamie so, but—"

"Why did you, then?" I demanded.

She stared into my eyes, challenging me. "Life is not always black and white, Daughter. Sometimes we just have to find the shade of grey that we can live with. The sooner you learn that, the better." She frowned and looked away. "I thought the demons would take you and any who cared for you. My own life I never feared to risk, but I could not bear that they should hurt either of you, whom I"—she stopped and wrapped her arms about herself—"either of you, whom I loved."

"I see. You loved us," I mocked. "You loved us so much you abandoned us for twenty-four years."

Maran sighed, and in that moment her whole armour of self-control dropped away, leaving only a middle-aged woman with a weary heart. "Bloody stupid, isn't it? Hells, Lanen. I know I'm too late," she sighed. "I know I've done damn near everything wrong, but"—she caught my gaze again and said very quietly—"my soul to the Lady, Daughter, I loved you and Jamie so much that I murdered my own heart and left you. I could not bear to be your death."

I shivered again, blinking back tears—and my new deeper vision shocked into me against my will. I had been fighting it, not looking deep into her eyes, not wanting to know, for now I could see the truth of her: the desperate fear, the courage it had taken to dare this meeting, the resolve that held her to her course in the face of such pain, risking all in the name of hope.

"That's it, and all the truth of it," she said. "I found out about eight years ago that I need not have left you. The Farseer didn't work the way I thought it did." She managed a wry smile. "Berys was just being enthusiastic. By then, though, I feared—well, this." She shrugged, her hands turned palms up and open in surrender. "Should have faced this the moment I learned the truth, shouldn't I? Got it wrong again. That's no great surprise."

She stood there, waiting. When I said nothing—how could I speak in the face of this revelation, with twenty-four years of thoughts and feelings still fighting to get out?—she nodded, and those broad shoulders slumped even as her chin rose. "As you will, Daughter," she said, and turned to go.

I was ready to curse my new sight, for I could see pain scoring her soul like terrible weals from a whip. *Odd*, I thought. *That's how I feel.*

Well yes, idiot. That's the point, isn't it?

"Mother?" I whispered after her.

She stopped and turned back to me slowly, hardly daring to believe what she had heard.

"Mother, please, I—oh, Hells, don't bloody leave again!" I cried. She was back in a moment, and we finally dared an embrace.

What ever happened to the strength of lonely despair? I asked myself mockingly, even as I felt my mother's arms around me for the first time, even as I clung to her. *I thought that was what made us strong?*

No, I corrected myself. *That was what helped us survive. Knowing that love had not deserted us, even when we couldn't feel it—Jamie and Varien, our babes unborn, now perhaps Maran/Mother—that's what has always made us strong.*

We did not hold each other for long, and we both knew as we drew apart that this was only the beginning, but—I cannot speak for her, but I felt something very small, very deep inside me, change. As if a wound deep within had stopped bleeding at last; as if a loose brick deep in a well had been mended and the clear water could begin to find its true level.

We were not given long to consider our meeting, for at that moment Jamie and Rella came striding up to us.

"Thank Shia you two have finally stopped shouting," growled Rella. "I'm sorry, but there is no more time for this. We need your help *now*, Maran."

She grabbed each of us by an arm and drew us away, past where Rikard and his students were laying out the body of poor Donal. There was quite a crowd of the townsfolk starting to gather.

Varien appeared again at my side. I took great comfort from his presence, though I still felt—detached from myself. Everything seemed so unreal.

Rella was busy explaining to Maran about the corrupt Healers, and why she and Jamie needed the Farseer. "Can you find him?" she demanded. "I never have understood the limits of that thing."

"Oh, I can find him, certain sure," said Maran, frowning. She seemed to be having as much trouble as I was, trying to wrench her mind back to the matter at hand. "The dragons aren't going to like the smell of me doing it, though."

"I feel certain that Shikrar will forgive its use in so worthy a case," said Varien, a crooked smile on his face.

Maran shrugged off her pack and carefully withdrew the Farseer. I remember thinking it had no business looking so normal. Just a big glass ball. "There is a difficulty, however. I may well not recognise what I'm seeing." She turned to Rella. "This is where you get to work for your information, my friend. I gave up wandering twenty years ago."

My mother—how strange, to say that!—my mother knelt down, putting the smoky glass globe on the ground before her knees, and we all gathered round. Will had wandered over to see what we were doing. Jamie and Rella were nearest, as they had travelled most.

I think I was expecting some kind of ritual. Far from it. She put her hands on either side of it and said clearly, "Show me Berys," and instantly an image formed in the globe. It was him, sure enough, in an airy, well-lit room, asleep in the middle of the day on a luxurious bed. I thought of sleeping on the stone bench in my bare cell and wished him seven kinds of ill.

"It could be anywhere," said Jamie, fidgeting in his frustration, trying to see around the edges of the image. "Can you—does the thing move?"

"What do you mean?"

"Getting a look out that window would be a good start," said Rella, shivering. I looked up. The morning was starting to cloud over and a nasty cold wind was gleefully searching out every loose seam and unmended tear in my old clothing.

"I'll try," said Maran doubtfully, turning back to the Farseer. I noticed she had to be touching it for it to work. "Show me the view out of the window there."

I blinked. Berys was gone, and in his place there rose up high, snowcapped mountains, ridge upon ridge stretching away into the distance, the bright sun gleaming full on the white peaks. Away below and to the left was a large placid lake, the far shore lost in a haze. In the center of the lake a small hillock, an island ringed with trees, boasted a high and ancient oak in its centre. That wooden monarch stood tall and leafless yet, only a haze of green about it showing that spring was well under way.

Jamie cursed, roundly and creatively. It helped a little, but not enough. "He's in the East Mountain Kingdom," he spat. "Hells' teeth! And damn me if I don't even know the place. It's only bloody Castle bloody Gundar! Where else? Marik's ancestral home." He rose to his feet and stamped about, beating his frustration upon the ground as he paced. "Curse it! If I'd had half a brain I'd have guessed they'd go there, but how in the name of the Lady did they get that far away that fast?"

"Demonlines, of course," said Vilkas quietly, and I wasn't the only one who jumped. He, Will, and Aral had joined us silently, while we were absolutely focussed on the Farseer. Vilkas sounded grim. "Berys must have set this one up a long time ago. You need to travel the distance in the real world to set the things up in the first place. He must have been planning this for *years*."

Jamie gazed up at Vilkas, his eyes alight again for a moment. "Just remember, lad, I'm first in line." He swore. "If we manage to get to him in our lifetimes. It's on the other side of Kolmar, hundreds of long leagues from here. How in all the Hells are we going to get there this side of winter?"

"I'd have thought that part was reasonably obvious," said Varien dryly. I shared a glance with him and smiled. Varien raised his chin in the direction of the mournful little group around Donal's remains, and there stood Shikrar, all the lovely size of him, his great wings folded neatly over his back.

"Oh," said Jamie. Then I swear, for the first time in my life, I saw him blush. "I really am an idiot," he murmured, grinning.

"Shikrar cannot carry us all, of course," began Varien.

"Truly," interrupted Vilkas. "It seems clear who must go. Jamie and I . . ."

"We are therefore fortunate," continued Varien more loudly,

"that there are a hundred and eighty-six others nearby from whom we may request assistance. I would not ask it of the Aiala, though some of the Dhrenagan may wish to be of assistance." He grinned. "It will give them something to do."

Will, who was watching Salera and paying more attention than the rest of us, said, "That crowd's getting bloody noisy for mourners."

We turned as one. There were quite a few raised voices. I exchanged a glance with Varien and we hurried over to where Shikrar stood.

Shikrar

It did not surprise me that they took the Healer's death ill. Those who had been there—Rikard, the students, a few of the townsfolk who were sifting the ruins of the College—knew the truth. The rest of those gathered knew only that a Healer had been killed by a dragon. I had cleaned my talons of his blood as best I could, but there was no water nearby. Dark stains remained, testimony that could not be denied.

To my surprise I noted that many of them bore small weapons—tiny blades, or slightly larger ones that must surely be swords. I had heard of swords but never seen one close to. The largest was not the length of my least talon, and it was thin and weak beyond belief. Some carried what looked to be thick tree branches, others had long sticks with many-pronged heads. I breathed a sigh to the Winds that they might not descend to an attack. It would dishearten them so.

Rikard explained again and again, but there were some in the growing crowd that would not believe him. "He is in thrall to the dragon!" some idiot cried out. "Rikard is corrupted!"

"Rikard is one of the few who isn't," retorted Lanen, loudly. She and Varien led the others, as they all came to stand by my side. Rikard let out his breath. I think he had been growing anxious.

"Haven't you been listening?" asked Lanen, her voice laden

with scorn. I was most impressed at the sheer volume she managed to achieve. It was—arresting, and that was what was needed, a moment to stop and reflect.

"Most of you weren't here. I was. I *saw* the demon using Donal's body," said Lanen, only the slightest quiver in her voice showing her remembered revulsion. "When Magister Rikard banished it and Donal returned for a brief moment—my soul to the Lady, he begged desperately for death ere the demon could take him over once more." She raised her head, frowning, her arms straight down at her sides and her hands curled tight. "I have been at the mercy of demons. It is a terrible thing—and I was not taken over as Donal was. For a Healer to be in the same body as something so obscene, so opposed to everything in the soul of the Lady's chosen ones, and to know of no end and no way out . . . I can well understand that death would be welcome. Even desirable."

There was a moment of silence. *Perhaps she has touched them,* I thought in wonder. *She is a truth-speaker, Lanen, and such truths can be very powerful*—but then a strident voice from somewhere in the crowd called out, "Is the dragon to get clean away with it, then? It killed a Healer! Donal's blood yet stains its claws, and it would talk its way out of paying for murder!"

To my surprise, Salera bespoke me. Quite clearly, too. Aside even from her words, I could not restrain a surge of pride in her ability, so newly won and already so well controlled.

"Lord Shikrar, do you focus their attention on you. The Raksha smell is strong now, where it was not before. I go to find its source. Distract them!"

Very well. I would distract them.

I rose up on my back legs, spreading my wings wide, in the Attitude of Defiance. Not appropriate, perhaps, but it most certainly caught their attention.

"What would you of me?" I cried loudly. Some raised their hands to their ears. *Ha,* I thought, *let you ignore that.* For sheer volume, we of the Kantri are difficult to surpass. "I and my people are the life-enemies of the Rakshasa: you may have forgotten that, but it is as true now as it was thousands of winters past.

Healer Donal confessed his corruption, he admitted before witnesses that he had sold his soul to Berys the demon-master and Marik of the House of Gundar." *Quickly, Salera, I can only bluster for so long no matter what Akhor says.* "The Lady Lanen has the right of it, he longed for—"

Towards the back of the crowd, a man cried out as Salera wrapped her tail about his waist. "Thiss isss anotherrr," she hissed, her voice sliding out of the difficult Gedri speech, her wings rattling with anger, her deep blue eyes blazing. "Rakshadakh!"

The people round about her scuttled away. Just as well, perhaps.

"Don't hurt him, Salera!" cried Varien. Vilkas and Aral were fighting their way through the crowd, as was Rikard. Rikard reached them first.

The man, held helpless in the coils of Salera's tail, was very young even to my eyes, but he bared his teeth in a snarl at Rikard. "Will you destroy me as well, then?" he spat. "You and your pet dragons! Who have you sold your soul to, Rikard?"

"No one, Rathen," Rikard sighed. "Which is more than you can say." Rikard raised his power about him and sent a shaft of purest blue to surround the man, who cried out. "Rathen of Elimar, Rathen of the South Kingdom, Rathen ta-Seren, speak to me, in the name of the Lady!" said Rikard. His power blazed. Rathen gave a great shuddering cry and wilted.

"Let him down gently please, Salera," said Aral as she and Vilkas arrived. They caught Rathen as Salera loosed him from her tail, and lowered him carefully to the ground. "Rathen?" called Aral.

There was no response, though the body twitched. "Come on, man, fight it!" urged Aral.

Rathen moaned, opened his eyes, and sat up. "Mistress Aral?" he said, frowning. "Rikard? Name of the Lady, where am I?"

Vilkas

"You're in Verfaren," said Rikard harshly. "And I know you have made pact with Berys. Have you not even realised that you have been worn by a demon?"

Rathen went white. "No," he whispered. "Mother Shia, I thought that a nightmare."

"It is truth. I have called you back but I do not know how long the creature may be banished."

"Save me!" cried Rathen, grasping at Rikard's robes. "I swear, Rikard, I only ever used the power when I was desperate. I used it to heal, in the Lady's name! Surely that is not so terrible?"

No, I thought. *The terrible part is that I know you, Rathen. You only got your warrant last year, as a Healer of the first rank. A low level, to be sure, the lowest warrant there is, but sufficient for most ills. I never knew you were so desperate for greater power.* "Rathen, was mention ever made of what you might do should you wish to break the pact?" I asked.

"No," he replied miserably. He started to shake as with an ague and gazed up at me, imploring. "Vil, you've studied demons, I know it. What can I do?" He began to weep. "Vil, how shall I ever escape?"

"You can begin by renouncing the power you have received," I said sternly, and without much real hope. At least it would be a start.

"I do! I renounce, in the name of Mother Shia, the power granted me by this pact!" he cried aloud. For a moment he looked a little better. For a moment.

Then, horribly, he began to shrivel. Before our eyes he grew weak and starveling, his eyes sunken, as if he had not eaten in a year. "Vilkas!" he screamed, his suddenly bony hand clutching desperately at my robes. "Help me!"

I summoned my power and poured it into him. The drain, and his need, were terrible. It was as if every act of healing he had performed in the last year, each of which had its own cost in strength of body and will, were being taken out of him again, all at once. I sustained him as best I might, but I had never known so arduous a task. I had always been proud of my inherent power. In my years at Verfaren I had never truly been taxed by any effort required by my studies.

This was exhausting. No matter how much I gave, it was not enough. Like pouring water through a sieve.

Ah!

I used my Sight to look deep into Rathen, and there it was. A wound in his soul, a link, sustaining something. The demon? No, there it was, fighting to regain the mastery over him, nothing to do with that wound. No, the link went elsewhere . . .

Berys.

Without stopping to think I cried out, "Blessed Mother, Shia, Goddess, sever this bond and deliver your servant!"

The bond was broken. Rathen screamed once and fell to the ground. The demon also screamed, frustrated to find defiance where it had expected nothing but ease, and disappeared in a gout of well-aimed Fire from Shikrar.

With the Sight upon me I saw the flame of Rathen's life reduced in that moment to a tiny spark, barely present, flaring its hopeless defiance against the endless darkness that surrounded it.

Still I let my strength flow into him, protecting that flame, encouraging it to life again . . .

I was not expecting Aral's slap in the face. My concentration was broken abruptly and I shuddered at the sudden withdrawal from deep healing. She hit me again, and I realised that she had been shouting at me for some time. "Stop, Vilkas! Stop it, you'll kill yourself!"

I glanced down at Rathen. He was terrifyingly thin, but he breathed yet.

"Good, he's alive," I said, and fainted into Aral's arms.

Aral

"Fetch food and drink for them both," commanded Rikard sharply, and I saw several hurry to obey as I lowered my beloved Vilkas to the ground. It struck me in passing that I had never had him in my arms before and might never again. I desperately desired to hold him to me just a little longer—raining kisses on his face occurred to me as well—but I knew that he would recover best if his head was level with his heart. I banished my ill-timed longing. Vilkas was pale as death. I started trembling.

No, no, don't be stupid, he'll be fine, I stopped him in time. Just.

"That was well done, young Aral," said Magister Rikard as he knelt to help me make Vil comfortable. "He's always been a stubborn so-and-so. At least he had the good sense to listen to you."

"He's going to be furious with me when he wakes up," I said, trying to make my voice light. I'm not at all sure I managed it.

"Then he is an even greater fool than I thought," muttered Rikard, "and I shall be happy to tell him so if you so wish."

I grinned. "Thank you, Magister, but I'd rather deal with him on my own."

Vil, with his usual timing, managed to rouse just as the food arrived. Rathen we had to restrain from eating too much, lest he overburden his newly frail body, but Vilkas ate as though he hadn't seen a morsel in weeks and was all the better for it.

And as he began to recover from his work, I locked my heart away again, hidden, safe, unknown. I did not dare listen to its strident voice. I knew Vilkas too well, knew that he felt nothing of the sort for me; but I still could not give over my stupid longing, hoping—dreaming—that perhaps, one day, he might recognise his folly.

Magister Rikard stood, brushed down his robes, and addressed the crowd. "They will both live, though Healer Rathen will take some time to recover." He frowned at those nearest him. "I trust that this has brought you all to your senses. Blaming the dragons, forsooth! They are creatures of Order. Our oldest wisdom preserves that at least."

"But, Magister," said Tolmas the stonemason, stepping forward, "what now?" He gestured to take in all the ruin of the College. "What are we to do? The town has always looked to the Archimage for guidance."

"I will meet with any who wish to look to the future in an hour's time, Tolmas," said Rikard firmly. "Until then, let each help as they may." He sighed. "There is surely enough for us all to do."

Rella

I have to say, if I had tried to stage that revelation I couldn't have pulled it off nearly so well. In the general milling about I hauled Hygel off to a quiet corner and told him rapidly what I suspected about all the House of Gundar Healers. "Get the word out fast. I don't know how to fight them, so best to tell everyone to keep out of their way."

"And what are you going to be doing, hey?" he asked.

I allowed myself the faintest smile. "Ah, now. Privilege of rank, you see. I'm going with this crowd to get Berys."

"You cheat. I've always said so," he said cheerfully. "I live a stone's throw from that rat bastard for six years and you get to take him. It's not fair."

"Never mind," I said. "There's every chance we'll end up as demon fodder. If that happens, I'm counting on you."

Hygel snorted. "Ha! With yon bloody great beastie on your side?" He gestured at Shikrar, who was even then taking to the air on some errand. "Even Berys can't stand against that, surely!"

"I truly hope not," I said. "Spread the word, my friend. I think you'll have your hands full here as it is."

ix

The Black Dragon

Shikrar

"Go where you will, Shikrar, go even with my blessing, but go. I am weary beyond measure," moaned Rinshir. I sighed. The petulance in his voice was annoying me. "Has the world not changed sufficiently for you? We all need rest before we undertake another such journey."

"I do not demand your presence particularly, Rinshir," I replied as calmly as I could. "Only a few are needed—the rest may surely remain and recover their strength."

Those around him had the good grace to be embarrassed at Rinshir's whinging. I saw several looking at my newly healed wound. No matter, the scales would darken with time.

"I do not ask you to cross the Great Sea again," I added loudly, addressing the Kantri. The Dhrenagan listened, but I would no more ask such a thing of them than ask my grandson Sherók to fly to the bright fields of the sun. They had so much to encompass— so much time passed, so much life lost, the world so changed—I would not dream of challenging them further by asking them to assist the Gedri. "True, there is no way of knowing how far there is to fly, for we have only the Gedri's knowledge of the distance. We go east, towards the far mountains." Still there was silence. "I need only two more to assist me," I repeated, "as the Lady Idai has offered to come for the adventure."

"Can it not wait, Teacher Shikrar?" asked Trizhe wearily. I knew him for a good soul, but I could tell that he was genuinely exhausted. He could barely lift his head off the ground to speak. "Give us but a fortnight and you will have us all at your service."

"We leave in a bare hour, Trizhe my friend," I said. "But I would not take you even if you offered. You have nothing left to give beyond your goodwill."

"Then let me help you," said a quiet voice. It was Dhretan, the youngest of us, aside from my son's son Sherók who had not yet seen six moons. His willingness touched me but there was scant time for tact.

"Dhretan, I thank you from my heart, but I fear you could not keep pace with us, especially burdened," I said as kindly as I could. However, his was the last voice that spoke. I sighed. So much for volunteers. *"Gyrentikh?"* I called softly in truespeech, bespeaking him only.

"I was hoping you wouldn't think of me," he said wryly, aloud. "I wouldn't mind being lazy, and I swear I could sleep a full moon round; but yes, Hadreshikrar, I will come with you," he said. "Were it not for you I might never have wakened from my last Weh sleep when the Isle of Exile was dying." Despite his words, he did not look or sound as worn-out as many of the others. "In any case, I do not believe the Gedri will be much of a burden," he added with an amused hiss. "They are too small."

"Two of them together are perhaps a quarter the weight of a bullock," I said, keeping my voice light. "There are few of us who could not manage so little weight without effort, even over a long journey."

"Father, let me come with you," said Kédra again. "I am rested enough, I am strong—"

"And you will be the Keeper of Souls when I go to the Winds,

*my son. Our people cannot do without you. I cannot do without
you. Stay here and be for me the voice of Reason with our people,
and with the Dhrenagan,"* I replied to him alone. Aloud I said
only, "No, Kédra. You must stay and look after your young son. He
has much to learn and he needs his father."

"Very well then. If no one else will help you, I'll come along,"
said a disgruntled voice, and to my astonishment I realised it was
Alikírikh who had spoken. I did not know her overwell, but I
knew her history. She was among the older of us. Her mate Lirh
had been a good, kind soul, but he had gone to the Winds soon
after the last of his younglings was born. She had turned bitter
at his passing and for many a hundred winters now had kept
her own counsel and company, seeing only her children and
shunning the rest of us. She was the last creature I would have
thought would volunteer for such a task, but I was in no position
to argue.

"Blessings upon thee, Alikírikh. Of your kindness, my friends,
prepare yourselves now, for we must go to Verfaren to collect
the Gedri and be on our way as swiftly as may be." Turning to
the others, I said, "As for the rest of you, O my people, and ye
Dhrenagan, ye Restored, whose presence is such balm to our
hearts, rest well and recover yourselves. I would beg you all to
have patience with the Gedri, should you have dealings with
them while we are gone, for they are intensely curious and will
almost certainly seek you out. Remember of your courtesy that,
here and now, however foolish it may seem, we are legends in
this place. Most of those who see us are likely to be terrified
first and angry after. Try to think of them as younglings, and remember that we are new-arrived in their land. I will see you all
when I return."

I let Varien know who was coming. *"Alikírikh? Shikrar, are
you certain?"*

"I am as surprised as you, my friend," I said. *"Perhaps our
voyage here has reminded her that the world is full of new experi-
ences, and that there are many kinds of good in the world."*

Lanen

We snatched some food, for it was now long past midday, then joined Vilkas, Aral and Will, Jamie and Rella, and my mother Maran. Jamie, Rella, and the Healers were all desperate to get away, to get to Berys as swiftly as possible to stop him. I could understand it but I can't say I was convinced.

My heart misgave me ferociously. Only by the grace of the Lady, Jamie, and Shikrar was I alive at all. I could not forget that Berys had said I was the most precious thing in the world to him when he learned of my mingled blood. I couldn't help but feel that the most sensible thing for me to do was to stay as far away from him as humanly possible. I took Varien aside for a moment and put it to him.

"I cannot argue with you, dearling," he said solemnly, "and I would not place you in danger for all the world. Perhaps we could remain with the Kantri until the others return?"

"What, you mean rest?" I teased. "Together? In safety? Surely not." I grinned at him. "If this were a proper bard's tale we'd be going along with the others, intent on revenge to the exclusion of everything else, including good sense."

He laughed. "Ha! Let us confound the ballad-makers, then, and take our ease." He kissed me lightly. "We have surely deserved it. Very well. Let us go and tell our comrades of our decision."

They were all assembled in the shelter of the one corner of the College that still stood: there was at least a portion of roof to keep off the rain that threatened, and there was room enough for Salera and Shikrar, though Idai, Gyrentikh, and Alikírikh had to wait outwith the crumbling walls. Tolmas the stonemason and several dozen others from the town were there as well, to hear what Rikard might say about their future, that for so many years had depended on the College of Mages. The assembled Gedri—I shook myself—*people* stared at Shikrar in astonishment, and at Salera in disbelief.

Rikard took a deep breath and began. "There are two chief matters before us," he said. "First and most obviously, I have much to tell you of the destruction of the College and our hopes to rebuild, but that will have to wait, for there are those here who must leave as soon as may be." He nodded to us. "There is news that will be hard to hear, but hear it we must. Ignorance would be folly. Pray you, hearken to Mistress Rella."

"Those of you who were around earlier saw what happened, with the Healers Donal and Rathen," said Rella, and speaking quickly, she told them of the demon-haunted Healers. Over the shocked swearing she continued. "We know beyond doubt that Magister Berys, he who was Archimage, has been the source of their temptation and the one who must bear the blame for this obscenity." She drew a deep breath. "What this means is that you cannot trust *any* Healer, apart from Rikard and those students whom you see before you, not to be the victim of demonic possession." Now *that* brought a hiss of indrawn breath. "Berys has taken even that fundamental surety away. Those who serve the House of Gundar are almost certainly tainted. For the rest, we cannot tell, but the dangers are too great to take chances. The best we can do is to recommend that you only trust Healers who wear a Ladystar in contact with their skin. The demons cannot bear the touch of that symbol of Her power."

"We cannot live thus for long, surely!" cried Tolmas, the others echoing his words. "And even if we are so fortunate as to have Rikard and the others, what may be done for those who live elsewhere?" His brow was deeply furrowed. "My sister's son dwells in Elimar, and his young lad is not well. What is he to do? How will he know who to trust? And how shall we deal with any of the tainted ones who approach us?" He lowered his voice. "Surely we need not kill them?"

"We leave this very hour to seek out Berys and destroy him," said Jamie stoutly. "The death of the demon-master breaks the spell. They will be free."

"Aye, well, if you manage it, all well and good," countered Tolmas. "But the Archimage as was, he's a powerful man. He may not be so easy to kill, and in the meantime how are we to protect ourselves? Demons walking in the shapes of men. Shia preserve us," he muttered.

"We will keep watch, day and night," replied Rikard heavily. He opened the top of his clasped robe to reveal the new Ladystar that hung above his heart from a silver chain. "It will take more than one of us to restrain them, so we will move in groups of three. We are very few, alas, and I fear . . ."

"Magister," said Salera, raising her voice only enough to be heard clearly. "I hight Salera, of the Aialakantri. My people and I have spoken of this, and we believe there is a better solution."

Those who had not heard Salera before stared, slack-jawed, at this impossibility. Surely that was one of the little dragons, speaking!

"There are not full five hands of the true Healers who yet live," she continued. "If one or two of you are able to subdue these creatures, rather than three, it would leave more free to watch and ward, perhaps to go abroad in the world to seek them out if that is needed. I have found"—here she paused to concentrate—"three hands of my fellow Aiala who have said they will assist. If we work together, surely we all will benefit."

Rikard's eyes were nearly as wide as those of the townsfolk and he obviously could not speak, so I did.

"Salera, you are most generous, and I know the Healers appreciate your offer. Are you certain that this is best for you?" I added in truespeech, for Varien had told me that she could hear it, *"Dear Salera, this is a great work and a great danger you undertake. What so moves you to generosity towards the Gedri? It will be hard, and not all will accept you for the reasoning creatures that you are. If you seek to do this as a kindness to my people, for my sake and Varien's, know that it is not necessary."*

"I know that well, Lady Lanen/Mother," she replied, her mindvoice calm and clear. *"It is because they do not yet know us that it must be done. For our own protection, the sooner we are able to assist the Gedri, to speak with them for longer than a brief moment, the sooner will they come to see us for who we now are."* I could hear the determination in her thoughts. *"There is also an undeniable pleasure in knowing that we will be working against our life-enemies. Fear not, Lady/Mother. This is not*

misplaced gratitude. I have spoken with my people at some length, and it has been decided."

Aloud she replied only, "It is decided. If the Gedri will accept our offer, we will work together against the Rakshasa."

Rikard had mastered himself and said solemnly, "Your offer is a blessing beyond hope, Salera of the Aiala. We accept gratefully."

"The blessing of the Winds and the Lady go with you then, Salera," said Varien, his glorious voice balm and benison. "The Wind of Change has blown roughly across us all of late. I rejoice that you and the Aiala are called to be the Wind of Shaping. Good fortune attend you," he said, and in broadcast truespeech he added, *"Remember that truespeech is not limited by distance, and that the Kantri for the most part will be near. Lanen and I will be among them. If ever you have need of us, you have only to call upon us."*

She stared at him in surprise and responded in the same broadcast truespeech he had used. *"Lord Varien, have you not seen? You and the Kantri, all save a few, journey east this very day with the whole people of the Dhrenagan."*

Idai responded while the rest of us stood speechless. She hurried into the courtyard, pushing Shikrar aside in her haste. "What say you, youngling?" she demanded, agitation rattling her voice. "That was the true voice of vision, I know it. Whence comes this?"

Salera seemed confused. "Lady, it is—it is knowing. It is true. It lies ahead as surely as the sunset. Why do you question?" Faced by our blank expressions, realisation dawned on Salera. She blinked in surprise. "Do you tell me that this Sight is not known to the Kantri?"

"We live in ignorance of our future, Salera," replied Varien, masking his astonishment as best he could. "I gather from your words that you do not."

She was projecting confusion and uncertainty. "We thought—I thought—Lady Lanen, surely you of the Gedri can see as we do?"

"Not even slightly," I replied, trying to keep my voice light. Salera appeared to be deeply disturbed at this revelation. "I wouldn't mind a bit of warning, but we can't see ahead." I smiled at her. "To be honest, most of us have trouble enough seeing where we are, much less where we are going to be."

"This requires thought," she said, slowly. "We have made assumptions that do not appear to be true."

"Then think on it while we are gone," interjected Jamie rudely. "Your pardon, Mistress Salera, but this lot would talk the sun down. We must go."

"Jamie!"

"We are losing the daylight, Lanen," he said impatiently. He was practically dancing to be gone—and I had to admit he was right. "Did I hear that you're staying here?" he asked quietly.

"It seems the most sensible thing to do," I replied. "Varien will be with me."

"Thank the Goddess!" he responded fervently, hugging me. "A battlefield is no place for you, with your babes to protect." He released me, and there was a curious look in his eyes. "Though I have never known you to be so sensible before. You're not growing wise, are you, my Lanen?"

"Surely not," I replied, smiling. "Perhaps I'm simply being forced to grow up, eh? It would be nice to think that I'm balancing the fact that I'm being forced to grow out as well."

Jamie grinned and turned to go. I caught him, hugged him again, and kissed his cheek. "Go you safe, Father, and keep you safe, and come safe home to me," I said softly, our traditional words of farewell.

"So I will, my girl," he said, and hurried off to join Shikrar.

Will

I stood beside Salera while the Healers made their plans. We had begged the time from the dragons who had offered to carry us. I knew in my bones that I had to be with Aral, that she would need me soon, but oh! After all those years of missing her, I was loath to bid Salera farewell so soon. Even to leave her side was hard.

"I tell you, we can manage with one just one Healer with each of the little dragons," insisted Mik—he always hated being called Chalmik—to Vil and Aral as Jamie and Lanen were bidding each other farewell. "Trust me, we all paid attention in Magister Posrik's classes. That's how we survived the first attack in the Great Hall." His voice grew lower and grimmer. "Think of it as a test. Those of us still alive can deal with demons."

"And what about the times when you can't?" replied Vilkas sternly. "Not all the Rikti respond to the same restraints. And I am here to tell you that the creature that dwelt in Rathen was one of the Rakshasa. They are a different problem altogether, and we know not how many like him there may be."

"How would you know?" said Mik, stung by the implied criticism. "I'm sure you're well up on theory, Vil, and you did well enough today once the actual demon was gone"—Vilkas started to protest volubly, which Mik ignored—"but I haven't forgotten a thing about Posrik's classes," said Mik, sneering. "You turned white as a sheet the one time we dealt with a real demon. Damn near fainted."

I would have smiled if I dared. Mik and Vilkas always put on a great show of not being able to stand the other's presence. Idiots. And at such a time! Still, it made a kind of sense. The world they had known was literally lying in ruins at their feet. Their old rivalry was familiar, safe. Known.

Ah, and here came Aral, eyes snapping, to puncture the raucous pride of the young men's display. I was proud of her.

"Oh, for goodness' sake, can't you two give it a rest even now?" said Aral, exasperated, turning to Vilkas and frowning. "Vil, you know Mik's right, demons make you lose your reason. Don't snarl at Mik just because you—because you weren't thinking straight last night. He survived. That took skill." Then she turned to Chalmik, who was beginning to look rather smug.

Ai, I thought, cringing. *Mik, you're an idiot. For Shia's sake, don't smile at Vil's discomfort! You ought to know Aral better than that.*

"And don't you *bloody* well pick on Vilkas," she said, rounding on Mik and looking for all the world as if for two pins she'd slap his face for him. I swear, you'd never believe such concentrated defensive fury could exist in so small a frame.

"Leave it, Aral. I don't need your help," growled Vilkas. She ignored him.

"He's dealt with more demons in the last week than you've ever seen in your life, including last night. We've been working without cease since Berys murdered Magistra Erthik. Vil's done things people are going to write books about, if any of us get out alive. Back off." The two young lads exchanged a speaking look over her head, male commiseration over the peculiar habits of the female, but she reached out and took each of them by the arm. "No more classes, lads," she said, her voice low and solemn. "No more stupid rivalry. That world is gone. It's all too bloody real now. We need to stick together."

"It's not enough, Aral," replied Mik, more subdued now that she had forced him to let go his mask of scorn. "Vil's right. I know I can manage the little ones, but—I'm still learning to be a Healer. I'm not gifted like you two, I'm just one of the crowd. I learned last night that I can hold off demons, and I've a reasonable idea of how I managed it, but what if I have to face a Healer with twice my strength?"

"There are only two ways to get rid of a demon," said Vilkas, starting to grin. He could see over Mik's shoulder, of course. "Run or have a dragon handy."

"I can't run very bloody fast," grunted Mik.

"Then let us not depend on the strength of your legs, Master Chalmik," said a clear voice from close behind the young Healer. He jumped a foot, and Aral howled with laughter as Salera stepped forward.

"Forgive me, Master Chalmik," Salera said. "Magister Rikard said that I should speak with you regarding the partnerships we seek to create." She gazed into his eyes, her soulgem bright in the late afternoon sun. "He suggested that I should work with you, setting up teams, planning our—our strategy." She sounded proud, though whether that stemmed from remembering the word or being able to pronounce it, I was not certain. "I am willing if you are."

Mik blinked. Knowing him, he was too touched to speak. I knew only a little of his history, but from what I could recall there was precious little of kindness in it, and less respect. *You've caught him on the hop, Salera, you clever soul,* I thought. *Well done, lass!*

"She's the leader of her people, Mik. You won't get a better offer this year," said Aral, gently teasing.

"I've a feeling you may be right, Aral," declared Mik, finally allowing a slow grin to cross his face. "I'd be honoured, Mistress Salera. Though I still think we need another Healer. I'm damned new at this."

"I have seen your heart, Chalmik of Durrum," she replied, "and others have told me of your kindness. You are not nearly so limited as you choose to believe."

Mik's grin widened. "Very well, then," he said, raising his hand, palm out. Salera touched her palm with his. "As long as you stop calling me Chalmik. That's my dad's name, it sounds like you're talking to my father. I'm just Mik."

"Very well, Chustmik," replied Salera as she let out a great hiss. Mik jumped back several feet.

"It means she's amused, lad," I reassured him as he caught his breath and let his heart slow back to normal.

Mik turned to me, annoyed. "And that's another thing. How in all the Hells do *you* know what that means?"

I ignored him, for the others were preparing to leave. The time was come.

"Salera, my lass," I began, but she was already moving towards me. Despite the lack of expression on her bright face, the young Healers all turned away. Salera did not speak at first and nor did I, we simply gazed at one another for a moment—and then she bowed her head, like any daughter wanting the kiss of benison from her father at parting. I leaned in and touched my lips briefly to her brilliant blue soulgem, then threw my arms about her great long neck.

"It'll all come right, littling," I said, trying to keep my voice steady, the strange, spicy smell of her hide awakening a hundred memories from when she was a kitling. "We've found each other after all this time, haven't we? We'll manage it again when this is over." She did not reply, just rested her head against my back for a moment. "Your life is all before you, and a great work awaits. I know you will do all things well," I said softly. "I trust—I know all will be—" I faltered for a moment, then moved a little away and gazed deep into her eyes. "Salera, my heart's daughter. I am so very proud of you."

There was a moment of utter stillness between us, when we did not breathe and I'd swear our hearts didn't beat, and for that timeless moment there were only the two of us in all the world.

But time still flows, and we stood back from one another—and the dratted creature got in the last word. "She does not know, my father, but have patience," she whispered to me. "Aral is very clever. She will see you in time."

She dropped her jaw and grinned at me, then turned to walk slowly away with Chalmik.

It was time to go.

Shikrar

Before I could question Salera further about this astounding ability the Lesser Kindred seemed to possess, Idai glanced up and said, "Shikrar, behold, one comes from the west." She sounded puzzled. "But it flies in from the sea. Surely we are all here? It cannot be Nikis!"

"I cannot tell from—this range—" I replied as my words began to falter. I felt a cold wind rising. That distant form cast a shadow over my heart.

"May all the Winds preserve us," whispered Idai. I felt the shiver that trembled through her. "Shikrar, it cannot be!"

The shape was right for one of us, but this creature was too high up and too far off and moved—oddly. It flew stupidly, impossibly, vast black wings flapping like a crow even at that height,

where it should soar on the kindly winds. It looked to be twice my
size and black as night, and when it passed between me and the
lowering sun I shivered from horns to talons, and for that moment
I felt as though my heart were turned to stone and would never
beat again. In that desolate silence one of the oldest legends of
our people whispered through my heart like the hiss of falling
snow.

*"When the Black Dragon comes, when the Eldest of the Kantri
falls from the sky, then will come the ending of the world."*

"May all the Winds preserve us," repeated Idai, shuddering, as
the thing flew eastward out of sight. "This is an evil day."

"Shikrar!" cried two hundred voices in my mind.

I was about to reply when a wave of sheer hatred crashed over
my mind, followed by a cry from voices I did not yet know. A single word, shouted in fury by hundreds of minds and throats, as a
mere ten miles away the great cloud of the Restored rose into the
air to give chase.

Demonlord!

Kédra

A terrible shudder rippled across every soul there in Timeth's
field when that vast black shape passed over. We had lost the only
home we had ever known, we had flown across the Great Sea for
our very survival, beyond hope the Lost were restored to themselves and to life the very day we returned—and now when even
we, even the Kantrishakrim, required rest and time to think, the
shadow of our ending swept over our heads a bare day after we
had arrived in Kolmar.

I saw Tréshak look up when the shadow passed over; saw her
flick in an instant from the Attitude of Calm, which had finally
graced her after many long hours of talk and food and rest, into
Fury. I watched in amazement as she went in a single fluid movement from being at rest to being airborne.

"Demonlord!" she screamed, aloud and in truespeech, and a
second and worse shudder took us all—but we who had returned

from the Isle of Exile watched in amazement as all the Dhrena-gan echoed that cry and, rising up in a great cloud, flew after Tréshak towards the distant black figure.

And behind them, but gaining fast, my father Shikrar.

Shikrar

Tréshak was insane. She it was whose name was most remem-bered of the Lost, for she was the first to be changed by the De-monlord. Her fury, like a furnace when he murdered her mate Aidrishaan, had made her first in the attack. This had happened five thousand winters and more ago.

To Tréshak, it was a raw wound made but two days since.

Her grief, her fury, were unabated, and she flew on her new-made wings straight towards Death. I shouted to her, sending truespeech that could be heard halfway around the world, but she would not listen. I cried out then to the rest of the Restored, commanding that none should take away Tréshak's honour of the first attack. I knew my thoughts were full of my fear of her death and I did nothing to conceal it. Perhaps that would convince them where mere sense had no sway. It seemed to work, for they broke off the pursuit and circled high, a great column rising in a spiral, all eyes fixed below on Tréshak.

As I bespoke them, I used every advantage of size and strength I possessed to try to catch up with Tréshak, but there was not enough time. The Black Dragon was too near to her and I too far away. I had barely passed the great mass of the Restored when she had come level with the thing and dove at it from on high, scream-ing wordless defiance, talons outstretched and mouth agape, to rend, to kill with a single strike.

It heard and turned its head over its shoulder. It opened its jaws and a terrible sound came out, short unconnected bursts of noise, as Tréshak fell upon it. Just before she could strike, it changed its flight angle, rolling and pulling up to face her, and spoke a single word as it rose. The sound was sickening, and it was clearly in the language of the Rakshasa. Dread took me. If this was in truth the Demonlord, had it just uttered the word that created the Lost in the first place?

Were we all doomed?

Tréshak flinched but was otherwise unaffected, and hit the Black Dragon at an angle.

It all happened so quickly.

Because it had changed its orientation, her trajectory took her straight at its underbelly. When she hit, she sank her front talons and her upper fangs into its wing, striving to tear the membrane, and let her momentum carry her back claws into what, on us, would be the soft flesh just in front of the back legs.

Then she started to scream.

She could not free herself from it. Her front talons and her fangs were embedded in the black wing, but it was not flesh. Where her talons tore frantically at the surface, I saw a white-hot seething mass, just before her forelegs disappeared into the creature. It was terrible. Her screams redoubled, ringing hideously in my ears. It seemed that the thing had caught hold of her body and was actively pulling her into itself as they fell earthwards. It was plain that she could not get away, and I watched in sick horror as she began to burn—but she denied it the final victory. She chose of her own will the Swift Death, and cleansing Fire took her instantly from within.

The Black Dragon cried out briefly in pain then, as pure Fire, sacred to the Kantri, took Tréshak to sleep on the Winds with her lost Aidrishaan. I saw something small drop to the earth and marked where it fell. The great black thing pulled out of its dive, and flapping clumsily but otherwise unconcerned, it returned to its eastward course as if nothing had happened. It ignored me. It ignored the great mass of the Restored, flying high above and watching in agony.

"*Back. Go back. This will not be overcome by fury, my people,*" I said sternly. "*Let us go back and think how we may defeat this creature, lest we all be taken down into darkness.*"

"*We will not let it go, Shikrar!*" cried Naikenna, the Eldest of the Restored after Tréshak.

"I do not ask it of you, Naikenna. Follow at a distance and mark where it flies," I said sadly. "And bespeak us, as we will you. We will follow soon. I pray you, use what restraint you may and do not attack the creature again as Tréshak did." I could not conceal the deep grief that weighed down my heart. "We have longed for your Restoration for many lives of our people. I pray you, do not desert us for the sake of vengeance. We will find another way to destroy the creature, we will all bend our minds to it—I beg you, practice what Disciplines you may, Restraint and Calm if you can bear them, Forbearance if all else fails, but I beg you, do not go down into death for no purpose."

"We will do what we may," said Naikenna coldly. "Follow soon." And she closed her mind to me.

I turned back sadly and flew low, coming to land where I had marked the fall of Tréshak's soulgem. It took me only a little time to discover it where it lay at the side of a field, half buried in mud. I wiped it clean on the grass and gazed into the depths dreading what I might find.

Clear. It was clear.

I breathed again. There was no flicker, she was not trapped again, it was like all the soulgems of those who have gone before. I gave silent thanks to the Winds from the depths of my heart, clutched it to my chest, and flew back to Timeth's field and my own people. I bespoke all of the Kantri and told them what had happened, in every detail. We needed to know what we faced.

It was in my heart to speak with Salera as well. She was proven disastrously correct in the vision she had revealed to us. If she knew aught of the creature we faced, or could assist us in any way, I would beg it from her before we left.

Kédra

My father's words were meant to help us understand, and they did, but we all work differently. Some at least there were who became desperately afraid. I could understand, for we all felt horribly exposed, resting as we were in the northern end of Farmer

Timeth's field. Nearly thirty souls rose up when Hadreshikrar described Tréshak's passing, their weariness forgotten, scattering in all directions as their fear took them, seeking shelter in hills, in caverns, in the heart of whatever forest they might find. I could not blame them. If I had had neither mate nor youngling, I might have even made one of their number.

My father returned soon with Tréshak's soulgem and reverently made room for it in one of the casks that contained all the others of our people who slept on the Winds.

The rest of us took what courage we could muster and did what small tasks there were to do before we departed, clearing away the remains of our feeding, taking a long drink ere we set off after the Dhrenagan and whatever dark destiny awaited us.

It was in this hour that my mate Mirazhe proved the usefulness of forethought. She had spent the morning arranging for the lansip trees and seedlings, which had been carried at such great cost of weariness across the Great Sea, to be planted in a large corner of Timeth's field. We watered them in by the mouthful, carried from the nearby stream. By the time we needed to leave, the lansip was as well cared for as we could manage. It was an important task for many reasons, the practical among them, but to me at that moment it was a powerful expression of faith in our future. Lansip, Lanen had taught me, was worth more to the Gedri than its weight in silver; with it, we might have some useful coin in which to treat with those who must see our arrival as a kind of invasion.

The trick with lansip is, of course, that it cannot flourish except in the presence of the Kantri. I do not wish to be crude, but it had astounded me over the centuries that those Gedri who had come to our island and taken seedlings or saplings back with them, against all experience (for the young trees always died), had never considered the matter of—fertilizer.

Farmer Timeth, however, had summoned his courage and come out to ask what we were doing to his land. He did not object, especially when we told him what kind of trees they were. He watched carefully and said he'd do all he could to look after them, but as I had learned from Lanen how valuable lansip leaves were to the Gedri, I would not follow our fate eastwards without making certain that the trees would be protected. Some of our number would have to stay, and one choice at least was obvious. The youngest of us, and his mother, must remain behind.

My parting from my beloved Mirazhe and our young son Sherók was the darkest and most desperate moment of my life, and I will not dwell upon it. Her spirit showed its true colours in that evil time, for I knew well that she would have come with us in a moment had it not been for Sherók, and because he was there she would not leave his side. He had barely seen six full moons, and already he had crossed the Great Sea. He should have been running on grass and diving in shallow pools for many years, not having to hide from death and danger. My beloved swore to keep herself and him safe and far from harm. A few others also decided to stay, for they were kind and would not leave Mirazhe and Sherók alone.

I was also intent on making certain that Dhretan agreed to remain behind. He was the youngest apart from my son, and although he had come of age he was yet very young in spirit. I was forced to take him aside and ask him to protect my beloved Mirazhe before I could make him stay. I warned her that I had convinced him so, and I delighted to hear her mindvoice lilt with delight as she assured me she would do her best to appear helpless for Dhretan's sake. At least for a few hours.

My father rose up and flew the short miles to Verfaren, there to collect the Kantri and Gedri who sought the demon-master Berys. It seemed that, at least for the moment, our paths lay together, but I did not doubt that we would be parted ere long. I wished them good fortune, but in the face of the dark evil that threatened to overwhelm us all I am ashamed to admit that all my care was for the Kantri. A single Gedri life, even that of so dark a soul as Berys, suddenly seemed to weigh little in the balance.

When all was done that might be done, I again bespoke Naikenna, who gave me the best directions she could, and as the sun rode down into the west, we rose and followed our destiny eastwards into the rising dark.

Even at the time I thought of it as the Last Flight of the Kantrishakrim. Only a hundred and fifty of us took to the air, singing a wordless song of battle and determination and courage

The legend of the Black Dragon was simple and terrible. From our earliest times, it had been said that the Doom of the Kantri would rise up, in shape and form as one of us, pure black in hue, but with killing fire in its veins. A great battle would rage in the skies above terrible mountains like talons of our enemies, but it would last no more than a single day, sunrise to sunset—and when it was done, when the Eldest of the Kantri fell from the sky, then would come our doom and the ending of the world.

Lanen

To say that I was torn barely touches the surface. My heart was raging, now in one direction, now in another. I knew that safety lay with Mirazhe and those few of the Kantri who were going to remain in the west. That delightful vision of peaceful rest among the gardens of Elimar had seduced me, in my heart of hearts I was willing Shikrar and the others to get on and leave, and then that damned Black Dragon showed up.

I heard them, of course. The Restored had yelled "Demon-lord" so loud I'm surprised Rikard hadn't heard it. And then they all took off after it—sweet Shia, only bloody *dragons* would fly as fast as they could *towards* their greatest enemy! Anyone with sense would run the other way. I was ready to do just that, with a song in my heart, but then I hit the stone wall that was my husband.

He had turned to me, his harrowed soul in his eyes, and said, "I must go, Lanen."

"What?" I said, confused. "Go where?"

"It is the legend. When the Black Dragon rises, filled with killing Fire, a great battle will come—*the* great battle—and with it our doom." He bowed his head and added quietly, "Our doom, and the ending of the world."

"Don't be ridiculous!" I snapped. "I don't care how powerful it is, it can't bloody well bring the world to an end." I spat, disgusted. "Legends indeed! Legends are no more than stories, and they grow with every telling. If there is a grain of truth in your legend, it's more than I expect."

"Natheless, *kadreshi*, I must go with them," he replied, abstracted. "A moment. Shikrar bespeaks me. Even now Tréshak flies to do battle with—no!"

I winced. I heard that as well, saw as if I flew with him the dreadful images that Shikrar was sending. Tréshak bursting into flame, unable to escape, choosing the Swift Death after surviving so many long ages trapped and Lost. It was terrible, it was heartrending, and it set Varien's resolve as nothing else could have done. "Surely you see it, Lanen?" he said, trying to sound reasonable. "Would you have me wait with you, safe and at our ease, while those I love face death?"

That was it. Here I was, shaking with terror, and he wanted to play the hero. As usual, I turned fear into anger. Anger is so much easier to deal with.

"And what will you do, while they are fighting?" I asked, suddenly furious. "What can you do against the Black Dragon that they cannot? Where are your wings, to fly against it as your people will?" I cringed even as I said that. It was a cruel thing to throw in his face, but just at that moment I'd use any weapon I could reach. "Has it occurred to you that the nearer we come to Berys, the nearer I come to death?" I cried. "Why put Shikrar and Jamie to the bother of saving me if we are going to go back into the teeth of that evil? Will you throw even our children on the pyre of your loyalty to the Kantri?"

"Enough," Varien growled.

"No, it's not enough," I snarled in return. "We said we'd speak truth to each other, Varien, no matter what," I reminded him. "The Kantri live too long! You, even *you* lose track of how fleeting life can be." I could no longer control my voice, it shook so that I could barely speak. "I fear Berys to my bones, Akor. He wants me for a sacrifice. He said he'd take my soul, wed whatever is left—though I suppose he'd have to murder you first—and use my blood for Goddess knows what. By now Marik has surely told him of my pregnancy." I was shaking head to foot now, my arms wrapped about me as they had been in that terrible cell. "Goddess, how can you ask it of me?"

"I ask nothing of you," he said, his voice utterly calm, his gaze cold now and shuttered. "Wait here in safety. I will bespeak you when there is news, and if I survive I will return as swiftly as I may."

"Damn you!" I screamed. "Did you hear a word I said?"

"Of course. If you fear Berys, you need not be anywhere near him. Mirazhe will be glad of your company, as will young Sherók."

I reached out with my mind, but his was closed to me. I could not reach him. *Oh Hells. Is he lost to me, so suddenly?* I was shaking, whether with fear or anger I couldn't be certain. *Just like that, to have him turn from me?*

"You must do as your heart tells you," he said quietly. "So must I."

Thank the Goddess, just then he reached out to touch my cheek, and his hand trembled as well. "There are some things in this world, Lanen, that must take precedence even over the truest love that ever was. For all that I have the form of a child of the Gedri, I am yet the Lord of the Kantrishakrim, the King of my people. I have been so for more than seven hundred winters. How then? Shall I turn my back on my people in their hour of need? Even if I cannot fly into battle, yet I know them. I know their hearts. If I am with them, I may not make any real difference to the battle, but, Lanen"—he reached out for my hand and held it between his two as gently as if it were a rose—"if I am a thousand leagues from them and they facing the worst evil our race has ever known, how shall they have the heart for battle? The Kantri choose their King in each generation. It is a sacred trust. I cannot break it, *kadreshi*," he said, and his voice shook just a little, "even if keeping faith with my people breaks my own heart and yours."

For a fleeting moment as I reached my own decision, I wished with all my soul that we had been willing just this once to stick to comforting lies; that just this once we might have done what we wished rather than what was right.

"Oh, Hells' teeth," I muttered, swearing rather more than that. "Come on, then, we have to catch Shikrar."

"But—" he said.

"Don't be stupid," I said. "I'm not letting you out of my sight. Shia only knows what you might get up to if I left you to your own devices."

"And what of Berys?" he asked quietly.

I lifted my chin and stared intently into his emerald-green eyes, so full of hurt and sorrow.

"Just don't bloody well lose."

Shikrar

When I landed in Verfaren I found the others ready to depart on my word. Of all of them, it was Aral alone who came forward to meet me, her eyes full of sorrow. "Varien told us, Shikrar," she said, reaching out to touch me. I took a strange comfort from the gesture, though I could not feel it. "I am so sorry to hear of Tréshak's death. May the Winds and the Lady preserve us all. This is a terrible day."

"All hath gone ill this day, truly," I replied sadly. "Let us hope that our fortunes will improve."

"At least the Healers and the Lesser Kindred have made their peace," she said, doing her best to speak something of hope to me.

I nodded. "So much good at least is done. And you remind me, I would speak with Salera before we leave. Forgive me."

Aral nodded and hurried off to join Gyrentikh. The Healer Vilkas awaited her.

I bespoke Salera. She flew swiftly to meet me, showing me gleefully Mik's surprise at her abrupt departure aloft. She landed neatly before me. "How may I serve you, Eldest?" she asked.

"Lady, forgive that I am so abrupt, but time presses. Have you any knowledge of what lies before us away east?" I asked.

She bowed and closed her eyes. "It is desperately hard to tell,

Eldest," she said apologetically, speaking with her eyes closed. "There are so many images, so many possible ways that the future might go. But a few things are surely to come. The battle will take place on a bright day, with clouds of smoke. Vilkas rises, but whether Sun God or Death of the World I cannot say, for he knows not. Lanen crushes that which was stone." She opened her eyes, and I felt a terrible sorrow pouring from her. "Many of us will never return, Eldest," she said, her voice suddenly rough. "Far too many. Forgive me. I have seen no more."

I bowed to her, my heart weighed down as with great stones. "It is enough, Lady. Thank you."

Lanen and Varien stood together outside the ruined wall of the College, their arms about one another, waiting for me. From a distance I could not be certain where the one ended and the other began, and it struck me as a good thing. The moment Salera left, they hurried up to me.

"Do you come to bid me farewell, my friends?" I asked, surprised.

"No, Shikrar. We come to beg you, of your kindness, to bear us eastwards," said Lanen.

"Lady, I thought you both meant to remain here," I began.

"How could we disappoint the ballad-singers?" said Lanen lightheartedly, but I had known her longer than any other Gedri, and I could see the dread that wrapped her round.

"Shikrar, how should I wait here when the Black Dragon is come?" said Varien, his words full of resolve, his heart awash with fear and sorrow. "It cannot be. I will not abandon my people."

"And if you think I'm going to let him leave me here," said Lanen as they climbed into the shelter of my hands, "think again. We've been apart long enough. What if Berys should have a demonline ready to return here? No. Together. It's the only way." I noticed that she carefully did not meet my eyes, or use truespeech.

"It is well, then, my friends. Together," I said, crouching. I spread my wings and leapt into the sky. Idai, Gyrentikh, and Alikírikh with their charges followed close behind.

The winds were behind us, for a blessing, blowing light rain away east. The moment I reached soaring height I let out the breath I had not realised I was holding. I could not really feel those I carried, as they were so light, but their minds were far more open to me than I think they realised.

Varien/Akhor felt a measure of joy to be aloft once more, riding the spring wind, studying the land as it passed below him— but that joy was tainted with fear for Lanen, fear that he should have tried harder to persuade her to stay behind, fear lest we should lose and Berys rise triumphant.

Lanen's thoughts were harder to read, but I caught them when they were wrapped about her babes. She, too, feared Berys to the depths of her soul and was terribly upset and unsure of her decision. She knew that she had made it based on sheer emotion, but even as we flew I felt her resolve strengthen. She was with her husband. Whatever else might happen they would not be parted again, and that was good.

I kept to myself the visions that Salera had spoken of. It was her sorrow that most moved me, and I had the very strong impression that she had lied when she declared she had seen no more. I have to say that I did not envy the Aiala that very strange ability. I would far rather go into battle with a heart full of hope.

I found an obscure source of comfort in the fact that I was ignorant of my own future as I rode the sky, with the wind and the sun behind me, eastwards.

Following the Black Dragon.

x

A Brief Respite

Shikrar

I soon outdistanced the other three. I could not help but smile, and bespoke Gyrentikh with a small jest regarding the flying lessons I had given him so long ago. He laughed and suggested that perhaps the fact that I was half again his size with near twice his wingspan might have something to do with the matter. True enough, he did have a point.

The sun was nearly gone down in the west when my companions and I saw in the distance a great mass of the Kantrishakrim, flying slowly and wearily. I bespoke Kédra and learned they were seeking a place to land for the night, and indeed they began to descend even as we spoke. I caught a late updraft and wheeled, rising, as they all began to land upon a vast grassy plain.

"We are all desperately weary in body and in spirit, my father," Kédra said to me privately. "The strength of the Dhrenagan we cannot yet fathom—indeed, I am not certain that they yet know it themselves—but it seems that for this night at least they are willing to rest with us."

"Where is the creature?" I asked, resolutely ignoring the wash of sorrow that swept over me. Poor Tréshak.

"Not far ahead. It looks neither left nor right, it has ignored us entirely. Eastwards, ever eastwards, in unbroken line. Forgive me, my father, I can do no more," he said, and I watched as the last of the small figures below went to land. The ground so far below was falling into shadow as I sped on. I sought greater height, that I might not come upon the thing in the darkness by accident. Twilight did not last so long here as on our vanished home, and the moon would not rise for many hours yet—wait! there!

Varien, Lanen, and I watched it, flying low to the ground, flapping stupidly—I wondered again that it could remain airborne. It flew like the veriest youngling, expending vastly more energy than it needed to. At the size, I had thought it must exhaust itself soon with such wild exertion—but no. We watched it as it flew and flew, in a straight line, working ten times as hard as it needed but showing no signs of weariness. I fell off a few points north, that I might not fly directly over the thing. The Raksha-stink was terrible, even so high up as I was, and I could not answer for my instincts if I came any closer. So I flew far around it, going some way north then turning back east. Now that I was not trying to keep it in sight, I fell into my normal rhythm. It was vastly easier than having to hang back at the pace of the evil thing. It was soon far behind us.

That in itself was a blessing.

"It is not alive, Shikrar, it cannot be," said Varien at last. *"Nothing that breathes could fly like that. It would fall from the sky. It is a golem, it must be."*

"Your thoughts echo mine. Animated by the Demonlord, given the energy to continue by who knows what obscene arrangement with Berys." As weariness overtook me I could not keep the plaintive note out of my mindvoice. *"Akhor, what is there to do? It is made of molten rock! I cannot think how to defeat it."*

I heard his mindvoice laugh a little. *"Is this my old friend Hadreshikrar, come to despair so soon? I cannot believe it. We have only known of its existence for a few hours, my friend."*

"It is no laughing matter, Akhor. You know yourself that time is short. It flies towards something with a singleness of purpose, and I expect that something is Berys. I cannot imagine what is going to happen to it when it finds him, my friend, but I would wager that things are only going to get worse for us all."

"I fear you have the right of it, Shikrar. But though it may be inanimate, you are not. How fare you?"

"I am weary, I must confess," I replied, though that was not the entire truth. I was exhausted.

"Then let us take our ease and go to land," he said. *"The morrow will be time enough to pursue."*

"Surely the best strategy is to get wherever it is going before it does?" I said, trying to sound as if I had the strength to fly all the night through.

He snorted. *"Don't be an idiot, Shikrar. You need rest, and by all accounts it is a very long way to the East Mountains."* More solemnly he added, *"Lanen and I are weary as well, my friend, and it would be useful to spend some time in careful consideration. We must find some way to fight so fierce a fire, where our own strength avails not."*

I began to look for a landing site and discovered that there was a sizeable river below us, running northwest-southeast. I began to spiral downwards, faster than I would have liked, but the air here was very still and it was hard to keep altitude. I fear that my friends had a bit of a rough landing, but when they found their breath again they assured me that they were not injured.

We had came to ground in what appeared to be an uninhabited stretch of land beside a tributary of the great river that divides the north of Kolmar from the south. There was a small wood nearby from which Lanen and Varien gathered fuel for a large fire, and the river graciously provided both drink and food. The fish were much smaller than I was used to, but there were enough for all.

"Idai and Gyrentikh are together," I told Lanen and Varien. I lay curled around the fire, they sat together on the other side and ate. "Idai bespeaks me. They have not seen our blaze yet. I will build it a little higher, that it may be more readily seen from aloft. Alikírikh comes also, but she despairs of finding us before dawn because of—oh!" I was pleased to find that even at such a time, I could still find amusement in the little things.

"What has delayed her?" asked Varien grimly.

"No, no, there is nothing amiss—it is only that she has had to deal with Will," I said, starting to hiss with amusement. "It seems that Will—well, Alikírikh reports that he is a typical useless Gedri, and that he hates flying." I rejoiced to see a real smile cross Varien's face. "The poor soul grew ill and demanded to return to land after the first hour. I gather that after he rid himself of his last meal he felt a little better."

Blessed be the Winds, they both laughed. "Poor Will!" said Varien. "Is he still so convinced that he must come with us?"

"He is," I replied. "Though I cannot fathom his reasons."

"Can you not, Eldest?" asked Lanen quietly. "It seems clear enough to me." Varien and I stared at her blankly and she sighed. "Man or Kantri, it obviously doesn't matter, you are both blind as moles at noon. Have you not seen the way Will gazes at Aral when she's not looking?"

"I confess I had not noticed," I said, intrigued.

"It breaks my heart," she said sadly. "He's a good man. If only she could see past Vilkas. She desires to be warmed by that furnace that burns in her friend, and she will not turn and see the home fire and welcoming hearth that await her lightest word." She yawned then, hugely, and smiled up at me. "Forgive me, Eldest. I am weary beyond belief." She moved nearer Varien and rested her head on his shoulder.

"Alikírikh says that Rella has mocked Will unmercifully," I reported, speaking quietly so as not to disturb Lanen. "Strangely, it seems to have given him comfort."

"Good for Rella," replied Varien, grinning. "Thank the Winds that she at least can keep her sense of perspective."

"I will confess that I am finding that difficult," I said slowly. "The legend . . ."

"The legend of the Black Dragon indeed!" Varien snorted.

"A story to frighten younglings into behaving. I am not a great believer in legends, Shikrar, and now that I have seen it—well, there may be a grain of truth in the centre of every old tale, but I do not think that our world is going to end."

I looked up, stretching my wings and my neck, working out the knots in the long muscles. "Perhaps you are right, and legend is . . . exaggerated." I sighed. "The air here is sweeter than at home," I said wistfully. "Have you smelled the flowers on the night breeze, Akhor? Even so early in the year. They are intoxicating." I breathed deep, savouring the heavy scent of the blossoms, the clean smell of the river, the sparkling glory of the brilliant star field above us in the deep sky. "The water is good, the land is good, and I rejoice with all my soul to see you and your beloved together again."

"As do I, Hadreshikrar, as do I," he replied, kissing her hair lightly. She slept.

"I believe there is much of good in most of the Gedri, and much that may be done between our two races for the betterment of both." Another sigh escaped me. "Truth be told, Akhorishaan, I would prefer not to die just now."

"Surely you cannot believe that old nonsense?" he scoffed.

"Perhaps not—but my thoughts have been much concerned with death, of late." I could not stop myself from shuddering. "You did not see it, Akhor. Our home died in flames. That green gem of an island was covered in fire and molten rock, there was no hint of green left—it was black from side to side before it sank below the waves. There is a part of me that died with it, I fear. I cannot tell you how that image has burned into my heart."

Varien bowed his head for a moment, in deep thought, when Lanen let out a snore. He grinned and gently lowered her to the ground, covering her with his cloak and resting her head on his pack. I was faintly distracted by the shifting gleams of the firelight on his long silver hair, so different from his scales yet so similar, and on his brilliant soulgem gleaming in the golden circlet I had made for it when he was new-made a man—but when he looked up from tending to his wife he astounded me, for there in

Gedri eyes was shining the warrior soul of Akhor, my soulfriend of nearly a thousand winters.

"Do not let them win, Shikrar," he said, rising, his voice deep and powerful, defiance in every line of him. "You know what the Rakshasa use when force is not enough. Despair is their greatest weapon and our final defeat. The world, our lives, are changed, not over!" He stood and, moving away from Lanen, began to pace before the fire. "You are right, you know. This is a good land, and surely with goodwill and a little assistance from those Gedri who know us, we will make a new homeland for ourselves." He glanced over towards his beloved, fast asleep, and lowered his voice. "I am already bound to this land by ties of marriage and blood, and I rejoice in it, but what future awaits my childer if they have not Grandfather Shikrar to teach them? And what of your own Sherók, our cherished youngest? Will you so easily desert your grandson, so new-come to this world?"

"Of course not," I snorted. "You know me of old. I will fight with the last breath of my body and the last beat of my heart to protect my family and our people. But sometimes courage is not enough, old friend." I shivered, snout to tail-tip, and not from the cold. "My word on it, Akhor, that great black thing has shaken me to my core. My soul is more bleak than I have ever known it, and I begin to think of Yrais more and more."

Varien did not speak, but he walked around the fire and stood next to me. I lowered my head to his level to see him better, and for the only time in all our years of friendship, he leaned forward and touched my soulgem with his. I was shocked, for it is a delicate intimacy, more normal between a mother and child. I had not known such a contact, aside from Kédra, since my beloved mate Yrais left this life to sleep on the Winds, but at that moment, somehow, it was entirely appropriate. At the touch of his soulgem, the torrential river of his loving concern came pouring over my parched soul. True friendship, born of long knowledge, born of knowing all the faults and accepting them as part of the whole— such a thing is rare and precious, and that was the gift he gave me that night; the full knowledge of the depth of his love for me, as mentor, as friend, as father to him since his own went to sleep on the Winds.

For the most part, we are a reserved people, as befits those who can speak from mind to mind. I was staggered, and honoured beyond words.

He stepped back and stroked my faceplate with his soft Gedri hand, just once. "And so, Hadreshikrar," he said, smiling upon me, and his smile like his eyes was a thousand years old. "Let the Black Dragon shake that. I dare it."

"What Black Dragon?" I replied, my soul rising on wings of joy. "Akhor—I—"

"It is well, my friend," he said, smiling. "You have always known it in any case."

"Yes," I said, blinking at him in the firelight. "But sometimes it is well to be reminded. May the Winds bear you wherever you—I mean—"

He started laughing. "If the Winds bear me wherever I wish to fare, I hope you will be there to catch me when they let go!"

It was the fire of my laughter that guided the others to us.

Vilkas

Aral didn't so much sit down on the ground beside me as plop. Then she threw herself full onto her back with a great sigh and gazed up at the stars in a clear sky. I too looked up from our roaring fire into the deeps of the night. The brighter stars shone like candles on a distant hillside, beckoning weary travellers to warmth and rest. The fainter ones were little children, peeping shyly into the night sky, as if making sure that all was safe ere they came out to dance.

Astoundingly, Gyrentikh and Idai had found Shikrar and the others and we were told that Alikírikh was near. We were camped beside a good-sized river with a rocky shore and a little wood on the near side. Idai had gone upstream to look for fish or whatever else might appear. Gyrentikh, who had borne Jamie and me, had started a separate fire for us before disappearing into the wood, declaring that he sought "something larger than fish." I hoped he would be willing to share whatever he found. I was ravenous.

However, both Aral and I needed sleep even more than food and the others were likely to be awake for some time, so we stayed by this smaller fire. I was still thinking, stupidly, of offering to help Gyrentikh when I realised that he and Idai were already gone. To be honest, despite being so hungry, I wasn't exaggerating. I needed rest desperately. I felt like I hadn't stopped running for a fortnight. When I thought about it, Aral and I really *had* done an insane amount of work in the last few days. Healing Shikrar's wing, then a mere few hours later treating that terrible demon gash, and Goddess help us all, rescuing Rathen nearly killed me. Going but a little further back, I realise that mere days before we first helped Shikrar we had been up all night sealing the Lesser Kindred's soulgems; a few nights before *that*, I had done something that I still could not fully believe. I had changed a woman's blood, Lanen's blood, to match that of the babes beneath her heart. Half human, half dragon.

Goddess preserve us, I thought. In the mad rush I had almost forgotten. *What in all the wide world is going to come of that?*

And what kind of power dwells within me that I could do such a thing?

I had been running from my own power most of my life, for a very good reason. Since I first manifested as a Healer, very early, I have had recurring dreams. In them I—I fight my way to the top of a mountain and I can touch the sky. *Really* touch the sky, reach out and feel the soft blueness of it. I am the ruler of the world.

After that, the dream can go one of two ways. In some I become a kind of Sky God, or a Sun God, like the one 'tis said is worshipped by the tribes of the Far South. In these dreams I use my power to its fullest extent, the land is blessed and I help make the world a glorious place.

In the *other* dream I also use my full power, but I become the Death of the World. I am fighting a demon, and when it stabs me I do not die—instead I become a demon myself, a thousand times worse than the one I fought. I destroy it with a flick of my power, for I am grown strong as worlds, and then—I kill every living thing, joyfully, and at the last I reach out and crush the sun in my hand, and the world ends.

And I laugh. Every time. Sky God or Death of the World, I laugh. Because either way, it feels wonderful. The use of my full power is the ultimate release, complete fulfillment and complete self-indulgence—and it is my fate, inexorable as night following day. And I have been running from that fate ever since I was come to manhood. The single exception was that night when I saved Lanen. It was change her blood or let her die, and Aral challenged me, and I—well, it was hard, yes, but once I had started, I—I felt as if I had entered my dream. It was so obvious what had to be done. I did not think about it, I simply did it. My memories of that night are very strange and blurred, almost as if I were drunk at the time.

Or as if I had called at last on the power that lies within me, churning, roiling like Hellsfire, that it takes all my control to restrain. Every moment of every day.

I did manage to control it that one time I used it, because Aral was there to keep me in line. I don't know if I can restrain it without her. She keeps urging me to accept my power, even though I have told her the risk. She believes in me utterly. That is very . . . seductive.

I often feel guilty about Aral. She is dearer to me than anyone, now that my family is gone, but I know she wants more. Damn it.

She is in love with me. I've seen it in her eyes. I've never done a thing to encourage that, but Hells, I don't know much about women, maybe she has just misunderstood. Of course I love her, if you want to use the word that way. But I am not *in* love with her. I value her friendship beyond words, beyond understanding, but it's friendship rather than anything else. I feel no unrequited longing, as I fear—as I know—she does.

Sometimes I think I should say something. In fact, before all of this madness broke out, I was on the point of telling her—but life has been moving at a dead run since we and Will barely escaped from Verfaren with our lives, and I really don't think she needs to hear this now. And to be honest, I don't think I want to deal with it right now either.

Mind you, there is a lot I don't want to deal with right now.

"Blessed Lady," said Aral eventually, still gazing at the night sky. "Did you ever, in your wildest dreams, think that you'd fly like that?"

"In my dreams, I fly all the time," I replied truthfully. "But no," I said, to her quiet *ha!* "No, I never imagined I would do it in real life. It was—"

"It was bloody terrifying, that's what it was," she interrupted, earnestly. "And horribly uncomfortable. And cold. And I've *never* been so scared as I was in those first few minutes."

"Right enough," I said, smiling. "No argument there. But the rest of it was more exhilarating than anything I have ever done, waking or sleeping—and that, my girl, is saying something." I held my hands before the fire, rubbing them together, in the earnest hope that I would soon be able to feel my fingers again. "I wish they had warned us how bloody freezing it was going to be up there," I added.

"Idai did warn us," she said, surprised. "Didn't Gy—Gy-what's-his-name tell you?"

"Gyrentikh, and no, I just told you he didn't."

"Mmm, sorry," she said, not really paying attention. "Anyway, it wouldn't have made much difference. All we could do was keep our hands under our cloaks. Idai was really nice about it, though, she held us right up against her chest, when she thought of it. It was a lot warmer that way."

"Who were you with?" I asked. "It was all such a scramble when we left, I didn't even notice."

"Lanen's mother, Maran," she replied.

"Did you get a chance to talk?"

"Not really. We tried yelling back and forth a few times, but the wind was so loud it wasn't worth it. We ended up pointing a lot." She gave a grunt and heaved herself with a great effort back into a sitting position. "Besides," she said rather more quietly, "I'm not the one she wanted to talk to." She nodded in the direction of the riverbank, where two dark figures, some distance away, stood together in the moonlight.

I glanced at Aral. "I'm surprised you're not trying to hear that," I said quietly. "I know you're working on learning more about how people think and feel. I'd have thought that would be a master class, one way and another."

She gazed at me across her shoulder. The firelight flashed in her eyes. "You forget, Vil. *You're* the one with the good shields." She dropped her face into her hands for a moment, mumbling, "I don't need to hear what they're saying. I can feel it from here, Shia save us all." She inched nearer the fire, pulled up her hood, and wrapped her cloak more closely about her.

"Aral?" I asked. "Are you alright?"

"Oh, Vil," she whispered, her voice catching in her throat. "Oh, Goddess. I can't bear it. Talk to me, please, now, about anything. Quick."

"You never could shield worth a tin ferthing," I sneered. "Honestly, all the time Magister Rikard spent with you, he might just as well have been teaching the desk."

"Ha, O Great Mage Vilkas," she shot back, rising to the challenge and desperately cheerful. "And you're just the same in the other direction." She did a decent imitation of Magister Rikard's slightly nasal voice. "*No*, Vilkas, you must *feel* the power, not just use it. Let it *touch* you as it passes through. That's what makes us *hyooo*-mn!"

We both managed a bit of a laugh, though it was fairly pathetic. "At least Rikard is still alive," she said.

"Thanks for reminding me," I said, feigning a snarl. "Have you any more gloom? I'll have it as well, as long as you're passing it around."

"Oh, Hells, Vil, I'm sorry," she said, instantly contrite. "I know. I can't bear to think about it, not in detail." To my astonishment she snorted. "But Stone Mik, of all people, to get out in one piece!"

I had to laugh. "Aye. Chalmik, indeed! Never heard his formal name. Poor bastard."

Aral grinned. "That and all. Can you believe it? And everybody who didn't call him Mik called him Stoneface. Some folk just can't enjoy themselves. I always thought he had a terrible time dealing with real people. I have to admit, I was amazed this morning. He handled that poor woman so well."

We fell silent again, just for a moment, then Aral piped up, "Did you see that town at the bend in the Kai? It was a long way down, but it looked huge! Was it Kaibar, do you think?"

"Must have been. It certainly looked like there was another river joining just there, and the Arlen meets the Kai at Kaibar, doesn't it?"

We spoke frantically about our trip, about flying—anything that would keep us from dwelling on the thought of our friends and colleagues, dead at the demon's hands—but we could not sustain it for long. Silence fell again, and for a while neither of us could think of a way to lift it. Trust Aral, though, when she spoke she found a subject that would get me as rattled as she was.

"So, Great Mage Vilkas," she said, lightly mocking, "what are you going to do when the moment comes?"

"What moment?" I asked, because that was one of the chief things I didn't want to think about.

"Vil, I know they're following that bloody great black thing, but the truth is that these dragons are taking us as fast as they can fly towards Berys. He's a demon-master. Hells, he's probably the next best thing to the Demonlord himself, now. Whom he seems to have summoned, Goddess help us all, in the form of a Black Dragon, and don't you want to know how he did *that*."

"Not really, no," I replied sharply.

"Vil, you know what I mean," she said gently. "I know you fear demons . . ."

"I don't damn well fear them," I snarled. Unfeigned this time.

"Eh?" she said, astounded. "But you can't fight them. I know you can't. I thought you said . . ."

"I don't fear them, Aral. I *hate* them," I replied fervently, rising swiftly to my feet. "Being anywhere near any of them makes my skin crawl and my eyes itch." I was breathing hard, and my heart hammered in my chest as I spoke out the real truth at last. "I told you I feared them because the truth is so much worse. I hate them so hard it makes my gorge rise up and my throat close. I want to kill them all, Aral," I purred evilly, kneeling right beside her and dropping my voice to whisper the dark truth, finally, to her startled face. "Every one of them. Slowly. Squeezing, choking, crushing, making sure it suffers agonies before I grant it the mercy of death."

Aral used a word I didn't know she knew and stared up at me wide-eyed. "Damnation, Vilkas," she said at last, her voice shaking. "That's sick."

"I know," I snarled, rising and turning away. "Why do you think I hold back? If I kill one I'd feel the need to kill them all, and by Shia's toenails, I probably could."

Goddess. My own words were making my stomach churn.

"That doesn't change the fact that we're going to be facing them soon," she said flatly, getting to her feet and brushing off her clothes. "Day after tomorrow, if Shikrar is right."

"Damn it, Aral, don't you think I know that!" I shouted at the top of my voice.

"And what are you going to do when Berys summons a Lord of Hell, or we have to deal with the Demonlord?" she asked, her voice now harsh and unrelenting. "I don't care how loud you yell, Vilkas ta-Geryn. It's not going to go away. Tomorrow or the day after we're going to have to deal with Berys, and he's going to have emptied half the Hells to protect his precious skin. We need to think what to do. *You* need to think what to do."

I started to shake and swiftly crossed my arms to hide it.

She must have been weary, rattled, for she saw me tremble and against all sense she reached out to me as if to take me in her arms for comfort. I shrank from her proffered embrace as from hot iron. At that moment it would have been as welcome.

She closed arms and heart and mind and all, in the instant, for which I was profoundly grateful. "Just remember, Vil," she said, her voice calm and reassuringly normal. "Dreams are just dreams, no matter how powerful. They're not predictions."

I did not reply. I could not, I was still shaking, and it would have shown in my voice.

She reached up and laid a hand on my arm. That was bearable, though revealing. I could feel her shaking too. "I know you. I've watched you for two years, I've worked with you at a depth even you are hardly aware of." I looked at her then, and saw in the dim firelight that she was smiling, albeit rather crookedly. "Sweet Shia, I've opened my spirit-self to you more times than I can count. I know you can be trusted." In a moment of wild daring, in spite of the rejection I had thrown at her only moments before, she raised her fingertips swiftly to her lips, kissed them, and touched my cheek softly as a butterfly. "Maybe it's time you learned to trust yourself."

I could hear her voice shaking with emotion. I had told her long ago that I didn't like to be touched casually. Even putting her hand on my arm was greatly daring. Planting a once-removed kiss on my cheek was practically an invitation to share her bed.

I knew perfectly well that now would be a good time to take her in my arms for comfort's sake, to give her what she needed because I knew she needed it. We might both be dead soon, and dear Goddess, who was I to refuse her?

She didn't give me the chance. She felt me flinch from her hand on my face and turned away, to put a few more sticks on the fire and sit close to it, her arms about her knees. No matter what her heart was shouting at her, she was too good a friend to blame me for her own feelings. She had offered what I could not accept, and she knew it, and she closed in once again.

In the silence we could still hear the soft murmur of the voices by the river. Jamie and Maran.

"Damnation," sighed Aral from the heart, resting her head on her knees. "Idai, Lady, be quick, I beg you. I'm bloody starving and bloody exhausted and those two are breaking my heart."

Jamie

I'd just started filling my waterskin at the river's edge when I heard someone on the shore behind me. Old habits die hard, don't they? I had my belt knife ready to throw when she spoke.

"It's just me, Jamie."

I put the knife away, but to be honest I wasn't any the less shaken. Worse, if anything. I knew what to do with a foe.

"Maran," I said, by way of greeting.

It was getting dark, but I could see her grin. "Aye, well, at least you remember my name."

I said nothing, and she sighed. "I see. You remember other things as well. So do I." When I didn't reply, she sighed again. "Ay me, here we go. Yes, it was my fault. No, I never sent word to you or to Lanen. And I never—" She stopped herself, and after a moment went on, more gently, "By all the leaves of spring, Jamie, did you ever in all your days think we'd meet again like this?"

"I never thought we'd meet again at all," I said. I hadn't meant my voice to be that harsh. I'd forgotten that rogue vein of poetry in her. It came out at the damnedest times, and it summoned our past together as nothing else could have done.

I heard the faintest grunt, as though she were in pain. "Aye, well, that's fair. Neither did I," she said. "I've had the easier part. I've been able to watch you both over the years. I wish the damned thing had sound as well as sight, I'd have given a lot to have heard some of those arguments," she said, a hint of lightness in her voice. It went warm and gentle again when she added, "I saw you teach her to use a sword, Jamie, in the middle of the night when Hadron couldn't see. I watched you when you held her as she cried. I saw the look in her eyes when she was learning how to ride and went over her first jump—and it wasn't Hadron she looked to with all the pride of her soul, it was you."

"She is not the child of my body," I growled. My heart was aching as though someone held it in their fist and was squeezing. If it had been daylight, perhaps I could have kept up my guard, but in the starlit darkness there was only Maran and me, and twenty years of pain.

"I only knew for certain when I saw Marik capture her on the Dragon Isle," she replied quietly. "She must be his firstborn. And mine." Her voice caught. "I swear, Jamie, I thought she was yours," she said. "I begged the Lady—"

"She *is* mine!" I cried, throwing down the waterskin. "Damn it, Maran! You think a few weeks' dalliance makes a difference to who her father is? Never!" I paced away from her, and swiftly back to stand before her. "He may have made her with you, the heartless bastard, but *I'm* her father!"

"I know," she said, her voice steady. The distant firelight gleamed on the tracks down her cheeks. "And never a day passes but I thank the Goddess that she had such a father as you."

"She needed a mother as well," I snarled. "You should have been there, Maran. What in the Hells is wrong with you? Why didn't you come back?" I grabbed her shoulders and shook her. "She needed you, damn it!"

I needed you, damn it!

She just stood there, gazing down at me. I couldn't bear it, I turned and walked away before I was tempted to violence. I didn't get far, though. Her voice stopped me.

"Jamie. Jamie," she called softly, as a lover calls her beloved, all her heart in her voice. "I know. My soul to Mother Shia, I know. I needed her too, and I needed you. Dear Lady. I needed you as a drowning man needs air." And she was starting to gasp a little, for air, to keep her voice under control. She stopped and just breathed—when she spoke again her voice was calm and steady and as inexorable as the water flowing down beside us, and my heart pounded to every word. "I thought the Farseer attracted demons, Jamie. The first ones came for me, and I fought them off, but then one hurt Lanen"—her voice faltered for an instant—"I couldn't take the chance."

"You never told me," I said, turning to her, shaken. "Maran, you never said there were demons come after you."

"I must admit, I wasn't exactly thinking clearly," she said. "I didn't know how to hold off demons then. I'm better at it now. But I swore that if the things were going to take whoever stood near that damned Farseer—then by the Lady, they weren't going to get either of you." Her voice grew thicker as she spoke, now, and her pauses for breath stopped my very heart within me. Her throat was so closed it seemed near to choking her. "I married

Hadron so that . . . that if they took my husband they wouldn't take you. When I left and for sixteen years after, I feared I would draw down death upon us all, Jamie, so I stayed . . . I stayed as far away from you . . . as I could."

Every part of me longed to go to her, to take her in my arms, the idiot, to make all our pain go away, to make those years disappear and make her mine again—but I stood where I was, and I knew it was right.

"You are the best man I have ever known, Jamie," she said, her voice forcing its way through her tight throat. "I know—I know you and Rella are together now, and I'm glad of it. She's a fine woman, and a good friend." She coughed, and turned it into a tortured laugh. "But if she ever loses her mind and tells you she's done with you, I'll be by your side in your next breath, and by every star that ever shone, I swear I'll never leave you again."

My head was swimming, my body shaking with a hundred memories. I could bear it no more, all my best intentions melted into air, I swear I could hear her heart beating with mine. "Maran—" I began, moving towards her.

"No!" she cried, and swiftly backed away. Her voice was shaking now, along with the rest of her, I guessed. "Goddess, no—" Her voice dropped to a whisper in the darkness. "If you touch me I am lost. Please, I beg you. I am holding true by a thread as it is."

"Come, Maran," I said, trying to speak lightly. "Do you tell me the men in Beskin are all blind? I cannot believe it. Surely you have someone to walk beside you, to keep you company in the long nights of the northern winter?"

There was a moment's silence, and she answered, "I have never loved another man, Jamie. Ever. In all my life, apart from that madness with Marik. By my life I swear it. And there is only one in all the world I love more than you, and she lies asleep by that fire yonder."

"Goddess, Maran—" I croaked, my heart wrung. All those years alone beat upon me worse than fists. I at least had known the love of my heart's daughter. She had had nothing.

"So now you know how I feel, and I won't say anything else

about it again," she said, her voice growing stronger. The firelight was dying a little, I could see nothing but her shape in the starlight. "Let us meet only as friends, Jamie, working together with these others to finish Berys. Goddess knows, it's time the world was rid of him. I have done so many stupid things in my life," she said quietly. "Together let us do this one good thing. For Lanen. For you and Rella."

"And what of Maran?" I asked gently, but she had turned away and was drawing near to the large fire the dragons had built.

I stood in the darkness by the river, listening to the echoes of her voice in my heart, knowing that she was right and there was nothing else to do. I picked up my waterskin, knelt by the side of the water, leaned over and filled it, and wondered idly as I corked it if it would taste even slightly of salt.

I spent some years as an assassin. I learned long ago how to weep silently in the generous darkness.

Idai

I brought back the carcasses of the two deer I had found. Gyrentikh and I had a gracious plenty to eat, and there was easily enough left for the Gedri. They all came, some roused from sleep and yawning, and carved steaks for themselves and for the absent ones. That still left most of the meat for us.

"Where is the other dr—the other Kantri?" asked Jamie. "I thought he had only fallen behind a little. It's been more than an hour already."

"Alikírikh has seen our fire, they will be here soon," I said. "Will did not take easily to flight, and he has delayed them."

"Is Rella with him?" Jamie asked.

"Alikírikh is a lady," I corrected gently. "And yes, Rella is with her. She is well and hearty, and laughing loudly at Will, as I understand it." I explained Will's difficulties with flight, and Jamie also laughed.

"Once they do arrive, I assume we're to have a council of war?" said Maran.

"Surely that can wait for the morning," said Vilkas, yawning.

"No, Mage Vilkas, it cannot," said Varien emphatically. "The Black Dragon appears to need neither food nor rest. It flies like nothing I have ever seen—like a creature that has seen flight but never learned how it is done—but for all that, it will arrive at its destination all the sooner." His voice grew heavier. "The Winds alone know what madness is brewing in the East Mountains, but my life on it, as soon as it arrives at its destination we will be the worse for it."

"Your pardon, Master Varien," said Aral meekly. "No disrespect to you, but can we not sleep until the others—arrive—oh," she ended quietly, as Alikírikh and her charges came to land.

Rella and Will were offered food, which she accepted and he did not at first. A brief blue healing glow from Aral, sent gently to Will, repaired his appetite.

Once we were all assembled, round a roaring fire in the deep night, we held the first Great Council of the new world. True enough, we never thought of it in those terms at the time, but that is what it was. A meeting of Kantri and Gedri together, to solve troubles that afflicted both. For all that we accomplished little, for all the awkwardness of it on both sides, there was a sense of rightness as well. It was at least an effort to plan, to work together to overcome a threat that faced us all. I believe we all found comfort in it, even Alikírikh. I had never been so long in her presence before without hearing a single complaint.

I was most pleased to see Shikrar come back to himself. I had been worried about him, and though I had tried to bespeak him, he would not hear me all day as we flew. I do not know what he and Akhor had spoken of while I sought food, but when I returned all awkwardness was past and Shikrar was himself once more. That yawning darkness that had been growing in his soul was healed now, by whatever means, and I was grateful for it.

We always assume that life will simply continue as it is. I have seen this same assumption among the Gedri, but for us it is worse, for we live so very long, and life for us can flow along unchanged for long years together. I did not believe that the coming of the Black Dragon was truly the end of the world, but I was absolutely convinced that it was the end of the world as we knew it, and that all the careful plans Shikrar and I had made for our people in Kolmar were going to have been so much wasted breath.

My use-name means "She who knows without knowing."

Sometimes I wish I didn't. I understand that ignorance can be a great comfort on occasion.

Shikrar

"The part I can't understand, Shikrar, is *why* you have to fight the Black Dragon? It goes against all reason," said Rella. "If it's that dangerous, why not just run? Scatter to the four winds! You can all talk to one another, distance isn't a problem. Go in a hundred different directions, make it do the work to seek you out while you think of a way to defeat it."

"It is the Demonlord," I said simply. "Even if we cared only for our own hides, even if we were willing to choose cowardice and let the Demonlord murder countless numbers of the Gedri while we sought only safety, we would only buy ourselves a little time. Perhaps your people do not remember, but we do. The Demonlord took great delight in death. He murdered hundreds of his own people before ever he killed Aidrishaan, and he could not be touched by our Fire, as true demons can."

"If that is indeed what animates that creature," muttered Rella. "I can well believe it a demon, but how did Tréshak know? She could only see it pass overhead, at a distance. Surely—"

"Tréshak was right," I said firmly. "Even if I had only her instinct to believe, I would trust that; but I have proof."

Varien looked up sharply. "What proof?"

"The Demonlord began life as a child of the Gedri," I said heavily. "He was human. I heard the Black Dragon today, when it looked up and saw Tréshak diving towards it. The sounds it made—I think it was trying to laugh. As humans do. And I would swear on my soul that it said the word that created the Lost, but for some reason the spell did not work this time. My soul to the Winds, my friends. Tréshak was right. It is the Demonlord returned, in the body of a golem of fire."

Perhaps we were all too weary, perhaps too much had happened that day, but not one of us could think how we might defeat a creature whose body was the fire of the earth itself. We all vowed to consider it while we were flying the next day, and the others went apart to sleep. The Gedri composed themselves around the two fires.

I watched, greeting the moon when it finally rose, singing in my heart with the stars that slowly wheeled overhead, making sure that no danger came nigh them.

Rella

Jamie and I spread our bedrolls, and he let me lie nearer the fire. What a gentleman.

We lay close and kept our voices low, that we might not disturb the others. There was a great deal to talk about, but in the end we were both too weary to say much about anything aside from the obvious. I was angry at myself, ignoring matters of great moment to deal with matters of the heart, until I realised that up until that time I had never had a matter of the heart that was so desperately important to me.

"I know you've spoken with her," I said, doing all in my power to keep my voice neutral.

"Yes, I have," he replied, his free arm about me. "And you were right. That kind of love is hugely flattering. Dear Goddess, Rella. I never dreamed that she was so true to me in her heart."

My own heart dropped like a stone. I must have stiffened, for Jamie leaned forward a little and kissed the back of my neck. "I said it was seductive, my lass, not that I was seduced."

I breathed again.

"I swear to you, Rella," he said, in that voice of utter truth that undoes me every time he uses it, "if I had been in any doubt about the two of us, if I loved you one whit less than I do, I'd have gone to her. Shia knows, I pity her with all my heart, and—well, you know I have never stopped caring for her."

"Then why are you here with me?" I asked. Of course I knew, I knew fine. I just had to hear it from him.

"Because you are my match, Rella my girl," he muttered into my ear. "I swear I can all but hear your thoughts. You complete me somehow." I smiled as his arm tightened around me. "My soul to the Lady, I never knew there was such an empty place in my heart until you came along and filled it." He sat up a little, leaned over, and kissed me sleepily. "I love you, Rella."

"Thank you for that, heart," I said, leaning back against his warmth. After a few moments I added, "I love you too. Can we go to sleep now."

For answer I heard his near-silent snore in my ear.

Good enough.

Maran

I thought I had pitched my bedroll far enough away not to hear them, but even around so large a fire there was only so much room.

I knew how it was. I had known before ever I caught up with them, and in my more rational moments I was happy for them both.

But, dear Lady, to hear his voice again, speaking such words to her! No dagger could be as sharp, or anywhere near as painful.

He asked me to wed him, all those years ago. Several times.

That was the worst of it, that life could have been so different for me—for us. I curled up physically, as if around a wound, and I remained so for some time, when at last a quiet thought came to me.

If I had wed him, Lanen would never have come to be.

And that was it, finally. I had known for years, in my heart of hearts, that I could never truly reclaim the love Jamie and I had shared so long ago. Seeing him again had been so much agony—but I could not wish Lanen unmade. She was the best part of me, however that might have come about, and somehow that was enough to soothe my heart. I sighed one last time, for love long since lost, turned over, and fell deep into blessedly dreamless sleep.

Lanen

My little sleep before supper had left me far more wakeful than I should have been. Varien lay beside me, but he couldn't sleep either. I heard Rella and Jamie talking quietly. Will and the Healers had their own smaller fire, leaving the five of us to take what comfort we could from the larger one. Maran was restless as well, but even she eventually lay still.

I found that the other two silent members of the party were also apparently awake. There was nothing so obvious as a kick, the movements were far more subtle. Hardly more than a flutter, but I felt it and gasped. Varien asked me if I was well and for answer I put his hand on my rounding belly. After a moment or two he sighed. "Alas, it is too soon for one so far removed to feel anything, even with Gedri hands," he said, a little sadly. "And yet, there are other ways." I felt his soft touch in my mind, and then— it was a most curious sensation. As if he were searching for other minds within me—which, I suspect, he was. After a moment he gave up and grinned at me. "Perhaps it is a touch too soon for that as well," he admitted.

"They're not even big enough to kick, you idiot dragon," I murmured. "Though whether I should expect to be kicked by four legs or eight, I haven't yet decided," I added ruefully.

"Lanen!"

I lay back, trying to find some comfortable place on the hard ground. "Well, don't you worry about that?" I drew my blanket about my shoulders and mourned, briefly, for the real bed we'd slept in the night before. I could have used the comfort of it. I was in a most peculiar mood, I remember—able to speak lightly of things that were desperately important to me. It was very odd.

"Dear one, does that fear haunt you, truly?" asked Varien, concerned at the genuine note of worry in my voice. Damn.

"Of course it bloody well haunts me," I said, exasperated. "Varien, even women married to normal men worry about their unborn babes. Will they be healthy? Will they grow strong in my womb, or do they wither within me? Will they have just the one head, and the two arms and two legs?" I snorted, torn between amusement and more than a drop of genuine horror. "Of course, in our case, Goddess only knows what grows in there. Hells, Varien, are they going to be born with wings?" Despite myself I shuddered. "Poor little scraps. Half Kantri, half Gedri. Alone in all the world."

Varien sat up and took my face gently between his hands. "Lanen, *kadreshi*, think. When Vilkas changed you, remember? He said then that they are perfectly human creatures. Human, and healthy." He smiled. "Two arms, two legs, one head each, and not a wing in sight."

"But that was so long ago!" I moaned. Foolish, I know, but what would *you*? Pregnancy does awful things to a woman's feelings. Mine seemed to be changing with every breath.

Varien grinned and stroked my hair. "*Kadreshi*, it was but a se'ennight since. It may feel as though an age of the world hath come and gone, but my word upon it, no more than seven days have passed."

"A se'ennight! Are you certain?"

"Certain sure, as Jamie would say. My word upon it."

"Nonsense," I snorted. "I don't believe it. You're lying. It's been a full moon since then, at least."

"As you say, then," he responded placidly. "Your word is law, my wife." I giggled. "But you must not be surprised, dearling, if the moon hath foolishly lost track of time and thinks that only a quarter of her cycle has come and gone."

"You're humouring me. Stop it," I said, pleased at the banter.

"As you will," he said, bowing while seated, which is quite a trick. I batted at him, but he caught my hand and kissed it, and was suddenly more serious. "Lanen, I do most deeply apologise that I could not—humour you this morning." He sighed. "We are creatures of habit, we of the Kantri. I have reacted in a certain way for a very long time, and I can forget that old responses are not of necessity the correct ones." He sighed. "I heard your fears, my dear one, but I reacted as though I had never changed, as though I were yet Akor, and Akor alone." He forced himself to look into my eyes. "I very much fear that you were right—are right—and that by taking you within a thousand leagues of Berys I am putting at risk not only your life but the lives of our childer."

Ah, damn it. In my weary heart I had been hoping that we could just let this one go, but no. We had already sworn to speak only truth to each other, however spiky and unwelcome it might be.

"Yes, you are putting us all at risk. I told you that in Verfaren, and I wish to goodness we'd had more time to think about it. But Varien—I don't seem to recall you having to drag me kicking and howling away from Verfaren, or forcing me at knife point to go with Shikrar."

He looked confused. Poor dear. He was still a bit slow when it came to understanding heavy sarcasm.

"Love, it's true, you gave me very little choice," I said. "But that is not the same as 'no choice.' I could have decided to let you chase this damned Black Dragon with the rest of the Kantri and stayed safe and warm in a real bed in Verfaren. I didn't. I, of my own free will, chose to come with you. So both of us must bear the consequences."

He relaxed a bit at that.

"That doesn't mean that I'm not annoyed at you for putting your people before your family, by the way," I added, turning onto my side with my face to the fire and wrapping myself in my blanket. "I can understand it, and I'm here because in this one particular instance I agree with you, but it's not a habit of mine I'd care to encourage."

"As you say, *kadreshi*," he replied. He lay down alongside me and put his arm around me. Even on the cold hard ground, even in that lonely place, his presence was comfort and safety to me.

I lay wakeful only a little time, until the weight of Varien's arm assured me he slept, and I matched the rhythm of his even breathing until I too fell into sleep's kind embrace.

Salera

I heard my elder brother sing up the moon. I lay, as he, beside a fire, watching over a child of the Gedri, and I joined my heart's voice to his. I would have sung aloud, but I had already learned that the Gedri require far more sleep than do we of the Aiala. There was a little breeze, a light spring wind, with the promise of warmth even in the night. The sap was rising all about us, pounding up the trunks of trees, whispering in the growing grass. Great changes coming, great changes all around us with every spring, but surely never before so many as in this spring that was changing the world.

There was much to ponder in the quiet of the night, beneath the shelter of a few trees. I still was teaching my heart that no others among the Kantri or the Gedri could sense the future rising before them. That Lord Shikrar had been so astounded at so simple a vision. That he could be facing that future and not have at least the shape of it to guide him surprised me.

Clearsight is not a gift of our Awakening. Even while we yet lived our half-lives before, I and others knew of this ability. We do not all have it—or perhaps it is more true to say that we have it to greater and lesser extents. I am not among the most gifted of us; Erliandr sees furthest and deepest, and there are many others whose Sight is clearer than mine. Still, like most I can see best when my own future forms a part of the vision. I knew I would not remain here in the west much longer, but I had yet one task to accomplish ere I might leave with the rest of my Kindred who were not partnered to Healers.

I would miss Mik. He and I had spoken long with Magister Rikard, and by sunset there were three hands—no, what were the words Mik taught me—five and ten—yes, fifteen pairs of Aiala and Gedri gone out to challenge the corrupted Healers. He had not objected when I asked him to accompany me, but he did seem confused when I asked that we leave immediately, ere the sun should set, and that we should go north as several others were planning to do. I had been forced to ask him to trust me.

That was when I realised that there was one aspect of clearsight that I had brought forward with me, through my Awakening, and that it was right. I knew, deep down, that I must not speak of particulars to the individual soul. I had not told Lord Shikrar the full truth of what I had seen of his future, and I had not told Mik either. True, I was with him, and that might change things—I trusted that it would—but I must not speak of what I had seen.

The future is always in motion, like a flowing river or a branching path. The slightest thing can direct the flow or choose the branch a person takes. Speaking of specific events can—it is difficult to express this—can stop the river, freeze it like ice, into the one particular version that has been spoken of. Speaking the future can lead a soul down a particular path, even if that is not the best one for them to take, or the one they would have taken if nothing had been said.

The night was moving towards dawn before it came. I was lost in contemplation when I heard an incautious footstep, far too near.

Finally.

"Mik, you must waken," I said quietly. He did not stir. Too quiet, perhaps.

"Mik!" I shouted.

He was on his feet in a single movement, crying out, "What, what is it?" He looked around. There was nothing to see apart from me.

"What is it?" he asked. "What happened? Did you see something? Hear something?"

"Both," I said. "'Ware, Mik. Something comes."

And so it did. An arrow flying towards Mik through the darkness, as I had seen in my vision. I batted it out of the air with my faceplate.

"Come," I hissed, and sped towards the source. It cursed when it saw me coming, which helped me find it. The creature tried to fire another arrow, but I moved quickly to the left, out of its path, and pulled my right wing close in. Then I was upon it.

My instincts told me to kill it, but that was not so easy as it once was. Instead I wrapped myself about it, holding it unmoving until Mik ran up, panting.

"What in all the Hells are you playing at, you idiot? Who the Hells are you, anyway, and why are you shooting arrows at— damn it! Gerthayn!" he cried.

"You know this man?" I asked.

"Of course I know him. He was in the year above me," said Mik, clearly confused. "He left at Midwinter Fest last year," he said, slowly. "Said he'd got himself a fine post." Suddenly Mik cursed. "Gerth, tell me you didn't take on with the House of Gundar."

"Gerth issn't here," hissed the creature.

"Damn it!" shouted Mik. He summoned his power to him, a clear blue glow, and sent it to cover his erstwhile friend. The creature writhed in my grip. Mik called his true name thrice, as Rikard had done, but the creature only laughed.

"I told you, he isn't here," the thing said. "His spirit ran away when I came to live here. I'm just as pleased."

Mik looked to me, pleading. "Salera, what can I do?" he asked softly.

"Call your friend once more," I suggested, but I held out little hope. The creature in my coils smelt purely of the Rakshasa, barely human at all, save for the shell it wore. Mik's summons was answered by a more determined writhing, but it changed not at all.

"I fear me your friend is truly fled," I said, as gently as I could. "He will not return."

Mik couldn't help his instincts. He sent his power to cover the Raksha, trying to let the Lady's healing drive the thing out. Certainly he made its life hard for the Raksha, but Mik swiftly began to fail. He had not the vast resources that Vilkas possessed.

I sighed. "Forgive me, Mik," I said, "but I cannot allow you to throw yourself into death for one who has already departed."

And with that, I broke the Raksha's neck. It cried out and disappeared, leaving only the two of us in the company of the body of one who had been a friend to my companion.

Mik raged. He struck at me with his fists, he kicked me and shouted at me and cursed me. I let him do so. Had I been in his position, I would have been as hurt and angry at knowing that nothing else could be done for one I had cared for. When he finally stopped from sheer weariness, the sky was lighter than it had been.

"Forgive me, Mik," I said. "I share your sorrow that the Raksha have claimed your friend, but I could not allow you to destroy yourself to no purpose. Your friend died when the Raksha took over his body—I would guess that he fought it and perished in the attempt."

"Knowing Gerthayn, that's very likely," croaked Mik, his voice hoarse from yelling at me.

"Then honour his deed, and mourn him. And," I added dryly, "give thanks that you do not follow him."

He looked up at me, and in the growing light I could see clearly the deep pain that he bore. "Maybe it wouldn't have been so bad," he replied. "Damnation! It's all gone so wrong. So many dead, so many poor souls corrupted, just for being weak. Damn it. It's not fair. It's not *fair*!"

I could not help but hiss my sympathy. "Truly, we are not so different, your people and mine. I agree, it is not fair, but it is the truth." I reached out carefully and touched his jaw, making him look at me. "All that is left to us, Mik, is the way in which we decide to react to that truth."

He stared at me, pain and anger still raging.

"Throwing a life after a life is not the path of reason," I said gently. "Rejoice in the life that was, mourn its passing, honour the memory and live. Life is the greatest gift of the Winds, Mik. Do not dare to cast it away for no better reason than an excess of sorrow."

He swore again. "Damn it, Salera," he said, his voice unsteady now. "Gerth was a good man. He didn't deserve this."

"Berys has much to answer for," I agreed. "But I would have you take note: you did not summon your power instantly when you woke. If you had, you could have shielded yourself, and I would not have had to deflect the arrow. Next time such a thing threatens, do not hesitate to call upon your power. It will save your life."

"I'll remember," he said groggily.

"Do so, for I will not be here to remind you," I said. False dawn was swiftly giving way to true sunrise, and I heard the wings of the Aiala as they gathered upon the Winds. My own wings fluttered in sympathy, almost against my will. "I am called away east, Mik. I did not know it before, but I must go. The others who partner the Gedri will remain with them, but the rest of us must join the great battle. Not a mile away west of here you will find Erliandr of the Aiala and Ferdik of the College of Mages. Go you safe and keep you safe," I said.

"Damn. I was looking forward to talking with you some more," said Mik, half a smile on his face.

"There will be long and long to talk, after all is done," I replied.

"Go well!" he shouted as I took to the air. "And kick the bastards twice for me!"

It was as good a benison as any. I met the rest of my Kindred, spiralling up on the Winds, and we struck out away west. We could not fly nearly as swiftly as the Kantri, but we would arrive when we were needed.

Of that I was certain.

The Eve of Battle

Berys

I am still exhausted. The Black Dragon seems to need more sheer strength over land than it did to fly across the ocean, even more than I had planned for. I was summoned by a minor demon soon after I woke. It seems the Demonlord was angry that its body was going stiff and would need much more power lest it fall from the sky. "Not that those mouldy dragons can hurt me, but I thought you wanted me there swiftly, little demon-spit."

"I do. You have fought them, haven't you?" I asked. I meant only to buy time, and was a little surprised by the answer.

"It was good practice," it replied smugly. "One of them attacked me. I had to do a little more than fly in a straight line. It's not so easy as you might think."

"Fool!" I snarled. "Every beat of your wings is held up by my hand. Do not waste your strength."

"Why, little demon-spit, do you grow weary?" it purred. "If you are so weak, why do you waste your time with me? Release me from the bond, I will find strength enough on my own to fly as I like."

The threat was always there with demons. One moment's weakness, true or perceived, and they pounced on it. I laughed.

"Weak? I have defeated nearly every Mage alive, I have brought a golem of stone and fire across the Great Sea to do my bidding, and I have you bound to me as my slave. I have strength in me yet to conquer worlds, witless creature. Here, be filled." So saying, I lifted my arms and sent of my own native power to the thing. It absorbed all I sent and sucked at me, demanding more. I closed the stream and denied it. "You must make do with that, for now," I said. "When you get here, I shall provide you with all you will ever need. In the meantime, fly straight, don't go too high, don't damn well fight the Kantri, and hurry."

"Yes, O great one," the Demonlord sneered. "I come." It cut the connection.

Once I was certain it was gone I collapsed. It had absorbed every drop of my strength. I had not counted on that. I managed to summon a servant to bring me food and wine, and told them that I was not well and to let me sleep. One of them asked me a moment ago where Master Marik was, and I quite truthfully responded that he was resting and was not to be disturbed. No need for him to be put into a cell and arouse the locals, after all. I have arranged for the guards who came with us to look after him and to report to me what he says and does, until I require more of him.

It is annoying that the book of Marik's thoughts lies buried in the rubble of the College of Mages. I will have to get him to tell me what he knows before the Demonlord arrives and I give it his soul.

I really must rest and make my preparations.

Tomorrow is the turning point.

Lanen

I woke in panic from a dream of war to find myself alone, though I didn't have far to look. Most of them were gathered around the fire having a hurried breakfast. I packed my bedding and went to join them. Travel rations again, I thought, sighing just a little. Never mind, at least the water was fresh.

Vilkas and Aral still slept. The sun was not long risen, and the tail end of the dawn chorus of noisy little birds fell like sweet refreshing rain from the eaves of the wood as I hurried to join the others.

"Varien, Shikrar, I'm a fool," I began. Everyone laughed at this announcement and I had to raise my voice. "There is much I should have told you yesterday, it's important, especially for you two."

"Yes, love?" asked Varien gently in truespeech.

"Don't!" I cried. He looked startled. "That's the problem. You and Shikrar must not use truespeech if you can possibly avoid it."

"Why, Lady?" rumbled Shikrar. Damn, he looked huge in the morning light. "What do you know?"

"Marik can hear you. Anything you say, either of you, he's been listening for months now." I explained swiftly how Marik had come to have truespeech.

Jamie cursed. "That's one of our greatest advantages gone," he said bitterly.

"Not entirely," replied Shikrar, sounding thoughtful. "Akor and I may not use it, but there is nothing to stop the rest of us, or Lanen, from bespeaking one another."

"I may not be safe either," I responded miserably. "He heard me too, when I was in that prison. He said he hadn't before. I don't know if it was because I was shouting or because I was barely ten feet from him, or if he's getting better." I turned to Varien and clasped his forearms in mine, wanting an anchor, wanting him to have one. I felt distinctly light-headed. "Varien, love, he also learned that I'm pregnant. Berys didn't know before, but I'd wager anything he does now," I said grimly. "I'm so sorry, love. I cried out to you in truespeech and he heard." I looked up to Shikrar. "But as far as I know, that's all. You, me, Varien. Everyone else is safe."

"We cannot so assume," said Varien.

"I was hoping to plan our strategy against the Black Dragon as we flew this day," said Shikrar.

"And so we shall, Teacher Shikrar," said Idai. She turned to me. "Know you if Marik can hear what we tell Shikrar?"

I thought about it. "He said he could hear you two, he reported what you said," I answered. "He didn't mention anything about hearing what you heard. Although," I admitted glumly, "that doesn't mean much. Marik lies as easily as he breathes."

Varien

"Indeed." Idai hissed her amusement. "Perhaps it would be best if we assumed that he can hear, and will report, anything that you hear or say, Shikrar. Very well—then let you consider the most tedious subject you can think of, in great detail and at length, and speak to Marik of it all the day long."

"Lady Idai, I like the way you think," approved Rella.

Idai continued. "The *rest* of us will consider how to defeat the Black Dragon." She glanced at Lanen and winked. "I know that we have not your years, that we are the merest younglings, but we must needs struggle along this once on our own. No doubt we shall falter without your guidance, O Sage of the Kantri, but think of us in our hardship and have pity . . ."

Shikrar laughed, a bright tongue of Fire in the broadening day. "Enough!" he cried. "It is all quite true, of course, and no doubt it will be a terrible struggle for you to manage so trivial a task without my assistance, but you must take courage and remain hopeful. If life and the Winds are merciful, you may one day attain to my years and my wisdom—though my natural modesty forbids my ever saying such a thing aloud."

"Your natural modesty would fit neatly in Lady Lanen's palm with room to spare," said Gyrentikh merrily.

Shikrar snorted. "Very well. I abjure pride from this moment. You kitlings come up with a grand plan to defeat our Doom and I will obey blindly!"

"Ha!" barked Rella, finishing her chélan, shaking the last drops from her cup onto the ground. "Even *I* know you better than that, Shikrar."

Varien laughed loudly. "Poor Shikrar! Even the Gedri tease you now!"

Shikrar's eyes gleamed in the morning light. "Alas, all my secrets are known, my character discovered, my faults made public, and I have not been here a fortnight! Where shall I hide from such infamy?"

"Please, Lord Shikrar," growled a deep voice, "have mercy. Waking to the hissing of laughing dragons is bad enough. I beg you, speak lower." Vilkas, groggy and bleary-eyed, poured himself a cup of chélan and drained it at once. Aral, behind him, grinned and drank her chélan more slowly as he was inhaling his second.

"In truth, Idai," continued Shikrar, more quietly out of mercy for Vilkas, "if we look to be drawn into battle before day's end, I think we must chance Marik overhearing what is said."

"Of course, Shikrar," she replied. Looking to Rella and Jamie, she said, "Have either of you any idea of how much farther there is to go?"

"Quite a long way," Rella said, and Jamie nodded. "I think I have a rough idea of where we are. Castle Gundar is hundreds of leagues northeast of here, through Mara's Pass—though if you are flying high enough, perhaps you won't need to worry about the pass. But I shouldn't think you could reach Castle Gundar before tomorrow in any case."

"Ah, but, Mistress Rella, you have not seen us at our best," said Alikírikh unexpectedly. It did my heart good to see her taking part in this. "We are still weary, but a night's rest will make a vast difference."

"Then let us be at it," said Shikrar. "Idai, will you wait for these heroes to break their fast? You have the best chance of catching me up."

"I will," she replied, "though I recommend they break it quickly."

Aral and Vilkas ate faster.

"Then let us be gone," he said to Lanen and me. Gyrentikh gathered up Jamie and Rella, Alikírikh took Will and Maran—and we were aloft.

Will

That day was years long. The morning was decent enough, clear weather and warmed by the sun, but clouds dark with rain rose before us ere noon. We stopped briefly just before the rain came on, to take some food and let the Lady Alikírikh catch her breath. I took the chance to take my blanket out of my pack and wrap it around me. For all that spring was now well along, it was bloody cold up there.

After we went back up, it rained almost constantly. Of course, Alikírikh sheltered us from much of it, but there was no escaping it all. After an hour we were soaked. When she remembered, she held us near her, and we warmed up and dried off a little—but it seemed not to be a natural position for any of them, and she often forgot.

Northeast, Rella had said. I didn't know if it was chance, but we seemed to be following the river. It had to be the Kai. I stared, delighted. I had always wanted to see the Kai, though I had to smile. I'd planned to be rather closer to it.

It would have cheered my heart to have passed the time with Maran, heard her story, maybe found out what she and Lanen had been yelling about, but the constant sound of the wind in our ears was all but deafening, and speech all but impossible.

Northeast. How any creature could tell directions in that downpour I know not, though of course the river lay below. And eastwards it must surely have been, for the hills rose steadily higher before us.

Shikrar

I sought the Black Dragon from the moment I took to the Winds that morning. We soon, to my sorrow, came upon it and the Dhrenagan together. Even as I approached, two of the Dhrenagan broke off from the rest and flew straight towards the Black Dragon. I could see their comrades trying to dissuade them, but to no avail, and as I watched the Demonlord laughed and caught them, burned them until all they could do was to choose the Swift Death, cheating him of their souls but throwing their lives away to no purpose. I could not bear it. I did not care if Marik heard every word.

"Naikenna, can you do nothing?"

Her mindvoice was disconsolate. "And how would you stop one of your own who was determined on death, Shikrar?" she asked, soul-weary, heartsick. "They are the seventh and eighth of our people to choose their deaths in this fashion. Each is a soul I have known for many long winters, each was a link to a past that is else lost forever. By my soul, I assure you, I would stop them if I could."

"Can they not even await our Council this night?"

"Most can," she replied. "Those of us who slept can wait. Those of us who waked, even in part—ah, you cannot know. To taste blessed freedom at last, to breathe, to ride again on the Winds! Thus far we are in paradise, after long ages of torment undeserved. To see the founder of that torment so near, in a travesty of our own shape, and know that we cannot even now extract revenge—it is more than some can bear."

"I hear you, Lady," I answered sadly. "Can you at least convince them to keep out of its sight? Let it not know where we are or what we do."

"I will try, Shikrar," she replied. I thought she had closed her mind to me, but—well, perhaps she was not shielding as tightly as she might. "Alas for Hyrishli and Orgalen," she mourned. "Hyrishli, soulfriend, heart's-sister, what darkness so overshadowed your soul? We are alive again, we are free, released from our torment at last. Was life so frightening after all these years? O Hyrishlianareli, my sister, sleep on the Winds, sleep soft and gentle where you are gone." Her mindvoice dropped to the merest whisper. "Hyrish, dear one, why could you not let me say farewell?"

I could not keep silence. Quietly, I bespoke her with the only words I had.

"May the Winds bear them up, where the sun is ever warm and bright."

We finished the Blessing for the Dead together. If Marik heard, much comfort may he take of it.

May their souls find rest in the heart of light.

I bespoke Kédra, for my heart ached for the sound of his voice. *"Where are you, my son?"*

"Far ahead and higher up," he replied shortly. *"Fear not, my father."*

It was enough.

We flew on. I would fain have joined Kédra and the others, but we four had to stay low for the sake of those we carried. We swiftly passed both Black Dragon and Dhrenagan and settled into a steady rhythm, following the river far below.

It came on to rain just after noon, and soon after we reached that place the Gedri call Mara's Pass. It is an excellent landmark for flight. It is not truly a pass, for the hills to the north and south fall away to flat ground for some leagues, but it is the only sensible place to cross that range of mountains if you cannot fly above.

I became more and more unsettled as we approached it. It looked—familiar. I could swear I knew the place, even to the extent of knowing that there were better updrafts on the northern side. I rose swiftly on the thermal, anticipating the jog to the left that I knew lay before me just past the highest point of the surrounding hills. I swooped away left, caught the rising air as though I had lived there all my life, and nearly dropped Lanen and Varien when I saw the vista before me. Their cries in my mind brought me back to myself, but all was changed.

There in the distance were the true East Mountains, of which these hills were mere outliers. They stood, snow-topped and menacing under the dark sky, looming at the edge of sight like a threat, and I realised between one breath and the next how I knew this place.

My Weh dreams.

Dreams that occur in the healing Weh sleep are important. The Weh sleep is our time of regeneration: the longer we live, the larger we become, and it is impossible to grow surrounded by armour. Thus, about every fifty winters the Weh comes upon us, with little or no notice—perhaps a day, perhaps a few hours—and we have no choice but to find a safe place and go to sleep. It is the only time that we are vulnerable to the Gedri, when our old armour becomes brittle and falls away and the new armour underneath has not yet had time to harden. It can take up to six moons for one my age to rouse from the Weh sleep. In most cases we do not dream, or do not remember it if we do, but sometimes a dream will come to haunt us. If it comes more than once, we consider it worth paying attention to.

I had dreamed of this place four times, over the space of three hundred and fifty winters. I knew the way to Castle Gundar from here, I knew what it would look like and what surrounded it.

And I knew now, to my sorrow, that my destiny awaited me there.

Idai

The rain lightened and gave way to clear skies just before the sun began to set. The high mountains before us began to glow in the golden light as we drew nearer, and the wind changed, blowing now from those distant heights. The air was cold and clear and bracing. I took a breath like a faceful of snow and was revived.

"Kédra, how fare you?" I asked.

"We are well, Idai, and we are here!" He sounded quite pleased. *"The castle rises above a huge lake right at the edge of the mountains. If you veer north-by-west when the lake appears the size of a soulgem, fly a double hand of heartbeats then roll a quarter right, you will find yourself above a long curving valley between two ridges. At the end of the valley is a grassy field, almost like the Summer Plain. There is a waterfall to the south and a little stream running from it."*

"Have you spied out the land around the castle?" I asked.

"I considered it, Lady," Kédra replied, *"but it is still light. Surely it is best if we are not seen?"*

"True. Ah, well," I sighed. *"The moon is with us, at least, she nears the full. We must trust that it will be enough."*

"Shall we light a fire to guide you, Lady?" he asked. "I would not hazard our discovery on such a thing, for all the comfort it would bring."

"If our enemy can see a fire through a mountain range, we surely are doomed in any case," I replied dryly, and Kédra laughed.

"Very well, then. Come to the fire, and bring my poor father as swiftly as you may. He will be suffering agonies at this enforced silence!"

I sent a swift thought to Shikrar, no more than "all is well," and shut my mind to him. Our plans, such as they were, would not take long to communicate to him once we came to land.

It seemed likely that all would be over and done by the morrow's sunset. I shuddered, making Aral and Vilkas cling more tightly to my foreclaws, the poor souls. I longed to turn from this path, fly on powerful wings in any direction that did not take us to our fate.

I could no more turn away than fly on my back. Our path was determined when the first Kantri who ever breathed chose order over chaos: thus we balance the Rakshasa, our life-enemies, who chose the path of chaos. The poor doomed Trelli chose not to choose, and they have vanished from the world. The Gedri alone among the Four Peoples from the dawn of life had chosen choice itself—each individual soul was free to decide if it would follow order or chaos.

The Kantri could no more abandon the Dhrenagan to their fate than walk on water. We are bound, by blood, by honour, by our very nature, to stand by them.

I took some comfort in the knowledge that for all the suffering the Lost had endured, for all those endless years of captivity, the balance that is in all things decreed that there was a terrible price yet to be paid. I for one intended to make sure that the Demonlord and that Rakshadakh Berys paid it as painfully as possible.

It did occur to me that the battle that loomed before us could be a blessing from the Winds, in a strange way. As if we were being given the chance to undo the great evil that had created the Lost all those long ages ago.

It eased my heart to think that, at least.

Berys

I have slept nearly a full day. The sun was setting when at last I opened my eyes, fully rested and ready to welcome the Demonlord. I sent a Rikti to find out when he would arrive. The useless creature said that he could see the East Mountains only as a mist in the distance, and that it was not possible that he should arrive before the morning.

"What delays you?" I demanded sharply. "Are you lost? Have you fought the Kantri again though I forbade you?"

"I haven't fought them, but what should I do when the damn things throw themselves at me?" he complained. "There have been at least half a dozen of them that couldn't resist the urge to kill themselves today." I could hear the pleasure in his voice. "I have let this body do most of the work. They do burn nicely."

"Are all the Kantri close to you?" I asked. "Do they follow you or precede you or fly by your side?"

"Damned if I know," he said, snorting. "I've been flying through mist and rain and cloud most of the day. Until the last half hour I have only seen the ones who attack. The rest could be anywhere."

"The skies are clearer now?" I asked.

"Yes, enough at least to know I can't see a trace of a dragon, but clouds still obscure the moon. Even now I can barely see to fly."

"I care not for your excuses. Keep coming. On the whole, I would rather you got here before the Kantri."

"I don't know why you are concerned about them," he replied. "They are just as stupid now as they ever were. They are doing now exactly as they did then, throwing their little lives away in a temper." He laughed briefly.

"Are you entirely stupid, or have you forgotten how to count?" I snarled. "Only six of them! There are hundreds more left."

"There would not be if you would let me engage them."

"Patience, foolish one. You are not yet at half the strength I have prepared for you. Get you here as swiftly as you may. This castle is vulnerable without you to serve as my guard."

"Guard! Little demon-spit, you have much to learn," he hissed. "I come because you promise me the Kantri, all together, all at my mercy."

"You bore me," I said, yawning. "Boasting is so tedious. You come because you are bound to my service, whatever your pride might wish were the case. Come swiftly and be ready to destroy the Kantri. If they are not here before you, they will not be far behind."

"I have been ready to destroy the Kantri for thousands of years," he snarled. "Let them come when they will. I will throw them from the sky, each and every, until they fall upon the earth like drops of rain. I will tear their souls from them and take them back with me to the deepest Hell, there to feast upon that rich harvest down the long ages."

I had never asked, and I was curious. "You were man, you are now demon for the most part—how long do you expect to live?"

In a low, drawn-out voice, it replied, "Forever."

Lanen

I have to say, it's quite handy travelling with the Kantri. True, we were all still damp and cold from the morning's rain, but if you ever want to get warm fast, talk to a dragon. Gyrentikh, who seemed to be enjoying the adventure, brought a young mast for firewood, broke it up, and lit it as well. Dragonfire burns hotter than normal fire, so the wood was consumed swiftly until it settled down to being normal flames, but that first blast of heat was more than welcome. Still, I'd have given a great deal for a hot bath.

While the Kantri were making their preparations, we humans all sat around the fire and tried to come up with some way of taking Berys out of action. Maran used the Farseer to check on him, and the image was the last one any of us wanted to see. He stood

before a makeshift altar, obviously preparing something important, and all around him fluttered a small army of Rikti and a few
Rakshi fetching and carrying. Jamie cursed and Rella shook her
head. "That's work for the Kantri," she said. "I'd happily carve
Berys into steaks, but I couldn't get anywhere near him like
that."

We all looked to the Healers. Will and Aral looked to Vilkas,
who sat very still indeed. It was left to Varien to ask, "What say
you to that, Mage Vilkas?" His voice he kept carefully neutral.
"Can you do aught to dispel those creatures?"

He took a long time to answer. "Yes, I can," he said, "but
whether I will be able to do so on demand tomorrow is another
question." He frowned. "I cannot in all conscience let you make
any plans depending on my abilities," he said calmly. "I cannot
give you my assurance that I will be able to do anything at all
about Berys's demons."

Aral opened her mouth to protest, but Will put his hand on her
arm and she held her peace.

Varien nodded. "It is as well we know this now, Mage Vilkas. I
appreciate your honesty." He glanced around the circle. "The
Kantri have said that they will bear us to a hill near the side of the
lake tomorrow morning, that we may see with our own eyes
everything that occurs. We should keep well away from the water's edge."

"Damn it, man, do you mean that we are to do *nothing* tomorrow?" cried Jamie. "If Berys is left to work unchallenged we will
all be the worse for it. Surely there is some way, between the
eight of us, that we can defeat enough demons to at least distract
Berys."

Aral began to protest, as did Rella. Vilkas scowled at everyone.

The most peculiar idea occurred to me.

"What if *Berys* were attacked by a demon?" I asked loudly.

Well, it got their attention, but not a soul there looked pleased
at the idea. Vilkas glared at me and said sternly, "Mistress Lanen,
do you tell me that you are versed in the summoning of the creatures? I would be surprised to hear it."

"Of course not," I snapped. "Only Healers can call the things, surely. I thought that perhaps you—I mean—uh—"

Vilkas's and Aral's brows were two black thunderclouds, and I was hugely relieved that it was Aral who spoke first.

"No, Lanen. Anyone can call them." Her eyes were hard as stone. "All it takes is a blood oath in which you revile the Lady and reject Her utterly. I'd rather not, thanks. Are you volunteering?"

My mother stood, slowly, and opened her mouth.

Jamie, not seeing her, said, "Lanen, it is an entrancing idea, to burn him with his own fire, but there are some ways closed to us. Would you rid a kingdom of a despot by torturing his subjects into rebellion? We cannot so debase ourselves as to use demons. We would be no better than Berys."

Maran turned and wandered off, as if to stretch her legs, but I knew perfectly well that she had meant to offer herself and risk her soul as a demon-caller. I wasn't certain whether I was proud of her courage or worried that she had so low an opinion of her own worth.

A few more idiotic ideas were put forward and demolished, until finally Will spoke up. "The truth is," he said practically, "that none of us wants to admit that we're useless in this." He stood and paced a little. "Believe me, I find this as maddening as you do, Master Jamie, but—I at least admit that I am completely out of my depth."

Maran, composed again, returned to the circle of firelight. Will continued. "I'm a decent hand with a longstaff and not a bad shot with bow and arrow, but I don't have either, and in any case a bit of wood isn't going to bother a demon. And I shouldn't think Berys would leave himself vulnerable to physical attack."

"He has before," said Jamie.

"When?" asked Vilkas, quick and sharp.

Jamie sighed and then grinned up at Will. "Twenty-five years ago, I suppose it was. You don't reckon he's learned anything in the meantime, do you?"

"Even if he hasn't, we'd have to get to him first," said Rella practically. "I suppose one of the Kantri could drop us fairly near the castle, if we had any idea of being useful, but I'd hate to give the bastard a chance of taking any of us prisoner again." She sighed. "I'm afraid we're just going to have to wait tomorrow. Wait and watch." Jamie began to protest, but she silenced him. "I don't like it any better than you do! But unless you can think of something we can be sure of accomplishing, we will best serve our cause by keeping out of the way. I shall keep my sword loose in its sheath and my wits sharp about me, but to throw ourselves into Berys's path unprepared is surely the worst kind of folly."

"I wish you were wrong," said Maran heavily, "but I know better. Goddess, to come so far and be so helpless!"

"Do not despair, Lady Maran," said Varien, smiling grimly. "The day lies before us, and nothing in this world is certain before it happens. It may be that we will all have something to do before the end."

With that we all had to be content. The rest settled down to sleep for what was left of the night. Varien and I walked along to the little waterfall arm in arm, taking our time in the starlight, walking in silence. The water sang a merry tune as it fell, heedless alike of demons and dragons, and it comforted me. Varien walked beside me, silent still, but I swear I could feel something rising in his soul. I just couldn't tell what it was.

"Varien, love, how fare you?" I asked him, finally. "Funny how I have grown so dependent on truespeech so quickly. I would bespeak you if I thought Marik wouldn't hear, but—"

"To the Hells with Marik," said Varien roughly, taking me in his arms. He kissed me passionately, desperately, and I could feel his mind singing in mine, a counterpoint to the whispered endearments so wild and intense that I grew giddy. "Lanen, *kadreshi*, beloved, *beloved*." He all but sang the words. "Come, my dearling, come, hold me, let me feel your dear arms about me. Bear me up this night, beloved, of your gentle mercy, for my heart is weary unto death with care and thou art my only rest."

We kissed and clung to one another and the world went away, just for those few moments. Alas that such distractions could not last.

Varien suddenly broke away and started walking, as if he would walk away from the dread in his soul. I kept pace with him, trying not to feel hurt that my love and care were not enough. "My heart tells me that this could be the last night that there are Kantri in the world, Lanen," he said bitterly. "On the Isle of Exile I often worried that there were so few born to us. It seemed to me that in several generations, perhaps as long again as it has been since the last coming of the Demonlord, we might be no more, and that was a dark evil." His voice was like a whip, but it was himself he was lashing. "And behold! I fall in love with you, I choose change rather than death, the world seems brighter than it ever has been—and now all my people face death on the morrow. All of us, even the Lost, Restored for a paltry few days and lost again forever because of me!"

I grabbed his arm and stopped him. He sought to tear himself loose but before he could I slapped his cheek. Not hard, just enough to shake him out of himself.

"Don't be so damned full of yourself," I snapped angrily. Bloody dragon. "If we had never met, if I languished still in Hadronsstead, do you think your island would somehow yet be above the waves? Nonsense. The Kantri would still be here in Kolmar, Berys would still have summoned that damned Black Dragon, and here you would be, all of you, just as we are now." I let go his arm. "The only real differences would be that the Lost would still be lost, the Lesser Kindred would still be asleep on the borders of reason, and—I wouldn't be carrying your children."

"And you would not be here, in terrible danger, carrying our children," he echoed, all contrition. He wrapped me again in his arms. "Oh, Lanen, how do you bear it?" he murmured into my ear.

"One breath at a time, my love," I said, holding on to anger that I might not weep. "One breath at a time."

We walked slowly back to the fire. The Kantri had begun to return by that time, and I felt safe enough to rest. We lay near the fire beside Idai. I had no idea what lay ahead, though I dreaded it—but for that moment I was content to sleep beside my husband, held close in each other's arms.

One breath at a time.

Kédra

We did not even seek to rest until the moon began to sink, weary, towards the mountains. Our plans were laid, our preparations, such as they were, completed. We would fight fire with earth, air, and water. I think that none of us truly believed we could prevail, yet still we worked deep into the night, flying by moonlight, piling the largest boulders we could lift into a cairn on the flat top of a low hill beside Lake Gand. Idai and I found a small wood that would serve our purpose, and made certain that as many knew of its location as possible.

A few of the Dhrenagan yet kept pace with the Black Dragon, still several hundred leagues away and not likely to arrive before morning, but for the most part they joined us that night. Nearly.

Naikenna it was who thought to use smoke to our advantage. She was saddened by the deaths of her people, but the Dhrenagan as a whole had given themselves up to the single purpose of destroying the Demonlord.

I found it both frightening and deeply distressing. They would not be swayed by reason. I had never seen that in our people before. They would not keep close company with us that night either, because of the Gedri among us. I saw the hatred in some minds, the barely controlled longing to destroy any human merely for the crime of being of the same race as the Demonlord had been. It did not bode well for our future in this place. I spoke to Lanen, and we ensured that all of the Gedri slept within the protection of at least one of the Kantri, lest any of the Dhrenagan be moved to seek revenge in the night.

When at last all was done that could be done, I joined my father and Idai, Gyrentikh and Alikírikh. The four of them watched over the Gedri most dear to me—Varien and his Lady, Lanen Kaelar, who had saved my beloved and my son. The humans had talked long into the night, but now they all slept near the fire. There was Vilkas Fire-soul and Aral the Valiant, who together had saved my father; there the Lady Rella and her dear one, Lanen's Jamie; and there a little apart, Maran Irongrip and Will the Golden.

The night was growing old. The stars in their ordered dance wheeled steadily above us, to the music of the nearby waterfall. There was a bird that sang as well that night, all the night long. I had never heard a night bird or its lovely, liquid song before, but it soothed my spirit as much as anything could. There was no more to be done but wait until the morning. Gyrentikh and Alikírikh were obviously using truespeech so as not to wake the Gedri.

My father, though, was restless. He could not settle after the work was done. I knew how he felt. The morrow held battle, something only the Dhrenagan had known. The prospect of severe injury, of death, of maiming, was very much in my mind no matter what I did to ignore it.

Finally he stood and left the circle of firelight. I followed him, a little way down the valley. The sky was still bright with moonlight, though she would set very soon.

"Will it ease your heart to speak, my father?" I asked quietly.

"Ah, Kédra," he replied wearily. "This night is as long as years." He stood in Sorrow, and his eyes were solemn. He did not say more but, to my astonishment, came near to me and gently twined his neck with mine.

It is a family gesture, parent to child. He had not touched me so since my mother Yrais went to sleep on the Winds. I was deeply moved. The gesture brought back a hundred memories, of the time when my mother still lived, of a time when my greatest concern was how soon he would teach me to fly. A hundred Midwinter fires blazed in my heart, when in the way of our people we sang together a song of home and family, of a love deeper than time that would never fail, love stronger than death.

It was at that moment I knew. He was saying good-bye.

"No, Father!" I cried, pulling away. "No, you can't believe a legend! It's foolishness." I tried to keep my wings from rattling with my agitation. "Why should you not prevail with all of us, Kantri and Dhrenagan, to fight beside you?"

"Kédra," he said softly, "this has nought to do with the legend." His Attitude softened. "As it happens, I think it very likely that we may prevail tomorrow, if the Winds are blowing our way, and the Gedri may well prove the turning point. Akhor's folly, that brought us Lanen and those around her, may prove our salvation." He sighed. "Alas, my son, I have seen this place in my Weh dreams."

"No," I breathed, stricken.

"Time and again, Kédra. Four times, and each ends in much the same way. I know what awaits me."

My heart dropped like a stone. I could only shake my head. *No no no no no.*

"I do not know all that will happen tomorrow, and by all the Winds I will fight with every drop of my strength, but"—he gazed then upon me with such naked love in his glance that I could hardly bear it—"it is in my heart, my dear son, you whom I love most in all the world, that I am going to die tomorrow. I would not leave without saying farewell."

I could hardly breathe. I knew somehow, deep in my heart I knew that he spoke bitter truth. I tried to deny it, I longed to deny it, but the words would not come.

"You know that you have been the light of my soul since the day you were born, Kédra," he said gently. "That has never changed, nor the light ever dimmed. Know that, remember it, and know that no matter what happens to me, a father's love never dies. I simply go before you to sleep on the Winds, and when after long years your time here is done I will be there to greet you in the Star Home, the Wind's Home, the place of all Songs, with your mother at my side."

"Father," I choked out, through a throat painfully tight. "Must this be?"

"It *will* be," he said gravely. "I know not precisely how it will come to pass, but—it is battle. I may not be able to speak with you when the time comes."

And at last his calm resolve cracked, and he bowed his head, and I saw that he was weeping.

We are creatures of fire. Tears are agony to us. We only weep when our hearts are wrung beyond bearing.

In a moment he looked up again, gazing into my eyes, his voice barely a whisper. "I say farewell to you now, my dearest son. I pray you, give me your farewell in return, that I may know you have heard the truth I tell you."

I could not, just then. My heart was too full. "Not yet," I whispered. "Not yet, I beg you, while night covers us."

He nodded. "Until dawn, then."

While darkness lasted we lay close together, my father curled around me for comfort, as around a youngling. We spoke of so many things: of memories, of hopes, of sorrow and of delight. Of life and death. Time seemed to spin around us, unheeding, as my heart begged it to slow, to stop, just for one more moment.

At last, away to the east, light began to creep silently into the darkness. It spread like water, slowly washing away the night, until false dawn filled the sky. For the first and only time in my life, I cursed the dawn.

We both fell silent, and my father looked to me. Waiting.

I would have given my wings to deny the truth of what he had said. I longed for him to be mistaken, for him to live long years yet with me—but I knew that my father was the truest creature I had ever known. To deny his truth was to deny him, and that I could not do.

"Farewell, my father," I whispered, barely able to speak. "May the Winds bear you up."

He touched his soulgem to mine and we stood thus in communion for a long moment while day grew broad about us. Then he drew back, nodded to me, and turned to rejoin the others, who were rousing with the dawn.

That moment has remained with me all the days of my life.

Even now, as I stand here removed by so many years, I can feel his soulgem against mine, a benison beyond words. These moments shape our lives.

I am glad I had the chance to say good-bye.

Aral

"Vil?"

"Mmm?"

"Vil, you can't ignore it. Tomorrow."

"Oh, yes I can," he replied, both eyes still tight shut.

"What will you do, Vilkas?" I asked, keeping my voice neutral. "When the demons come?"

"I'll be able to decide then, because I will have had some sleep," he growled. "Not much, but some. Please, do shut up."

I said no more and he feigned sleep for ages, until at last exhaustion claimed him.

I would not have had his dreams for all the world.

The Wind of the Unknown

Berys

Marik arrived just after dawn, nicely annoyed.

"What the Hells do you think you're doing, sending for me at this time of day!" he yelled as he strode through the door of my rooms. I smiled.

"Good morning, Marik. I thought you would like to join me for breakfast," I said. "I thought we might venture to celebrate this morning."

"This is *my* home, Berys. In future please assume that I will seek you out if I want to talk to you, and I bloody well won't at this time of day." He threw himself into a chair and helped himself to food. He made quite a good meal of it. Very appropriate, I thought, considering.

"Have the dragons said anything of interest?" I enquired.

"Not a damn thing they couldn't have said aloud." He grinned, wolfishly. "Though one of them at least is nicely miserable. Weary at heart, it seems, poor bastard that he is." He took a savage bite of bread and butter. "So, what news of your flying friend?"

"The Demonlord is nearly upon us, I am delighted to say. He

reported this morning that he neared the mountains. I expect him here within the hour."

"Well, better late than not at all," Marik said easily. "Tell me, is he going to start killing the Kantri right away, or do we have to feed him first?"

"He must be fed," I said.

"What does a creature like that eat?" he asked, draining his cup of chélan.

"People, for preference," I replied. "Specifically—you."

Marik stared at me for a moment and then laughed.

"Hells, Berys, I thought you bloody meant it!" he crowed. I smiled at him.

"Come on then, tell me," he said, brushing the crumbs from his lap. "What does it really eat? If I need to send for a cow or six, it will take a little time."

"No, Marik," I said cheerfully. "I meant what I said. It's going to eat *you*. Oh, perhaps not physically, that depends on what it feels like, but you are going to feed it."

"What, yet more blood?" he asked, annoyed, and entirely incapable of believing what I said to him. It was delightful. "This grows old. I'm amazed you have anything at all in your veins."

"Come into the courtyard," I replied, rising, and calling over my shoulder as I left, "I will await you."

Marik

I waited for Berys to go, waited a moment longer lest he be listening outside the door, and slipped out through the hidden door in his bedchamber.

I'm not a complete fool. I grew up here, I know every foot of this castle, and I'd had him put in these rooms for a very good reason. It's one of only three that connect to the concealed passageways between the walls. You can go practically anywhere in the place, including out. I was soon scrambling out the little concealed door and up into the mountains. Hells' teeth, he was going to feed me to that damn thing without another thought! Me!

Bastard. He'd pay for that in time, but first I had to get a very long way away.

A voice rang in my head.

"It comes! Rise up, my people!"

I cursed and hurried on. *Stop bloody posturing and get on with it,* I thought wildly. *Bloody dragons! If you'd just damn well kill the thing I may live to see another day.*

"Bloody hellsfire! Marik?"

What the—somebody *heard* me?

Lanen

We rose just after dawn, not that anyone slept much, and broke our fast together. Shikrar and Idai took wing to see that all was prepared, and Maran announced that she was going over to the waterfall to have a quick word with the Lady and if anyone wanted to join her they'd be welcome. Vilkas and Aral wandered along, and after a moment so did I.

We said little, each in the privacy of our own minds addressing the Goddess. Being so near a waterfall, of course, the Laughing Girl of the Waters was uppermost in my mind. It seemed odd, addressing so weighty a subject as battle to the lightness of Mother Shia, but somehow it cheered me. If the Mother of us All had sent us the Laughing Girl, perhaps it was to remind us of hope. That's how I chose to think of it, in any case.

Aral was deeply moved, kneeling, her hands cradling the leather bag around her throat that held the soulgem of some lost Kantri, and her corona surrounded her for a moment as she prayed. To my surprise, her power was no longer plain blue; it was still bright and clear, but there was a depth of colour that suggested purple. I had seen corrupted Healer's power. This seemed the opposite.

My mother Maran seemed to have a very rough and ready approach—she didn't kneel, she didn't even stop moving, just kept walking back and forth in front of the little waterfall, muttering, gesturing, as if she were addressing someone who stood beside her. An impulse took me—I'm sure it was because of the danger we all faced, rather than a kick from the Goddess, but I went up to Maran, stopped her for a moment, and kissed her cheek. Just like a daughter.

Tears sprang into her eyes, sudden as a spring shower, and she wrapped her arms about me. "Oh, Lanen," she said, just for a moment holding me close. "Bless you for that."

Our devotions were soon done, and as we walked back to rejoin the others I happened to glance at Vilkas. I never meant to look at him with my new depth of vision, but so it was. I shuddered. I had once watched a travelling silversmith ply his trade, and I swear that under the surface Vilkas was like nothing on earth more than molten metal burning off impurities; white-hot and boiling, dangerous, beautiful, and waiting to be shaped by the hand of the maker. How he could bear it I will never know.

And suddenly a clarion call ringing in my mind.

"It comes!" cried Shikrar. *"Rise up, my people!"*

We started running when to my amazement I heard another voice.

Stop bloody posturing and get on with it. Bloody dragons! If you'd just damn well kill the thing I may live to see another day.

A voice I had heard before, but never with my mind. *"Bloody hellsfire! Marik?"*

"My name somebody heard me Hells what is this?"

His mindvoice was shrill with panic. Varien waited beside Idai, who was to bear us to a safe place on the far side of the mountains. I took Varien's hand and opened my mind to his.

"It's Lanen, Marik. You said you could only hear."

"It was true up to this moment where are you how can you hear me?"

"Can you hear him?" I asked Varien as we scrambled with Vil and Aral into Idai's impatient hands. The instant we were all together Idai launched herself skyward, throwing us all off balance.

"Hear who?" shouted Varien, struggling to keep his footing.

"Marik!" I yelled.

Varien obviously couldn't hear what I was saying: it wasn't

worth trying to talk. Idai and Gyrentikh were flying as fast as they could, but because there are no thermals so early in the day they were having to fly to the end of the mountain ridge, south and a long way west of where they wanted to be, then back around east and north to Lake Gand. It was sheer hard work. It didn't help that they were also burdened with the eight of us.

However, it did mean that we saw the arrival of the Black Dragon. It headed straight for the castle nestled up against the mountains' roots. Castle Gundar. My father's home.

It was not alone. Behind it, above it, flew many of the Dhrenagankantri. They watched closely as it aimed itself directly at the castle, then held back. They all knew the basics of the plan of attack, and praise Shia there didn't seem to be any more of them who desired death so strongly that they must needs pursue it.

We came to ground on a hilltop, near the shore of Lake Gand. Idai dropped us as gently as she could as she came to land. She did not rest, but launched herself immediately off the edge and aloft again. Gyrentikh did the same before joining the gathering cloud of Kantri.

Idai swooped past then, returning with the last and largest boulder to lay on top of a cairn of stones that she and many others had carried from the mountains' feet by moonlight in the small hours. Many of the Dhrenagan and the Kantri took this fleeting moment of quiet to fly into the mountains, searching, taking this brief chance to learn the lay of the land in daylight.

We all watched as the black thing circled and landed behind the high walls of the courtyard. It barely fit. Even as we prepared, insofar as we could, we could see its wing joints above the walls.

"The Winds and the Lady help us all," I muttered.

Varien stood at my side and put his arm around my shoulders. "They will, surely," he said.

"I'm glad you think so," murmured Rella. "In my experience they tend to stay well out of such things."

Varien gazed unblinking at the distant creature. "The Wind of Change has blown over us, the Wind of Shaping we have been part of," he said quietly. "This is the Unknown, *kadreshi*. It is the hardest to bear."

"You Gedri keep away from the lake," said Idai's mindvoice in our heads. *"It begins. Keep well back. We will fight the better for not having you to worry over."*

Speaking of worrying. "Varien, before Idai brought us, did you hear—" I began.

Then I heard him again, Marik, my father. His thoughts spilled into my mind. I tried to shut him out, but no matter what I did his voice was there. Goddess, it was terrible.

Berys

When Marik didn't follow me, I raised the alarm. His castle, after all, his people. "Your master is missing. His mind is not stable, he has not been well, help me find him, there are *dragons* out there!"

The presence of the dragons had not escaped the denizens of Castle Gundar. They were petrified, and only Marik's reassurance stood between them and panic. They were desperate to get him back.

I was seriously annoyed with Marik. Of all times to develop an independent mind! No, I was not amused at all. Fortunately one of his old family retainers came forward—one Mistress Kiri—and told me that as a child he used to be fond of the hills, and when he went missing they would always find him in a certain place.

I was impatient. Waiting in the main courtyard of the castle, I called up a Messenger Rikti and sent to the Demonlord.

"Your future has escaped into the mountains," I said without preamble.

"My future lies where I choose, demon-spit. What are you on about?"

"I have a soul here, ready to join with you and make you less dependent on my power," I said. "But the current owner has escaped."

"Why are you telling me this, fool? To expose your weakness before I have a chance to find it out myself?"

"Don't waste time. Legend calls you Demonlord, with power over every Raksha ever spawned."

"Only the Lord of the Last Hell does not owe me homage," it said smugly.

"Then send me a winged Raksha to fetch me your soul carrier," I demanded.

"Why should I use my power to assist you, little demon-spit?" it asked haughtily.

"I will waste no more time in debate," I growled. With a thought I was in the realm of the spirit, where Healers see all things in metaphor. There soared the Demonlord like a vast high-flying hawk. A tethered hawk. The line was woven of all the binding spells I had cast about him: it was interwoven with cruel spikes, poised upon his back to cut him to the bone should he disobey me, and the line led to my hand. I had made the binding tight and true: he could not shake it off, try though he might. I grasped my hand about the tether and pulled. Hard.

The spikes of the bargain he had agreed to were driven into his flesh. He screamed, and with my real ears I heard a distant dragon roar. It was good.

"Bound to me, in bonds unbreakable. Do as I bid you or suffer more," I commanded.

"I am not a demon, fool!" it cried.

I pulled the binding leash again.

"I don't give a damn what you think you are. Do my bidding as was agreed, or suffer the True Death."

It laughed, even in its pain. "You cannot threaten me with that! My life is as safe as ever it was."

"Your life is in your heart, which you bear even now within your form."

It laughed again. "Fool! Do you think the power of the Distant Heart is in its physical location? There is only one creature in all the world and time that can inflict the True Death upon me. It is the stricture to the spell, and you know it not."

I smiled as I pulled the binding tighter. "Fool, thrice fool and damned! I know exactly what is required, and I have her under my hand: she who, when cut, bleeds both Kantri and Gedri blood."

The Demonlord reeled, in the realm of the spirit. Luckily my mind was closed to him, at least enough that he could not see that I did not physically have her by me. Enough that I knew the stricture and had a demonline to her. I knew I could take her when I needed her, and that is all he would see in my mind.

"If you are done with your posturing, send me a Raksha to bear to me my prey," I growled at him. He cursed and spat and writhed in the bindings, prophesying my sudden demise—and sent me a Raksha.

"Fetch Marik," I told it. "He will be in these hills. A man, running away from this place."

"Too many Kantri!" it cried. I'd never seen a Raksha terrified. Interesting, but I had no time for this.

"Then fly low and find him swiftly," I retorted. "Go!"

It flapped up to the wall, looked about, and took off towards the southeast.

I stood alone in the courtyard, drew my poniard, and waited.

Marik

Height. Must get higher, so I can see and not be seen. I can't shake the feeling that Lanen is right behind me, but I've looked back ten times and she is not there. My mind is playing tricks.

My mind. How did I get to this place? I was steadily gaining wealth, I was doing well as a merchant, then Berys came along and I made that damned Farseer and my life was ruined. I'd never have been as rich as I am, but who knows, Marik, you might have lived longer, eh?

There is no pursuit. Hells! I'm not as young as I was, I can't run up the side of a mountain without catching my breath. Damn—but I've come a long way up, he'll have a job finding me—what's that over the castle—oh, *Hells*.

It's the sodding dragon. It's too big to be alive, nothing that big should be able to move. It's circling to land, it's—

Damn it what's that something's got *hold* of me

it's a demon NO *NO* Let me go damn you let go of me oh *Hells* we're *flying!*

It's taking me back. I just came all that way I got away I was nearly away it's taking me BACK—to Berys, Berys is standing there in my courtyard smiling, and the dragon is waiting.

I'm struggling against the demon but I can't get away, the second it drops me one of Berys's own guards holds me, I kick I fight to get free but it's done—

Oh, shit.

A second of pain, a deep thrust with a knife like a terrible needle—the sight of it sticking out of my chest is surprising, my heart stumbles and stops—thought flies away, it's like a dream my mind is loosed my body drops away I'm free at last . . .

Gahhhh!

I was dead. I know it. Dead, just now. A terrible, eternal, burning moment of pain, and then freedom. No more agony, no madness, no fear. No self. It was—comforting.

But Berys has dragged me back, half healed. Hells, the agony! I cannot breathe, my chest is on fire—and Berys is calling my name. I ignore him, but am forced to open my eyes. He is standing above me, smiling.

"Ah, Marik, welcome back," he says happily. I struggle, I long to leap up and throttle him, but I cannot move. "Just in time. Here is your soul mate. I hope you like him."

Something huge has fallen to earth behind me, with a great commotion and a gust of hot air. The Black Dragon. The Demonlord. It is so near I can see its eyes, but I cannot focus for more than an instant, the pain is everywhere. I cry out with it but nothing happens. I force myself to look at the creature, take my mind off the searing agony in my body.

Close to like this, it seems to be no more than a thin shell over something that flows horribly beneath the surface, ever changing. And it is hot, a haze rises from it, it bleeds heat like a hundred days of summer violently crushed into one, scorching heat streams from it, merciless, more cruel than death.

Berys is chanting. Why isn't he healing me, the bastard? The thing seems to nod in reply to Berys, while I lie here in agony, dying again as they go through some stupid ritual. And at last, here again is Berys. He is speaking to me.

"You are chosen, Marik of Gundar. Your soul will blend with the Demonlord, you will fly with him, you can kill every dragon ever spawned. Do you consent?" he asks, as unconcerned as if he asked about the weather.

"Let me die, you bastard!" I scream.

"No, no, we must have consent," says Berys evenly, as if he corrected an errant child. "That is the way to end the pain, Marik."

Pain pulses through me, endless, agonizing. I half open one eye—he's keeping me alive, bastard, I can see the thin stream of healing—not enough to do any more than keep me on this rack. "Bastard," I croak. "Let me go!"

"Consent, Marik," he says, "or you will live forever."

I can barely hear him. What is he saying? Consent. Forever. The prospect of living another instant is torture upon torture.

He wants me to say I consent to something. What was it?

I don't know. I don't care. I will say anything that will end this torment.

"I consent, I consent, damn you forever let me *die*!" I scream, my voice thin—but it is enough.

A voice unimaginably deep rumbles through the courtyard, shaking through me. "Your wish, brother, is my command," says the great black beast.

No!

It reaches for me, I am lifted from the ground, I can smell the burning and hear the sizzle of my flesh where its skin touches mine.

I turn my face away, towards the cool blue sky, and close my eyes on my last glimpse of the world of life, as I am pulled through that thin shell and into the body of the beast. AAhhhh, it burns, it burns—but what . . .?

Marik/The Black Dragon

And behold, we are one. I-Demonlord I-Marik, we are in one body, powerful, free of pain. As we are joined, I-Demonlord find a mind not unlike my own—weaker, unstable, but not so very different in kind, and rather than send that half screaming down into madness I listen to it and we both learn. We are one, and we have a soul again.

I-Demonlord realise immediately that this poses a problem. The Distant Heart spell requires that the heart cannot inhabit a body that has a soul. If that should come to pass, the heart would become mortal once more.

Swiftly I-Demonlord reach into my chest and remove the Distant Heart from the molten rock of my being. It shines in my claws, an unlovely thing the shape and size of a human heart turned to silver-black stone. It remains unchanged: I have acted in time. Berys's eyes glitter. Ah, yes, he would see this as a desirable object.

I leap into the sky. The mountains here are high and perilous and the range extends over a huge area. I can drop the heart somewhere in the trackless heights for now. I will find it a safer resting place later.

For the second time in this hour, I feel the force of Berys's binding spell like spikes driven deep into my soul. This body cannot feel pain, but he is not working in the realm of the physical.

He's a clever bastard.

Berys

"Back you come," I declare, pulling the binding tether. It rages, it spits fire at me that slides off the shield I have raised against it, it screams defiance.

"For one reputed to be so wise, you are an arrant fool," I say.

"Whatever your pride may make of things, you are bound to me."
I feel a triumphant grin stealing on to my face. "And by the power
of that binding, I tell you that I will not release you to the pleasure of destroying the Kantri unless you leave that ugly silver-
black lump of stone with me."

It hisses like ten thousand serpents. "You cannot force me to
this!" it cries.

"Fool, I tell you I can," I respond. I jerk on the binding, driving the spikes of the spell ever deeper into the tender flesh of the
bound soul. "You required my living hand for the binding spell,
Demonlord. Blood and bone binds deep." I dropped my calm
mask and growled, "Give to me your Distant Heart, Demonlord,
or I will tie the binding at its sharpest and leave it there forever."

It screams. It curses me a thousand times, it writhes, it flails
about—but it knows that I have spoken truth. At last, the agony
wins over its defiance. It flings the Distant Heart at my feet.

"Thank you," I say to it, secreting the thing in a deep inner
pocket of my garments. "I was certain that you would see reason.
Fear not," I add. "I will put it somewhere very safe indeed when
time allows."

It tries to tear me with its teeth. I shrug it off.

Ah, life is sweet.

Marik/Demonlord

I will kill him. I will find a way, for he must sleep sometime.

For now, I-Demonlord must admit defeat. However, I-Marik
know that Berys did indeed have beneath his hand the only creature in all of time who can control me, that she is our daughter,
and that Berys has no idea where she is. I-Marik have realised
that for all our new strength we are yet bound to Berys and for
the most part controlled by him. I-Demonlord learn from my
brother that we do not know where the Lanen is, but she will not
be far from the Kantri, and once they are dead she is defenceless.
I-Marik remember that I could hear two of the Kantri, but when
we listen, there is nothing. I-Marik am truly changed.

The best we can do in the present moment is to turn to Berys and say, "You are dead, demon-spit."

"You are bound to me, beast. You serve me," he replies.

"Fool! I keep telling you that I am not a demon," I-Demonlord reply. "Your lies are made plain. She is gone out of your hands! And when she is dead, I owe you only enough allegiance not to destroy you." We laugh. "Perhaps I will leave enough of the Kantri alive to do that for me, for once she is dead I will have all the time in the world in which to destroy the few I will leave alive."

The Kantri. There, in the sky above us. If they are here, she must be as well—but for now, they stand between us and our prey. We will have to fight them. It is good. We are strong, we share thought and will, we share hatred.

We rise with a thunderclap, beating vast wings that do not grow weary, and fly straight toward the largest assembly we can see. We breathe fire upon them, and three are stricken at once. Our fire is thick and viscous, it clings to them and sears them to the bone. The three fall from the sky screaming and burn to powder before they strike the ground.

We dance on the wind with delight, just for a moment, then we scan the ground for humans—but there are too many dragons forcing us into battle. They are many, and the spell we once used works no longer to tear them from the sky. We will have to fight them—but ah, Berys never knew. We have a soul again, we are the Demonlord once more. A price once paid to demons is paid until death, and I-Demonlord have never truly died.

I can call upon six of the Seven Princes of the Hells to aid me.

Lanen

I heard every word, every thought, felt everything that Marik went through. I fell to my knees, retching, when Berys stabbed him to the heart, when Berys would not let him die and fed him to the Demonlord.

As deeply as I hated my cursed father, surely no one deserved such a fate.

Blessedly, when he merged with the Demonlord, his voice in my mind was silenced. My mother Maran was at my side, full of concern, Aral right behind her.

"Can I help?" asked Aral quickly.

"I'm alright," I said shakily. The others had gathered round. Varien gave me his hand and I pulled myself to my feet. "It's Marik. He's dead, but he's not—oh, Hells!" I cried. My gut was wracked with spasms. "There is part of him that's still alive, and it's in that great black beast. His mind has merged with the Demonlord's, it knows everything he knows or ever knew—Goddess!" I shuddered from head to toe. "There are two of them in there!"

Varien

Do not believe the songs: they were made many years later, by those who were not there.

The battle was nor glorious, nor simple, nor swift. It was hideous. It began when the Black Dragon first took to the sky, murdering three of the Dhrenagan, dancing with delight and then turning to destroy wherever it could.

Watching my people and the Restored fighting for their lives against something that breathed death, and against which our natural weapons were useless, wrung my heart and my gut until I could barely draw breath. Lanen, at my side, was hardly in a better case.

Our strategy—the strategy of all the Kantrishakrim—had been decided. The question was simple enough. How do you fight the fires of the earth? That is what the thing seemed to be made of, to our sorrow. We had never defeated the molten stone on our own Island of Exile, despite thousands of years of trying. We had often tried to drown the advance of flowing rock, but we could not carry enough water swiftly enough.

Thus the basis of our strategy for this battle. Lake Gand was deep and its waters cold, Rella had told us. Perhaps the sudden cooling of being dashed into the water would render the creature immobile. Idai had another thought, about using the Black

Dragon's poor powers of flight combined with a screen of smoke in the mountains, but that depended even more upon swift pursuit of one or more of us.

We could only hope.

Shikrar

From the moment the Black Dragon rose from the castle courtyard, it was plain that it had changed. Most noticeable, alas, was that it flew a great deal better, as though it were no longer under the control of a spell that compelled it to fly only in a straight line. It seemed more alive, less like a golem—but it was still plain that it was not a natural flying creature. That was one of our few advantages.

"All keep well apart," I said yet again, gazing down at it. The dead weight of the stone in my claws was reminding me more and more of Nikis. *"Do not present a target. Naikenna, see to your people!"* I cried, for three of the Restored had begun flying together.

It only took an instant. The Black Dragon arrowed towards them, breathed its unholy Fire onto them all three, and danced on the wind to see their deaths. I too watched, and saw the Swift Death take them all ere they could be killed by that solid fire.

Three too many, and they were only the first.

I dove at the thing, dropped my great rock onto its back, and was rewarded by seeing it lose height swiftly. However, I had managed to get its attention. *"Ready, as many as may, above the north end of the lake,"* I cried, riding up on the momentum of my dive and wheeling around towards the water. I was pursued rapidly; the thing was fast, with those huge wings, but it flew stupidly, trying to gain height in a straight line regardless of the air currents. I rolled away left and into a shallow dive, rising up again after two swift wingbeats, and felt the heat of its attack pass behind me as I gained height. When I glanced back it was slowing down—its great size and weight worked against it while climbing, despite its wingspan. Still, it was coming directly towards me. In a straight line. Over the water.

Surely it was not that stupid?

There again, I would take any advantage I could get.

I went into another dive, much steeper this time, straight at the surface of the lake—and pulled up, for the Black Dragon was no longer behind me. I had hoped that it would pursue me, that its obvious unfamiliarity with flight would betray it to simple manoeuvres, but no, it had turned away towards the northwestern shore, towards where Varien and his company of Gedri stood.

It also became apparent that even Naikenna had not taken complete account of the bone-deep hatred of the Dhrenagan for the Demonlord. Some, it is true, had barely noted the passage of time, but a few now come back to the world yet remembered being trapped, voiceless and alone, all down the long centuries. The death of their three comrades struck deep, and for all that counsel and reason might urge, our instincts incline us to physical battle.

The moment it was clear that the Black Dragon was not blindly pursuing me, a large group massed above it and all loosed their burden of stone at once. Some missed, but many struck their target, and it was forced down nearly to the surface of the water. So near, so near—

Then, of a sudden, I saw that six of the Restored were not leaving this to chance. They fell on the beast, all of them, from a great height, and like Tréshak were trapped. Also like Tréshak, they forced the creature down by their sheer weight. The moment those of my Kindred touched the thing, they began to burn, but they did not choose the Swift Death until the whole mass of them fell into the cold waters of the lake with a great hiss and a cloud of steam. The waters closed over them all, and boiled at the spot where they had fallen. I felt in my deep heart the sighs of the Restored, as they welcomed the Swift Death once their task was done.

Someone is going to have to dive into that lake to recover their soulgems when all is over, I thought stupidly as the steam cloud roiled below me. Those who had fallen upon the Black Dragon had done so in full knowledge of the price to be paid. I bowed my head and vowed in my aching heart to honour their courage and their sacrifice more formally, if I lived.

The thing was huge and made of molten stone—it must be vastly heavy, and surely only kept aloft by demonic power. It could not possibly swim. Did it need to breathe? Would it drown? Would the cold water freeze its limbs forever?

Then the steam cloud rising from the lake began to move towards the shore.

There was work yet to do. I had feared it would not be so easy. As I dove and plucked the topmost boulder from the great cairn of them we had created, I bespoke Idai.

"It is time for your plan, my friend. Set your Fire where it will do the most good, that our enemy rising from the water may be confused."

"Your words fly to the Winds and become truth," replied Idai as she led a number of the Kantri in a long line, swooping low behind the nearer hills and sending Fire into the heart of the wood they had marked by moonlight. The wood grew at the foot of a great flat cliff face that rose high above the trees. There would be an impressive updraft there on a sunny day, even before we did anything about it. In a very short time the wood was alight, a cloud of thick smoke rising into the clear air like a burnt offering for the dead. It shrouded the cliff face very effectively. If you were new-come to flight and knew not what you were doing in that maelstrom of air currents, it would be quite a hazard. With luck and the blessing of the Winds.

The water boiled in a straight line, more vigorously now, and the creature's head rose from the lake. By the time the whole creature was out of the water I soared high on the rising air, watching to see the result of our efforts and the sacrifice of our Kindred.

The Black Dragon was covered all over with strange black extrusions, some very large indeed, especially where its limbs met its body. As it walked, steaming gently, onto the shore, I saw great lumps of black stone fall away and shatter on the ground.

It was decidedly smaller. Who knew what masses of the fabric of that body had had to be discarded, gone cold and dead in contact with the water, that it might move again?

Before I could even begin to rejoice, however, before I could think what we should do next or call off those of the Restored who dove at it and hurled stone, I heard its voice. It spoke with great difficulty, as if it were not used to the shape of its mouth, but the words were clear enough, as was the malice with which it spoke.

"By the price that was paid, by my mastery, I summon thee, Ur-kathon, Prince of the Sixth Hell! Take unto thee the woman Lanen and wrap her in hellfire until her bones be ash and her heart blows away on the wind!"

xiii
Hadretikantishikrar

Lanen

We were all ranged along the edge of the hilltop when we heard the Black Dragon scream out its summons, damning me, and I learned then how much I had changed. Fear had no more power over me. I had faced hopeless despair and found fire in my soul, sacred Fire, like the Kantri whose blood I now shared. I drew the dagger Rella had provided me with, useless though it would be against even a minor demon, that I might at least face my enemy armed.

I did not stand alone. Varien's sword rang as it flew from its scabbard, making a bright harmony with Rella's and Jamie's swords as they were drawn. Vilkas and Aral stood surrounded by the blue glow of their power, and as I watched they strove to cover us all in a kind of shield. Varien, considering, nicked his arm slightly and let his blood flow onto his sword blade. Good point, I thought, and did the same for my dagger. Seems we both bled Kantri, at least in part. That seemed to work on the Rikti. It almost certainly wouldn't kill a demon prince, but if it banished the Rikti at least it might give the creature a bad taste in its mouth.

There came a deep rattle of metal on metal and I turned to find my mother, Maran, standing like the others with her long heavy sword at the ready. Against all sense she grinned at me, a wild delight in her eyes. "Well, girl, we'll likely lose," she said, her eyes fixed fondly on me, "but Hells' teeth, won't it make a good ballad!"

Even there, even then, we laughed—grim laughter, but laughter—and lo, all was changed. I knew death stalked me close, but for that moment I was surrounded by those I loved, in the free air, on a glorious morning in spring.

I reached out with truespeech.

"Varien, kadreshi na Lanen," I whispered.

"Kadreshi na Varien," he replied simply, reaching out to take my hand. His love, real and solid and unchanging, washed over me like clear water.

It was a good day to be alive.

Suddenly on the hillside there came a disturbance in the air, as though a small storm cloud were forming before our eyes. It grew swiftly until it was a dark upright oval, three times the height of a man—and from that darkness emerged a gigantic figure, the size of the portal, to stand on the very summit of the hill.

My stomach churned. It was an obscene mixture of dragon and human. It stood on two legs but from its back sprouted large leathery wings, like those of a bat. Its face was covered by a mockery of a Kantri mask—what in the Greater Kindred looked like worked metal armour, beautiful and unchanging, was here attenuated and become a threatening deformity. Great fangs protruded from its jaws, long talons tipped its hands, and it reached out for me, getting through Vilkas's barrier with no trouble at all. Vilkas cursed and dissipated it.

Jamie's sword struck the thing just after Rella's thrown dagger bounced off of it. It spat at Jamie, who had to dodge balefire.

"Nice try, Jamie," said Aral firmly, "but this one's ours."

Behind her I could see the Black Dragon leap into the sky once more, assailed by our people with every wingbeat, breathing death among the Kantri. Another fell even as I watched.

Aral, concentrating, sent a stream of blue flame to encompass the creature. The demon barely shrugged and Aral's flame winked out. Vilkas shuddered.

"Vil, help me!" cried Aral, reaching out again with her Healer's power. The thing tried to move but Aral's will opposed it, and for a moment or two it was held in place, but I watched the colour drain from her face in a heartbeat. "I can't hold it!" she cried, even as the demon prince shook itself free of her web, flapped its batlike wings, and was beside her faster than eye could follow. It wrapped one great hand around her and started to lift her towards its mouth. Will, horror-stricken, tried to hold on to her and was lifted high in the air, clinging to Aral's waist. The demon prince took only enough notice of him to toss him aside. He cried out as he fell. He struck the ground with a sickening thump and lay still.

Aral screamed as Willem fell, her voice rising unbearably at the end. *"Vilkaaas!"*

Vilkas

There was no more time for soul-searching or hesitation or fear. I watched the demon lift Aral to its mouth and I knew that what would follow even I could never heal.

I had to stop it. Now.

Time slowed to a terrible crawl, and I realised that all those dreams, all those nightmares of stepping into my full power were come upon me. I had to choose. Would I let fear decide my fate and Aral's, or would I leap into the unknown and hope for the best?

I am not well endowed with hope. It seems to elude me, for the most part.

I decided to go with love instead. I might not love Aral as a man loves a woman, but by the Lady, I knew perfectly well that she was part of my soul, and I loved her as I loved air.

It wasn't a difficult decision, on the face of it; but the next time you decide to change your life at a crucial moment, truly change it at a fundamental level, no matter how obvious the need, you will learn just how hard it is to leave what you have known. Even if what you have known is pain and anguish, it is *familiar* pain and anguish. I felt a thousand demons of doubt and fear rise up within me, *what if you destroy your friends what if you fail how many will die at your hands what if you cannot control this power once you accept it Death of the World what if-don't-what if-don't.*

I fought the real battle then, in that timeless moment, though it took less than half a breath. All those years of self-control, all the terror of that which dwelt within me, all the wildfire passion in my soul screaming to get out, burning within me now in truth as before only in dreams—

I held out my arms and chose to be whole, and for the first time in my life I raised my full power about me.

The high thick walls I had built so carefully, to protect both myself and the world, the armour so thick I could barely live within it, all, all were gone as smoke in a high wind, leaving only the searing blaze of the power that I had run from since I came of age. I was dizzy with the change, shaking at the terrible sense of nakedness as my true self settled into my body at last.

It was as if I had spent my life wandering blind, stumbling, crashing into the unseen on every side, and I had magically been given sight. It was like diving into deep cold water on a summer's day. The Lady's gift coursed through my body from head to foot, light and life and power, oh, yes, power, and I knew that this was what I was born for.

It took a moment to adjust.

It took *years*.

It was now, and Aral was nearer death, her terrified voice still caught on my name.

With a thought I immobilised the demon long enough to release Aral from its grasp and bring her safely back to solid ground. It struggled—I could feel the lash of its powerful will, and was surprised—but I was adamant.

Once she was safe, the true battle began.

Berys

Damnation! I wasn't expecting the Demonlord to do *that*. Still, those who protect her will almost certainly be able to prevail against that prince long enough for me to steal her away while they are engaged elsewhere.

Drawing out the amulet that holds the near end of the demonline, I draw my power to me and throw the amulet on the ground. Grind it with my foot. My eyes are darkened for an instant, and then the demonline is there before me, shimmering in air, connected directly to Lanen.

I step through.

Lanen

I had to turn away from Vilkas, for he was become the sun and I risked being blinded.

Just as well, for I saw Varien swinging his sword at—

"Berys!" I cried. He stood beside me and reached out to grab my arm. I aimed a kick at him but I was beaten to it by Jamie, who knocked me out of the way. He didn't even stop to consider, he just stepped in, whirled, and slashed at Berys.

Berys raised a hand. Jamie's sword bounced off the shield of Berys's power and Jamie howled with frustration.

Varien, who had missed his first stroke, strode up to Berys shouting, "He's mine!" Jamie cleared off and Varien swung back his sword and struck a horizontal blow with all his strength. Berys didn't even try to get out of the way.

I nearly fainted. I saw that huge heavy sword, driven by Varien's terrifying strength, go through the barrier as the demon prince had gone through Vilkas's. Without slowing in the slightest, Varien's sword swept right through Berys's body like a bread knife through a loaf. My husband cut Berys in half. He should have bled like a butchered cow and landed in two pieces.

Berys's eyes flew wide with shock, just for an instant, but even as I watched the wound was gone. The only trace of it was a thin line of blood along the line of the cut, all around his torso.

"Have you forgotten that I'm the best Healer in all the world?" he asked cheerfully. "You really are stupid. You can't touch me, any of you. You might as well give me the girl. She's not much to look at, it's true, but I can make use of her." He looked directly at me, so deep in his own madness that he looked absolutely normal. "You don't even know what you can do, you poor fool."

For all that the demon and the Black Dragon had frightened me, this mad immortality shook me to my bones. Staggering back from the thing that had once been Berys, I called in shaky true-speech, *"Shikrar, Idai, we need your help! Can the battle spare you?"*

"I come, Lanen," said Shikrar instantly.

Despite Berys's protection, he didn't seem inclined to throw himself on the collective swords of Jamie, Rella, Maran, and Varien to get past them to me. He frowned slightly at me. "You're going to call for help any moment now, aren't you?" he said, annoyed. Then a slow grin spread across his face and I swear his eyes twinkled.

"Tell you what. I'll go first, shall I?"

He raised his arms and cried out in a terrible voice, "Come unto me, ye legions of darkness! Come, I command thee! By my power, by my name, I, Malior, Master of the Sixth Circle, do summon to my service all ye of the deep Hells to my aid. Come swiftly!"

On the instant, the air was black with legions of the Rakshasa. I could barely see the Kantri for all the demons. There must have been twenty to every one of the Kantrishakrim.

These were not the Rikti, who could be dispelled by the touch of the Kantri's breath of Fire: these were the Rakshasa, the mirror image of the Kantri in creation, shaped roughly like winged Gedri and only slightly larger than humans. Although Kantri fire can wound them, they are much harder to kill, and although they are much smaller and do not fly as swiftly as the Kantri, they are more manoeuvrable. The Rakshasa breathe balefire as well, the only fire aside from molten stone that can wound the Kantri.

There were so *many* of them, and the Kantri so few.

For all that they were beset on every side, however, a good quarter of the Kantrishakrim would not leave off harrying the Demonlord. They flamed and fought the Rakshasa even as they pursued or enticed the Black Dragon, flying like mad things to avoid its deadly fire, those who still had them throwing those great stones at it whenever they could to try to force it to ground, or better yet to douse it once more in the deep waters of the lake.

I saw in that brief time more carnage than I could bear. The Kantri, those wise, ancient creatures, attacked from all directions by evil incarnate, fighting back with tooth and claw and the Fire that is sacred to them. So many wounded, so much of blood and agony on both sides. I have never heard that the Rakshasa ever wanted, truly, to take over the world, except in old legends. I think they were forced to it by Berys. If that was the case, every drop of blood, Rakshi and Kantri, was on his soul.

And suddenly there was a great shout and a second deep splash and boom, a second great cloud of steam. The Restored, led by Naikenna, had managed even in the midst of battle so to harry and anger the Demonlord that it had flown out over the lake once more. I saw in the instant I turned to look that some five or six of the Kantri had thrown themselves on the thing and forced it down. I could hear their agony, but there was triumph there also, and a fleeting sense of peace when they chose the Swift Death once the beast was under the surface of the lake.

Berys called out something in a sibilant speech, and a group of the Raksha came for me.

"*Shikrar, swiftly!*" I cried, in truespeech—and aloud. Would to heaven I had held my tongue. Would to heaven my tongue had withered in my mouth ere I had spoken.

Shikrar arrived, covered in wounds, and with fang and talon he bit and crushed the Rakshasa who threatened us, ignoring the fresh cuts they inflicted on him. He spat, when he was done, and turning to Varien said, "It tastes worse even than you remember." Varien grinned up at him.

Then to my astonishment, Berys spoke. He had been watching

the battle with delight, distracted perhaps, or perhaps simply keeping out of the way of Varien, Jamie, and Rella. That kind of healing must wear him out eventually, and they all three would cheerfully kill him again and again until it worked.

"You are Shikrar?" he said, looking desperately pleased with himself.

"I am, *Rakshadakh*," growled Shikrar, drawing back his head to strike.

"No," said Berys smugly. "The true name is binding, knowing the true name is power over the named, truth in essence holds the soul and thus I bind you to my will. You are *Hadretikantishikrar*, and you will be still!" Berys cried.

Shikrar froze. He was screaming in truespeech, he was fighting with his entire being, but for once in his life Berys spoke truth. The true name is the essence of the soul. He who knows the true name has a terrible power over the named. True names are kept secret, told only to a soulfriend or a loved one.

Marik had overheard Shikrar's true name when Varien bespoke Shikrar in the Language of Truth. If Shikrar and Akor had not forced open Marik's mind out on the Dragon Isle, Marik would not have been able to hear their truespeech to report to Berys. If Marik had not been trying to kill them both, they would never have done such a thing. If, if, if . . .

Berys grinned. "How delightful," he said, seeing his foe immobile. With a casual gesture, he called a hundred of his demons down to him and threw them at Shikrar.

Varien screamed, *"NO!"* and ran towards Berys, but there were too many demons in the way. Varien, my beloved, fought like a madman, but he made little headway. Too many demons. Not enough time.

"IDAI! KÉDRA! SHIKRAR NEEDS YOU NOW!" I screamed in truespeech, kicking myself that I had not called before, putting all my horror into my mind's voice, and even I could hear the underthought that ran through my call. *"Help help help he's held by his true name Berys has him quickly quickly they'll kill him help help help!"*

They flew, desperate, fury and terror driving every stroke of their wings. Time seemed to slow as I watched them approaching from two different directions. Too far away. Too slow.

Too late.

My breath stopped as I looked upon Shikrar held helpless. *No, it can't be—Goddess, help us—O ye Winds, blow that word back into Berys's mouth and let him choke on it, let it not have been spoken, oh no, oh no . . .*

The demons tore Shikrar's flesh with their teeth and with their claws and he could not fight back. He could not even cry out in pain. When they broke his wings, laughing, I heard his mind's scream, a sound that shook my bones to the marrow and drew an answering scream from my own throat. I swear that sound will haunt me every day of my life.

At the last instant, just before Idai and Kédra arrived, they broke his neck. I heard it go. My knees would no longer hold me up, and I landed hard on broken stone, gasping for air, as if I could breathe for Shikrar. My throat ached as if some great hand choked me.

Shikrar collapsed. Berys and the demons cackled, and then Berys said, "Enough of pleasure. Bring me the girl."

Vilkas

It was harder than I thought.

I reached out in all my pride and power to destroy the Prince of the Sixth Hell and found myself somewhere else entirely. I was thirteen years old and it was summer. My friend Jon and I were wrestling, as was our wont. I had him in a lock and had started to squeeze.

"Ow, Vil, too tight!" he cried. "Let go!"

"You're such a baby, Jon." I laughed, squeezing tighter. He started to choke. Suddenly I realised that I was grown furious with his weakness and had let go of my self-control. To my horror, I was on the very point of killing him before I forced myself to release him. "Jon, no, I'm sorry," I began, and the world shifted again. The demon prince laughed.

"Sssuch a fool you are," it hissed.

I threw my power at it again and found my hands clasped around Aral's throat. She was beating at my arms and kicking my legs. I squeezed tighter, and suddenly found myself unable to move. My hands were forced apart and Aral dropped back, her hands protecting her neck. She released me.

"Damn it, Vil!" she cried. "What's wrong with you!"

"Where are you from, Aral?" I shouted, convinced that she was some phantom of the demon's. "Where were you born?"

"Berún, you idiot," she snapped. "What in all the Hells is up with you? You let it go and went for me!" She pointed up to the demon prince, who was laughing again. Or still.

Once more I sent fire to envelop it, and this time there was a great light. I closed my eyes and turned away that I might not be blinded, but when next I opened my eyes, I lay in bed. Clean, crisp linen sheets, gentle sunlight at the window filtering through the young spring leaves of a rowan tree.

"Welcome back, Vilkas. You had us worried," said Magistra Erthik. She smiled, the crooked smile she saved for those moments when she was feeling most maternal. "I am glad you have come back to us. I'd rather not lose my best pupil just yet."

I sat up in the bed. I was in the infirmary at Verfaren. Magistra Erthik was alive.

"Magistra?" I asked, quietly. My throat began to close but I fought it. "What happened? Where is the demon prince?"

"Gone with your waking, young man, and not before time. You've been feverish for nearly a month." She reached out and touched my forehead. "It has truly broken at last. Thank the Goddess."

"A dream, was it?" I asked suspiciously. "What of Aral?"

"Was that someone else in your dream?" Magistra Erthik asked, politely curious.

"Stupid," I said. I called on the Goddess and sent my corona to cover Magistra Erthik, who screamed and vanished. I was back on the hillside above Lake Gand, with the demon prince almost near enough to touch. I backed away.

"Vil, what's wrong?" asked Aral frantically. "I thought—I *felt* you change, I know you aren't restricted any longer. What are you waiting for?"

"It's playing with my mind, Aral," I said quietly. "Changing time, changing appearances. Its illusions are horribly real. How shall I know truth when I see it?"

"As you ever have, Vilkas," she said, and her voice had taken on the strange cadence it sometimes did when she was speaking not entirely for herself. "Trust those who love you. Here. She wants to help. We both do."

And with that, Aral put the soulgem of Loriakeris into my right hand.

It was astounding. No wonder the Kantri are so good against the demons. I could *see* the demon prince twisting reality, changing shape, trying to govern my mind and make me drop my guard or injure myself or Aral. The touch of that ancient mind, Loriakeris of the Kantri, granted me for that brief time the vision of the Kantri and acted as a talisman of truth.

Or perhaps it was the touch of Aral's hand and soul.

I bowed my head briefly, committing myself to the Lady, and lifted my hand. Blue flame mixed with red surrounded the demon prince and swiftly constricted about it. Its screams, I am ashamed to say, were music to me. I squeezed harder. I kept expecting it to dissipate, but Berys must have performed quite a spell. It died the True Death.

In my defence, once I realised that it was not going to disappear back to its Hell I killed it swiftly. Even demons require some mercy, after all. It is their nature to bargain and they are forced to obey their master's commands.

It is people who deserve no mercy. They can choose, after all.

I turned to find Berys advancing swiftly on Lanen, a company of Rakshasa with bloody claws before him. A sight that would have moved me to frustrated terror such a short time ago. I raised my hand and Lanen was shielded from their attack.

"Take him first!" cried Berys, gesturing, and a score of demons flew at me, roaring, fanged mouths agape, talons raised to rake and rend.

I blessed them in the Lady's name and destroyed them all with Her power, flowing from me as light from the sun. It was—trivial. Berys looked on impassively, as if he were judging me.

"Berys," I said quietly, saluting one about to die.

"You're that pup Vilkas," he said calmly, drawing his power around him. The blue of the Healer's aura was gone entirely; that which surrounded him now was a black cloud, through which he could barely be seen. "You should have taken the horses. You could have been imprisoned and died with all your friends back in Verfaren."

"I have sworn myself your enemy," I said. In the full flow of my power, looking at him was like looking at a patch of red-shot darkness distorting the world. "For all the evil you have loosed upon the world, for all the murders, for all the corruption of that which was worthy, death is too small a price."

"Then you can pay it," he said, and sent the full brunt of his malice against me, to sear my soul and rend my body.

I was surprised at his strength, but not nearly as surprised as he was at mine.

For that first moment it was a battle of raw power against raw power. The battle of a bully grown proud, believing that he possesses the greatest strength, striking at one he knows cannot fight back. The battle of a coward. He expected me to fall before him, helpless. He expected me to die.

"Your pride has ever been your weakness," I said quietly, as I deflected his strike. It was harder to do than I had thought. Perhaps my own power was not infinite.

As long as it was greater than his, I was not concerned.

Varien

I joined my mind to Shikrar's from the moment his true name was used against him. There were no words left to say between us, but I was there with him for every breath. He was never alone.

I fought beside Maran, Rella, and Jamie to keep Berys away from Lanen as Idai arrived, flaming Rakshasa as she came, to land beside the broken body of Shikrar. Kédra was behind her by only a wingtip. Their arrival worried Berys enough that, for the moment, he backed off. He left his Rakshasa to continue the fight; Idai swiftly despatched a score or more of them while Kédra moved carefully to stand beside his father.

Jamie and Rella were having trouble with the demons. Maran was much better at fighting them, but Lanen had smeared her dagger with her half-Kantri blood and was doing best of all, especially as Aral was now at her side. Vilkas seemed to be well in command of the Lord of the Sixth Hell. I trusted them all to the Winds and the Lady and turned back to my dying soulfriend.

Shikrar's mind began to relax, as the pain left him and he realised that his time was come. *"Kédra, my son,"* he said, his mindvoice soft but clear.

"I am here, my father," said Kédra calmly. *"Be at ease."*

"Farewell, my dearest son. The Winds blow ever kindly on you and those you love."

Kédra's eyes never left his father's. His strength humbled me. *"I love you, my father,"* he replied, his mindvoice calm and clear. *"Rest upon the Winds, and know that you will live always in our memory, Hadretikantishikrar."*

I breathed again. It was well that the last time Shikrar heard his true name, it was spoken with love. I was grateful that he could not see any longer, for the great hissing tears wrung in agony from Kédra's eyes would break a heart of stone.

"Akhor? Idai?" Shikrar called weakly. We who had known him longest, through all the years.

"Here, my friend," I replied quietly, and *"Here, Shikrar,"* she said. I knew that oceans of grief awaited me, a thousand years deep and broad as all time yawning to swallow me up, but as yet I stood on the shore.

"Fight on," he said, and died.

I could not speak aloud, so in truespeech I sang, *"Sleep on the*

Winds, Hadretikantishikrar," honouring him with his true name as he passed from us. Leaning forward, my hands on his faceplate, I closed my eyes and gently went to touch his soulgem with my own one last time, in token of the depth of our lifelong friendship.

To my horror I felt his soulgem *move* under mine. My eyes snapped open, my bones turned to water, and I saw the brilliant ruby fall to the earth. I could not stop the movement I had begun, and my own soulgem touched the place where Shikrar's had been.

And I fell, and fell, and fell forever.

Lanen

That happened which could not happen.

I saw Varien lean forward to touch Shikrar's soulgem, saw Shikrar's red gem come loose and fall to earth, saw bright emerald touch the hollow where it had lain—and saw Varien *fall* into Shikrar's body, as a man falls into a grave, and be swallowed up. The great body that lay before us shuddered along its length, once, then lay still.

What in the name of all heaven was happening?

"Varien!" I screamed idiotically, turning my back on Berys. "Goddess! Varien! *Varien!*"

Then the green soulgem, resting in the hollow where a soulgem should be, began to glow. From a tiny gleam in the depths, as a light rising through deep water, it brightened and flowed until it filled all the space in Shikrar's faceplate. The light grew brighter yet, green as clear emerald, green as leaves in deep summer, bathing all that vast body in its radiance. The dark bronze of Shikrar's face did not look so dark as it had. Under the green light, just around the blazing soulgem, it seemed much lighter—almost—

Silver.

I laboured to breathe as I watched, for miracles, good or ill, are not easy to bear. Starting from the slight silver stain around his soulgem, the dark bronze of Shikrar's hide was washed in a coating of silver, sweeping ever more swiftly from nose to tail. Where the green and silver touched the great wounds Shikrar had borne, light flared as flesh and blood and bone were healed. The terrible broken wings blazed green and silver and were made whole. The neck bone came to its right place with a snap very little less terrible than that which had broken it.

It all took little more than the blink of an eye, and when all was done—Akor lay before us, but not Akor. He was the size of Shikrar, and all his body glowed yet fire-bright with emerald radiance.

Then he opened his eyes.

Varien/Khordeshkhistriakhor

I woke as from a long sleep, instantly aware, myself again after some dream of another life. I stood and stumbled, as one who has not moved for some time. I flexed my wings, glad to find that they were not as stiff as I had feared. Only then did I look about me.

My beloved Lanen stood staring up at me, her eyes huge, her mouth slack. She—she looked terrified. Astounded.

Desolate.

"Akhor?" said a voice, quietly, behind me. I turned to see Idai gazing up at me, her eyes like Lanen's full of fear and wonder.

Wait—Idai gazing *up*?

I reared onto my back legs and stared *down* at Idai, and far, far down at my own Lanen. Her lips moved, but it was not the voice of the body I heard. It was the voice of her mind, soft and dry as death, in motionless agony, and so terribly alone.

"Akor. You are Kordeshkistriakor once more. Sweet Shia, no!"

And then she cried out in her desolation, a scream of pain torn from her as though her heart had been wrenched from her breast. She fell to her knees and hid her face from me.

We were parted once more, as I had never thought to be parted from her again in life. Parted forever.

Sorrow fell before fury.

I never wanted this.

Wrath rose in me then, fire unquenchable, and I looked up to where the battle raged. I did not try to understand. There was no time to mourn Shikrar, to mourn anything. With a heart blazing with death and fury, I leapt into the sky and trumpeted a challenge to the Black Dragon, not nearly so huge now as it had seemed. I flew twice as fast as ever I had flown before, I flew as one gone mad, and I felt light as a bird's feather. I swear the Winds blew solely to bear me up.

Marik/The Black Dragon

I dragged myself out of that damned lake once more to find that Ur-kathon was no more. The sun had turned blue, it seemed, and come to rest on that hilltop. For the moment, the girl was beyond my reach. Still, I-Demonlord had faced any number of Mages in my day. Eventually they grew weary, as I would not in the body of this golem of fire and ash. The largest of the Kantri, the big bronze one, lay dead on that hilltop as well, which gave me joy. I rose with a great leap into the sky and began pursuing the others, one by one. The big one had been a lesson in flight; the smaller ones were good, but they were not the match of their dead leader. I danced on the air and destroyed some thirty or forty, one after the other, glancing back to that hilltop after each one died, waiting for that Mage's glow to die down, or at least to withdraw from the figure of the girl.

There! He was busy with something else—of course! Berys! Excellent! I wished that Mage all success, as I dove straight as an arrow for the key to my death/my daughter/Lanen, who stood now unprotected and unaware. I drew breath and sent a lance of flame to scorch her to bare earth—and a wind blew up from nowhere. The molten stone of my fire was blown back at me, I was thrown nearly onto my back by the fierce wind. Recovering, I stared in amazement.

Their leader was dead, the big bronze one. I'd seen it lying still as stone with a broken neck—but here it was rising before me, glowing green and shining silver.

I-Marik remember. It's that damned great dragon that came through the wall, I thought it was dead what is it doing here alive again *no it's coming for me!*

I-Demonlord fight to retain control of this body. I-Marik is taken with soul-deep panic, for a moment I-Marik am in control and I fly as fast as I can away from the creature.

But I-Demonlord look deeper into my other half and find the hatred below the fear. I fan it, I encourage him to remember what has been done to him and what this body can do to the beast. I-Marik slow, thinking, and when I-Demonlord show him an image of the silver one dead I-Marik peel away right and return the way I came. I-Marik gladly let my other self take control.

The silver one sees us coming and takes fright, turns to escape. We pursue with a light heart.

xiv

The Word of the Winds

Lanen

Jamie, Rella, Maran, and I took advantage of a brief pause in the fighting to catch our breath. Most of the Raksha that had been harrying us had been dashed on the rock of Vilkas's power and destroyed. Others would no doubt replace them soon. Aral was kneeling by Will, her power bright around her. Even as I glanced at them, he sat up, his hand to his head. "Hold still, you idiot, I'm still working," she told him.

He let himself be told. It was as well Aral was looking at his wounds and not his eyes. Even now, I thought, the greater wound is there. He gazed at her the way Varien—Akor—no, I can't bear it . . .

"You'll keep now," she said briskly, rising, and she returned to us, swiftly cleansing and sealing the worst of our wounds.

I longed for more Raksha to fight. Anything that would not let me stop and think.

Kédra stayed for only a brief moment after—after—"Lady Lanen, I pray you, assist me here."

I hurried over. He reverently lifted his father's soulgem and placed it in my hand. "Keep it safe, Lady. I cannot stay."

"As my own life, Kédra," I replied.

He leapt into the bright morning to join the others in the aerial battle. I put Shikrar's soulgem in my scrip and turned back to find the others watching me. Behind them more demons approached— I cried out and pointed. We all prepared, and I drew my dagger across my arm yet again, letting the blood fall onto my blade. I welcomed the pain. Anything that kept me from thinking.

Vilkas

I had never been so happy, or so free, or so completely myself in all my life. There I stood, fighting for my life against the powers of darkness, and I was filled with a joy so vast I could barely contain it. Only the smallest part of me remembered that in my dreams I laughed as I destroyed the world.

Berys was more powerful than I would ever have believed, certainly far stronger than he had ever revealed himself to be. He screamed and cursed and sent dark flame like daggers to pierce me to the bone. Most I deflected, but those that got through and injured me I healed at once.

At first I let him do all the work, restricting myself to defence while I tested the extent of my own powers. Before I welcomed them, a few minutes and an age of the world before, I would have been terrified. Now—ah, now I felt the Lady's power flowing into me through my feet, through the top of my head, through my very skin. I formed it into a shield that soon deflected everything he flung at me.

Berys turned from smug to angry very quickly. "You foolish boy, you cannot hope to equal my power!" he cried. "Bow before your master!"

"I have already made my devotions to the Lady this morning," I replied, turning away the forest of knives he had conjured to throw at me.

"This is some trick!" he screamed. He paused to draw a deep

breath, moved his hands into a semblance of a claw, and reached for my heart. I had never seen such a thing, his arm grew impossibly long and his fingertips appeared to touch my skin. I battered against the claw, moving away from it; it followed me, and suddenly I felt something tap my abdomen. I looked down.

If he'd had two hands I might have been done for, but even Berys could not make a claw from a stump.

I laughed and poured the healing light of the Lady into the very substance of his extended arms. He cried out in pain and released the spell before it could travel up his arms. In panic, to buy himself time, he sent a cloud of choking blackness to cover me. I summoned a wind to blow from behind me, returning the cloud to its maker, who had to disperse it as swiftly as he had called it into being.

I seemed to have the defensive part worked out.

Berys glared at me, wild-eyed, desperately summoning yet more strength for some new attack.

"My turn, I think," I said, and grinned. I relaxed and breathed deep, feeling as if I were sustained by a brilliant beam of light shooting through me from the very heart of the world. I drew power from the very *air* as a lamp draws oil through a wick, ignited it at the raging bonfire in my soul, and sent it forth to batter down the thick defensive walls around Berys's soul. He fought me, beating away my initial foray. I leaned into him, sending my power deeper. He did not laugh anymore, he was focussed absolutely, but he turned aside my attack.

How could this be?

I sent again, concentrating harder, thinking to tear his shields from him.

He remained unharmed.

Stop we cannot win we must not lose control hold back do not attack do not let go

Old voices chattered their old song in my mind, insistent.

Strange. I had thought they were answered.

I concentrated, astounded that there was yet some vestige of that in me—and yes, there, for all my new freedom, I was still holding back. Thick walls yet surrounded my very core, where lay the deep roiling center of the flame.

But that is our secret heart! cried my soul in terror. *That is the fire, that is the searing flame that protects and that we protect. It rages ever in control. That is our power. That is our* **truth**. *We cannot let that be touched or known, we cannot let down the barriers, once that is loose we may never call it back.*

Berys was fighting with all his strength as I threw at him everything I could think of, but he did not seem to be more than— inconvenienced. If I did nothing more he could surely fight me off forever.

No this is terrifying we cannot show who we truly are it will hurt we will be overcome we will be derided it will fail we will fail we will do something terrible we will kill again and again and again!

I had never paid any attention to that poor frightened part of my soul. The voice was my voice, yes, but as a small scared child, the one who had so horribly killed the first demon-victim he had treated, the one who had been having nightmares about it ever since and been terrified of the power that could boil blood in living veins.

Who was this who said "we"?

Berys, sensing that my attention was turned from him, gathered himself to attack once more. With a thought I held him motionless. It was hard work, he cursed and fought back, but I could sustain it for a short time while I investigated this last barrier.

I turned my Healer's vision on myself, moving into the realm of the mind where all is metaphor and outside time stands nearly still—and there he stood. A skinny ten-year-old boy who had made a horrific mistake and had been running from himself ever since.

Me. Ten years old, though I looked younger, shaking, white-faced with terror and self-loathing.

I stopped before him and looked down, and found myself moved by deep pity.

"Vil, lad," I told him gently, "it wasn't your fault."

"I killed her!" he shrieked, beating at me. "We killed her, remember!"

I knelt down, that I might not loom over him. "I remember, Vilkas. But it was a terrible accident. Our mentor Sandrish should have realised that we could not control a power we barely understood. He should never have let a child, however powerful, take over so difficult a case."

"He didn't kill her, we did!" shouted the boy.

I held out my hand to him. He hesitated, but took it, and finally looked into my eyes. I think we both took comfort from that.

In the back of my mind, Berys began to work free from my binding. I didn't have long.

"Yes, Vilkas," I admitted heavily, his hand clasped gently in mine, that he might withdraw it at any time. "We killed that poor woman. You are right."

He burst out weeping and grasped my hand in a painful grip. "I'm sorry I'm sorry I didn't mean to it must have hurt her horribly I can still hear her screaming oh please let me not have killed her . . ."

"Vilkas, we made a mistake," I said, putting my free hand on the boy's shoulder. "The one we trusted allowed us a freedom he never should have allowed. We made a mistake and we have been devastated for ten years and more because of it—but, Vil, it is done. She is dead. We cannot bring her back, no matter how sorry we are for causing her death. But we can honour her by putting that wild power to its proper use. I am older—we are older now. I understand control, I have worked hard to learn it ever since that day. And now we need the wildfire within us." I showed young Vilkas the great legions of demons harrying the Kantri; I showed him the Demonlord; and lastly, I pointed to Berys in the realm of the spirit, a demon struggling out of a net and beginning to break free.

"I know him, he tried to kill us he killed so many of our friends Magistra Erthik he is bad!" my younger self cried.

"Yes, Vil," I said quietly. "And we are fighting him now. This is our chance to right the balance, to honour the woman we killed. Let us release that power to its proper use."

"I'm scared I'm scared we can't make it do what we want . . ."

I was profoundly moved by the lad's fear. "It's alright, Vilkas," I said, and putting my long arms around his skinny body, I held him close. The first instant it was like hugging a plank of wood, but after that first shock the lad relented and clung to me. "I can control it. Truly."

He drew back, staring frightened into my eyes. "But what if we kill someone else?" he whispered.

"I promise I will not ever use our power to kill anything except demons," I swore to him. "Ever."

I felt his gaze sear along my mind, down into my deepest heart, as he searched out the truth of what I said. It was there. Something began to dawn in his eyes, so brilliant blue, so large in that young face. He reached out, and tentatively he put his light little arms around my neck. "You promise?" he whispered.

"I promise," I whispered back.

"Then what are you waiting for?" he demanded, shoving me away with vigour. "Look, he's getting loose!"

I stood and grinned down at my young soul. "Shall we stop him, Vil?"

The lad grew to meet my height, changing swiftly into the self I knew from the mirror. His identical grin began to meld with mine.

"Oh, yes," he said, his voice no longer its boyish treble but my own.

And we were one.

A sharp pain ripped me back to the real world. Berys was free, shooting black power like swords into me as fast as he could. His eyes were bloodshot with fury but he was laughing.

"Poor little lad, killed someone did he? And you impotent because of it ever since. How wonderful!"

I felt young Vilkas grow to fill my skin, and the cage around the core of my true power grew thinner, thinner, like reeds, like gossamer—gone.

I averted Berys's attack with a contemptuous flicker of thought.

He drew back his hand and started to chant something hideous, his face a mirror for the words.

"Oh, do shut up," I said, suddenly tired of the sound of his voice. I sent silence around him, as he had kept Lanen silent. He struggled to get away. I found it surprisingly easy to hold him still.

I gazed into his soul with my Healer's sight. It was revolting. In among the swirls of bloodred and poisonous bile green and pus yellow there was a centre of solid black—no, a silvery black—oh! That wasn't him, it was something he carried. I ignored it and forced myself to look deeper. There! There were the shields, like overlapping armour wrapped around him. Like the layers of an onion gone soft and stinking.

I began to remove them. I worked slowly and carefully, for I did not know how closely these touched him and I was determined not to harm him with my power.

I had promised.

Khordeshkhistriakhor

Sacred Fire rose within me as I flew from the Black Dragon, drawing it after me. I went to breathe my Fire onto the Winds, that this act might be consecrated—but when I opened my mouth no flame came forth. I felt the air currents change, a sudden headwind—no, my *head* was forced back. I tried turning my head to the left and breathed flame—a sudden gust forced me to the right.

My thoughts reeled. I lived in a body that could not be. Shikrar, turned to Akhor all in a moment—no flame, though I am a creature of fire, but the power of the Winds at my command.

I never wanted this.

There again, I didn't recall anyone asking what I wanted. The Wind of the Unknown blows hardest of all, it is said.

I turned to face the thing behind me, breathed the Winds at it, and flew faster. I felt its contempt, heard its unnatural laughter as it pursued me in my terrified attempt to escape. I heard it start to roar and swerved left. The edge of its solid flame caught my tail-tip and I screamed in agony.

Well, perhaps it didn't hurt quite that much, but it pleased the Black Dragon and stopped it thinking.

I veered right, it followed me close. It was flying much better than before, but it was still clumsy in the air, and so huge. So huge, so intimidating, so very . . . *heavy*.

Shikrar—*oh, my soulfriend Shikrar*—had made us all learn to fly carrying weights when we were young, that we might come to understand the changes that we would need to deal with as we grew older. We learned swiftly that with greater weight, we could achieve far greater speed; indeed, that was the first half of his lesson.

The second half is that with all that momentum it is very, very difficult to manoeuvre, and even harder to stop.

I put on a burst of speed, rejoicing in the midst of my fury at the feel of the Winds bearing me up, at the strength in these great wings, speeding me onward towards that great cloud of smoke. Some careless flame must have set fire to those trees. Oh dear, oh dear.

I concentrated, focussed my voice, and sent a sudden loud note to ring in that spot in my faceplate where it would resonate just . . . so . . . *there*.

The echo told me I was upon it. Heart racing, I flew into the cloud and instantly folded the greater part of my wings in close and, using just the tips, pulled up at the sharpest angle my body would bear, praying to the Winds that my speed and the updraft would allow me to change direction. I scraped the cliff with my belly and legs, and bashed my poor tail, but I did it. Flying straight up for a brief moment, then flipping over and rolling away left—I was right way up and heading back the way I had come when I heard the Black Dragon fly into the cliff at speed. It barely had time to scream before there was a terrible thump and a hiss, and black smoke made a thicker screen than the white.

I rode the updraft, spiralling into clear air. *Always gain height, the advantage is always in height*—I could hear Shikrar's voice in my head even after all these years. I was oddly untroubled by Rakshasa as I rode the winds, trying to see through the billowing smoke and learn what damage Idai and I had wrought.

A smaller thump, the sound of one taking to the skies—and the Black Dragon emerged.

It was half the size it had been. No, less—it had lost much of itself in its two dunkings, and only half of what was left now flew.

Straight towards Lanen.

Jamie

We fought on, Maran and Rella, Lanen and I, beating away at the demons that beset us, all the while watching Vilkas out of the corners of our eyes. Aral protected us as she could against the demons. At least she slowed them down to manageable numbers. We fought with all our strength, all of us, and the dragons did what they could, but there were just too many. Maran fought like a madwoman, her sword flashing in the sun, the graven runes upon it at least as deadly to the Raksha as the blade. Lanen kept cutting her arm and blooding her dagger—Goddess only knows what *that* was about, but it seemed to work. It was Rella and I who fared worst, for all our skills. Raksha are hard to kill.

Vilkas

The layers of enchantments surrounding Berys came off slowly, almost physical in their intensity of evil. Some made him writhe, some made him scream—but none made him weaker.

I stopped to think. He saw this as weakness and struck out at me, snarling now like an animal. It was a very powerful attack, as though he were the stronger for losing the enchantments I had removed. I had to work a little harder to fend it off, and it drew blood.

The fool. I was in the midst of my Healer's vision even as he attacked. Perhaps I did not defend myself as well as I might, but now I could see where much of his power was coming from. The shape of it, the flow of it, jogged my memory—where had I seen that? I sought that shape, that particular spell, hidden as it was among the others, woven around with misdirection. He attacked more viciously, managing to stand, but I paid only passing attention to what he was doing. Where was it now, a flow, almost like a funnel—a soul's memory of the smell of burning hair—*got it!*

Rathen. It was the other end of the flow of power that had been draining Rathen, that had so devastated him when I closed it from the wrong end. Close it from this end, though, and all the other Rathens would be free.

Berys fought me, furious now, sweating heavily, drawing every drop of power he could pull into himself. He gestured and a cloud of Rikti surrounded me. I dispelled them with a wave of my hand. His mouth moved, still caught in silence, and even then a dozen of the Rakshasa converged on me. I drew a deep breath and felt the Lady's power flow through me, from the great Mother earth, from the Crone now hidden in daylight, from the Laughing Girl—a sudden flash of that morning by the waterfall—fanning the white-hot fires of my soul let free at last. I gestured and bathed the Rakshasa in Her power. Screaming, they disappeared back to the Hells, where by rights they belong.

But I was being distracted. I held Berys still—it took more strength to do that than I had hoped—but still I could search through the stinking morass of his soul—wait. Something blue flashed in my vision. Was that some vestige of Berys's, own native power? Some particle of soul still uncorrupted? Surely not . . .

I looked deeper. Ah. No, it wasn't Berys. It was foreign to him: the funnel that supplied him with the reserves he needed to command so many of the Rakshasa. Rathen had escaped at his end by renouncing the pact. I could see no way of closing that source. I tried all the obvious ways, but nothing touched that vast river of strength. I could not close it or stop it supplying him with ever-renewed power.

I released Berys, allowing him to move. Instantly he drew out a demonline I had not seen and opened it.

"No," I said, and reaching out, crushed it.

It closed. They can only be used once. It disappeared.

Berys screamed and threw himself at me physically. I had not considered that, and it was not a trivial attack—he had the body of a man in his prime, and he easily outweighed me two to one. It might even have succeeded if he had had two hands. As it was, I was able to wrest his dagger from him and throw it over the side of the hill.

That was enough of that. Ruthlessly I stripped away his remaining armour, all in a moment, until all that remained to him was that source of power. He shook as he stood there, trying to say something.

I removed the silence. I was shaking myself. The power that raged in me felt as if it would tear me apart. *I promised I would not kill him. I swore it, I must not kill him with this power.*

The restraint threatened to unman me.

"Let me live," he said instantly, going down on his knees.

I sighed. *Honestly, how stupid does he think I am?*

"I can give you more power even than you have now," he said. "There is a spell—I can give you all my own power, I will go through the world blind and weak, but let me live!"

"Fool," I said, and my own voice surprised me—it was deeper and more resonant, it was grown huge. I felt as if I were growing physically, as if my body could not possibly contain it all. "Are you even now so blind? Behold," I said, and let him See me. The flame that I had held caged those long years roared now, searing what it touched, blending with the Lady's healing power and reinforcing it. A lick of blue flame snapped out, of its own accord, and struck Berys like a physical blow. He fell back, measuring his length on the ground.

"Master," he said, as if in awe. "You are the greatest Mage that has ever lived. Let me serve you!" He scrabbled to his knees. "I have ways of learning that which is hidden, I can help you to your heart's desire, I can give you that which no other knows of . . ."

"Be silent!" I commanded, angry with myself that I could still not stop the flow of the corrupted Healers' power to him. "You could have nothing that I would ever desire."

He smiled and reached inside his robes. "Indeed? What of this?"

He drew out—Goddess, it was a human heart! No, no, it was only shaped like a heart, made of that stone the jewellers call bloodstone, that seems to bleed red when it is cut. It was incredibly detailed, for a carven stone . . .

Berys's eyes gleamed when he saw my curiosity. I realised full well that he was regaining his strength as he played for time, but I was intrigued. I did not fear anything that Berys could do to me.

"The Distant Heart," he whispered. "It is the Distant Heart of the Demonlord. Say you will spare me and it is yours."

Jamie

Berys was down. He had been down before, screaming even though Vilkas didn't touch him physically, but he'd gotten up again and gone to stab the lad. He failed at that, too.

I thought at first I was seeing a cruel streak in Vilkas, playing with Berys like that, but in the midst of trying to keep out of the reach of demons, and as Vilkas dragged things out, I realised—he's barely twenty. He doesn't know what to do now he's got Berys in his power. And he's a Healer, they can't kill intentionally without corrupting themselves forever.

I, on the other hand, owed Berys recompense for half a lifetime of wrongs. I owed him for teaching Maran what fear was; I owed him for the demons he sent that chased her away from my side and kept her from knowing her daughter; I owed him for all the ills that had beset my Lanen this last year, and finally, least but greatest, I owed him revenge for the life of the innocent, nameless babe he and Marik had sacrificed to make the Farseer, without a thought to its parents, without a care for its wasted life, a quarter of a century ago. To a fiend like Berys, life was a game, and it did not matter who was murdered or trampled underfoot, so long as he won.

Berys was on his knees now, but I'd seen Varien's sword cut him in two with no effect. There had to be some way to get to him—oh. Oh, *that* might work.

I reached over to Lanen, who was fighting still but growing weary even as I watched. I must be quick.

I sliced open her scrip and caught the soulgem Kédra had given her as it fell out. She didn't have time to notice.

Somehow I didn't think old Shikrar would mind helping one more time.

It was harder than it sounds to stab Berys to the heart and push the gleaming red soulgem into the wound before it could heal, but I managed it.

At first Vilkas cried out nearly as loud as Berys, the difference being that Berys kept on screaming.

I have never in all my years before or since taken joy in ending a life, but by all that's holy, I did that day.

The edges of the wound began to turn black and shrivel. Berys was still alive, still screaming, as he began to smoke. Suddenly Shikrar's soulgem was surrounded by flame.

Berys was burning. He had enough strength to try to heal himself for quite some time, but there was never any question what the outcome would be. He was too terrified to realise that he was prolonging his own agony.

I was rather surprised when Maran stepped forward and struck his head off.

But then, she always did have a soft heart.

I collected the head and put it on the body, where the flames burned most fiercely. No sense taking chances.

Marik/Demonlord

Free! We are free from the bindings put upon us, free to loose the legions of Hell on that cursed silver dragon that has so diminished us. I-Demonlord feel my old powers return with a shock, and we know that Berys is no more. I scream the words into the air, I sing them, I take joy in the chaos that will rule when all the Kantri are gone down into death and demons rule the world.

I-Marik reel. I did not agree to this. Kill the girl, kill the dragons, yes, but not demons to rule the world. Where would be the gain for me? I fight for control.

I-Demonlord effortlessly thrust that mind away and take the body for myself. At last, I can do that which I have longed to do, all down the centuries of darkness. Berys had summoned many of the Rakshasa. Time to bring in the rest.

"Let the gates of all the Hells be flung open! Come ye great Lords of Hell, come great and small, Raksha and Rikti, come feast on your life-enemies—behold, I, the Demonlord, summon you all here to me!"

There was a soundless clap. The air shook, for all I know the ground shook, and all in a moment the sky, the ground, the very waters of the lake, were full of the screaming hordes of all the Seven Hells. The noise was immense, the numbers uncountable. I laughed with delight.

The Kantri fight, desperately, outnumbered a hundred to one. And there upon that little hill hard by, about to die among a cluster of her companions, stands the one creature I need most desperately to kill.

I start to fly towards her—she is so close!—when that huge silver beast rises before me. It tries to scorch me, fool, but it has no flame. Just then a great gust of wind throws me nearly on my back in midair. I have to fall away and glide for a moment before I recover. The silver one follows me, choking out its hatred from a dry belly, spitting nothing at me—and before I can make any headway towards the girl the wind turns against me again, blowing a gale from my left forward quarter. I yell my frustration, flying as hard as I can against the wind. I am battered by gusts from all sides, forcing me ever down. I cannot react quickly enough to recover, I happen to look up—

—and see the silver dragon circling above me, its mouth wide, spitting nothing at me but hot air. Air, winds, air, the damn thing is controlling the winds with its *breath*!

"That one!" I cry to the nearest demons. "Kill me that silver one!"

Nothing happens. The Rakshasa do not move. I look around—none of them are moving. Damnation!

I ignore all else, I must reach that hill. The silver dragon flies better than I do, it gets ahead of me, the wind slams me back and down, again and again. I am moving forward, but so slowly, so horribly slowly. I roar my frustration. It is exhausting, and several times I nearly fall out of the sky—but she was not that far away to begin with.

I am near enough to the hill.

I draw in a deep breath, ready to pour the molten stone in my gullet over the bowed and bloodied girl, for her death is my freedom forever.

Wait—no—*NO!*

Lanen

The sky turned black. For an instant I thought a sudden storm was come up out of nowhere, but then it began to spread out. The Kantri were going frantic, fighting—oh, dear Lady.

For all that I had been through up until that moment, I give you my word, I was never so certain that I was going to die as at that moment. The Rakshasa filled the air like a plague of insects, biting and clawing the Kantri and the Dhrenagan, who fought back with vast courage in the face of impossible odds.

It seemed to be raining blood.

And there was a large contingent of Rakshasa coming our way. I drew my dagger lightly over my arm one last time, committed my soul to the Lady, and waited for death to claim me. I had cut myself so often there was blood all over my hands, but I swear I didn't feel it.

They never reached us.

It was Vilkas, of course. I had watched in amazement as he brushed off a legion of Rikti, a dozen of the Rakshasa—but when Jamie had stepped forward and killed Berys, Vilkas seemed to go into a kind of shock. Aral tried to help him, but then the Demon-lord unleashed the Hells and he snapped back into focus, after a fashion. He put up a barrier between us and the demons just before they reached us.

And he did nothing more.

Outside the barrier, the Kantri began to fall from the sky, bloodied, dying, mobbed by demons.

I did not know which would break first, my heart or my mind. "Vilkas, do something!" I shouted. "You cannot leave the Kantri to die like that!" Every muscle in my body was tense as a bowstring. "Goddess, you're the only one who can help them!"

"You don't understand, if I start—" he began.

"They will all *die!*" I screamed, my heart in my throat. "In the name of the Lady, stop them!"

He raised his eyebrows and smiled. "Very well," he said. He raised his arms above his head and made a gesture as of throwing something away—

And every demon stopped moving, apart from the Demonlord. It was madly fighting Akor to reach us, that was clear enough.

But why?

"What do you think that damn thing wants?" asked Rella. Her voice was ragged with weariness, and when I glanced at her I realised that her voice was likely the strongest thing about her.

Maran was—eh?

Maran had put down her sword and taken off her pack, and now she was drawing out the Farseer. Her movements were careful but swift. I think we all knew there was not much time.

What in the world does she want that thing for now? I wondered.

She knelt, the globe before her on the ground, and said clearly, "Show me what the Demonlord fears."

Damn my mother was a bright woman.

She looked up at me. "Everyone, here, come look," she snapped. We all hurried over.

There in the murky globe was a picture of me holding something in my hand. But what the Hells—

"Ah," said Vilkas. He was trembling as he reached into his scrip and drew forth a shiny black stone. "You'll be wanting this, then."

"What in all the Hells?" I wondered aloud. "It looks like . . ."

"It is the Demonlord's heart," said Vilkas. "The Distant Heart. The reason he didn't die all those centuries ago when the dragons burned him to a cinder."

There was a roar from the skies. I looked up. The Black

Dragon, for all that Akor was throwing it about the skies, was nearly upon us.

I took the Distant Heart from Vilkas. The blood on my hands, from all the shallow cuts on my arms, began to smoke when I touched the thing, a great cloud of acrid smoke that I batted away with my free hand. There was something happening—

I swore loudly and profanely and nearly dropped the thing.

It was beating.

No longer stone, no longer dead now but flesh and blood, it beat steadily in my palm, almost like a bird fluttering.

The Black Dragon, near enough now that I could see its blazing sulphur-yellow eyes, cried out, a great *NO!* that rang in the mountains.

I raised my hand, that it might see better.

"Die, you bastard," I snarled, and crushed the heart to a pulp.

The Black Dragon fell from the sky and landed in a heap. True, a moment later it was aloft again—but this time it was flying *away*.

Vilkas

I spoke to all the demons at once. "The creature that called you here is gone," I cried. "Return to that place granted you by the Powers and I will allow you to go in peace."

I was trembling harder now. Every part of me, heart, body, and soul, longed to destroy them all. I held myself back with a terrible effort. *Aral, Aral, you cannot know, I have let loose the fire and it threatens to burn the world . . .*

"Stupid mortal!" cried one of the greater demons. A lesser prince, perhaps Lord of the Second Hell? "We are free here at last, with no strictures to bind us! Tremble and die!"

It threw itself at me. I brushed it away. I longed to swat it to the ground like an annoying wasp, crush it, hear it scream . . .

"I give you all one final warning," I said, my voice shaking with the effort of restraint. "If you stay here, I give you my word, by the Lady's grace, I will destroy every living soul among you. Go now. I cannot hold back forever."

"We fear no mortal!" came a chorus of voices. "This world is ours, we are come to kill and then to rule!"

That was it. I cared no more that I might do a great wrong. I knew only that I was all that stood between the demons and the death of the world of men. Not much of a decision.

I let go. Of everything. All restraint, all self-control, burned away like straw as I became the flame that raged within me.

I struck out at the princes first. They were dust and ashes in that first moment. Then I began with the ones that harried the Kantri. I burned them in swathes, like scything a field, brushing them off the fallen Kantri like flies. They died in their tens, in their hundreds, and it was good.

No. I lie.

It was *wonderful.*

It was better than cool water in the desert. It was better than sleep to the exhausted. It was better than food to one dying of hunger, better than sex, better than the dawn—my body, my mind, my heart and soul, all working together seamlessly, all using the vast power that had been forced into hiding all my life, finally set free.

I have never known such incredible, transcendent joy.

I killed hundreds. Thousands. I was not banishing them back to their place in the Hells. No. It was the True Death. *I* was the True Death.

I laughed as I beheld my dream come true.

Eventually they realised what was happening and many fled back to the Hells. They were the clever ones. I would pursue them later. For now, I slaughtered those that were stupid enough not to run away. I laughed again as I slew them, I rejoiced in their deaths. I *was* Death, and it was good.

Marik

I wake as from sleep, find myself on the ground, leap aloft and try to fly away. The Demonlord has forced me into darkness. I have no idea what has happened since he and his servants declared war on the world—except that the world seems still to be here, the Demonlord is gone and the demons are dying in droves. I am now in sole possession of this body.

I wonder if there is any chance of me getting my old one back? Especially since I don't know how long this one is going to last without demon-strength to support it. Already it begins to cool, to stiffen, around the edges.

Death soon, then. Real death this time. Release at last.

I shall fly into the mountains. They do look beautiful, so welcoming, so calm. There aren't very many of those big dragons around to stop me, either—except for that damned silver one. Again!

I flap harder, trying desperately to get away.

Lanen

I threw the horrible thing from me. It burst into searing flame the instant it left my hand, and was dust before it could fall to the ground. My hand was scorched. It was a small price to pay.

I looked around. Vilkas was yelling something, briefly, but I think the demons proved how stupid they were and defied him. In any case, they weren't bothering us anymore. I think they were too busy dying.

And the Black Dragon, still alive somehow, was flying away. Akor flew in pursuit of the creature, but I did not fear for him.

Goddess. It was over.

By all the Hells, my poor battered heart ached as if its pain would never cease.

He was a dragon again. My love. My husband. The father of my children.

A detached part of my mind watched his graceful flight. He was a glorious creature, gleaming silver in the late afternoon sun—how had it come to be so late?—and he seemed to be borne aloft like a leaf in a breeze. He was so huge. Shikrar's size. Akor would have grown that large in the fullness of time, as one of the Kantri, but not for hundreds of years yet. He was—he was—

I ignored the rage, ignored the despair that pressed against my heart. Ignored my lonely future, though a scurrying thought danced past the vision of that vast dragon faced with children half the length of one of his talons. He was himself always, no matter his form. Varien kadreshi na-Lanen. My beloved. With a strength that came from I knew not where, I drew myself up and began to sing. Aloud.

I sang—very badly—the wordless song of love that we had made between us on the Dragon Isle. I sang to remind him, to remind me, of that love that does not change save to grow deeper and stronger with the passing of the years, no matter what else might happen. I let the music echo in my mind as well, and felt it when the bond of truespeech locked between us. The song had changed yet again and was awash with sorrow, but it held the truth of love as well.

Akor managed to get in front of the Black Dragon and turn it, or the Winds were blowing it back in this direction. When he turned to me, I realised Akor was singing too. He joined me in the song of our making, adding to it the Tale of Lanen and Akor that he had composed for our wedding as my bride-gift. As I watched, those of both houses of the Kantri who still could fly joined him in the air, melding their voices with his, weaving harmonies around and about the song. It grew wilder, deeper, higher, until there was a sudden shift—from one moment to the next it changed, from a wild symphony built around a story of two lovers into the pain and truth and deep joy of love itself, and the sheer power of the music thrust me to my knees.

The music took on a life of its own then. There were yet echoes of the Tale of Lanen and Akor but other voices wove a wondrous tapestry of sound about it now. I heard the jangling chords of the Lost, rattling against the music, until in a blazing chord they were resolved. Restored. And they joined in the vast sound, so many-layered it was hard to make out the melody—but—but it still wasn't right. Something was missing, some vital part of the tale untold.

The Black Dragon tried to escape the music, charging Akor

time and again, but Akor floated light as a bird's feather and danced away from it on the air with barely the flick of a wingtip. They all moved with Akor, the Restored singing now their lives rediscovered, their suffering redeemed with the death of the Demonlord. It was wondrous, but it lacked something—something—

Away in the far distance a sound arose, so faint as to seem more like a memory. It came from the west, where the sun sank slowly towards the distant sea—for a moment, it almost seemed as though the Sun itself were adding his voice to the music. I squinted, trying to see around the edges of the blazing light. Was that a flock of crows flying swiftly towards us?—no, it must be eagles surely, moving so swiftly— Ah. No. Not eagles. Brighter than eagles, gleaming in the light, copper and steel and bronze and golden, their soulgems scattering light of ruby and emerald and sapphire as the sun caught them.

The Aialakantri. The Lesser Kindred.

They soared in, singing, joining the complex pattern of flight as though they were joining a dance; and the music grew, made full, made bright and sparkling with the higher voices of the smaller creatures.

Made whole.

I probably should have stopped singing, but I could not. They were now most truly my people as well. My voice could not be heard by any save Akor, but I sang with all the peoples of the Kantri in a wild rejoicing.

The Black Dragon was confused by the music, stiffening even as I watched, trying to find a thermal to rise upon, trying to find a way out—but the music grew and grew, until the very stones echoed with it, until the mountains joined in the song and the Kantri wove even the echoes into the full glory of that sound. My throat closed in the face of more beauty than I could bear. I fell silent as the great mass of dragons, all three Kindreds united, surrounded the Black Dragon in an ever-moving spiral. Their unearthly music, so full and triumphant, woven of voices silent for long ages of the world and voices new-come to life, danced until it came to a single chord, complex beyond imagining—and there it locked, shining, all but visible. I heard notes that not even the Kantri could possibly sing ringing in the air, right at the edge of hearing, and in the lowest range I finally heard the voice I knew to be Akor's adding the deepest note of all. I felt it through the soles of my feet, I felt my babes resonate to it in my belly, I felt it in my deepest heart. That chord shook the earth. That chord the creator sang when the world was brought into being replete with joy.

And as I watched, the Black Dragon, caught up in that unimaginable music, caged, surrounded by music, began to shake. Every separate mote of the creature, every bit of ash and speck of sulphur, every drop of molten stone, quivered in the grip of that sound until, between one breath and another, it gave one last cry that faded upon the instant to a terrible sibilant hiss as it disintegrated. A great cloud of dust rained softly down upon the earth, and it was gone.

All that remained was the music.

I am not sure when the Kantri stopped singing, for to speak sooth that chord has never left my heart, down all the years. I became a struck bell, resonating forever to the truth of it. No matter what else may distract me, what life may throw my way—in my deepest being, that living glory of music rings ever within my soul to remind me of beauty and creation and the fundamental wonder of life.

There was only one distraction, as the sound echoed in the mountains, dancing between hills alive with joy. I would swear that in the silence behind the music, I heard my father Marik's mindvoice one last time. It was less than a whisper in my mind, the merest ghost of a breath.

"Thank you," it said, and disappeared.

And the Kantri, rising in a vast spiral, opened their throats again and began their lament for the dead. I should have realized that they would sing their first farewell to him whose loss they most would feel. The music was solemn, composed of equal parts of sorrow and hope inextricably entwined. It would break your heart even if you knew not for whom they sang. And it was Kédra's voice that led them, with Akor's in the second line.

"May the Winds bear you up, Hadretikantishikrar, Keeper of Souls, Eldest, soulfriend, Father, to where the sun gleams ever warm and bright. May your soul find its rest in the heart of light. May you join your voice to the Great Song of Time, and may those you love, who have flown before, meet you and welcome you into the Star Home, the Wind Home, the Place of All Songs, where all is well, and all is joy, and all is clear at last."

He has found his Yrais again at last, I thought, and bowed my head, and wept.

Aral

I watched Vil as he changed. Sweet Shia. I know I urged him to use his full power, but—heaven keep us, it was terrifying. He had dealt with a demon prince, then held Berys at bay and stripped his works from him (I reminded myself to thank Jamie from the bottom of my heart). But now . . . now he was killing without let or hindrance, and the expression on his face was terrible to behold.

He was in bliss.

I had heard his exchange with the demons and given thanks then for his strength, that wildfire that raged in him—but now—now he was pursuing the demons that fled. He was even stopping those that tried to return to the Hells. It was wrong.

Never mind that they were demons. This was *genocide*.

Damn.

I strode to his side. "Vilkas!"

He never twitched.

"Vilkas, damn it, man, you have to stop!"

He laughed. *Goddess,* what a horrible sound.

"Vilkas, you listen to me, you have to stop right now! This isn't right!"

He turned to face me, his eyes blazing that incredible blue, his raven hair blowing in a wind I didn't feel. "Aral, you were right! I should have done this long since! Look, they cannot stand against me!" He gestured again, and another score of demons died screaming.

"They are trying to get away, Vil, you have to *stop*!"

"Stop? Why should I stop? You were the one who said I needed to let go." Another gesture. More screaming, more death, and the smile on his face was becoming a terrible rictus.

I shook him. "Stop, Vil! Listen to me! You're not killing them to protect anything now, you're killing them for the joy of it!"

"Yes, isn't it wonderful?" He grinned.

I struck him across the face, once, hard. "Vilkas, stop it!"

He turned to face me then, holding me motionless along with all those demons, gazing at me as though he'd never seen me before. The power running through him made my hair stand on end even from two feet away. "Why? Why should I stop? They are demons, they don't deserve to live."

"Vilkas ta-Geryn," I said quietly, "you listen to me. They deserve life as much as we do, as long as they stay in their own world. They're trying to get back there. Let them go."

He looked at me for a moment, considering. "No," he said, dropping me to the ground and turning back to the demons. More screaming.

I raised my power about me, stood directly in front of him, and put my hands on his shoulders. He did not react. Damn it.

I reached up and grabbed his hair, tugging it down hard, forcing him to look at me. He was taken by surprise and actually looked into my eyes. I let go his hair, I barely knew what I said. I would have said anything to stop him.

"By the Lady, Vilkas, I charge you—by the friendship between us, by the power of the Goddess that rages within you, I beg you to stop this slaughter. You are not dreaming this time, Vilkas. This is real. If you kill all the demons you will be the Death of the World in truth. Remember the balance! If all the demons die at your hand, what will come to take their place? Balance in all things, Vil! You have used your power to save us all, the whole world owes you its life. Thus far you are the Sky God, Vil." I seemed to be weeping. "Do not do this. Stop with the Sky God." A mad giggle fought to escape me. "You can be the Death of the World some other time."

There was a faint flicker, I could see it deep inside him. A moment of hesitation, a moment of his real self.

Oh, Hells. Oh, Goddess. I had no choice.

I threw all restraint aside and spoke the words I had sworn I would never say, knowing as I did so what it would do. To both of us.

"I conjure you, by Mother Shia, by all we have been to each other, by every moment of friendship—oh, Vilkas—oh, Hells—" I had to push so hard to say the words aloud that I practically shouted it. "I love you, Vilkas ta-Geryn. I love you with all my heart and soul, I always will. And now, here, this moment, by the endless love I bear you that you cannot return, by that pain I must bear every day of my life for love of you, I require you. Stop this. Now."

It was like stabbing him with so many daggers. I watched him wince, watched his mind reappear in his eyes. Watched as that unutterable joy drained out of him and left him desolate.

He turned to the demons and growled, "Return to the Hells that spawned you or die the True Death." He gestured them free, and in the instant every single one disappeared back to their own rightful place.

He turned back to me. *Oh, Hells, here it comes, and I bloody deserve it . . .*

"I do not love you. I have never loved you and you know it, but it's not my fault." He shuddered. "Damn you. You had no right to do that. How could you throw that in my face? I *trusted* you, Aral!"

He came right close to me, he took my chin in his hand, his face a thundercloud. *Goddess, what is he doing?* I wondered, even as a stupid, traitor part of me that had nothing to do with my mind prayed that he was about to kiss me.

Far from it. He was returning the favour. He forced me to look at his eyes, and as both of us were still in the depths of our healing power, I saw him.

No. No, you don't understand. I *saw* him. We merged as we always did when we were working together, and I felt it: felt for an instant that incredible delight, that transcendent bliss that had been his for so fleeting a moment, felt it tear through me like a hundred swords, so sharp was the joy—and then I felt it stop. Ten thousand swords, all poisoned, ripping me apart. Ten thousand thousand demons wrenching me from that pinnacle and throwing me down, twisted and broken, mourning, into a dark pit.

I was sobbing so hard I couldn't see his face when he turned away, but I heard him.

"You have only ever been second-best and you know it. I could never love you. You have used me, used our friendship, and I have paid the price. Why should I ever speak to you again?"

Someone put their arms around me and held me as I mourned. I think it must have been Will.

Lanen

That was my mistake, of course. I wept. Not tears seeping out for the beauty of the dragon-song, but true weeping, for Shikrar's passing, for Varien lost forever—for too many things. The only problem was that I couldn't stop.

Akor, the Lord of the Kantri now again in truth, came spiralling down to land as soon as the lament for Shikrar was done, but I could not look at him. The others sang for their own dead. I heard them, but I heard nothing, I felt nothing beyond myself. My world encompassed only my own body, and my own pain, and a sorrow beyond words. Beyond living. Even then some part of me, some last rational voice, reminded me that he was changed, not dead, but at that moment I could see no difference. I knelt there on the cold ground, my arms wrapped around my chest, rocking back and forth in a vain search for comfort, my body forcing me to breathe, great ragged breaths rattling painfully into my chest.

Gone, gone, knelled my ravaged heart. *He is gone beyond any hope of returning. I will never hold him in my arms again, our children will be alien to him forever. He is lost to me forever. Unbound our vows, unbound our future, the pain I have borne, the children yet in my womb fatherless.*

I am told that I screamed. I must believe it, for my throat was raw.

And as suddenly I found myself on my feet, and it wasn't only my throat that was sore. My right cheek blazed pain at me. My eyes flew open, and there before me, her right fist closed about a thick fold of my tunic, her eyes locked on my face, her left arm drawing back to strike again, stood my mother Maran Vena.

I threw up my right arm to stop her hand. She loosed me instantly.

I shouted and threw a punch back at her. She avoided it neatly and caught my hand. Damn she was fast, and strong as iron. "What in all the Hells are you doing?" I screeched. "Leave me alone!"

"No, I think you've had long enough," she said, letting go my hand as she calmly looked me over and obviously found me wanting. "I've seen this sort of thing before. If I let you indulge yourself it will only get worse."

"Damn you!" I cried, furious. "My future just disappeared before my eyes!" I wrapped my arms around myself again, cold at the thought, and my anger left all in the instant. "He's gone, Maran. He's gone. Mother. He's gone from me forever," I said, my eyes stinging with yet more tears.

She took me by the shoulders and shook me. "How dare you?" she said, her eyes lighting with anger. "He is here, idiot child! He stands before you, whole and unhurt," she said, gesturing towards Akor, who stood yet some way off, his face turned away from me. "Unhurt save for your words, that are like to kill him more surely than any demon ever spawned," she added. She put her hands on either side of my face and forced me to meet her gaze.

"Lanen, since the moment you took your first breath I have known your warrior soul," she said sternly. "You have been my shining daughter all these years, you have borne more than I could ever have done. Do not fail now, here at the bitter test." Her eyes blazed. "Goddess knows, I have failed in every kind of love, but you are better than that."

"I am weary of being better, Maran!" I cried, and in my extreme of passion I let slip the childish cry of my heart. "It's not *fair*! I've been alone all my life, with none but Jamie to care if I lived or died, until I met Akor. I nearly died a dozen times on that island, and then he changed, and—I thought we would have our whole lives together!" I was weeping again. "It hasn't been the half of a year! Is that all the happiness I am to know in life? One half of one year? Goddess, what have I done to deserve so little?"

"Life is not fair, Lanen," she said quietly. "That is no argument for a woman grown. Did you expect life, or love, to be perfect? Or easy? In my experience it is seldom either. Only in bards' tales does anyone live happily ever after. You have had a whole six moons of happiness. Some never even know that much."

"Hells, even you and Jamie had three years!" I cried.

"That is enough, Lanen," said Maran. She stood square before me, her anger plain. "Think you that you are the only one whose heart is riven by this? Listen to him!" she said, pointing to Akor. "Hells, girl, I don't have truespeech and even I can hear his heart breaking."

"So is mine, damn it!" I cried.

"You cannot give up now," she said, implacable. "Broken or no, your heart must yet beat. You bear his children under your heart. They need you. You cannot fail them. You must not."

And suddenly she stepped in and held me tight, her arms strong about me, her words softer than I expected in my ear. "Lanen, for all that you have done, you must yet do one more thing. One last thing, dear one, dear daughter, and all is done." She held me again at arm's length. "You must forgive him."

I burst into sobs, my whole body shaking, out of my control. "I can't! I can't bear it, I can't face him, I beg you, no . . ."

"You can and you will," she said firmly, and dragged me bodily to the place where Akor lay upon the ground. He still faced away from me, his head held at its natural level, far, far above my own.

"Turn around, damn you!" shouted Maran, making a fist and striking as hard as she could at the nearest bit of him she could reach.

Akor ignored her and kept his face firmly turned from me.

"You Hells-be-damned coward, you *will* face the mother of your children or you'll answer to me!" cried Maran, as loud as she could.

He turned then and looked down. He still did not speak, but his eyes, deep as the sea, old as time and wild with all regret, were locked on mine.

Maran left us to it.

His soulgem gleamed a little in the last rays of the dying sun, and his vast silver faceplate shone with tears.

Tears. From a creature of fire.

It was as if a human were to weep blood.

The sight shook me as nothing else could have. Greatly daring, I attempted truespeech.

"Akor?" I said, tentatively. No response. *"Akor my heart?"* I said. Nothing.

Aloud, then.

"Akor?" I said, my traitor voice cracking.

"I am here, little sister," he answered, finally. His own voice shook me. It was much deeper than it had been when last he wore his natural shape, and with my new perception I heard far more than his words. By speaking at all he laid his heart naked before me, and I saw in it all that roiled in my own—hurt, anger, weary sorrow, longing. Despair. And over and around all, through the pain and behind it, love.

Little sister. So he had called me when first we met on the Dragon Isle.

"And still you leak seawater," he said, bringing his great head down to my level. His soulgem was dark, now, and somehow that touched me more than almost anything. "I wished long ago that all your tears might be tears of joy. Alas, that I have been the means—" And the last of his control broke, and he bowed his head. "Lanen, *kadreshi*, my own heart, I am as confounded as you. I know not how this has happened. Some cruel trick of the Winds, some price perhaps required for the death of that terrible beast—Lanen, by my soul, it was never my wish that this might happen, but I know not how I might undo what has been done. I hear your anger, I share it, but I can do nothing—" And then, the true cry from his heart, "I beg you, Lanen, my wife, do not turn from me." He lifted his great eyes again and I felt the touch of his soul, my husband, my lover, and felt his despair sweep through to meet mine. "My only soulfriend in all the world is gone to sleep on the Winds this day, my Lanen, and I am severed from your arms forever. Do not leave me alone here in this desert, lest I run mad, or die of sere loneliness and sorrow."

Maran was wrong. Forgiveness was not enough.

I could not think how to answer him for a moment, when the words of our marriage vows rose up in my mind. *I take you as my husband and my mate for as long as life endures.* Well, life still endured in us both. He had not broken faith with me. He was changed, it is true—and, Lanen, what if he had been merely human, and returned from some terrible battle alive but unable to move without help? Would you leave him then? Abandon him to his fate because he could not hold your children?

Goddess, I cannot bear this! I cried silently. I looked away, closed my eyes to shut out the vision of him just for a moment, and at last paid attention to what else was happening around about me.

The earth trembled yet, resonating to the glory of the music of the Kantri. The great Mother Shia who bore us upon all Her broad back was shaken with wonder. Glancing below the lip of the hill, I saw the Laughing Girl of the Waters whispering up to us in a mist, rising from the lake into the twilight. I glanced behind me—and yes, there, just rising over the mountains, rode the Crone, the full moon in all her glory. The first rays of her loving light bathed us both in brilliance and struck gleams from Akor's soulgem. The Goddess in all Her aspects breathed in me, I was filled with Her presence, and I heard again—in my mind? in my soul? in my memory?—the words I had heard when Akor and I sought to understand why we had been so drawn to one another against all reason.

Daughter, have no fear. Let not this strangeness concern you. All will be well. All will be well. Follow your heart and all will be well.

No word of "he will be changed." No word of "you will know his love for only six moons, then be parted forever." No. All will be well.

All will be well.

Akor spoke again, his own eyes closed, his voice now soft with grief. "Lanen?"

I reached out to him, the same gesture I had used half a life and six moons ago, and touched his warm faceplate. His eyes flew open, wild with hope, and I swear I could hear his heart beating as though he had run a race. "The Winds and the Lady aid me, Akor. I am lost as you are lost," I said. The words, too, were an echo, and to my astonishment a tiny smile touched my lips. "We might as well be lost together, eh, my love?"

I stroked the smooth bone below his soulgem. "Damn and blast them all, my love. We're caught in this together. Shia forbid I should leave you now, when things are darkest." I stretched up and embraced as much of his neck, at the thin point behind the faceplate, as I could manage.

With that touch he opened his mind to me, unleashed a great flood. I could hear his thoughts as though a multitude spoke, a thousand voices at once, a thousand thoughts but each of them barely audible, as though he were shouting through a stone wall.

Lansen, I never meant this / my heart is broken even as yours / I feel your heart in my own breast its beating is all that keeps me on live / beloved, those who sought our death are defeated beyond recall / the Black Dragon is dust and ashes and the Kantri still live / Shikrar, Shikrar, soulfriend, my life is changed forever with your passing, sleep on the Winds, O friend of my heart / beloved, for all that has passed we yet live, our babes yet live / our future will not be what we expected but at least we are both here to have a future / was I not this shape when we first pledged ourselves to one another? / I will never hold our babes O ye Winds, have pity, have mercy / my heart breaks anew / Lanen Kaelar, Lanen, kadreshi, can you bear it? Can I bear it? By every Wind that ever blew, how in all the world are we to survive this parting? / for all that is, for all that will be, you are my love.

At that last, he drew back and fought for control of his voice. It took him a moment, for which I was deeply grateful, as I fought for speech as well.

"Lanen," he said, his voice far deeper than it had ever been, "Lanen, how shall we bear it?"

"One day at a time, *kadreshi*," I replied. Perhaps it was the Lady, perhaps I had touched again that strength of fire I had found when I believed I faced death in my cell in Verfaren. "If necessary, one breath at a time. It will not be easy, but—one breath at a time, I can do this thing."

He raised one great hand and wrapped it around my shoulders, as gently as he could manage. "One breath at a time, then. It is well." And then the great idiot added, "At the least, you know that I am not changed towards you."

Damned dragon. How *could* he say that with a straight face?

I felt one corner of my mouth turn up, then the other, then I snorted, and then I let loose with a great laugh, right from my toes. I felt his shock at my reaction, felt him hear the wild inanity of his own words, and watched as a column of flame shot into the darkening sky. A dragon's belly laugh. Goddess help us all.

By the time I finally wiped my eyes and he had regained some measure of composure, the worst of our souls' darkness had passed, at least for that time. I grinned at him. "Well, we did promise each other the spiky truth, didn't we?" I said. "Damn it, Akor, I didn't mean it literally!"

He hissed his gentle amusement, but was soon solemn again. He gazed into my eyes, far calmer now, thank the Lady. "I bless you for your loyalty, *kadreshi*. One breath at a time it is." He sighed. "Name of the Winds, Lanen Kaelar. What have we done that we must ever be faced with such ungentle choices?"

"Shia alone knows, and she's not telling," I said, sighing. "True enough, we have neither of us chosen the easy path in this life."

He cocked his head at an angle. "There is an easy path?" he asked.

"So I hear," I replied dryly. "I hope for their sakes our childer are blessed with better fortune. Or possibly better sense."

He hissed a little. "Hear us, ye Winds, and protect our babes from our ill fortune!"

"I hope they're listening," I said, my voice trembling. I was starting to shiver, for now the sun was down it was growing cold. Away on the far side of the hill a small fire began to gleam. "I'm getting bloody cold, Akor," I added. "And I'm tired and hungry and I could drink that lake dry, I think."

He hissed. "Some things have not changed. It is well. Shall we go to join the others? I believe many of our companions have moved down to the shore."

"Not all of us," said a voice, and my mother Maran came to join us in the moonlight. "There's a fire closer than that."

"Have you been here the whole time?" I asked, suddenly angry, afraid that she had overheard all we said.

"Not near enough to hear anything, Daughter," she said, "so you can save your anger for those who need it. Though I'm glad you're up to anger," she said wryly. "It's an improvement."

She turned to Akor, as if to learn how he fared. He raised up his head enough to look down at her.

"Lady Maran, I seem to recall—did you threaten me just now?" he asked.

I didn't think Maran would hear the slight teasing note under his scold, but she did.

"Don't be absurd," she said, her smile gleaming in the moonlight. "I may be daft, but I'm not stupid enough to threaten anyone whose head is larger than I am."

"Of course not. How foolish of me," he replied.

"And if I ever do it again, you'd best listen," she muttered, shrugging her pack from her back.

"Listen to what?" asked Akor innocently.

"Good lad," she said, pulling out a familiar cloth-covered shape. "I do have one request to make of you, if you have a moment."

"Of course, Lady," he replied with a little bow.

I couldn't resist. "Goddess, you're stuffy now you're back in that shape," I said out of the corner of my mouth, pleased and surprised to find that I had yet some remnant of humour within me.

"Silence, Gedri. You will show the proper respect for the Lord of the Kantri," he teased, mock-solemn, until Maran unwrapped the Farseer. "What would you of me, Lady?" he asked cautiously. "I wish to have as little to do with that globe as possible."

"I couldn't agree more," she said, holding it out. "It's a kindness, really. I thought I'd give you the honour of doing what I've longed to do for years." She smiled. "Destroy this for me, will you, my son?"

Akor took the Farseer, which looked absurdly small in his great claws, and tried to crush it. I thought it would instantly be powder, but it was too small.

He looked about at the green sward on which we stood and handed the globe back to her. "Come," he said, and flowed over to a large outcropping of rock. He moved astoundingly fast for something so huge.

We followed. Maran handed the Farseer to him once again and we stood back. He drew himself to his proper height, lifted his arm high, and brought the demon-haunted thing down with all his strength against the native stone of the mountains. It shattered with a splintering crash.

Maran gave a great sigh, as of one who has toiled long and hard come at last to rest, and fell senseless to the ground.

xv

The Healing of Wounds

Will

I'd seen it coming for more than a year now, but that didn't make it any easier when it came. Aral clung to me like a drowning man clings to anything that will keep him alive without noticing what it is. I held her close, I breathed in the sheer perfume of her like a guilty pleasure, and let my shirt and then my skin grow damp from her tears as she sobbed.

I was growing angrier by the minute. Good thing Vilkas had made himself scarce. I'd have felled him for a tin ferthing and let you keep the fee, no matter what he did to me after.

Rella waited until Aral had settled down to plain crying, then she brought over a waterskin and some bandages and ointment and sat down with Aral and managed to get her to take a drink. I wandered about and found just about enough sticks to get a fire going, though my hands shook a little with the flint and tinder. The little fire wouldn't last long, but it was better than nothing. I took the waterskin off of Rella and drank deep. That water was purest nectar.

With a sigh, I sat down with Rella's little pot of ointment and a few bandages. I'd barely begun when Aral croaked, "Here, Will, let me help." The poor soul, her eyes swollen with crying, her nose bright red, still managed to call up her power and clean the worst of the cuts for me and speed their healing. She soon realised that Rella was in worse case than I and insisted on treating her as well. When Rella was patched up, Aral went along to Jamie and did the same. Then she looked around.

"Where's Maran?" she asked.

Jamie and Rella looked around as though they expected her to appear from the darkness.

As it happens, she did. After a fashion. Akor joined us, Lanen at his side, Maran draped gently across his neck, unconscious. He lowered his head and I helped Lanen lower her mother carefully to the ground in front of the fire.

Aral

"What's wrong with her?" asked Lanen. I was strangely glad to hear normal concern in her voice. Goddess knew they had a long way to go, these two, but at least they'd made some kind of start. With all she had been through, Lanen still found it in her heart to be worried about this mother she barely knew. She is a great soul, Lanen.

Drawing my power to me, I gazed swiftly at Maran's limp body. Exhaustion, weariness of soul, demon claw, all of these were obvious, but there was something else, something I could not see properly. I treated the Raksha bites and gouges first, cleansing and healing. She breathed easier, but still she did not move.

It is so hard, with those who have withdrawn. Still, I owed it to her to try.

I drew in a deep breath and focussed my sight, traversing all the systems of the body in turn. Wait, what was—there—a faint shadow, elusive, moving, but there.

Normally I'd have asked Maran herself if I could go so deep, but she was not there to permit. I put one hand on either side of

her face, my palms to her temples, and went within. The landscape of her mind rose round about me, where all is symbol made
manifest.

I was in a dark place, but there was a large fire and the smell of
hot metal—oh, of course. A smithy.

Maran, clad in thick leather shirt, trews, and apron, stood at
the forge, shaping metal on the anvil. I watched as a Ladystar
magically took shape under her hammer. When it was complete,
she picked it up with a pair of tongs and thrust it into the water
barrel, where it made the water boil. A great cloud of steam
arose, shaping itself into a small smoky globe. She sighed, lifted it
out, and thrust it back in, but the same thing happened. A smoky
globe of steam above, the Ladystar glowing an angry red in boiling water, refusing to be quenched. "I was afraid of that. Too hot
for water," she said, and calmly turning the tongs around, she
pressed the hot iron into her flesh.

The shape of the Ladystar fell into her chest. It did not cause
her pain of itself, but she began to thrash as it went deeper into
her soul. "No, it's gone, I swear it's gone, I'll never use it more!"
she cried. "I never used it for gain, never!"

Smoky globe. Of course. Staying deep, I spoke aloud. "What
has become of the Farseer?"

"I destroyed it, as she bade me," said the voice of the dragon.

I saw it then, all clear before me. A demon artefact, used on
and off for years by a good soul for what she perceived as good
reasons, would yet forge an unseen bond with the user's soul. If
we did not act swiftly, she would follow the damned thing into
oblivion.

I withdrew from her mind, shaking myself, back in the real
world. "Will, find more wood for the fire. Maybe Vari—maybe
you could help him," I said, looking up at the dragon. The two of
them hurried off down the slope, towards a nearby stand of trees.

"I'll go with them," said Jamie, but I stopped him.

"No. I need you to call to her," I said. "She is—the country folk
would call it elfshot. Away with the fairies. In her case—she was

connected to the Farseer, and when it was destroyed something in her gave up." They all three stood about, slack-jawed. "She's lost part of her soul with the Farseer, damn it," I yelled, resisting the urge to slap all of them. "More than anything right now, she needs to hear the voices of those who give a damn about her. Talk to her." I sank down, weary beyond belief. "Give her some reason to stay."

Rella spoke up first, taking Maran's hand. "You get back here, Maran Vena," she scolded, as only good friends can scold one another. "Don't tell me you'd come all this way and live through the battle just to give up now? Hells, woman, you're free of that damned Farseer at last! Would you leave iron half shaped after you had done all the work to draw it down?" To my astonishment, Rella lifted Maran's hand and lightly kissed it. "I don't have so many friends I can afford to lose one, you stubborn blacksmith," she said. "Get back here."

"Maran," said Jamie. I could only admire him for managing to get any words at all past that lump in his throat. "Maran, I've so much to tell you yet. Don't go, heart's friend. Don't go before I can speak to you of our daughter's childhood."

Maran twitched a little, and a small moan escaped her lips.

"Oh, bugger it," said Lanen. She elbowed the other two aside, knelt beside her mother, lifted her under the shoulders, and clasped her mother's limp form to her heart. "I'm here, Maran," she said. "Thank Shia you've come to find me. I need you. I've always needed you, but more than ever now. I can't look after these babes all on my own, and Varien won't be able to help. Please, Maran. Stay to help me. Stay to know your grandchildren." Lanen sighed. "I know it's early days yet between us, but—please, Maran. Mother. Stay and let me learn to love you."

The soul can be healed as swiftly as the body. Sometimes. Maran rose to consciousness and tightened her arms about Lanen. Then, as if only then realising she no longer dreamed, she released her and sat up.

"Lanen? I was dreaming—I thought—did you say . . . ?"

"I surely did," said Lanen, rising to her feet and giving her mother a hand up.

Maran stood and gazed at her. "Lanen . . ."

"And I'll say it again later, but only after I've eaten something," said Lanen. She managed to find a grin. "Come on, Mother dear. I don't know about you, but I'm starving."

Maran returned the grin. "I could eat a bear, claws and all," she said as we all started down for the lake.

"I'd fight you for it," I chimed in. "Wait, shouldn't we tell Will—"

"They'll meet us by the shore," replied Lanen, sounding just a touch smug. "Truespeech is a wonderful thing."

"Thank you—and that reminds me, I must help you heal up after I've had some food, Lanen. You've had a hard time of it."

"I'll not object, Mistress Aral," she replied. As we walked, she suddenly started looking around, as if seeking something or someone. "Aral, I thank you for all your kindness, but why do you labour alone? Where is Mage Vilkas?"

I didn't know whether to curse or weep. "Mage bloody Vilkas was last seen heading for Castle Gundar," I replied. "I hope he thought to ask them to send us a few blankets and a bite to eat."

Then something occurred to me. I stopped dead, blinked, and looked at Lanen. "Wait. You *are* Marik's daughter, are you not?"

She stopped and turned to me. "Yes, alas. I am."

I grinned. "Then it's *your* castle. It was his, he was your father, he's dead, it's yours. Right?"

Lanen's eyes grew wide in the bright moonlight. "Now *that* is an interesting idea," she said.

We stumped on down the hill.

Idai

After all was done, after we had sung our dead onto the Winds and the sun was sinking rapidly into the west, I glided down to the shore and drank sparingly of the water of the lake. It was fouled but it was not poisoned, and I was desperate. Then, as Eldest, I began the terrible accounting.

The Lesser Kindred—no, the Aialakantri now, I must remember—were the only ones unhurt. Of the Restored, the precious Lost now come to themselves again after all the long centuries, eighty-eight remained alive out of two hundred, most with dreadful injuries. Twenty of those dead were those who had chosen the Swift Death upon their Restoration, but to my mind they were but the first casualties of this battle.

Of the Kantri, so lately arrived on these green shores one hundred and eighty-seven strong, just one hundred and twenty-six yet lived, including those who guarded the lansip trees with Mirazhe and Sherók in the east and Kretissh and Nikis on the Halfway Island. Here on the battlefield, one hundred and ten lay exhausted and in pain.

A hundred and seventy-three of us had fallen in battle, including one whom I could least bear to lose.

For that moment, I envied the dead. They slept on the Winds—*O Shikrar, my friend, may the Winds bear you up*—and we were left to go on, to live, to start again in this new world full of those who would not understand us. My heart was weary and my soul wrung beyond bearing. I came again to land and sprawled by the side of the lake, wounded and exhausted and weary nigh unto death at heart. There were no others by me, and I had only my thoughts for cold company.

Ah, Shikrar, you always did say we didn't fly enough to keep our strength at its fullest, I thought, sending my foolish truespeech to follow wherever he might have led. Now that all was over and there was time for thought, Shikrar and Akhor filled my mind. I lacked only a cent and a half of Shikrar's age, I had known him since we were younglings together, and now all those centuries rose up before me rich with memory. He and Akhor had been the dearest creatures in all the world to me. I cannot say the depth of all that was in my heart when I saw Akhor rise up from where Shikrar had fallen, but I fear that old foolishness sent up fresh shoots in the very instant. *He cannot be husband to Lanen thus, he is himself again, perhaps now, perhaps this time . . .*

As I say, foolishness. I was too weary then to discipline my heart, and it was soon forgotten in the battle that followed, but when that incredible music began to echo in the mountains, singing of love and the wonder of our three Kindreds reunited, I could not help but notice the tiny flame of hope deep, deep within, that even I hardly dared to recognise.

When, a little later, Akhor and all of the Gedri came down from the hill, I was the first soul they came to. For Akhor's sake I rose to my feet. I could not meet this wonder lying down.

"Akhor," I said, bowing. It was most strange, to look up to him. Akhor was younger than I, and so should have been smaller. *Does he wear Shikrar's body?* I wondered, horribly, but no—there was no mistaking that gleaming silver hide that scattered the moon-light.

"Lady, I rejoice to see you among the living," he replied. His voice was deeper, but it was *his* voice. My heart leapt even as I sternly beat it down. "Idai, my friend," he continued, "forgive that I intrude upon your grief. Know that mine is no less deep, but Shikrar would surely want us to help the living ere we mourn the dead."

"You speak truly, Akhor," I replied sadly. "Though I know not what may be done. There is a terrible toll among us, Lord," I said. "Many of our people are in pain, some in dreadful case, and all are wounded. What of the Healers?" I asked, raising my voice and looking to the young Gedri Aral. "Are you willing to assist?"

"I'll do what I can, Lady Idai, and welcome," said Aral, her voice so soft I could barely hear it. "It's Vilkas you want, though, and he's—I don't think he'll work with me anymore."

"For goodness' sake, why not?" asked Lanen. Then, gazing more closely at Aral's face, she asked, "Aral, why have you been crying?"

"It's a long story, Lanen," said Will the Golden, who had appeared with Akhor. He lay his hand on Aral's shoulder. "She's right, though. He's in no mood to be helpful, especially if it means working with Aral."

For all that I was pleased at last to see him in better case with Aral, the anger in his voice was plain.

"What's got into Vilkas?" asked Lanen, her own anger rising palpably. "Goddess, the man practically saved the world, what could possibly be bothering him? I'd have thought he'd be damned proud of himself."

"He nearly destroyed the Rakshasa, Lanen," said Aral wearily.

"Shame he stopped too soon," Lanen responded fervently.

Aral shook her head. "It's—it's not that simple, Lanen. I—he's angry at me, with good reason."

"I see," Lanen said. "And people who need his help can go hang, can they, while he goes off in a huff?"

"Lanen, it's not that simple," said Aral quickly, but Lanen was already hurrying down the hill after Vilkas. Akhor went with her. Maran started after them as well, but Jamie caught her sleeve and held her back.

"Wait," he said. Even to my eyes, his smile was peculiar. "Give her a chance. She's quite a lass, our girl Lanen," he told Maran. "Let's see what she can do." He looked around. "And in the meantime, I recommend we start a fire or six. It's going to get cold when the sun goes down, and I would happily maim for a cup of chélan."

Vilkas

I had no idea where I was going, as long as it was away from Aral. I found myself striding at speed along the north edge of the lakeshore, the calm water on my right, swearing at her under my breath.

I knew how she felt, of course I knew, I'm not blind deaf and dumb, but it wasn't my fault. How could she throw that in my face? I had trusted her with my deepest feelings as I have never trusted another soul. She knew I felt guilty, even if I never said so. To use our friendship as a—as a halter, as a weapon—damn the girl. I would never speak to her again.

Vilkas.

First she had nagged at me, nagged for more than a *year*, that I should let go the strong restraints I had placed around my power, and the instant I do so she loses her nerve and . . .

Vilkas, you idiot, you know she was right.

She had no right to say that!

No, that's true, but she had to shock you. You were too far gone to hear anything else.

She abused our friendship. She used emotional blackmail!

Yes. But no one else could get through to you at all. She was the only one who cared enough to try.

Cared enough to betray my trust?

And a deeper voice, a wiser voice from my secret heart, said, *She cared enough to rip her own heart out and throw it at your feet, man. To stop you from destroying yourself and half the world with you. I'd call that true friendship.*

"She stopped me!" I cried aloud, as though I could win this internal argument by sheer volume. "I was free for the first time in my life, I was *happy*, and she stopped me!" I clutched at my heart even as I walked. "I was in paradise. I will never know that bliss again. She took it from me."

She saved your life.

I would rather have died!

And would you rather have taken every last demon soul with you?

Yes!

That's why she stopped you.

I trudged on, stubbornly ignoring the fact that I'd lost the argument with my own conscience, when a vaguely familiar dragon landed a little way in front of me. It let off a human passenger and left. Anger swept through me. I didn't care who it was, I was spoiling for a fight.

It was Lanen.

She waited for me to come to her. Truth to tell, she didn't look very well.

I didn't care.

"Mage Vilkas," she began. "There are many yet who . . ."

"I'm only human, Mistress Lanen," I growled, sounding petulant even to myself. "I'm too tired to help anyone else tonight."

"There are many who wish to express their gratitude to you," she said evenly. "You have done a great work this day."

I said nothing but plodded on. The ground was heavy going just there.

"There is a greater work yet that awaits you," she said, striding by my side. The woman was a fool. Hadn't I just told her?

"I am exhausted, Lanen, didn't you hear me?" I snarled at her.

"Pah! Don't be stupid. You and Aral have quarrelled and you're angry at her. Fine, be angry, be bloody furious, I don't give a damn. But there are Kantri out there in mortal agony. I can do nothing to help them. You can."

I kept walking, but my anger was rising.

She hurried around and stood before me. I started to go around her and she reached out and stopped me by the simple expedient of planting her hands on my shoulders.

"Don't touch me," I said haughtily.

"Why not?" she asked, not moving.

"Because I said not to," I replied, trying to throw her off. Damn, she was strong. I couldn't shift her, which of course made me angrier.

"Vilkas, you must listen," she said, but I had come to the end of my tether.

"I don't have to listen to anyone!" I cried. I summoned my power and threw her off easily. She staggered back and landed with a thump. "You have no *idea* what I have suffered this day," I hissed at her. "I have been threatened by every demon in every Hell there is. I have saved Aral twice, by Mother Shia I have saved *every living soul in the world* this day, and for thanks the only person I have ever trusted betrays me. I am sick unto death of helping people. I don't care if the Kantri *rot.*"

I should have left then, I wanted to walk off and leave her there, but there was something about the woman that made me wait. Or something within me that knew she spoke truth, and stayed to hear it.

"Vilkas, you live," she said, rising to her feet. She walked towards me slowly, her hands outstretched to me in supplication this time, her honest face full of heartfelt pain. "Hundreds of them do not. Hundreds of them have died—O Shikrar—" She bowed her head for a moment, then looked full into my eyes. "Vilkas, their numbers were dwindling before. This may be their ending as a people. I beg you, of your mercy—surely there has been enough of death this day. You have been given power beyond measure. Use it to heal. They are in such terrible pain." She went down on one knee before me. "Please. I beg you."

It is a way to atone, my conscience said. Traitor that it was, siding with her. *You have done a terrible thing. It is a way to redeem yourself.*

I sighed. "Damn." I looked at Lanen out of the corner of my eye. "You sure you're not a Mage? I had no intention of helping you."

"I was tested years ago," she said, grinning up at me. She was nearly pretty when she smiled like that. "Not a trace of power anywhere."

"Oh, get up," I said, giving her a hand and helping her back to her feet. "Very well. Where shall I start?"

"A moment," she said. Her gaze lost focus. I was beginning to recognise that as an indication that she was using Farspeech.

"Idai comes," she said, even as Idai landed heavily a hundred paces away. She hurried to meet us, despite her injuries. I could not help myself, my power rose up in the face of pain, and I reached out to heal.

Nothing happened.

I tapped into that fire within, now banked a little, but there when I needed it. Nothing.

I poured my strength into her like a river, even a creature her size should have been restored from head to foot with that much assistance. I would have done better with a roll of bandages.

"Damn it," I muttered. "I can't do it."

"Are you well, Mage Vilkas?" asked Idai. *She* was concerned for *me*. I was beginning to feel a little ashamed.

"Your pardon, Lady, I can do nothing for you by myself," I admitted. It galled me, but I couldn't get away from the truth. Damn, blast and damn. "I need Aral."

Truespeech is an astounding thing. In moments Gyrentikh was aloft—I think it was he—and a very short while after, he landed by the lake with Aral.

She walked towards me tentatively, as though she trod barefoot on broken glass. When she came near enough in the failing light, I could see that her eyes were still red and swollen. She must have been weeping again.

Or still. You are not the only one who has lost something beyond measure this day.

She could not look at me. Aral, who had soundly berated me any number of times for any number of reasons, whose cheerful abuse had kept me from getting too full of myself for two years, could not raise her eyes to meet my glance.

"Have you treated yourself for shock yet, woman?" I asked, aiming for the tone of banter we had been used to use. It sounded brittle and angry. Ah, well.

"Didn't bloody well do any good," she replied. I could tell from her breathing that she was holding back tears. She knew I hated seeing women cry.

I have always enjoyed surprising Aral. I stepped up to her, took her by the shoulders, and kissed her forehead. "Vilkas, don't," she began, but I immediately let her go. She stared at me, uncomprehending.

"Now is not the time, Aral," I said gently. "We can address other things later. You were right. I was right. We were both very, very wrong. Come on. There is an awful lot of suffering going on that we can stop. I can't do it without you."

She nodded. We both turned to Idai, and Aral drew out the soulgem of Loriakeris. This time, though, she said quietly aloud, "Lady Loriakeris, will it please you to assist us?"

For answer the soulgem blazed once, briefly, in the darkness. Aral turned to me and grinned. "I'll take that as a 'yes'," she said. Holding the soulgem in one hand, calling her Healer's strength to her, she gingerly placed her other hand in mine. I gathered my Power about me, allowing the stream of that inner fire to fill me, grasped Aral's hand firmly, and sent the focus through the soulgem.

We found out later that we made quite a vision, Aral and Loriakeris and I. The evening star, turned blue and come to rest.

Idai's physical wounds were healed in minutes. Even I was astonished. It would take time, of course, for the new tissue to strengthen its bonds with the old, but she was healed.

"Don't get in any more fights for a few days, will you, Lady?" I said, and was rewarded by a blessedly warm hiss.

We went to treat Kédra next, but he refused. "There are others who need you more," he said.

"Take us to the worst," I replied. I kept hold of Aral's hand as we were borne through the air, in token of friendship, of apology. Of trust. We might never be able to rebuild that which had been, that first absolute trust, but there again, perhaps the new friendship would be based rather more strongly on truth.

We worked through the night. At first we were borne by Kédra or Idai to the worst injured, and we worked by the light of bonfires hastily provided by our escorts. Despite our best efforts another three of the Restored died, and another of the Kantri, but we saved ten who had been on the brink. We ate what we could in between.

When those in danger of imminent death had been seen to, when we were near dropping with hunger and weariness, Kédra whisked us away to a level field on the northwest shore of Lake Gand. Some blessedly practical soul had built a rough shelter, no more than a lean-to of branches but better than nothing, with a fire before it and a little more substantial food and drink laid out for us—fresh bread and butter, a gorgeous collop of venison stewed in wine, with cheese and dried fruit after. And some blessed soul had thought to send along both chélan and sweet water to wash it down. We fell on it as though we hadn't eaten in a hundred years.

Just as we were drinking the last of the chélan, Lanen stepped into the firelight and went down on one knee before us. "How fare you both?" she asked. Her voice was calm, but her eyes were filled with concern.

"I think we'll live, Mistress Lanen, thank you," said Aral. "Bless you for the food."

"Have you strength now to continue, or do you require rest?" she asked.

So that was it. She was afraid we had stopped for the night.

I rose on weary legs and clapped her on the shoulder. "Fear not, Lady. We have supped and drunk." I looked to Aral. "Can you go on?"

She stood slowly, brushing off crumbs, saying, "I could sleep for a week, to tell the truth, but not until we're finished." She smiled. "Come then, Lanen, call Idai and take us to the next."

To my surprise, Lanen rose and grinned. "We are better organised than that." She raised her chin and called out, "Now!"

In the instant the nighttime landscape changed. We beheld a field ringed with bonfires, set alight by the Kantri we had healed, who then wandered around the circle lighting yet more. At last we could see what we were doing, and I wasn't going to complain about the warmth either. Our next patient lay wearily in the firelight, Jamie beside it.

"Who has done this?" I asked, all astonishment, as we reached the bright centre of the field.

Jamie grinned. "It was Rella's idea. You're not the only ones who've been busy, you know. Lanen has even had the Kantri working away, bringing enough wood and ferrying her back and forth from the castle."

"The castle?" said Aral in wonder. Then her expression changed. "Bloody hellsfire! That's where the food came from!"

Jamie's grin grew wider. "Indeed. Seems there's a woman there who knew Marik as a child and can see the resemblance in his daughter." He laughed. "Of course, the fact that she arrived in the courtyard in the hands of a bloody great dragon almost certainly helped her case along."

We treated one after another, barely stopping save to admit

the next to the circle of fire. Lanen stayed with us to translate, for many of the Kantri had no human speech. The Dhrenagan, to my astonishment, spoke more fluently even than had Shikrar, though their speech was terribly archaic—I learned later that in their day, Gedri and Kantri lived together in peace. It struck me that their experience in this might be desperately needed soon.

Shadowy figures kept the bonfires burning bright, and Will and Maran, Rella and Jamie, kept us supplied with food and drink. Towards the end of the night, when we could no longer stand, they watched over us as we rested for the half of an hour here, a few minutes there.

I had thought, at the height of my glorious madness, that my power was infinite. Now I began to learn the merely human limits that surrounded it. As dawn grew pale in the east, Aral and I were finally forced to stop. Our joined Healer's strength was hardly diminished, which was astounding, but we were entirely exhausted. We saw the last of the dragons whose wounds might kill them and finally called a halt. I sank to my knees and was prepared to sleep on the bare ground, but Maran lifted me in her powerful arms as though I were a child and carried me to our lean-to. I had no strength to protest. Goddess, but that woman is impressive!

There were two piles of heather, covered with blankets, and a feather pillow each. I realised this when I woke, you understand. I was asleep the instant Maran set me down.

I think Will carried Aral.

Lanen

I woke in the late afternoon, groggy and confused. It took me a moment to remember what and where this room was.

The guest chamber at Castle Gundar.

My father's people had taken us in the night before, given us ample food for ourselves and the Healers, and when we returned at dawn they led us each to decent rooms and let us sleep. I don't recall whether Mistress Kiri really believed that I was Marik's daughter at that point or not, but she was kindness itself. Given the near presence of the True Dragons of legend, and the fact that Akor spoke to the lady in so courtly a fashion, I suppose her generosity was not surprising.

We had all danced attendance on the Mages until daybreak. I was still weary beyond belief, but I forced myself out of bed. I wandered down to where I thought the kitchens must be and found a maidservant who pointed me to the bathing chamber, O blessed civilisation! A long deep bath stood there, and two young lasses helped me fill it with steaming water and provided soap and drying cloths. I nearly wept when I lowered myself into clean water for the first time in what felt like years. My hair was shocking and my clothes were worse, and it was only when I had scrubbed off the grime that I realised just how filthy I had been. I went to scrub my clothing in the bathwater, but the little maidservant took away my horrible shirt, tunic, and trews and brought me a long gown. It was a good handspan too short, but there was enough room in the shoulders. The maid assured me that my own garments would be ready for me by morning.

Clean and warm at last, I followed my nose and found Jamie wandering about not far ahead of me. I hailed him, and he led me confidently towards the Great Hall.

"How fare you this morning?" I asked, yawning.

Jamie laughed. Goddess, it was good to see him laugh again. "It lacks but an hour of sunset, my girl. Morning, indeed!" He yawned along with me. "I am well, Lanen. Exhausted, but well. Nothing that another day or so in a real bed won't cure." He stopped in the corridor and faced me. "And before we meet the rest of them— how are you?"

"I am well enough," I replied solemnly. I didn't bother to tell him that I had wakened weeping. We were none of us unwounded. "And all three of us will be considerably better once I get some food inside me!"

The Great Hall boasted a long oaken table and individual chairs rather than benches. The table was well laden with food, though by the look of things it had groaned even louder before. Maran and Rella sat at one end, talking at speed. Jamie joined them, and I could only admire Rella's restraint. She sat back, for the most part, and let Maran and Jamie catch up on the last twenty-odd years. I caught her eye, and was satisfied with the calm smile and the nod she sent my way. All was well with her, then, too.

I joined Will, who was sitting alone at the other end. "Good morrow, Willem," I said cheerfully, once I had devoured a little bread and meat. "I pray you, forgive my lack of manners, but I seem to spend my days perpetually ravenous."

He laughed. "'Tis usual for a pregnant woman, Mistress Lanen," he said. "I remember my sister with her first. Her husband told me he was convinced she would bear him three sons at once, for she ate practically without ceasing for a full two months."

I grinned in sympathetic horror. "Three at the one time!"

He smiled again and shook his head. "No, no, it just seemed that way. In the end there was only the one! To be fair, the lad was big even at birth, but within three months my sister was back to being tiny. We still don't know what she did with all that food."

We ate and drank and talked, at peace for that time. Vilkas and Aral arrived, barely able to speak, just after sunset. They had exactly enough strength to nod to us all before they began to feed their ravening hunger. "You must understand, Lanen," said Aral, between mouthfuls. "In the normal way of things, we would heal a single individual of whatever ailed them, and then spend the next day or so sleeping and eating to restore our strength." She took a long swallow of good wine and sighed with pleasure. "I have no idea how many we healed yesterday, but, dear Goddess, I could sleep the full moon round."

On the heels of her words a young servant lad came rushing in, crying, "Dragons! The dragons are circling, they'll kill us all! Save us!" He threw himself at my feet. "Please, Mistress, we've treated you well, don't let them take us!"

I grinned and reassured him that not a single marauding dragon would come for him as we all hurried out into the courtyard. In the failing light of the westering sun the air was sparkling with dragons. Where yesterday even their rejoicing held the edge of darkness as they sang their loved dead onto the Winds, now they wove a sky-dance of sheer delight, to lift the heart and heal the spirit.

My eyes were drawn instantly to the great silver form that was the centre of the pattern. I opened my heart to him, sending no words, letting him know only the joy that I felt at the sight. In return I heard the great song, too distant for the ears of the body but full and wondrous in the mind. The high, light voices of the Aiala sang a song of sheer joy in life; the darker voices of the Dhrenagan sang of their redemption and of peace made with the Gedri through the healing of the Dragon Mages, Vilkas and Aral (*Goddess, just wait until they hear that*); and blended through all, the strong voices of the Travellers, the Kantri, twining all into a single glorious music that rang in the heart and echoed down the years. I heard Akor now and again as he struck the lowest notes, the foundation of the music, as though the mountains had grown wings and sang with the Kantri one last time.

I let the music wash over my weary heart. The sheer beauty of the dance was a blessing. The music, reinforcing the pattern of their flight, spoke of hope for the future of Kantri and Gedri.

All will be well.

The sun set. The three Houses of the Kantri glided gracefully through the twilight, coming to ground beyond the lake, and we saw light spring up on Shikrar's hill as bonfires were lit.

We all returned to the Great Hall, warm and welcoming, and as fresh chélan was passed around I told everyone of the song of the Kantri. Vilkas sat astounded and utterly delighted that they had mentioned him by name, and Aral grinned. "Amazing," she said, laughing. "Dragon Mage, eh? There's a new one. I predict my mother will faint when I tell her. Pass me those parsnips, will you, Maran?"

When the two of them finished gorging, they rose separately, bowed to us, made their apologies, and disappeared back to their several chambers to sleep once more.

After they left, I wandered down to the other end of the table and sat beside Maran.

"Welcome, child," she said, in great good humour. She looked ten years younger since she had been talking with Rella and Jamie. "I've just been finding out the worst of the tales Jamie has to tell on you."

"Oh, no!" I cried, in mock dismay. "Oh, Jamie, you didn't!"

He looked up and grinned, and my heart near stopped. I had never seen him so happy in all my life. "I did, and then some," he said smugly.

"You'll be wanting to leave again soon, then?" I said jestingly to Maran.

She laughed. "What, and miss the chance of seeing you lose your temper? I couldn't."

I smiled. "Shia save us, what has he been telling you? I'm a sweet, patient soul, gentle as the day is long. You'd go far to find anyone more softly spoken and even-tempered than I!"

I don't think anyone heard those last few words. Jamie, for one, was laughing too hard.

By the time we had all eaten, most of us were ready for more sleep. Aral never had helped heal my wounds, and they ached. The good folk at the castle had helped me clean and bind them the night before, and I knew no more than time and rest were needed to put them right.

I bade the company good night and wandered, replete, into the torch-lit courtyard of the castle, with some vague thought of a quiet walk before bed. To my surprise I found Kédra there. "Good even, my friend," I greeted him.

"Good even, Lady," he replied. "How fare you?"

"I'm well enough, thank you, Kédra," I said. "We saw you all dancing on the Winds. It was—extraordinary."

"And for us," said Kédra. "The first sky-dance of the Three Branches of the Kantri was a dance to end the life of the Evil One. The second we danced for our own dead. Tonight, without a word being spoken, we all rose up aloft for a dance of life and rejoicing. It is well."

"It was a wonder," I said. "Though that word is a lame horse with much to bear." I smiled. "However, I cannot believe that you have come here only to be complimented on your music." I composed myself and asked, quite calmly, "Where is Akor?" *Why is he not here, Kédra, instead of you?*

Kédra bowed, a short bob of his head followed by a little ripple of his long neck. "You have the right of it, Lady. Lord Akhor begged me to await you here, for answer to that very question. He bids me tell you that he is tending to his people." Kédra sighed. "We are all weary and wounded in body and spirit, Lanen Kaelar," he said. "Lord Akhor moves among us speaking reassurance, soothing wounded hearts, and letting all see that there is order yet to cling to. He sends his greetings by me, and begs that you will forgive him for not spending time with you this day." Kédra's voice was quite dry. "Truth to tell, Lanen, he is greatly weary himself, and I believe you would do him a kindness not to bespeak him until the morrow." To my surprise, Kédra dropped his jaw and hissed his amusement. I welcomed the warmth on my cold ankles. "Indeed, he has by now told the tale of his transformation to each individual soul, I believe, and thereby has accomplished the most important task of all. We now have something to think about."

"What, exactly?" I asked, faintly amused. "Whether he's truly a dragon or no? Whether having given up the Kingship he can now reclaim it?"

Kédra snorted. "Far simpler than that, Lady. The great question is, who is Eldest?"

"Idai, surely," I said, confused. "She was next after—oh!"

"Yes, you see it," he said. "Akhor is not in the body he was born to, but neither does he inhabit my father's remains, although his present form is the size my father's was. Idai has lived longer, of course—but we none of us are certain what to make of Lord Akhor anymore."

I barked a laugh. "Ha! You're in good company. Goddess knows I haven't the faintest idea."

Kédra hissed. "I think perhaps he does not know either, Lanen. He appears to be—stunned, by his new shape." He sighed. "At the least, let us be thankful that he is obviously Akhor, the Silver King, and not some dreadful hybrid of himself and my father."

I shuddered. "Kédra, I—I am so sorry . . ."

"Do not fear to speak of Shikrar," said Kédra kindly. He gazed at me. "He took me aside the night before the battle, Lanen. He told me of his Weh dreams, and that he believed that his time was come to sleep upon the Winds."

"Oh, Kédra!" I said softly. "I am so sorry that your dear father was taken from us. I knew him so very short a time, but he was always just and always kind to me, and I will miss him."

"It is considered a great gift among us, Lanen Kaelar, to know when your life is about to end," said Kédra, and his voice and his heart were calm, if sad. "My father lived a long and worthy life. His use-name was Hadreshikrar, Teacher-Shikrar, for he taught nearly every one of the Kantri now alive how to fly." Kédra paused a moment, and stood in what I eventually learned was the Attitude of Recollection. "I am told that he was a wild spirit in his younger days, always in the air, trying new and different ways to fly, to manoeuvre, to test his own skills in flight, and to try them against those of his companions who dared try to match him." His Attitude shifted a little, to include elements of Pride. "None ever did, not after his second kell. He served as Eldest of the Kantrishakrim for nearly three kells, as Keeper of Souls for seven, and in his last days he led us in our great return, flying home across the Great Sea to Kolmar." Kédra's voice quavered a little, then. "He was ridiculously proud of me, you know. I found it embarrassing, but that is who he was. And he was set fair to be even worse about his grandson."

Kédra looked into my eyes then. "I know not what happens to the Gedri soul after death, but we believe that the departing spirit is met by those who have died before, to welcome the traveller home. My father Shikrar"—he had to clear his throat, and I felt my own tighten in response—"my father Shikrar loved my mother Yrais with a love exceeding deep. She was taken from him so early. I barely remember her, only as a soft loving voice and a dear presence." He bowed his head for a moment, and when he looked up there was a peace in his eyes that I envied. "I mourn him, Lanen. I loved him dearly and I will miss him as long as I breathe, but I know in my deepest heart, as surely as I know that the sun will rise on the morrow, that he and my mother are together again in joy, where no pain or sorrow can touch them. It is well, Lanen Kaelar."

"It is well, Kédra," I responded. My heart could rest now, though I too would miss Shikrar's great soul.

I bade Kédra good night and returned to my chambers, with but a single thought before me that followed me into sleep.

Akor, Akor, my dearling. We have survived the most dreadful test of our marriage, short of death—but now that the light of day shines upon our lives, now that the dread of battle and its aftermath are over—what is to become of us, my husband? Whatever in all the world is to become of us?

xvi
Ta-Varien

Lanen

There was much to be done and decided before we all left Castle Gundar.

The matter of my patrimony was eventually established on a more solid foundation. Mistress Kiri, who had known my father since he was a child, began by being terrified of the dragons and deeply suspicious of me and my claim. After she spent half a day closeted with Maran, discussing Goddess only knows what, she was forced to admit that I was indeed the only known child of Marik of Gundar. It seemed that he had told her once, in his cups, that he had a daughter, but she had never managed to learn any further details. Maran, seemingly, supplied sufficient details of her own to content Mistress Kiri, who then became my staunch ally and introduced me to the entire household as the right and legal heir.

It was very peculiar indeed to realise that these people, some of whom had been kind and considerate even when they believed our company to be complete strangers, had known of my existence for several years, while I had lived in complete ignorance of theirs.

Mistress Kiri, to my astonishment, even went so far as to convince the steward to give me access to Marik's fortune. I tried to object. Mistress Kiri, looking at me rather more shrewdly than I would have expected, said, "Did your father, in his entire life, ever give you one single thing?"

"No," I replied simply, realising that she might not want to hear the true answer, which would be *Well, he gave me to a demon, or tried to. Does that count?*

"Then he can make up for quite a long stretch of neglect," she declared, handing me the key to Marik's treasure room.

I had a long talk with the steward, Kesh, who was harmless enough if you didn't expect much in the way of generosity. Marik had hired him for his grasping nature. I made him swear on his soul and in front of quite a few witnesses, including Mistress Kiri, to pay everyone in the place a better wage, thanked him for looking after the lands so well, told him to get in more cattle as we might expect any number of winged visitors in the near future, and left him to it.

I suppose I could have tried to live there, but it never even occurred to me. Spending more time than absolutely necessary in a place where Marik was honoured? No. I would presume far enough to provide myself and my friends with food and shelter for a week, and the staff with a decent living from my father's ill-got gains, but more than that I could not do. I did leave the staff with the impression that I might return at any time. Just for morale.

I saw but little of Akor in that time. He spent his days among the three Houses of the Kantri, teaching, learning, listening, and avoiding me as surely as I was avoiding him. We were coming to terms with our new life, but it was hard, Goddess it was hard, and there was so much else to do. We found a compromise, finally. Akor had taken to lighting a fire on Shikrar's hill in the evenings, and I joined him there, to talk a little, to consider what had happened to us both, to speak a little of our future, but for the most part simply to be in each other's company. It grew easier, over even those few nights. He could still make me laugh.

A full seven days after the battle, when even Vilkas and Aral had recovered much of their strength, we held a last council in the Great Hall at noon. Its generous windows were flung open, and the light and air that flowed into the room were extraordinary. Spring came late to the mountains, but it seemed to be trying to make up for lost time. The orchards were heavy with delicate apple blossom, and there was some plant that grows in those hills that had the most wonderful scent I have ever known. If the High Fields of the Lady are worth achieving, they must smell like that.

We were graced with Salera's presence as well, thanks in large part to those windows. Akor, too, could come near enough to see and hear. We had put it off for a time, while wounds were healed and tales told all round, but we all knew that the time had come to go our own ways.

Jamie and Rella announced that they were leaving on the morrow. "Where are you going?" I asked. This last week had been a blessing, having the pleasure of their company without a single deadly threat in sight. I knew fine that Jamie would not stay in the House of Gundar even if I did.

"Somewhere warm and green and quiet," said Rella. "Where they have real beds with feather pillows. You have spoiled me, girl," she said, grinning at me. "This week of living at ease has got into my bones. I could bear to live like this."

"We're going back to Hadronsstead first though, Lanen," said Jamie, smiling. "I shudder to think what that idiot Walther may have been doing to the farm. He's a born horse-breeder, but I wouldn't let him within smelling distance of the Great Fair at Illara." He put his arm around Rella. "Ilsa is green and quiet, and I daresay we will manage to make enough warmth between us to be getting on with."

Maran smiled, and only the slightest shadow darkened her eyes.

🐉 "As to that," put in Akor from the window, "I am to tell you that Kédra offers to fly you as far as Elimar. He returns to his family tomorrow. He has asked me to say that he would be honoured to bear with him any who wish to journey so far."

"Oh, excellent Kédra!" cried Rella, and Jamie went so far as to stand and bow to Akor. "We accept with deep and abiding gratitude, Lord Akor. Kédra is very kind."

I turned to the Healers. "And what of you, O Dragon Mages?" I asked, teasing. Vilkas winced and Aral laughed. "I don't think our services will be needed here for a time," said Aral. "I was going to go home for a bit. Berún's a fair step, but I haven't seen my family for nearly three years."

"Mistress Aral, might I have a word with you?" said Salera. Aral, taken by surprise, rose and joined her in a quiet corner of the room. They appeared to be discussing something quite solemn that was obviously important to Salera.

Vilkas returned my gaze evenly. "I think that where I go will depend greatly on where you go, Lanen Kaelar." He nodded at my belly; I was now growing more obviously pregnant, practically by the day. "I suspect that all will be well for some time yet, but if you can bear my company I would rather be nearby. Especially in the last two months," he added wryly, "lest I outstay my welcome before." He pinned me with that brilliant blue gaze, smiling for a change, and for the first time I had a glimpse of what Aral saw in him. I suppose he was rather good-looking, at that.

"I think Aral's idea is the best, for me," I said, turning to Maran. "Time to go home."

She nodded, resigned. "I suppose you'll want to be in Hadronsstead, somewhere familiar, now that—"

"No, no, I didn't mean that," I said hurriedly. "Not at all." I barked a short laugh. "Jamie, you know I love you like a father, but I cannot bear the walls of Hadronsstead. Maran, I know I haven't asked, and Goddess knows there will be quite some train of us if you'll have us, but—Mother, I would very much like to go back with you to Beskin." I grinned. "I expect I'll be tied down for some time over the next few years, and I've never seen the Trollingwood. Jamie tells me it's quite something."

Why it should have given me so much pleasure to see joy in Maran's face, I don't know. We still hardly knew each other, though surviving the death of the Demonlord had brought us sharply together. Perhaps now we would have the chance to put right what had gone wrong. Given enough time.

"What say you, Maran?" asked Akor gently. "Is there room in Beskin for a dragon? Can you take us both, and Mage Vilkas, and put up with two squalling babes when the time comes?" He hissed a little. "Though perhaps your home is too small for two babes *and* Lanen . . . ?"

Maran laughed. "It held me and all my brothers and sisters, it can surely hold my daughter and her family. Oh, come and welcome!" she said, taking me in her arms briefly. "Though you, dragon, are almost certainly going to be a problem."

"Hmmm," said Vilkas calmly. "I appear to be going to Beskin, near the Trollingwood." He grinned. "I always wanted to travel."

Aral

The moment I was near enough to hear her quiet voice, Salera spoke.

"Mistress Aral, I have said no word, but the time is come. What is in your heart for my father Will?"

"I beg your pardon?" I asked, taken aback.

She gazed at me. "My speech is much better than it was, I am certain that you can understand me."

I was going to feign surprise, but I could not, not in the face of that open soul. "I don't know, Salera," I replied honestly. "I can only guess at what he feels, and I don't like guessing. He has never said a single word to me about his own heart."

"Father," said Salera. Her voice was not loud, but he heard and wandered over. I tried to read him as he approached, but he was just Will, just there, big and calm and golden-haired, a good friend.

Goddess save us all, Salera really didn't know about human delicacy, for she greeted him with, "My father, why have you not spoken to Mistress Aral of what is in your heart?" Will spluttered. She ignored him and went on, "I know the depth of your feelings for her, but how can you expect to win her if you say nothing?" She turned back to me, leaving Will blushing furiously, and said in a conspiratorial tone, "It appears to be a male trait. My own suitor has waited a full year before speaking."

"A suitor?" said Will, amazed. "But—you've only been awake such a short time . . ." His voice faded as he realised the obvious.

"I was awake before, my father, and I remember Tchaeros well. Now that we have speech, he is more courtly"—and she hissed a little with amusement—"but it has taken him a very long time to ask me to join with him."

"Do you love him?" asked Will, frowning like any father at being informed so of a daughter's lover.

"I do, my father," said Salera, her wings fluttering. I could only guess that it was with pleasure. "I agreed to join with him this morning as the sun brightened. We will celebrate our—betrothal, is it called?—this very night, and I would that you might be there." She turned back to me. "I would see you there as well, Mistress Aral, if your heart allows."

She brushed past Will as she left, and I heard her whisper, "Speak your heart, Father. She is wise. She will hear."

"Aral, I—drat that child, she doesn't understand—"

I put my hand on his arm. He froze.

"I think she understands rather better than you or I," I said quietly. I was suddenly shy, but I managed to mutter, "Will, please—I—please, just speak truth to me. Is Salera right?"

He took my hand from his arm. "Aral, I'm a good few years older than you," he began.

"Not that much," I said, smiling. "Look at Varien and Lanen!"

He grinned back. "Right enough, I suppose. I—I've never said word these last two years, Aral, because I know fine how you feel about Vilkas."

I nodded. "I know how I feel about him too. Go on." I felt one corner of my mouth go up. "You haven't actually said anything yet."

I practically felt him crack. He stepped closer to me as if he would have swept me into his arms that very moment; I could see him tremble with the effort of not doing so, and I was suddenly very aware of him as a *man* rather than as a friend.

And there he stood, this tall, handsome man, not daring to touch me, but telling me all his heart, speaking such words of love to me as I had only ever dreamed of.

I had dreamed of hearing them from Vilkas, of course, though my rational mind had realised that would never happen. No, he was not Vilkas, tormented, wildly powerful, terrified of life and of love. He was Will. Strong, calm, reliable, capable Will, who had loved me for two solid years now and said nothing until this moment because he knew I cared for another.

I never meant to do it, but in moments of high emotion I seem to call my corona to me without thinking. I swear, I could see his love, flowing between us strong as a river from a high mountain, and still he did not touch me.

"I knew the time would come when you'd bring Vilkas to the point," he said, finally, when all else was said. "I feared it might happen when you were far from me, and I couldn't bear that. I let myself be carried by those great beasts because I would not abandon you when you needed me." He stopped and let himself smile. "Though I won't pretend it was for your sake alone. I damn well intended to be there to catch you."

"And so you did," I replied. I would never forget his arms holding me up when Vilkas cast me from him. Vil and I had come to a working truce, but in that awful moment it was Will who had held me close and supported me until I could stand again.

He finally let himself go so far as to take my right hand in both of his. "By my word, Aral, I will not die if you do not, or if you cannot love me." His eyes were alight, he seemed more alive than I had ever seen him. "But I tell you true, I would far rather live my days with you than without you."

No matter what sentiment might say, I owed him the truth. I spoke quietly, for the others were not speaking much just at that moment and I did not wish to be overheard.

"Will, I won't pretend I feel more than I do," I said. "You know I care for you, you've been a wonderful friend to me ever since I met you. But—" I glanced at Vilkas, smiling now and chatting with the others. His hold on my heart was less than it had been, but not by much. "You know also that my heart has long been his. I found out for certain that he doesn't want it, but—it will all take time."

I paused. I had been going to tell him that he should not hope, but as I was about to form the words, I found to my surprise that there might indeed be room in my heart for another. He stood, strong and true, his heart open and undefended, for me to wound or to heal. A curious thought occurred to me.

"Come with me out into the corridor, Will, I have something particular to tell you," I said, and went before him out of the range of other eyes.

The corridor was deserted. He closed the door behind us.

"Kiss me," I said.

For all his ardour, he was taken aback. "What?"

"Kiss me like you mean it," I said, challenging him.

Gracious Lady. I got more than I had bargained for.

When we came up for air, he reeled as one drunk. I suspect I did too.

"Come with me, Will," I said quietly. "Come with me to Berún and meet my family. I do not promise anything, and I do not yet have a whole heart to offer you. I would not offer you less."

"I have waited two years, Aral," he said, his voice lovely and deep. "I can wait a little longer." He grinned wildly. "I've always thought I should see the rest of the South Kingdom," he said, smiling and drawing me out into the broad spring day. "Tell me about Berún."

If that's how you always kiss, my lad, you may not have all that long to wait, I thought, and casually took his hand as we walked out into the sunlight.

Khordeshkhistriakhor

The next morning, all farewells said, the company of friends scattered to the Winds for that time.

I was not yet accustomed to my new strength and had some concerns about carrying Lanen, Maran, and Mage Vilkas all the way to Beskin, but I barely noticed them once I was airborne. I remember thinking that I had had no idea that Shikrar was so astoundingly powerful. I flew high, smiling as I heard his voice in my memory. *High air is the best—least work, longest flight.* His words were a part of me, they had been for many a hundred winter and would stay with me as long as I drew breath. The thought gave me comfort. *Sleep easy on the Winds, my soulfriend Shikrar. Your words yet ring in my heart.*

I was not prepared, however, for the sheer joy of flight. I had flown a few times near Castle Gundar, mostly short hops, and the great Celebration of the Three Branches—but that was a dance, not flight for the sake of it. This—this was freedom, this was life and all, and it filled me with unalloyed delight. I did not dare to bespeak Lanen, lest she feel my joy and gain a terrible understanding of what I had missed.

I felt she had enough terrible understanding to be getting on with.

In the meanwhile, I took intense pleasure from the feel of the wind bearing me up, the strengthening sun of spring on my face, the sheer power of these immense wings, and a new land below me full of promise and the unknown. I sang my joy to the Winds, and heard Lanen's mindvoice echoing the song.

We had spoken together several times in the kindly darkness of evening, up on Shikrar's Hill (it is called that to this day). There was a truce just then between my lady wife and me. We lived as we had said we would, one breath at a time, but so often still those breaths were bought with heart's pain.

It did not help matters that Lanen was even more passionate in her nature than usual. Vilkas had told me that this was normal for a woman carrying a child, but it widened the gap between us even more, for I found myself inclining in the other direction. The body shapes the mind in many ways. At rest, my heart now beat at a tenth the pace of Lanen's, and I took far deeper and far fewer breaths. How could my mind not be affected by this incredible change?

I do not say that my love was lessened, for it was not and never has been—but the expression of it was changed perforce, and that threatened to tear my heart in two. Lanen was the same, I know she was. I heard her thoughts while she slept, saw her dreams, knew her fears. From dreams of winged and clawed monsters she would wake with racing heart, calling out to me in fear, and the only answer I could make was to speak to her mind to mind, say her name gently, reassure her that all was well and that she had only been dreaming, bespeak her until her heartbeat slowed. She had had to wake the maidservants at Castle Gundar to bring her a warm cup of chélan. I knew not what we could do when we reached Beskin.

Beskin should have been three days' flight, but it took us full five days to find it. Maran, the only one of us who knew where it was, did the best she could, but as she reminded me, nothing looks the same from the air. She was quite right. Finally she laughed and said perhaps we should try walking for a few hours, in the hope of finding someone to ask our way from. After four days had passed, that is precisely what we did, though I decided to keep a little distance away lest I terrify any poor souls that should happen upon us. The great forest of the Trollingwood stretched trackless away to our left, but I needed more precise directions than "just keep going until you're near the mountains, then turn back a little."

In the end, Maran wandered into a little town and came back shamefaced. We were much too far south and west, it seemed. I gathered up my charges and rose up aloft, bearing north and east. I took pleasure in the smell of the trees rising to meet me, in having so vast a land to fly over. Our old island took less than three hours' flying, end to end. There was so much to see here!

Lanen and I began to consider, simply as an exercise, the possibility of some kind of harness that I might wear, whereby she might in future accompany me in more comfort. We whiled away quite a few idle hours on possible designs.

In the midafternoon of the fifth day, Lanen bespoke me to say that Maran had recognised a great stone house not far from Beskin. We came to land at the edge of a large field. The cattle galloped away, which suited me well. Maran led us—swiftly by her standards, at a snail's pace by mine—along the road for a few miles, and up. Beskin lies in a cosy valley, protected by half a ring of hills at its back, looking out over rich farmland, and behind the bare hills around Beskin lies an arm of the Trollingwood, the vast northern forest that sprawls over most of the width of Kolmar. Maran assured the others that the Trollingwood was just far enough away for the villagers of Beskin to be safe from marauding wolves and bears. Most of the time.

I walked with the three of them to the door of Maran's house. The village seemed deserted, but Maran laughed and told me that everyone was hiding. "We'll have the chance to sort it out later, Akor, never fear," she said. She seemed curiously pleased to be invading the village at the feet of a terrible marauding dragon. "That's what they'll think you are, at least," said Maran, her grey eyes alight. "I think I'll let you talk them out of it."

Her home was built on two levels with several rooms in each. I found Gedri buildings astounding and stared into each window in turn, but the little stone courtyard around the smithy was far too small for me. I could only stand there coiled about myself, with my wings tight furled and my tail firmly tucked out of the way. It would be like trying to live in a tiny cage.

Lanen, realising for the first time that I must dwell entirely apart from her, turned stricken eyes up to me. "Akor, what— damn, I thought you'd be nearby at least—" Her eyes filled with tears, which she dashed impatiently away. Her raging emotions, over which she had no control, made her furious.

"Do not be concerned, my heart," I replied. "We are but newcome here. There will be plenty of time for change." I grinned. "And possibly for building. Lady Maran, have you thought of a place nearby where I might rest, or shall I seek shelter in the Trollingwood?"

Maran met my gaze and replied, sadly, "For now, Akor, I fear it must be the Trollingwood. I have ploughed my brains for days, and I can think of nowhere large enough for you to stay. Forgive me."

"There is nothing to forgive," I replied, doing my best to keep the sorrow from my voice. "I will see what may be done. You are certain that none claim land in the Trollingwood?"

"Certain sure," said Maran, grinning. "It's said to be far too dangerous in there."

"How clear-sighted of people, to know in advance that I was coming to dwell therein," I said lightly. I leaned down and came within Lanen's reach. *"I am ever here, dearling,"* I said in true-speech as she laid her hand gently upon my faceplate. *"No more than a thought away. And if it may be done, perhaps we will make the smithy courtyard more worthy of the Kantri."* Aloud I added, "If you all will meet me at the edge of the wood tomorrow at dawn, I will guide you to whatever chambers I have been able to find."

By the next morning, I was pleased to show them my new dwelling. It was but a short distance from the eaves of the wood. I had found a cave nearly large enough to fit into, and there was a good clear stream not far away. With some effort on my part, it would be a comfortable enough place to dwell. I also asked Maran, who said that no other owned the land round about her house, and I was welcome to enlarge her courtyard to my heart's content if I would do the work of laying the stone floors and building walls.

I took it as a challenge.

Lanen

It was the oddest feeling I have ever known, walking into Beskin. I had never been there before, but—how shall I explain it? It began with the scent of the Trollingwood, whose western edge lay near my old home in Ilsa. I knew that smell and it was the same here, only wilder somehow. The air was fresh and sharp with the scents of pine and balsam, the ground was rich, the hills felt like old friends. I walked into Beskin and felt that I had come home, to a place I had never seen. It was very strange, but oddly reassuring.

Maran's house was huge. Her grandfather had built it with his sons, and there was room and to spare for all of us. The rooms were sparsely furnished, the furniture well made and lovely in its simplicity. One of Maran's brothers, Harald—Goddess, how odd, to have uncles and aunts!—Uncle Harald is a woodworker, and made all the furnishings in the house himself.

Maran gave me a room to myself on the upper floor, a large airy room looking to the hills, with plenty of space for the children when they came. She slept across the hall, near enough for a hail but far enough for privacy. Vilkas had the third bedroom on that floor to himself.

Maran and I settled in quickly enough, but Vilkas was like a butterfly that could not light upon a single bloom. After a few days, when he was certain that I was well enough and would keep, he went off on his own into the country round, a travelling Healer. During our first three months there, as spring gave way gradually to summer, he would disappear for weeks at a time, turning up suddenly of a morning with a scrip full of silver, looking a little more weather-beaten each time and a little more at peace with himself. He would give me relaxing herbs, examine me closely, make sure the babes were thriving, exhort me to eat more meat, and disappear again.

I managed to sit about the house resting, as ordered, for all of a week. The next morning I was up before Maran, making the porridge and starting the bread. She scowled at me for not following Vilkas's orders for exactly three breaths, then she grinned at me. "Bored, are you?" she asked.

"Put me to work," I begged. "Quick, before I get too big to do anything at all."

She laughed and led me to the forge, where she provided me with an ancient, scarred leather apron and a thick leather jerkin. I started like the rawest apprentice, working the bellows, but over the days and weeks she taught me how to stoke the fire, the smell and look and sound of iron when it is ready for the hammer, and one memorable day she handed me her second-best hammer and let me get on with trying to shape metal.

I have never known anything like it. I'd never done the like before, but I had watched Maran close for some time by then, and the movements just seemed—natural. The hammer seemed to fit my hand, the iron turned sweetly for me. My mother's eyes gleamed with pride. "By the Goddess, my girl, you've the making of a fine smith in you!" she declared.

"Oh, is that what they are?" I said, looking down at my bulge in surprise. She had a grand laugh, my mother, one that started at her toes and took her over entire when she was really amused. Impossible to resist.

When I came near to the start of the seventh month of my pregnancy, however, Vilkas returned and declared that his wandering was over for now.

"I've almost two months yet before anything exciting is due to happen, surely?" I said, panting a little. I was finding it harder to breathe, and Maran had banned me from the forge the week before, for her own safety as well as mine.

"You never know with twins," replied Vilkas, trying to keep a straight face but failing miserably.

"And how many twins have you delivered, O Great Dragon Mage?" I asked, teasing.

"Only one set, and that was at Verfaren," he replied, suddenly serious. "Lanen, now that you mention it, I would like your permission to bring in a colleague to assist me. Her experience with midwifery is much greater than mine." He grinned a little ruefully. "She is also less likely to terrify an expectant mother, though I'd hope you would be used to me by now."

I took advantage of my state to surprise young Vilkas and hugged him tight. "You dear idiot," I said, releasing him. "I'm married to the largest dragon in all the world, and you think I'd be afraid of you?"

He laughed rather well, all in all. "Still, I would like to call her in for the birth," he said, "and perhaps a few weeks before. Twins can come early." He looked about him. "If your mother wouldn't mind, I expect she'd appreciate a place to stay as well."

I laughed. "What's one more in this barn? Do what you need to, Vil. I trust you," I said.

I should have known, really. Idai arrived a week later, bearing Aral and Will and followed closely by Salera. Vil had gone to Akor, asked him to bespeak Idai and beg her to find Aral. There was a grand reunion, and the house was full.

I was quietly delighted that Will had come with Aral as a matter of course. They had progressed so far as to occasionally hold hands publicly. It was clear to all the rest of us that it only a matter of time. Aral was more contented than I had seen her, and Will stood at least a handspan taller, bless his good soul.

When the new arrivals sought their beds, I stepped out into the long twilight of the northern summer to walk Akor back to his chambers. He had been labouring on Maran's courtyard, but it was slow work, and not kind to the clumsy hands that attempted it. As we passed the latest disaster of a stone wall I smiled. "Perhaps we can find a stonemason who will trade his skill for raw lifting power," I suggested. It made Akor hiss with amusement, and for that I was grateful.

I was becoming grateful for anything that helped us to be together. We had begun to live disparate lives, and it worried me. When we were apart, we bespoke one another and we were knit as close as ever. Our souls have ever been the two halves of one whole. In truespeech we shared heart, mind, and spirit, and all was very well. It was only when we were in one another's presence that we could not ignore the eternal distance between us. Now and ever, Kantri and Gedri, between whom there could be only a meeting of the minds—except in our babes.

I waddled along the rough path, feeling better for the exercise but not able to keep it up very long. We came to an open space where there was a convenient stone to sit on, and I made use of it.

"Are they not yet prepared for the world?" asked Akor lightly, staring fascinated at my awkward body. "Surely you cannot stretch any farther!"

I laughed despite myself. "Alas that we cannot call to them and suggest that now would be a fine time to be born! The Lady knows I am ready for it." I sighed. "Right now, I'd settle for being able to see my feet."

I expected Akor to hiss, but he turned away with a moan.

"Dear heart, what is it?" I asked, adding dryly, "I mean, what is it more than we have borne these three months past?"

"Nothing more, Lanen, but—nothing less," he said. He could not look at me. "The time is nearly come. Our children are ready to be born. And I will never—I cannot—damnation!" He cried out, a wordless shout into the darkling sky. "Lanen, I can bear it no longer!" he groaned. His wings were starting to flutter in his agitation. "Here you are, more beautiful than ever, full of new life we have made between us—and I who have longed for younglings for a thousand years will never be able to hold my own babes." He began to pace up and down, as much as so large a creature could in the space. "It will be many years ere I dare even to touch them, lest a careless talon should rip through tender skin. I could murder them by mistake!"

"Please, Akor," I said, trying to compose myself. "Love, don't break now. I need you more with every passing day."

"I know it, I know it, but Lanen—Lanen, I cannot bear it! I am come to the end of myself." He roared, sending Fire into the night sky, and I realised that he was furious. "Ye traitor Winds!" he cried out. "I have given myself, body and soul and life and all, to my people, as you demanded. I never knew love until I knew her. Why have you given us to each other only to tear us apart?" His voice grew even louder. "I cannot bear it!" He was practically dancing on the spot, so desperate was he to be gone from me. I knew exactly what he was feeling, and I couldn't blame him in the least, and I blamed him with every word he said. He turned to me again, agony in his voice. "Lanen, I cannot bear it!"

"Then go," I said, stonily. "You have wings. You can go wherever in the world you wish." I stood tall, my belly prominent. "I am held down to earth."

I had sworn to myself that I wouldn't bespeak him, I knew it would be the last burden on a weakened back, but my anger rose to meet his. *"Your childer, Akor. Our childer. Do not turn coward on me now, damn you. I need you."*

He screamed then, a soul pushed to the limit of endurance. He rose with a thunderclap into the darkening sky, and his mind-voice sang its agony and its contrition as he flew away north, deeper into the great forest.

"Lanen forgive, forgive, I cannot bear it, I cannot bear it any longer. Lanen, my heart, you know that I love you beyond words, to be separate forever from you and from my only younglings, it destroys me, I cannot bear it, forgive, forgive . . ."

I felt as though I should weep, but there were no tears. Curious. I think I would have been more angry with him if I had not been so relieved. He was not the only one who could not stand it any longer. It was not his fault, nor mine. I bowed my head for a moment, my eyes closed. *Ah, Lady Mother Shia,* I whispered. *I heard the bards' tales but I did not understand. The love that is too wild and strong destroys the lovers every time, doesn't it? I don't think I could have stood his presence a moment longer, it was agony to see him, agony to have him so close and so infinitely far away.* I gazed up where he had gone. *Fly well, my heart,* I thought, carefully not bespeaking him. *Thank you for leaving. Your suffering made mine worse too. If you ever come back, I'll apologise properly.*

I walked slowly back to my mother's house. I got in just before the rain came.

The next evening I went into labour.

Khordeshkhistriakhor

I flew low, ashamed to be aloft yet as unable to stay with Lanen as to turn back time.

I had never thought of myself as a coward before, but I could not escape the evidence. The bravest thing I did was dare to bespeak my wife as I left. My heart burned within me as though it were truly aflame. I flew to escape my skin, to escape the torture of being so near to happiness yet forever separated from it.

I did not fly far. My strength seemed to drain away from the instant I left Lanen. I just managed to glide to a patch of open ground before I fell from the sky. I was confused and dizzy and my eyes didn't seem to be working very well. I felt rain begin to beat upon me, lightly at first, then harder and harder as the clouds opened. I was soon soaked, and I had the curious feeling that I was shrinking with every raindrop. *Perhaps the Winds have heard my plea and have sent this rain to dissolve me,* I thought, oddly cheerful. Eyes closed, shaking with fever, I imagined that I grew smaller and smaller. *Perhaps Lanen will have room in her womb for me,* I thought, but that was a very peculiar thought and I didn't like it. I decided not to think any longer. That was good. And after another little time, just before the end, I realised that I could no longer move my limbs or feel my wings.

It is over then, I thought, tolerably content for it to be so. *Farewell, my dearest Lanen. Even as I sleep on the Winds I will love you. Now awaken, Shikrar! I come!* I sang with my last thought, and my mind floated away into darkness.

Lanen

Vilkas and Aral managed to stop my body from continuing with the birth immediately, but at most they could delay it for a fortnight. Still, as Vilkas said, at that stage even three days would be useful.

Idai scoured the land round about, shocked and angry, but Akor was nowhere to be found.

I began labour in earnest ten days later. I was sufficiently terrified to be going on with, but—as Vilkas reminded me forcefully, several times—I had in attendance the two best Healers in all of Kolmar. Will spelled them at my bedside, letting first one then the other get some rest.

They kept the worst of the pain at bay, and they never left me alone, Goddess bless them. After full twelve hours of it, I'm told—the Goddess is kind, I have no memory of how long it took—my son and daughter were born within minutes of each other. She came out first, followed after a very few moments by her brother.

My mother helped Aral clean them while Vilkas looked deep into their tiny bodies, making certain that all was well with them. He nodded, smiling, and they laid my children in my arms. I wept with relief. I wasn't the only one.

"They're beautiful, Lanen. They're just beautiful," said Maran, grinning madly. "All their fingers, all their toes, one head each. Well done, my girl." And then she said, more than a little stunned, "Grandchildren. Goddess save us, I have grandchildren." She burst out laughing. "Oh, very well done, Lanen!"

"Are they meant to be this small?" I asked. I was exhausted, thrilled, worried about them, missing Akor desperately, and utterly enchanted by these two tiny people I held.

Everyone laughed. "They've been born a moon and a half early, Lanen," said Aral. "Yes, they are meant to be tiny. They're fine, believe me, they'll grow soon enough. And Vil and I will stay with you for a while yet to be certain that all is well with them." She grinned. "Have you and Akor chosen names for them?"

"Yes," I said, choking back a sob. "He is Trezhan, and she is Irian. They are to be called Ta-Varien, to remind them always of their father's love." My throat closed on the words. Thankfully, just then there was a knock at the door. Maran, muttering something about Will being a lax door warden, went to answer it. We all waited to hear the voice of the visitor, but whoever it was said nothing but came directly up the stairs. Maran was silent as well. That was unusual, certainly.

We were, therefore, all staring curiously at the doorway when Varien walked through it.

He strode to my bedside, leaned over, and kissed me—I didn't kiss him back, I was barely able to breathe let alone kiss him back—it was—he was human—Varien, caressing our children—

I'm afraid I blasphemed rather thoroughly before I fainted.

Vilkas

"Aral!" I shouted, catching up the baby nearest me. She was watchful and gathered up the other before Lanen dropped it.

I was tempted to bring Lanen back to consciousness immediately, but judged that she had been through enough and let her recover in her own time. In the meanwhile I dragged Varien—Goddess, it *was* Varien, wasn't it?—downstairs and more or less threw him into a chair. Aral stayed with Lanen, but Maran wisely brought down the other babe. In moments he held one in each arm, gazing at them in turn, lost in wonder and delight.

He was not alone. Looking around the room, I decided that a quick treatment for shock would not go amiss. I sent my Power out from me in a soft cloud, parting it around the newborns that it might not so much as brush against them. We all were locked solid in amazement, though, until Maran managed to speak. With difficulty. After clearing her throat.

"Varien, lad?"

He looked up at her, bemused. "Yes, Mother Maran?"

"Would you care to tell us just how in all the Hells you come to be here like this?" she asked. With admirable restraint, I thought.

Before he answered, he looked to me. "Lanen is well, Mage Vilkas?"

"Aside from an unexpected shock at a delicate moment, yes, she's fine," I said. "How in all the world did you manage it?"

He began to answer, but his daughter drew a deep breath and tried out her new lungs.

Good lungs.

Varien started violently.

"Take them back upstairs, you idiot," I said, restraining a rogue smile, as her brother took up the refrain. "They are hungry, and you're not equipped."

He grinned and started back up the stairs. Lanen's voice greeted him halfway up.

"Varien Kantriakor, you *bastard*, get back up here NOW and bring the children!"

In the face of all temptation, I held Maran back and called Aral to come to me. "What, Vil?" she asked, worried. "Lanen's alright, isn't she? Her colour's good . . ."

I smiled. At last, one up on Aral in the field of humanity.

"Her colour's fine. But I expect they have a few things to say to each other. A little privacy for the new family, eh?"

Aral had the grace to blush.

"Blast your delicacy, boy," said Maran grumpily. "I want to know how in the Hells he did that!"

Lanen

I had a thousand questions, a thousand demands, a thousand kicks and kisses to administer, but truth be told I could pay attention to nothing else once the babes began to suckle, and I fell asleep instantly afterward. When I woke again, only a little time later, it was to find mother Maran sat by my bedside.

She answered my expression before I could speak. "It wasn't a dream, he's downstairs having a meal. I'll send him up."

"What did he . . . ?"

"He's refused to tell us a thing," she pouted. "And I'm sure he's right, you should hear it first, but by every blade of grass that ever grew, I'm *this* far from threatening his life if he doesn't start talking."

When Varien was seated beside me, the babes asleep in our arms and the rest of the company waiting patiently and not so patiently below, he told me the tale of the night he left.

"I honestly thought I was dying, Lanen," he said earnestly. "I felt myself shrink, then I couldn't feel my wings, then I lost consciousness—and I woke in that spot some few hours later, cold and wet and human."

Fighting past the wonder, I managed to say, "What think you, love? How could it happen? Did the Winds and the Lady have pity on you? On us?" I laughed. "Goddess, do you think they actually did something *for* us?"

Looking a little self-conscious, my husband said, "Not precisely.

At least, not in the way you mean." He thought for a moment, choosing his words with great care. "You know how deeply you were changed when Vilkas saved your life?"

"Of course."

"Well—I appear to have undergone something of the sort when—when Shikrar and I changed places."

I stared at him, waiting. "Well? What? How are you changed?"

"The Gedri chose choice itself, did they not, my heart?" he asked in truespeech. His eyes blazed, now that he was come to it. *"I am of the Gedri as well, now, but for me, I am changed to—change itself."*

Bloody dragon.

"Would you kindly stop blethering and tell me exactly what you mean before the children are old enough to walk?" I said, exasperated.

He grinned like a maniac. "I'd prefer to show you, but there isn't room in here," he said. He was practically glowing. "Lanen—I can change. At will. Entirely at will." He laughed with the wonder of it. "I did not believe it when I woke. I was terribly confused, and consciously thought, *I should bear the shape of the Kantri.* Within the quarter of the hour, I was changed back. I have done it several times since, to make sure. Kantri or Gedri, whichever I like, when I like." He barked another little laugh. "I'm my old size, too, not as vast as Shikrar. Name of the Winds, how he ever managed to move on the ground I'll never know."

I had finally managed to find my voice.

"Bloody hellsfire!"

I think I yelled that a touch louder than I meant to, because there was a brief thunder on the stairs and Will, Maran, Aral, and Vilkas all piled into the room, the Healers with their coronas blazing, Maran with a hammer in her hand, Goddess only knew where she kept that hidden.

"All's well, all's well, my friends," said Varien, grinning like an idiot. "There's nothing to see. Not just now. Though I will give a demonstration later for those who are interested."

He told them then, in so many words, what had happened.

I will never forget the stunned amazement on all of their faces.
Vilkas was the best. I never thought to see that self-contained
soul so lose his composure, he was an absolute picture.

"Varien, you're not serious," I said finally. "You—I mean, it's
not possible—"

And Varien laughed, a great hearty laugh from his belly that
woke the babies.

"Lanen Kaelar, you never cease to amaze me. Of all that
has happened to us in the last year, how much is even faintly
possible?"

I smiled slowly. "Very, very little, to be sure," I said, kissing
Irian, who yawned and went back to sleep.

"Quite right," he replied, far more softly. He gently rocked
Trezhan until our son fell asleep again.

"Sweet Lady, Varien," I swore quietly. "What in all the world
and time are you meant to do with *that* gift?"

"I have no idea," he said, his face transformed by utter joy.
"But it will surely be a great adventure to find out."

There is so much yet to say about those times. The world and
everything in it was changing around us, faster than we could
keep up with it. It took a very long time to truly understand all
that had happened.

The twins were born when the harvest was ripe and the light
was warm and golden, a little more than a moon before my own
birth-day at the Autumn Balance-day.

Despite all my fears they did not have either wings or soulgems, but they did each have a tiny bump in the centre of their
foreheads where a soulgem would have been. Believe me, I
thought long and hard about *that* over the next few years. And I
only ever told Varien about this, but—a few weeks after they were
born, when we all were sitting outdoors and it began to be a little
chilly, I was sent what Mirazhe calls "a picture of their thoughts,"
in this case a sudden feeling of cold and fear, from the children.
Just like young Sherók's first efforts. *Perhaps he is not strictly the
youngest of the Kantri anymore,* I thought very quietly to myself.

The news from all quarters was good. Kédra, away in the

Súlkith Hills with his dear Mirazhe and Sherók and that contingent of the Kantri that chose to remain with them, bespoke us one day with the news that Kretissh and Nikis had arrived. We laughed heartily, though I felt sorry for poor Nikis. It was not her fault that she had been caught in the Weh sleep when the rest of the Kantri had flown the Great Sea! Still, Nikis the Weary she was and remains. The others have found chambers near the sea, and have tended the lansip trees on behalf of our whole people. Farmer Timeth takes lansip leaves for his rent, plays with Sherók, and bids fair to become quite disgustingly wealthy in a few years, when the trees have grown a little more.

Idai left Beskin soon after the twins arrived. She and a contingent of the Aialakantri have been working almost constantly since the day of Shikrar's death, seeking out the soulgems of those who died in and around Lake Gand. It took them three years, but they eventually found every last one. The first, of course, was Shikrar's, lifted from the midst of Berys's cold ashes and cleansed with dragon fire. It gleams now a brilliant, untroubled red. His soul rests upon the Winds, and hardly a day passes even now that Varien and I do not miss him.

Varien has been much involved with the resettlement of the Kantri throughout Kolmar. Idai consults him regularly, and from time to time she comes to visit. When she arrived with Will and Aral and stayed until the babes had been born, she of course wished us joy of our younglings, and told us some of the best news yet. A number of the Kantri and the Dhrenagan had taken mates in the last few months, and there were already several younglings on the way. "We have even found a hot spring in the mountains above Castle Gundar," she said happily, "and are digging out a birthing pool. The high mountains are riddled with caves perfect for Weh chambers for those who require them, and there are many who do. All is well. Oh, Akhor, all is well at last!"

"It is indeed," he had said, smiling up at her. I remember that daft grin of his. He had barely looked away from the twins since their birth, I practically had to tear them from his arms to let them sleep in those first weeks. I recall being heartily grateful to Idai, who at least forced his eyes to focus on something more distant.

Before she left, though, she reminded him that no matter what his shape, he was still their King. "Do not think that you are released from your service just because the Winds have given you this astounding gift," she said, pretending to a severity she did not feel in the least. "You are still our Lord and King, by acclamation, and you will not slip out of your duties so easily."

"You are Eldest, Idai," he said. "This is foolish. Let you call a full Council of our people and choose a new leader from among you." He grinned up at her. "Perhaps it is time that we had Queen Idai to turn to, rather than King Akhor."

She hissed. "Very well, Lord, if you so command. A full Council must be attended by two-thirds of the Kantri then on live. I suspect that enough will have wakened from their Weh sleep in, oh, perhaps twenty or thirty winters. I will do my best to remember your wishes at that time."

Things had changed by then, of course—but that is another story. Ever since the Kantri came to Kolmar they have insisted on calling Varien their King. When the bards came to hear the tale of the wild adventures of that time, they soon heard that part of the story, and the idiots assumed that that must mean that I should be Queen Lanen. Ha! Never trust the bards, for they will always change the truth to make a good tale.

One other thing did take me by surprise. When the twins were a few years old, Varien spoke long with one of the bards and bought the man's second-best harp from him. In the years between, he has worked hard to learn the old tales and has created any number of new ones. My Varien is well on his way to becoming an extraordinary bard, but then he has an unfair advantage to begin with. After all, the Kantri are the best singers in the world.

Trezhan and Irian ta-Varien grew and flourished as children will, though of course they were the most glorious children who have ever lived. Varien says that Shikrar always said that about Kédra, from the moment of his birth.

I think I understand Shikrar a little better now.

This is the true tale of the Redeeming of the Lost and the Second Death of the Demonlord.
There is more to tell, but then there always is.
True stories never really end.

ACKNOWLEDGMENTS

First and foremost, I must acknowledge the usual huge debt of gratitude to my wondrous editor, **Claire Eddy** of Tor Books. She has put up with writing delays due to my iffy health, and my getting slightly married, with a kind understanding that I probably don't deserve, and her sharp insight has, as ever, improved this book vastly.

My sincere thanks again to **Deborah Turner Harris,** dear as a sister, whose clearheaded advice and experience have gotten me out of any number of writing dilemmas—without your help, kiddo, this book would have been a darn sight more boring, and you may not realise it but your support and friendship have kept me going when I was ready to throw either the computer or myself out the window. You'll never know how much you've helped, Debby. Bless you.

Margaret Lynn Harshbarger for plotting sessions above and beyond the call of duty, for kicking me when I needed it, for hauling me back into the path of myth when I was getting lost in mechanics, and for her eye-opening insights into—well, too much to mention here. Much of life, actually.

Sandy Fleming, friend of many years' standing, for chatting to me when I just *had* to talk to someone, for reading a few snippets in the interests of a reality check, and for being my Webmaster out of the kindness of his heart.

Dr. Frank Prior, for stopping me from killing off the Kantri through ignorance, and for generally keeping me straight on matters of basic physiology—although to protect his professional reputation he has refused to let me quote specifics about which I have consulted him. Understandably. However, any medical idiocies perpetrated herein are my own doing, and have occurred despite Frank's kind assistance rather than because of it.

Catherine and John MacDonald, for their generous willingness to be interrupted and keep me right on matters of midwifery and pregnancy, and to **Kirsty Nicol,** dear friend, for information about being on the sharp end, as it were, of pregnancy. Again, any missteps are my own entirely.

Christopher, as ever, for putting up with frantic calls at all hours, for staunch friendship, for his delight in the language, and for being the voice of reason for me when I couldn't think in a straight line.

And finally, ever and always, my deepest thanks go to my best-beloved, **Steven Beard,** dear friend for many years and now my treasured husband, who has carried an infinite number of cups of tea up the stairs over the last three years and never once threw one over me, richly though I may have deserved it. The man brings me toasted apple and cinnamon bread to keep me going, for goodness' sake. What more could a girl want?

I couldn't have done it without you, my dears. I hereby owe you a beer. Each.

—Elizabeth

GLOSSARY

Aialakantri—OS for the Awakened Kantri, who were the Lesser Kindred.

Ceat—OS, a thousand years.

Chélan—name of a plant and the brew made from it. It is drunk as a stimulant. We would say it tastes rather like maté with a hint of cinnamon.

Dhrenagankantri—OS for the Restored Kantri, who for five thousand years were the Lost.

Ferrinshadik—the longing felt by (esp.) the Greater Kindred to join in fellowship with the Gedri, though it is described more generally as the desire to speak with other races.

Gedrishakrim—humans. Usually shortened to Gedri. OS, "the silent people."

Kadreshi na—"beloved of" is the nearest translation in English. An endearment between lovers.

Kairtach—a curse that is also an intensifier. I refuse to translate. The Kantri would not be pleased if I did, and it would not reflect well on them.

Kantriasarikh—the OS word for the language of the Kantrishakrim.

Kantrishakrim—the Greater Kindred of Dragons (originally all dragons). OS "the wise people." Usually shortened to Kantri.

Kell—OS, a hundred years.

Khaadish—OS word for gold.

Language of Truth—the telepathy natural to the Kantri. It also has elements of empathic awareness. The Gedri call it Farspeech.

Lansip—name of a tree and the brews made from it. It grows only where dragons dwell, all attempts at transplanting to solely human regions have failed. Made into tea it is a tonic and general remedy for minor ailments, from headache to heart's sorrow; taken in quantity, it is an elixir of youth. Lan fruit, the precious and rare fruit of the lansip tree, is a sovereign remedy, and when eaten fresh will heal nearly anything short of death.

Lesikrithic—a cripple among the Kantri, one who has lost a limb or sustained a wound that cannot be healed by Weh sleep and yet lives.

Old Speech—(OS) the name in the common tongue for the language created by the Kantri and used by all the peoples before the Choice. Since that time it has developed into distinctly separate languages.

Rakshadakh—demon droppings (that is the polite translation). It is the ultimate insult as far as the Kantri are concerned, and generally refers to a demon master or one who is tainted by the Rakshasa.

Rakshasa—(obs. form Rakshi) demons. Singular, Raksha (greater demon) or Rikti (lesser demon). OS: "people of chaos." This is plural because, at the time of the Choice, the Rakshasa were already differentiated into two distinct peoples.